PRAISE FOR LAUREN B. DAVIS

"Richly layered. It's not just a com_____ _____ ___e idea
of fighting back when one's belief _____ ___. The
way one's ideals might survive in a _____ ___e now
as it was thousands of _____
expertly re_____ _____.
— *Globe & Mail* on *Against a Darkening Sky*

"Set against an otherworldly, intimate backdrop, Davis's tale vividly brings to
life a near-mythic period of British history while speaking to
universal human experience."
— *Publishers Weekly* on *Against a Darkening Sky*

"*Against a Darkening Sky* is told in the clear, uncluttered prose that character-
izes Davis's other work . . . Never a false note is struck in Davis's detailing of
Anglo-Saxon life . . . The struggles of a steadfast pagan woman and a fearful
monk [are] captivating and entertaining."
— *Winnipeg Free Press* on *Against a Darkening Sky* ·

"Davis heartbreakingly renders the disturbed thought process of someone
trapped in addiction."
— *Quill & Quire* on *The Empty Room*

"An entirely accurate portrait of alcoholism . . . [It] is very real, and it is
believable . . . Davis is without a doubt an exceptionally talented writer."
— *Globe & Mail* on *The Empty Room*

"Davis' novel is raw and disturbing, yet we keep reading, spurred by the clarity
of the writing and intensity of the description. Davis offers a completely
believable picture of one woman's decline and helplessness . . . . As a writer,
Davis has the rare ability to mine her own experience and create fiction from
what she palpably understands. It is an enviable talent and her novel allows
those of us who have never been there to grasp the hell of being an addict, of
how sorry things can get when we waste our lives . . . [A] great psychological
portrait of a woman under the influence."
— *Toronto Star* on *The Empty Room*

THE GRIMOIRE OF
KENSINGTON MARKET

ALSO BY LAUREN B. DAVIS

Against a Darkening Sky

The Empty Room

Our Daily Bread

The Radiant City

Rat Medicine and Other Unlikely Curatives

The Stubborn Season

An Unrehearsed Desire

THE
GRIMOIRE
OF
KENSINGTON
MARKET

LAUREN B. DAVIS

A Buckrider Book

Buckrider Books is an imprint of Wolsak and Wynn Publishers.

Cover image, design and interior design: Kate Hargreaves
(CorusKate Design)

Author photograph: Helen Tansey at Sundari Photography

Typeset in Adobe Caslon Pro

Printed by Ball Media, Brantford, Canada

 ONTARIO ARTS COUNCIL
CONSEIL DES ARTS DE L'ONTARIO
an Ontario government agency
un organisme du gouvernement de l'Ontario
 Canada Council   Conseil des arts
for the Arts   du Canada
 Canada

The publisher gratefully acknowledges the support of the Canada Council for the Arts, the Ontario Arts Council and the Government of Canada.

Buckrider Books
280 James Street North
Hamilton, ON
Canada L8R 2L3

Library and Archives Canada Cataloguing in Publication

Davis, Lauren B., 1955-, author
The grimoire of Kensington Market / Lauren B. Davis.

ISBN 978-1-928088-70-7 (softcover)

I. Title.

PS8557.A8384G75 2018   C813'.6   C2018-903869-1

1 2 3 4 5 6 7 8 9 10

To R.E.D. The road always led to you.

SOME DAY YOU WILL BE OLD ENOUGH
TO START READING
FAIRY TALES AGAIN.
— C.S. LEWIS

‹GRIMOIRE: *NOUN* A BOOK OF
MAGIC SPELLS AND INVOCATIONS.›

CHAPTER ONE

PEOPLE DIDN'T WANDER INTO THE GRIMOIRE. It wasn't that sort of bookshop. People found it by some force even Maggie, the proprietor, didn't understand. If one was meant to find the shop, one did, otherwise it was unnoticeable. Alvin, the nephew of the former proprietor, Mr. Mustby, came as he pleased, as did Mr. Strundale, who ran the Wort & Willow Apothecary a few doors down, but on the other hand, Maggie's brother, Kyle, had never found his way, and she wasn't about to invite him.

Located at the front of the ground floor of an old house, the shop smelled of old paper, glue and wax, with slight undernotes of mildew and mice. It was *full* of books, as one might expect, but not just full of books in the general way of bookshops. Rather, it was full of books so that walking from the door to the corner where Maggie sat behind her desk was like navigating a maze. There were books on the shelves, books on the tables, books precariously balanced on the top of forgotten teacups on the aforementioned tables, books on the windowsills, books on the chairs, books piled on the floor shoulder high, if you were tall, over your head, if you were short.

This morning Maggie, dressed in her usual black turtle-neck and jeans, sat behind her desk, which had legs carved with dragons, and their clawed feet gripped marble globes. Across the edge of the desk, piles of books formed a sort of rampart, inside which were a scatter of items: a small saucer of stones and shells, an assortment of small creatures – a wooden mouse reading a bible, a rhinoceros-nosed dragon carved from coal lying on its back reading a book, a winged gargoyle, a crystal owl, a jade turtle – several candles scented with frankincense, a brass lamp and a very large nearly empty teacup, decorated with a blue narwhal. Maggie held a dark blue book with three silver moons embossed on the cover, in the waxing, full and waning aspects. As often happened when a book caught her eye, it was just what she hadn't known she was looking for. She ran her long pale fingers over the artwork. It triggered a memory of last night's dream. Something about a man cast away on the moon. The first story was about an old man who stole a bundle of firewood and then refused to give it to a freezing beggar. As punishment for the hardness of his heart more than the theft, the wind whisked him to the moon, where he waited for Judgment Day. He said he didn't mind. It could have been worse, for the moon only showed itself at night and so his shame would be seen only half the time.

"Huh," she said and fiddled with one of the two silver bird charms pinned in the honey-coloured braid that fell over her shoulder. She wore no makeup; they were her only concession to vanity. Several golden lights flashed, the size of the fairy lights people sometimes hung in gardens, and Maggie noticed two shelves, one housing stories about Syrian immigrants and the other stories of sub-Saharan Africa, lengthened just a tad.

Such was the way new additions to the shop were announced. Some days the shop seemed to sparkle, so many books appeared, other days a few flickers and nothing more. One would think that such a bookshop would eventually burst through its walls, since more and more stories appear in the world, and therefore in the Grimoire, every hour, with shelves expanding to accommodate each one, but it is a sad truth that stories also leave the world when they are forgotten, or when the last teller of the tale has died. When this happened, a small flame appeared above the book in question and as it burned, the book itself dimmed, lost its shape and, when the flame snuffed out, so did the book. In this way, although the inside of the shop expanded or contracted to fit the world's tales, it was always the perfect size.

Badger, the shaggy black-and-white mixed-breed dog curled near Maggie's feet, looked up and cocked his head, one ear flopping. He whined. Maggie scratched his ear. She turned the page. A very old tale. In one version God exiled the thief to his choice of either sun or moon. In another the wind made him spend eternity repairing hedgerows on the night's silver disk. No one gave the old man a chance to explain or offer a defence. Maybe he was freezing himself. Maybe he had sick children at home. He had no advocate; no one on his side. Maggie snorted. Wasn't that always the case? It was so easy to judge, to punish; so hard to find justice; and mercy never seemed to enter the picture at all.

She closed the book with a thump, causing a puff of dust to explode heavenward, and pushed it away. She slurped up the last of the tea and then went into the kitchen at the back of the shop to make more. While the kettle heated she let Badger out the back door into the stone-walled garden. Within it was a seat under an old oak tree, and rose bushes, lilacs, camellias and hollyhocks that filled the entire shop with fragrance when in bloom. Now, in late October, the garden was quiet and still, falling asleep at the approach of winter. Maggie stood in the doorway and watched Badger sniff around. She thought how Mr. Mustby, the shop's previous proprietor, the man who had saved her life, had loved mornings and how she'd often found him in the garden when she got up, a coffee in one hand, a book in the other, sitting on the bench under the tree. Three months after his sudden death she fancied she still saw him there.

A few minutes later she was back at her desk, sipping her steaming tea. She tapped her fingers on the moon-story book. Something to learn, certainly, from last night's dream. But what? Well, time would tell. She'd almost grown accustomed to dreaming in fairy tales. As a child, the dreams had been vague, mere snippets of glass mountains, talking frogs and handless maidens. But when she lost herself to the drug elysium all that changed. The boundaries grew thin. Dreams were no longer dreams; they were journeys into the Silver World, the World Beside This One. What was real and what wasn't blended. Fairy tales, holy myths, ancient figures from the imaginations of a million dreamers . . . they were as real as the hand at the end of one's arm. That was the deadly lure of the elysium. And even though she'd put down the pipe three years ago, her dreams had never returned to their pre-addiction vagueness. Perhaps she'd always had some genetic predisposition.

She pinched the bridge of her nose. It was exhausting, as was the grief she was experiencing after Mr. Mustby's recent death. No one ever talked about that. Pain she expected, but this fatigue! Her eyes burned. She didn't want to cry anymore. Maggie tilted her head and rolled her neck, trying to work out the cricks.

The little bell sounded over the door. Badger whined and stood. Alvin, maybe? Maggie's hands went to her hair, but she stopped herself. She hadn't seen Alvin in several days and although she didn't like to admit it, she missed him. More fool, she! Alvin, Mr. Mustby's nephew, who'd once inhabited the second-floor room she now called her own, lived on a charter boat docked in Lake Ontario. Sometimes he took out people to scatter the ashes of loved ones, sometimes wedding parties. If he knew how often she thought about him when he was gone, he'd only tease her.

Badger sat back down. Not Alvin, then.

A moment later a woman's face popped round one of the shelves. "Hello?" she said. "Quite a store you've got here." She was probably in her fifties, with grey hair cut in soft wisps around her face.

"Can I help you find something?"

The woman adjusted her turquoise-framed glasses. "Oh, what a sweet dog!" Badger trotted over and leaned against the woman's camel-hair coat in a position for ear scratches. The woman obliged and said to Maggie, "It's funny, I've never noticed this place before. Have you been here long?"

"Quite a while, but we don't really advertise."

The woman scanned the crowded shelves that went on, row after row, much farther than the laws of physics ought to permit. "What an odd place."

This happened when customers came in; they seemed befuddled, but it didn't last. Maggie concluded long ago that this was part of the spell of the Grimoire – a just-below-the-surface-of-consciousness reassurance people felt when they crossed the threshold.

"I like it though," the woman said. "Anyway, I was walking past and suddenly remembered a dream I had last night. Sounds crazy, I know, but . . ."

"Doesn't sound crazy at all," said Maggie. "I was just pondering a dream I had last night myself."

The woman cocked her head as though trying to recall. "I'm not sure, but there was something about, I know this sounds strange, but a lily and a snake, something about men dressed in blue flames." The woman looked over Maggie's shoulder. "Could have sworn I just saw fireflies or something over there."

"Lights under the rim of the shelves. Darn things are always flickering. Bad connection."

Maggie took the woman by the arm and led her to the back of the store, to a great wall of small wooden drawers containing index cards upon which were recorded, in a beautiful calligraphy drawn by an unknown hand, all the titles of the books, their authors and a brief description, cross-referenced and updated as books came and went. "I think I know a book you might like. Goethe, of all people, wrote a fascinating story called 'The Green Snake and the Beautiful Lily.' It's considered one of the great symbolic enigmas of world literature." She rifled through the cards. "This one. It's in his book *Tales for Transformation*."

"You know, that sounds right somehow. God knows I'm going through enough transformations right now – divorce, retirement, you don't want to know – and everything feels enigmatic. Might give me some food for thought."

"Follow me." Maggie found the book and handed it to the woman.

"You won't know what it all means until you read it. But it's not that unusual. You'd be surprised how many people come in here asking for books based on their dreams."

"Looks awfully old."

"Not so old. Nineteen-thirties, I think. First edition of the English translation."

The woman went to hand it back to Maggie. "I'm sure I can't afford it."

"I bet you can. How much would you like to pay?"

The woman blinked. "Gee, I don't know . . . forty dollars?"

"I think you were meant for this book."

At noon, Badger and Maggie took their usual constitutional along the crowded, noisy streets of Kensington Market. Opening the door was always a slightly unsettling moment. Behind the doors the world of the bookstore was hushed, calm, as though out of time entirely, and the street noises didn't penetrate. Stepping out into the world of brightly coloured

Victorian houses, the Wort & Willow Apothecary her friend Mr. Strundale owned, riotous second-hand clothing stores, cars and taxis – drivers leaning on their horns – bicycle couriers whooshing by, coffee shops and open-air vegetable markets, which even in winter filled the air with a note of overripe fruit and decay, was a bit like stepping through the looking glass. They walked past Kensington Market's Italian pasta shops and espresso bars, Chinese herbal dispensaries and French cheese shops. The sidewalk was crowded with people speaking English, Arabic, Portuguese, Cantonese, Somali – it seemed like seven or eight different languages at once – and no one paid the least bit of attention to either Maggie or Badger. The air was damp and chill and the few trees were leafless. An empty paper cup danced along the sidewalk in a gust of wind.

Badger trotted along. He had been rummaging through the garbage in the alleyway near the Grimoire when Maggie found him, and he'd chosen to accept her invitation to live with her. Maggie had welcomed him, malodorous and crawling with vermin, given him a bath, as much food as he needed and her love. Now they wandered round to Bellevue Square, where Badger discreetly performed the necessary functions, and then made their way back to the shop.

As they neared the Grimoire's narrow door, Badger lowered his head, flattened his ears and did a fair impression of a lion stalking something through tall grass. "What are you doing?" Maggie laughed, trying to ignore the chill up her spine. Badger stopped and growled. She followed his gaze. The sidewalk traffic looked normal – mothers pushing strollers, people talking into phones, a man walking a schnauzer. Maggie wondered if it was the other dog that disturbed Badger, although he was generally friendly to other animals. Then she noticed a woman.

She looked familiar, but Maggie couldn't place her. Her hair was a short silver halo around her head. Her gaze was downward, and Maggie couldn't make out her features, other than a slash of dark lipstick. She wore a long wool coat, open, showing a man's suit, and lace-up black shoes. Something about the way she moved . . . and then she raised her head. The ghostly skin, wide mouth, the deep dimples . . . the eyes, holding knowledge of some private joke. It looked so much like *her* . . . but different . . .

"Well, what a nice little shop," the woman said. "Maggie, dear girl, how are you?"

That voice, all honey and smoke, the accent something Eastern European, Ukrainian or Russian perhaps. Srebrenka looked different, yes, softer somehow, but no older than when Lenny, Maggie's old boyfriend, had first introduced her eight years ago. Maggie had asked her then where she was from, but Srebrenka said it was nowhere she would know and refused to say more.

"What are you doing here?" Maggie's mind spun. Srebrenka, from whom everyone bought elysium, knew where she lived? And she could see the Grimoire? How could this be?

"I heard about your loss," Srebrenka said, "and wanted to say how very sorry I am."

Badger growled. "Sit," Maggie said, and the dog did, although not without a reluctant little dance first. "What loss?"

"Oh, dear," said Srebrenka, shaking her head. "Why Mr. Mustby, of course."

"How do you know him?" Maggie's breathing was shallow and her heart beat too quickly. She took a deep breath and tried to relax her shoulders.

Srebrenka smiled and put her hands together as though in prayer. "I was so sorry to hear about his passing. Of course, he was very old, but that's never a comfort when we lose someone we love, is it?"

It was odd, how even though Srebrenka was such a striking figure, no one glanced at her, although several glared at Maggie. She realized she was standing in the middle of the sidewalk, making people go around her. She moved closer to the door.

"You didn't answer my question."

Srebrenka stepped to the side next to Maggie and smiled down at Badger. "I know a lot of people, Maggie. I have a lot of friends. And I count you among them. I've been hurt, frankly, that you disappeared."

"I had to get clean. Or die. That was the choice."

"A bit dramatic," Srebrenka laughed, the sound like little bells. "But you did surprise me. I mean, to be honest, you're the first friend to leave me like that, and I can't imagine what I did to offend you. Wasn't I always there for you?"

"Look, I have to get going. I wish you all the best, okay, but I'm not interested."

Srebrenka tilted her head and gazed into Maggie's eyes. She bit her lower lip. "No? Are you sure? I'm not. I'd love a cup of tea and a chat. Perhaps you could invite me in? Someone grieving, as you are, needs a friend."

"Some other time maybe. I have a lot of work to do."

Srebrenka, ignoring Badger's growl, stepped close to Maggie and whispered in her ear, "The elysium longs for you, longs to hold you, longs to dream for you and ease your grief."

Her breath was like cool silk on Maggie's ear. Badger barked, and Maggie jerked her head and spun away. "Leave me alone."

"I didn't mean to upset you. Another time, then, my dear. Another time." Srebrenka blew her a kiss and walked away.

Maggie ducked in the shop and slammed the door, her heart a wild thing in her chest. She sank to the ground and wept.

THREE YEARS AND THREE MONTHS AGO SHE HAD CRAWLED, thin as a grasshopper, into the Grimoire. She was still seeing visions and had only recently put down the pipe. When Mr. Mustby, white bird's-wing eyebrows bristling, shuffled to the front of the store to see what fate had invited in, she'd asked him, shivering, if she could just sit in a corner and read a book. His tortoiseshell glasses had gleamed and he smelled of something like cinnamon or spice cake. His grey, curly hair fluffed around his head (and around the fountain pen tucked behind his ear, which gave him a scholarly appearance) and his goatee was neatly trimmed. The knees and elbows of his brown corduroy suit bagged from long wear and, judging from the way his pockets bulged, they were stuffed with an inordinate number of objects. His shoes were polished, but one was brown and the other black. He asked her name, nodded as though he'd expected as much and said he didn't care what she did so long as she didn't throw up on the books. She curled up in a dusty corner with a copy of the fifteenth-century masterpiece *Tales from the Sleeping Fortress*, and read and slept, read and slept, all that afternoon and into the night, until Mr. Mustby finally brought her a cup of tea and toast and said, "You may sleep in the back. I've set up a cot near the stove."

The next day Mr. Strundale had come in wearing a burgundy smoking jacket and nearly fainted when he saw her. Seeing the small fox wrapped around his shoulders, Maggie assumed she was hallucinating and nearly passed out herself. "Good God!" Mr. Strundale said, "Cat's dragged in and all that . . ."

He and Mr. Mustby talked for a few minutes and then Mr. Mustby called her over and said, "I have discussed this situation with my friend and counsellor, Mr. Strundale. You are here, so apparently this is where you are supposed to be."

"It's that sort of shop," said Mr. Strundale.

"Indeed," said Mr. Mustby. "In any event, I think you'd best get to work organizing the section on addiction stories, subsection Dark Night of the Soul."

And so the Grimoire had become her home; Mr. Mustby, her foster father; Mr. Strundale, something of an uncle and Alvin, her friend . . . or more than a friend. Life was as full of people as she wanted, and she'd felt safe for the first time in years.

Now, Srebrenka had come for her. But surely, Maggie told herself, she wouldn't be back. Maggie had made herself clear. That part of her life was over. Srebrenka would give up. But of course she wouldn't, would she? Maggie hugged Badger and shivered.

THE NEXT MORNING MAGGIE TOOK A MOMENT BEFORE opening the door. She would open it, she told herself, and find nothing unusual. She and Badger would go for their walk and come home and nothing would happen. She took a deep breath. She clipped the leash to Badger's collar. He was coiled, vibrating, which she told herself was nothing more than a reaction to the unusual leash. She flung open the door, perhaps a little more quickly, with a little more flourish, than she'd intended.

Srebrenka was just walking past, or so it seemed.

"Maggie." She held her arms out, palms up. "I came to apologize. I think I alarmed you yesterday, and that was the last thing I wanted to do." She took a few steps forward, her white coat and trousers shining in the sunlight. "You must know I want to ease your pain. That's all I wanted to do when we first met, so many years ago, and it's all I want to do now." She put her hands in her pockets and opened her coat. "See, nothing to be frightened of. Please, why not invite me in? Let me make amends? I've brought you a little something."

Maggie fought her urge to slam the door. She would not show fear. She stepped out, shutting the door behind her. She walked past Srebrenka, her shoulders high, keeping Badger close, for the dog was trembling and ready to bite. Srebrenka walked beside her.

"This is almost rude, dear. We are old friends, and you're refusing a gift. I give it to you freely, asking no payment." The woman held out a small silver pipe, the bowl already filled with the shimmering black tar-like potion.

Maggie set her jaw. She would not speak.

Srebrenka trailed along beside her, murmuring about the sweetness of the dreams waiting. Maggie ignored her as long as she could, lasting half a block, before she ducked into Mr. Strundale's apothecary, slamming the door behind her.

Inside, the air smelled of peppermint and lavender. Around the walls stood shelves, some glass-fronted, containing white and blue and green jars filled with herbal and homeopathic remedies, as well as glass canisters of various herbs – burdock, dandelion root, angelica, fennel, chamomile and so forth. Gold and green scrollwork decorated the wall above the shelves and from waist-height down were drawers, each with little brass plates describing the contents. In the centre of the room rested a large, highly polished island with more drawers in it. On the island sat brass scales and weights. A chandelier with flame-shaped bulbs hung from the ceiling, creating a soft glow.

The front door remained shut. It seemed Srebrenka wouldn't venture in, just as she didn't walk into the Grimoire without invitation. Mr. Strundale popped out from behind a screen at the back of the store that was ornately embroidered with dragons and birds. He smiled, although on his basset hound–face the gesture was unpersuasive, then his features settled into their natural droop. Finnick, the fox, pranced around his ankles. Finnick was a bit of a mystery. When Maggie had asked about him, Mr. Strundale had chuckled and said that Finnick wasn't an ordinary sort of fox, by any standard, and that he had been a companion to the previous herbalist, so he'd always been in the Wort & Willow. "But," Maggie had said, "you've been here for forty years so that would make him, what?" "Oh, ancient," Mr. Strundale had said, "and so very wise." And that was that.

"Maggie, how lovely to see you."

Finnick chirped in greeting and Badger flicked his ears but keep his focus on the door. Finnick went and sat next to him, equally alert.

"Thought I'd pop in for a cup of tea. Is that okay?"

He frowned. "Of course, but are you all right? Badger and Finnick seem on guard about something." He tightened the belt on his smoking jacket.

"I'm fine. Just haven't visited for a while." It took effort not to check if Srebrenka was following her.

"Don't be silly. Look at Badger. He's practically ready to vault at the door. What on earth is happening?"

She didn't want to tell him. There was a weakness, a flaw in her, that had led Srebrenka here. Like a dog wanting to kick dirt on its feces, she wanted to hide this. She wanted to take a long bath and soak away whatever Piper-filth must surely remain on her skin, sending out signals like a beacon.

"There's someone outside I don't want to see."

Mr. Strundale's eyebrows met above his nose. "Someone found you at the bookshop? I see. Someone from your life before you came here, yes?"

The flush rising to her hairline gave her away.

"Unusual that," said Mr. Strundale. "Must be, I'm afraid to say, someone quite powerful. Stay here."

He moved toward the door and she reached out to stop him. "Don't."

He patted her hand. "Just wait here. No one will get past me, I assure you." He looked down at Badger and smiled. "Or Badger. And you'd be surprised how ferocious Finnick can be." The animal bristled and chittered. "It'll be fine."

When he opened the door, Finnick at his side, there was no one outside who shouldn't be there. Just a busy street full of people. He stepped out. Looked up the street and down, Finnick mimicking his gesture. "No one there now. Are you sure?"

"Yes, I'm sure. It was . . ." She didn't want to bring him into it, old man that he was, and she didn't want to admit how uncertain of herself the visit had made her. "No," she said, "probably not. Just old fears." Badger lay down at her feet.

"Well then, tea it is. Chamomile and lavender, I think." He put his arm around her shoulders. "You know, my dear, you're still grieving. The loss of Mr. Mustby was a great one, seismic even, and it will take a long time for you to come to terms with it. For any of us to come to terms with it. It's quite normal to be discombobulated."

Is that what he thought? That she was delusional with grief?

He smiled, led her into a little kitchen not unlike the one at the Grimoire. Like Maggie, he lived above his shop. He told her to sit at the small table as he plugged in an electric kettle. "Without my old friend the world is changed, and not for the better. But you must remember he trusted you. He left the shop to you, knowing you were the right person." He puttered about, getting cups and saucers. "It takes a certain inner fortitude to be the proprietor of a shop that is the cosmic nexus of the world's tales." He chuckled and sat across from her. "So, regardless of whether the person who came to see you is a function of your grief, or a ghost from your past, or a person with malicious intent, the same advice holds: you mustn't cower. You must, and will, be afraid many times before you're as old as I am. Fear isn't something you can avoid. But you can turn and face it. Bullies hate it when you simply stand your ground. Power comes from resolve, not might."

She hung her head. "And what if I'm not as strong as all that?"

"Then Mr. Mustby wouldn't have chosen you for the job. The Grimoire and, to some extent, the Wort & Willow are thin places, as the Celts say. You know, a place with a somewhat porous barrier between the sacred and the mundane. It is also powerful, and those who reside in it, who are charged with its care, are recognized by such power, and cannot help but benefit from it." He patted her hand and the kettle began to sing. "Now, we should talk of more pleasant things and leave the morrow to the morrow."

When she left, Srebrenka was nowhere in sight.

WHEN, THE DAY AFTER, THE BELL OVER THE DOOR SOUNDED mid-morning, Maggie nearly fell off her chair, but it was only a man looking for a book of stories about the War of 1812. She found him the book and when she walked him to the door she peeked out, but saw no one who shouldn't be there.

Later, she opened the door again, Badger's leash wrapped tightly round her hand.

Srebrenka had brought a wooden folding chair and set up on the sidewalk. Maggie's skin tightened. Srebrenka smiled, waved her fingers and then rose. "I come in peace. I can't bear the misunderstanding between us. We were so close once. You're like family, and you know how much that means. After all, we're both alone in the world, aren't we? Especially now."

"I'm not alone," Maggie said.

"Your brother, Kyle? He's a sweet boy, and my friend." She flicked a piece of lint off her fire-engine clothing. The colour matched her lipstick.

Perhaps it was hearing Kyle's name on Srebrenka's lips, but Maggie wanted to strike the woman, to gouge out her eyes, to tear her cheeks. She stepped up to her, so quickly Srebrenka stepped back, knocking the chair into the street. Maggie was shaking, Badger taut as a steel spring.

"Enough! Do you understand? Enough! I'm not coming back. Not now, not ever, and I'll make the biggest scene you can imagine if you don't leave me alone! I'm not giving up everything I've got. I'll tell everyone what you're selling and to hell with the consequences!" Badger was barking now. "How many people around here do you think have lost relatives because of you? How long would it take the cops to get here? Do you want me to make a scene? Do you?" She'd started screaming out of desperation, and hadn't thought it would do much, but whereas a moment before people hadn't noticed Srebrenka, suddenly people stopped and looked and began to gather and whisper and point.

"Pretty Maggie, calm yourself," Srebrenka said, her eyes darting from one face to another. "No need for all this."

"Leave me alone! I don't want you, I don't want it! I'm done!"

Srebrenka dropped her cigarette to the street and ground it out under her heel. "Well, scenes are so uncouth. You always did surprise me, dear girl."

"I'm calling the cops," said a man from the Korean market. He pulled out his cellphone. Someone else was taking a video on their phone. Maggie flinched and hid her face. She didn't like scenes any more than Srebrenka did.

Srebrenka walked to a silver Jaguar parked at the curb. As she got into the driver's seat she said, "You don't think this is over, do you, pretty Maggie?" Srebrenka winked. "It's not."

The car began to move away. People blinked and scratched their heads. They grinned a little sheepishly, as though they weren't quite sure what they were doing there. They didn't seem to notice Maggie any longer, which suited her just fine.

The wooden chair lay in the street and then a young man with a beard and a knapsack with a U of T sticker on it stopped. "You throwing that away? I'll take it if you don't want it," he said.

"Be my guest," said Maggie.

THE NEXT DAY, MAGGIE OPENED THE DOOR A CRACK AND peeped out. Nothing. Badger's tail wagged. All clear. And the day after that, and the day after that . . . Srebrenka disappeared as abruptly as she'd appeared. Maggie hoped she might, after several weeks, once again put it all behind her. She wanted it to be a small whitecap on an otherwise calm sea. Nothing to worry about.

CHAPTER TWO

TWO WEEKS LATER, IN THE EARLY MORNING, when Maggie let Badger out in the back garden, something looked off. The sky was clear. Still, it looked too dark. The sun had risen; she'd seen it from the bedroom window. She looked over her shoulder at the clock on the kitchen wall. Yes, just after eight. True, the sun rose late this time of year, but it was up. So why was the day so dark? Badger sniffed here and there, staring at the top of the wall as though at an invisible squirrel. The shadows were long and fell in the wrong direction. Evening shadows, not morning. She shivered. Just a funny trick of the light, surely. "Hurry up, Badger." She hugged herself and stepped back into the kitchen.

By ten o'clock, Maggie sat at her desk, perusing a collection of folk tales from India. Just then she noticed a small red flame hovering over a book. Oh, no, she thought and rushed over to see what it was. The light was brightening, about to burn out, in a moment it would be gone, as would the book. Even now it was becoming indistinct, fading, the writing on the spine was barely visible. *The Stubborn Season* by . . . but Maggie was too late. The tiniest puff and the book was gone. Forgotten. Lost.

The bookshelf contracted as though the story had never been. She preferred not to notice when a book disappeared. They disappeared all the time, of course, but if she didn't look, if she didn't know, then she could avoid the sharp cramp of sorrow in her stomach. Still, there was something almost holy about bearing witness to such a death even if one couldn't help, wasn't there? What happened to a story never told again? All she could think of was void.

The bell over the door chimed. Badger's head came up and he rose to his feet from his bed by the fire. Someone sneezed, twice.

"Excuse me . . . is anyone here?" A child's voice.

"Hello?" Another sneeze. "Look at the dust! Hello? I got a message for someone named Maggie?"

There were few people who would send her messages; she had no friends save for Mr. Strundale and Alvin. Her parents were long dead. The store received no flyers and no bills, since apparently the mailman wasn't intended to find the place.

"Hello?" The child sounded a little frightened. "Anybody?"

Maggie sighed. "Come on, then. Back here. Badger, sit."

A boy's thin face peered around a bookshelf. He was perhaps ten years old, wearing a too-large red plaid jacket and droopy camouflage cargo pants. Black hair stuck out in an impressive number of directions.

"You sure have a lot of books," he said.

"Really? I hadn't noticed." She wandered back to the desk, the boy following, and sat.

"Does your dog bite?"

"Badger's more his own dog than mine, but I've never known him to bite, have I, Badger?" Badger's tail thumped on the floor. The boy looked dubious. "Did you say you had a message?"

"Right." The boy held out a pale blue envelope. His fingernails were black rimmed.

"Do you work in the coal mines when not delivering messages?" Maggie regarded the envelope with suspicion. She refused to have a cellphone because having one meant people were likely to call you and she didn't want people calling her, not even Alvin. She didn't even have a land line. Alvin didn't seem to care and popped in when he wanted to see her. Kyle, her brother, told her he thought she was nuts, hiding away from the world, but what had the world ever done for her? Might be from Alvin, or Kyle, she supposed. She hoped it wasn't from Srebrenka or any of her acquaintances from her time in the Forest.

"Who gave it to you?"

The boy scratched his head just above his ear. "Just some guy." He waggled the blue envelope. "You gonna take it?"

She wasn't sure why, but she felt obliged, if only to reassure herself it was nothing to worry about, probably not even meant for her. But the boy was here, and no one came to the Grimoire unless they were meant to. "I'll take it." Odd, it was heavier than it looked. Sure enough, there was her name and address, written on the envelope in silver ink. Silver? Her heart fluttered. Her fingers tingled. She tore open the paper. In the centre of a small piece of blue paper were a few words written in a squiggly silver script.

Follow me

No signature, not even a period at the end of the short sentence. She turned the note over. Nothing. She looked at the handwriting. "I don't understand. Am I supposed to follow you?"

He frowned. "I doubt it. Maybe."

"Where are you from?"

"Where do you think?"

"The Forest?"

He shrugged. Maggie opened the desk drawer. She reached into a wooden box and pulled out a ten-dollar bill that she dangled in front of the boy. His eyes narrowed. "I'll give you another if you promise not to deliver more messages."

"I don't make promises. But I'd rather you gimme a book."

"Really?"

He glared. "What, you think I can't read?"

"What kind of book?"

"I dunno, like an adventure story or something."

"Have you read *Peter Pan?*"

"Is it any good?"

"It's about a boy who never grows up and battles a pirate who has a hook instead of a hand."

"I dunno. What's so good about never growing up?"

"Point. But he can also fly, and he's leader of the Lost Boys."

"Yeah, all right."

She got him the book. A nice edition, with full-colour illustrations.

"Thanks." He tucked the book inside his coat.

He was skinny as an eel. She gave him the ten-dollar bill as well. He hurried out as though afraid she'd change her mind. Poor kid. It occurred to her he might work for Srebrenka. Alarming thought. She picked up her tea. Silver ink? It almost looked like the silver swirls Pipers developed on their skin as the addiction grew. She'd developed just a few traces along her abdomen and chest, the kind easily covered with clothing, although they'd faded away after six months or so of being clean.

She snorted. Follow the boy back to the Forest? Not likely. But if she wasn't supposed to, then why had the boy been admitted to the store? Well, she didn't care. She wasn't going. She scratched Badger behind the ear and went back to her book.

THE NEXT MORNING AS BADGER AND MAGGIE RETURNED from their walk, Maggie noticed the boy from the day before pacing up and down the street, looking decidedly perplexed.

"Are you back?" Maggie opened the door of the Grimoire.

Given the shop's knack for being inconspicuous, she never needed to lock it. "Tell me you're not looking for me."

"Did you change something about the place? It looked different yesterday."

"I don't believe anything's changed here in a very long time," said Maggie as she stepped inside.

Although it wasn't quite true that nothing ever changed, was it? The darkness she'd noticed in the garden yesterday had remained all day, and today it seemed even darker still. On top of that, the garden looked smaller. Impossible, of course. It was just a sense she had, of the stone walls being kind of . . . compacted. Badger trotted into the maze of bookshelves, heading for his nest of blankets near the fireplace by Maggie's desk.

The boy followed Maggie inside and when he closed the door behind him the street noises immediately quieted. He pulled a blue envelope out of his jacket pocket. "Got another one for you."

He put the envelope in her outstretched palm. More silver ink.

"Look, who's giving you these? Do you know Srebrenka? Is this from her?"

The boy snorted. "I wouldn't do nothing for her." Then he looked a little uncertain. "That who you think it's from? Look, some guy gives them to somebody, who gives it to somebody else, who passes it to someone, who gives it to a kid I know, and he gives it to another kid I know, until it gets to me. I'm like a boss, kind of, to some around there, and they know to bring things to me. I know my way around. Thought there might be some cash in delivering it, is all."

She reached into the inner pocket of her black peacoat and pulled out some bills. She handed them to the boy without counting.

He looked at the bills and grinned. "This is turning into a pretty good gig. I'm your delivery guy if you want, okay? Don't matter how the streets are all funny."

"Meaning?"

"Haven't you heard?"

"Would I have asked?"

"Everyone's talking about it. Shifting buildings and shrinking streets . . . from the Forest, they say."

"What are you talking about?"

"Nobody knows what's up, right? But something is. I got to go." He gave her a quick salute and dashed away.

A few minutes later Maggie sat at her desk, still wearing her coat, staring at the envelope. She took a deep breath and tore the paper.

I need you. Follow me

She cursed and slammed the top of the desk with her palm. Badger barked. "Sorry, boy, sorry." Maggie turned to the fireplace, took a long match from the little brass container by the hearth, lit the match and held the flame to the page. When it caught, she tossed it into the ashes, where it lay for a moment, glowing and backlit, the silver going black, until the paper browned, curled and then burst into flames.

CHAPTER THREE

T HE NEXT NIGHT A BITTERLY COLD WIND
worried the corners of the house and rattled the windows. Maggie could almost imagine it as an elemental being, a
malicious spirit. It snuck under the door and was strong enough
to riffle the thin mat. For a moment she imagined this might be
the spirit responsible for the compacting of her garden and was
thankful whatever magic held the Grimoire together seemed
strong enough to withstand it.

She carried a tureen of chicken stew to the table. The steam
rose, fragrant with rosemary, onions and black olives. She placed
it next to the bowl of green salad. Badger sat by her chair, his ears
cocked, his mouth open. "You've had yours. Lie down. Go on,
now." The dog, grumbling a little, slunk to his bed by the stove.

Alvin sat at the table, slicing the crusty bread. He'd rolled
up the sleeves of his heavy grey sweater and Maggie thought
his forearms were quite beautiful, as she did his strong and
long-fingered hands. Even though they were calloused from
the hard work on the boat, there was something elegant about
them, just as there was something well worn about his big slab
of a face, the result of time spent in sun and wind. Deep creases

around the eyes and mouth. Skin not coarse, but a bit leathery. The thick hair that always looked wind-ruffled and was bleached from the sun.

"That smells good." His knee bumped the table leg and the plates shook. Alvin Mustby was a big man, with long legs and big feet and big hands, and he always seemed to be bumping into things. "I'm going to bring you chicken every week if you promise to cook like this." He often did that, popping round with a bag of groceries. He was the sort of man who could be counted on for such practical things as chicken and salad and bread and so forth. She did not expect roses or perfume, nor did she crave them.

"Is this your way of inviting yourself to dinners?" Maggie poured tea from the squat brown pot into their mugs.

"Well, it's only fair the hunter's fed, isn't it?"

"Stopping off at the grocery store is hardly the same as tracking a deer through the winter woods, now is it."

"You've never had to contend with the wilds of Whole Foods." He spooned the stew into their bowls. "What's been going on here?"

She considered telling him about the letters but decided against it. She had almost convinced herself it was a bad joke. "There's something strange about the garden. Sounds mad, but it looks smaller, and, well, darker.

Alvin forked a large, dripping chunk of meat into his mouth and made appreciative noises, then got up and peered out the window to the garden. "Hard to tell much in the dark. Odd stuff going on all over, I hear. Most of it just gossip."

"What about?"

He returned to the table. "Lots of cops on the streets over by the Forest."

The Forest used to be a social housing project called Regent Park, full of red-brick low-rises, mixed-income families and some petty crime, but since elysium had taken over the drug market, the neighbourhood had become something different – more menacing, more insular, a thousand times more dangerous. At first, because of the *park* in its old name, Pipers had started calling it the Enchanted Forest. But the more they used, and the more Pipers there were, the less enchanted it looked. Once there had been a sort of gritty, hardscrabble sense of community, but that was over now. Some low-income families had moved out, displaced, others had nowhere else to go. The place was a no-go zone for just about anyone else, even the police. Maggie knew it only too well.

"Some sort of unrest," Alvin continued, "but no one's saying for sure, and there's nothing in the papers. Rumours, though, which sound as nuts as your shrinking garden." He scratched his head. "People think the Forest is taking up more space."

"Pipers moving into buildings outside the Forest?" The only good thing about the Forest was its self-containment. One side of the street was a reasonable, if down-on-its-luck neighbourhood, the other, the Forest side, had become something out of that Hieronymus Bosch painting of hell.

"No, not that. More like the neighbourhood itself is . . . expanding."

"I don't understand."

"Neither do I. Streets getting smaller on the border between Cabbagetown and the Forest, and something about streets ending where they didn't used to. You know, the geographical confusion that's happened in the Forest for a long time."

Yes, Maggie knew. Space inside the Forest wasn't precisely static. "But not outside the Forest."

"Not until now, if the rumours are to be believed. Not that I do. Probably just what you said – more people on the pipe. You do realize you're the only person I've heard of ever getting off the stuff."

She considered that. She'd never heard of anyone getting off it either, not permanently, unless you counted death. And when

Srebrenka had come after her, hadn't she said as much? "That can't be true, can it?"

Alvin shrugged. "Well, no one I can think of has ever stayed off it like you have. Speaking of people who are still at it, no word from Kyle?"

"Why do you ask?"

"I don't know. I was just thinking about him. He'll turn up one of these days."

She considered. "Possibly. Then again, he's been so angry at me for so long, maybe not. He's been pissed ever since I left home and didn't take him."

"You were just a kid. You're not to blame."

Just a kid in the thrall of Lenny the Predator Poet, she thought.

So much might have been different if she'd not run away with Lenny. But then again, maybe not. Kyle had stayed with the cousins, who, after their parents' deaths had become their negligent guardians, and look what happened to him. Maybe even if Lenny hadn't put that first silver pipe between her lips, she'd have done it herself. If she refused to accept responsibility for Kyle's addiction, she couldn't put the blame for what happened to her on Lenny. Lenny died out there. So many Pipers did. But surely not all. Thinking she might be the only one who'd stayed clean this long was unsettling. It felt like a responsibility she didn't want. She'd done it, and all by herself, so why couldn't others? Why couldn't Kyle?

"Kyle cut down the apple tree in the backyard, you know. Just to spite me." How she'd loved that tree. How many afternoons had she sat beneath it, nose in a book, hiding from her cousins' varied tortures?

Alvin gnawed on a bone. "What will you do if he does come back?"

"I didn't tell you, but when I saw him a few weeks ago he asked if he could stay here."

"Did he?"

"Right. Look at your face. That's the point. I don't trust him any more than you do."

"Yes, well, I'm a jaded bastard. Not like my uncle."

Maggie blushed. "Your uncle was a saint, and you know God protects them, them and fools."

She put her bread down and pushed at the stew with her fork. "You think I should let him come here?"

Alvin reached across the table and took her hand. "I think you should do what you think is right, for both of you. I'm no poster boy for charity, or for family for that matter. Never had much experience with them, save for my uncle."

Alvin's father had been a gambler and sometime sax player, and when he'd married Alvin's mother her parents had disowned her. When Alvin was just a baby his parents were killed in a car accident one night when Alvin's father was being chased by unhappy loan sharks. His paternal uncle, Mr. Mustby, had taken him in, raised him in the Grimoire and was the only family Alvin knew.

Alvin ran his thumb back and forth on the palm of her hand, tracing her lifeline. "What are you afraid of, if he came here? I could take the money and keep it safe, if that's what's on your mind, but I don't think it is."

"No, not entirely. Besides, there always seems to be enough."

When Mr. Mustby died she found a trunk full of cash in the bedroom wardrobe, with a note inside saying, *Maggie, my dear, this is for you. This place is yours now.* It explained a great deal, all that money. For one thing, it explained why Mr. Mustby never cared there were so few customers. She had told Alvin about the trunk and told him she thought the money should be his, but he'd declined, laughing. "Not for me," he'd said. "Anymore than this shop is for me. I don't like being cooped up, and my uncle knew that. I don't need any more money than I can earn myself. That ever changes, I'll let you know."

"I've never felt it was really my money," said Maggie. "More like I'm a paid guardian."

Alvin nodded. "So, are you worried about what would happen if he started using again? If he was here and close to you?"

She nodded.

"I'm afraid I'd start again," she whispered. She wasn't scared she'd lose her money, or her brother, or her security, although all those things were tied up in it; she was afraid she'd lose herself. "If I did, I wouldn't come back." She could practically feel it, right now . . . the pipe between her lips, the rise out of her body, the silver shimmer of the World Beside This One . . . She'd never told Alvin about Srebrenka's visits. Srebrenka hadn't returned. Maggie had handled it.

"I wouldn't let that happen," said Alvin, toying with the end of her thick braid.

"Really? And how exactly would you stop it?" Save her, would he? It was so sweet of him. And so naive. Maggie knew full well that if elysium got a grip on her again no one, not even Alvin, would be able to stop her. She was the only one capable of keeping herself out of the Silver World. She was fond of Alvin. She was *very* fond of Alvin, in fact, and she supposed she trusted him as far as it went. He was a good man and an honest one, but he was a man who loved boats, here today and gone the next, up the St. Lawrence Seaway perhaps, to open water . . .

"I'm pretty good in a fight, you know. Did I ever tell you about the time I was in Tonga and got into a fight with this Samoan?"

"I thought it was a giant Scotsman in the Orkneys?"

"Oh, that was another time. He was big, for sure, but the guy in Tonga must have been seven feet tall and battered as a pound of cod. Can't remember what started the fight, but I finally picked up a bottle and bashed it on the bar, but the damn thing wouldn't break. Slammed it three times with this guy bearing down on me so I whomped him over the head

with it. That broke the bottle and he went down like Liston."
He laughed. "Course, I spent the night in the lock-up. Don't
recommend that. Centipedes the size of rattlesnakes with a bite
more painful, and since I've been bitten by both, I can say that
with all honesty. But anyway, listen, you're not going back down
the drain. I'd move in here, if I had to."

Ah, Alvin's adventure tales. Tonga, Macau, Barbados, the
Orkneys . . . "You wouldn't like that. There's no point glowering
at me, you know it's true. You'd be good for . . . oh . . . a week, a
month, and then if you weren't back on the boat you'd be thun-
dering around like a bear."

"Come on, you don't know that. I've already been to every
place in the world I'm interested in and several I wasn't. I'm not
saying I'd never go for a jaunt now and then. Besides, remember
what Marian Engel said: 'So this was her kingdom: an octagonal house, a roomful of books, and a bear.'"

He had grown up in the Grimoire and so, like her, he read
and read. Unlike her, he was fond of quotes.

"Nice try, but no, we might as well face it: we do not play
well with others, you and I, Alvin, and our lives suit us best as
they are." She stood up and took his hand. "Come upstairs and
let's forget all this. Trouble will still be here tomorrow."

IN THE MORNING, ALVIN KISSED HER AND LEFT HER STILL
in bed. He'd be gone for a while. He docked the boat for the season at the Marina Quay West by the massive Canada Malting
silo, and it was time to winterize. She didn't expect to see him
for a week or more. Maggie reached for the sweater hanging
from its place on the bedpost, and crossed the icy floor to the
smudgy, wavy glass of the front window. Alvin sauntered down
the street, his cap at a jaunty angle, his duffle bag slung over
his shoulder, his step light even in his heavy boots. He walked

with a boxer's bounce, and in fact had been a Golden Gloves light heavyweight champion when he was twenty. The street was busy with people hurrying off to early morning jobs, but no one looked up toward her window. He rounded the corner without a backward glance and was gone.

As happened after every night she spent with Alvin, Maggie was in something of a muddle and she did not like being in a muddle. As a woman of solitary preferences, she should have been satisfied with things the way they were, and yet she wasn't. Not quite. Her spirits drooped, watching him walk away. It was vexing.

The room was comfortably furnished with the four-poster bed, a bureau under the window, a Queen Anne chair beside that and a bookshelf (no room should ever be without a bookshelf). An old armoire boasted four drawers and a space for hanging clothes: more than enough space for Maggie's limited wardrobe of jeans, T-shirts, sweaters, turtlenecks, her Doc Marten boots, a pair of running shoes, a couple of scarves and a peacoat. All black. It made things simple. On the bureau stood two photos: One of Mr. Mustby seated at the leather chair by the fireplace in the bookshop with a large volume on his lap, and on the small round table next to him was a glass of what Maggie presumed was brandy, and his pipe and ashtray. The expression on Mr. Mustby's face was one of slight surprise, as though the photographer had come up on him unawares. Crinkled eyes, his mouth in a smile, which was just like him. He always expected the best and assumed every surprise would be a pleasant one. The other photo was of him and Alvin, standing on the deck of Alvin's boat, *The Storyteller*. They both squinted into the sun and their hair was tangled in the wind. The love between them was so obvious with Alvin's arm around the smaller, older man's shoulders.

Badger whined and pranced at her feet. "Walk, yes."

Downstairs, she walked out into the back garden. It looked like twilight, and there was no mistaking it, the garden was smaller. She could cross to the seat near the oak (which was shorter, she was sure it was) in ten steps, instead of the usual twenty or twenty-five. Only the stone wall seemed the same – or did it? Was the fact it encircled a smaller garden the reason it looked taller? It had always been over her head, but now? She reached up. She had to jump to touch the top. What was happening? She turned and found Badger sitting in the doorway. "Not coming out? I don't blame you. Come on, we'll go to the park."

Maggie and Badger stepped out the front door. The air snapped with autumn's nip and smelled of apples along with the usual scents of the market. Badger barked once and trotted off to the nearest tree against which to do his business.

They were passing the Wort & Willow Apothecary when Badger stopped and turned back in the direction from whence they'd come, his ears pricked. Maggie put her hand down to reassure the dog and, following his gaze, tried to see what he was fixed on, but there was nothing except the street – a few women carrying shopping bags filled with fruits and vegetables, a bearded hipster singing along to something on his headphones, two teenaged girls giggling . . . but wait, there, who was that? Badger danced a little, whined, looked up at her and then back again. A boy, wearing a plaid jacket and camouflage pants. A riot of black hair. Standing in the doorway of the Grimoire.

Mr. Strundale poked his long, lugubrious face from his doorway. "Maggie, did you find that book on honey mead I wanted? I was just going to bring you some cider. Dear, are you all right?"

"I'll bring it by later today, Mr. Strundale."

Badger ran up to the boy, who jumped and then reached out and scratched the dog under the chin. Badger stretched his neck in pleasure. "He's a good dog, isn't he?"

"Well, you're practically family. What's your name, anyway?"

"Peter."

"Hello, Peter. Peter Pan!" Maggie ushered the boy into the shop. "I suppose you've got another one?"

"Yeah. Weird, though. Just found it in my pocket. Figured I'd better bring it."

She stared at the handwriting. It was fainter than the second note, which, now she thought about it, was fainter than the writing on the first note. "Listen, any more unusual stuff out there? Streets moving and so forth?"

"Don't you have a TV?"

"No TV."

"Internet?" He looked as though she'd just said she didn't breathe air.

"I'm a freak. I get it."

He shook his head. "Big news. Like, you know the Rogers Centre and those figures of cheering fans, all gold, by the entrances? Well, they've disappeared. And those big cow statues down in the financial district went missing. Stolen, probably, although . . ." the boy grinned, "there were also reports of cows hulking around near the Necropolis by the Forest."

Maggie handed him a twenty. "Nonsense. Besides which, the Necropolis is up by Wellesley Street, not the Forest."

The boy shrugged. "It is now. Well," he turned to go, "guess maybe I'll be seeing you."

"It's possible."

She very much wanted to burn the envelope without reading it. There were a number of arguments as to why this would be prudent. She twirled her braid and fidgeted with the owl charm affixed to it. Badger leaned against her leg and sighed, gazing up at her. "I agree," she said, and opened the envelope.

I'm lost. Sister, follow me

The skin along her arms pricked and chilled. *Sister.* The last two words were barely legible and trailed off in a scrawl of ink.

"Oh, Kyle." Tears burned the back of her eyes. "What have you done?"

KYLE IS WRAPPED IN FURS IN THE BACK OF A LOW-SLUNG white convertible. The driver in the front seat, a silent man with ice-blue eyes and a fur hat, steers the car along the dark road. They move quickly. The evergreens on either side of them blur. He wonders where they might be going, but only mildly. It doesn't really matter where, or when, or how. He understands that now. So very little matters. The car skids and rocks on a turn, a patch of frozen blackness, and Kyle thinks that in another life he might be alarmed by such a thing, and smiles. How foolish. What a waste it is to be concerned. Why had he ever bothered? Why did anyone? The car settles down again and on they speed. The stars in the indigo sky above glitter, chilly and distant. The air smells of winter – the metal-sweet scent of ice and snow. He leans against the woman beside him and sighs. She holds a silver pipe to his lips and he sucks. The woman chuckles and calls him a greedy boy. She rakes her fingers through his hair and he shivers with pleasure. The fur envelops them both. Silver fur. Silver night.

"Everything is freezing fast," she murmurs in his ear.

"I am warm."

"Yes, sweet boy, I will see to it you are never cold again."

The pipe is at his lips. Deep, deep goes the smoke into the lungs, and through the tissues and into the bloodstream and look, up there, those stars are actually shining people, twirling, dancing, and animals, too, bears and great whales and an owl with the wingspan of all heaven, and their movements are music, one moment sweet and trilling, the next deep and thrumming into his soul.

The woman's skin is alabaster, cool as marble, but somehow her touch warms him, a golden trace along his neck, his chest . . . wherever her fingers trail. The furs are soft. His head lolls back to gaze upon the dancing diamond creatures of the sky and he lets her fingers wander where they wish.

"More, please." His voice is a wisp of fog.
The woman holds the pipe and tilts his chin toward it.

CHAPTER FOUR

THE LAST TIME MAGGIE HAD SEEN HER BROTHER, a few weeks ago, he'd been off the elysium. He was staying at a flop on Jarvis and had sent a message one night, arriving with a slightly baffled street kid, asking her to meet him by the greenhouses in Allan Gardens. She'd been loath to go, sure he only wanted more money, but then again, you never knew.

The traffic was light on Gerrard, even for a Monday night. As she walked, Maggie caught sight of Kyle rounding the corner from Jarvis. She called out to him twice, but he kept going, stepping through the pools of light from the street lamps as though he couldn't get back into the darkness quickly enough. He passed the Baptist church, eyes resolutely on the sidewalk. Maggie cursed, and started to run.

"Kyle, wait!" She reached out and grabbed his sleeve.

"Hey, didn't hear you."

A strange greeting, she thought, after not having seen each other in more than a year. He was thin as an alley cat, his shoulders sharp under the jacket. His skin was oysterish.

As though reading her mind he said, "Don't worry, I'm not looking for it."

She wanted to put her arms around him, her broken little brother. "I brought you a book." Kyle looked at it but made no effort to take it. "Poems. *The Song of Simplicity*." She stepped closer, practically touching him with the outstretched book. "I thought, maybe . . . it might help you find, I don't know, a little beauty."

How could she explain that although nothing would ever compare to the elysium visions, his only chance was to try and find beauty anyway.

He took the book and stuffed it under his jacket. The air was cold and damp. Maggie buttoned her peacoat.

"I didn't know if you'd come," he said.

"I'm here."

"Would have come to see you, but of course I can never find the damned bookstore. Kid said he went back the next day and even he couldn't find it again." He snorted.

"That kind of place. So," she asked, "where are you going?"

He half smiled. "To meet you." He looked a little like his old self then, like the beautiful fawn-like boy he'd been, his dark eyes twinkling.

She remembered how jittery and irritable she'd been when she was newly clean. They walked along silently. Their breath formed little clouds. Then he said, "If I have to stay where I'm at, I don't think I can make it, not without killing somebody. They're hollow, useless, whining . . ."

"Try not to kill anyone. It only complicates things." She affected a cartoonishly sincere expression, hoping to get a laugh, even a bitter one. He merely glanced at her, his eyes snapping. "I know it's hard," she said. "But it won't be forever. Just a little while. You'll get back on your feet. You'll get a place of your own."

"I need a job."

Kyle turned onto a path leading to the greenhouses. Under the trees, small groups of homeless people camped, using old

picnic tables and tarps. Two empty wheelchairs. Three backpacks.
A wire garbage can with a scatter of paper plates, plastic forks
and empty bottles nearby. They were a little dishevelled, but they
didn't look like Pipers. Not yet, anyway. It wasn't much of a slide
from here to the Forest. A van pulled up and four young men
got out, carrying Thermoses and sleeping bags. Maybe from the
nearby Anishnawbe Health Toronto or St. Stephen's Community
House. The men walked over to the group of homeless people. It
lifted Maggie's spirits to see such kindness.

She considered the glass-and-brick building in front of her.
It was astonishing that the palm house hadn't been vandalized
over the years. Maggie tried to imagine how grand the park
must have been in 1882 when Oscar Wilde gave a lecture there.
Kyle tried the door. It opened, and without saying another word
he walked through.

"Come on," she called to him. "We can't go in. The place
should be locked this time of night."

She looked around. No cops, just the homeless guys and
the men from the van. She blew out her cheeks and stepped
through, closing the door behind her.

There were no lights on inside and she had to wait for her
eyes to adjust. Somewhere off to her right gravel crunched as
Kyle walked into the shadows. Shapes formed in the gauzy
moonlight and weak puddles of emergency lighting. Inky,
sinewy tree trunks solidified. A low rock wall. Shrubs. Fleshy
tropical plants. It was humid and warm.

Where was Kyle? If he was playing some sort of joke on her,
she'd smack him. "Kyle? Where are you?"

She walked to the next room and found him sitting on a
wrought iron bench beneath a banana tree. She couldn't make
out his features. He rested his elbows on his knees, but his head
was up.

"What are we doing in here?" She sat next to him. His body
vibrated like a violin string, tightened to its limit, about to snap.

He bumped her shoulder with his. "Why don't I come and stay with you?"

"In the shop?"

"Yeah, the shop." He muttered something she didn't catch.

"Pardon me?"

He glared, all defiance and shame. "You're so goddamn selfish."

And there it was: the little toad on the ground between them. Maggie admitted he had a point. But have him live in the shop? Her theory was that if he were meant to find it he would. But should she invite him? Mr. Mustby had told her to take care whom she brought to the shop, that the shop would bring to it those who were meant to come, and if she were to interfere, inviting someone of her own, she must ensure the person was of impeccable character. By definition any Piper was disqualified. Her stomach cramped just thinking about having Kyle live with her.

Kyle had been clean when Alvin had given him a berth on his boat and a crew job – cleaning and so forth. It lasted a little over a month and then Alvin woke to find Kyle vanished, along with Alvin's cash box. Alvin had come to her, rubbing his hand through his hair, and asked for a loan, just to get him through until he collected the money owed him for a corporate charter. She'd had to pry the truth out of him. He denied Kyle's involvement at first. Said he'd lost his money playing poker, but she knew him better. Because of his father he never gambled.

She shouldn't have been surprised Kyle had let them down. That's what Pipers did. But still. She'd thought he wouldn't do that to *her*, and by extension, Alvin. As children, she and Kyle had clung to each other in the chill of their parents' lackadaisical neglect. It wasn't that their parents abused them; it was more as though the drama of their own lives and their own self-regard made them forget they *had* children. They'd died when scaffolding from the thirteenth floor of a construction site of a new condo building going up near Harbourfront snapped in half, sending four workers crashing to the sidewalk below, right on top of the Marchettes, who were on their way to the sales office to inquire about a lakeview unit. Maggie was fourteen and Kyle nine. They'd gone to stay with Horace Gallagher, a distant cousin with four children of his own all squashed together in his cramped rented house on Winchester Street. Horace seemed to spend much of the time with a woman in another part of town, and his wife, Phyllis, left Kyle and Maggie to their own devices, apart from the odd meal here and there. Their children, however, Ben, Brian, Carol and Karen, did not take well to the new members of the family and spent most of their free time thinking up new ways to torture them. Lit matches tossed into one's hair, dead mice in the bed, spit in the soup, shoves into mud puddles and walls, pinches and slaps and all manner of name-calling. And then, when Maggie was seventeen, she ran away in the mad illusion she had at last found protection and care elsewhere, abandoning Kyle. It had been a selfish act. Utterly selfish, although at the time it had felt imperative. Of course, Kyle had been lost. Of course, he'd been enraged. He'd been as terrified as a duckling left behind on a fast-freezing lake.

So Kyle tried to escape as well, to follow his sister down the elysium road.

Maggie had wondered how long it would take him to ask her. She would have done the same thing in his position. A good sister would take him in, would trust him not to steal, not to fill the bookshop with every ragged, dagger-eyed, silver-swirled Piper in a five-mile radius. A good sister wouldn't feel this acid-burn of horror at the idea of having to take responsibility for another human being. She was not a good sister.

"I was selfish. I shouldn't have left you and I've apologized a thousand times. But you need to be independent, Kyle. You need to stand on your own two feet. Get your own place. I'll help you find one."

He stiffened and pulled away. "So you haven't changed."

She stood. What boiled up in her was like hot tar. It stuck to everything in her gut, in her head; it scalded her lips. "Stop whining, Kyle." She bent toward him, her pointed finger in his face. Kyle looked startled and drew back. She was probably yelling, but she didn't care. "If it hadn't been for Mr. Mustby, I'd have died out there, and nobody gave a flying fart, did they? Did you? And now I should save poor little Kyle? Well, I know you, Kyle, because I know what I was like when I was on the pipe and don't tell me you're not using again, because you might not be using now but sure as hell you're going to be before the week's out and you know it, so don't give me that hurt little boy look or I'll slap you."

Kyle stood up now, too, and they stood eye to eye, the same height, the same sharp bones, the only difference was that whereas her hair was the colour of honey, his was dark as November.

"I'd like to see you try." His hands were fists at his side.

She should sit. She wanted to back down. She wanted to say she didn't mean it, to say they were in this turbulent sea together and she wouldn't let him drown, but instead she said, "Don't tempt me. If I'm selfish, so are you, nothing but a selfish little boy, sulking because you don't get what you want. You stole from Alvin and you'd steal everything I have if I was stupid enough to let you live with me. Goddamn it! You want the pipe so bad I can smell it on you. I've been where you are, remember?"

"Oh, nobody could ever forget how you've suffered, and how you've overcome, and how much stronger you are than I am, and how you never did the horrible things I've done."

His eyes shone with what Maggie was horrified to realize were tears. "Kyle, I –"

He shoved her, and she stumbled back.

He took off running. The door to the street opened, and

then slammed shut. She ran after him, her feet slipping on the gravel. The door stuck, and she wrestled with it, cursing, praying she wouldn't be trapped inside for the night. The hinge protested, then gave way, and she tumbled into the park. She looked right, and then left, but saw nothing but paths and grass and trees and three bums sharing a bottle. Wherever he'd gone, he was halfway there by now.

An image rose in her mind: Kyle in his striped flannel pajamas, curled up under her arm, falling asleep as she read to him from his favourite book of magical tales; the powdery, slightly animal scent of him; his weight in her arms; his thick eyelashes . . . and her chest felt bound by tightening ropes.

CHAPTER FIVE

M AGGIE STARED AT THE LETTER. KYLE, HER broken baby brother, was sending her messages from God-knew-where. She didn't understand how he'd managed to get a message through to her, but in her bones, she knew – Kyle was back on elysium. Lost in the Forest, probably, lost in his own mind and that warren of twisting streets. She wouldn't risk everything on three cryptic notes. Of course she wouldn't.

I'm lost. Sister, follow me

She almost laughed. What did he expect – that she simply stroll into the Forest and fetch him? Yes, that's exactly what he expected.

This day is over, she thought, and climbed the stairs to her room.

Maggie lay on the bed, Badger at her side, and stared up at the ceiling cracks, longing for Mr. Mustby's guidance. Long yellowish slivers of light slipped through the drawn shutters and sliced across the dark beams. Light from a setting sun. Although only God knew what time it was in the ever-darker, ever-smaller garden. She was cold. Still fully dressed, she pulled a blanket to her chin.

Badger's legs twitched, and he huffed, his jowls flapping. Maggie stroked his head and he started, yelped and then looked sheepish. "What were you dreaming?" His tail thumped.

She remembered nights after her parents' death when Kyle had such terrible nightmares, and she would comfort him, or try to. He screamed and screamed, saying machines were eating him, and talked of blades and saws and small steel rooms that contracted until he was crushed. She put her arms around him and told him he was safe, but he pushed her away, crying for their mother. He'd been all eyes and elbows and knees, prone to bumps and bruises on the jagged things of the world. One day he'd brought home a tiny, featherless, baby bird that had fallen out of its nest. He'd cupped it in his hands, and walked a mile home from the ravine, talking to it all the while. He put it in a little shoebox lined with handkerchiefs. Maggie warned him it probably wouldn't live, but he looked at her with that stubborn, frowning look and said, "No. I will save it. I'll feed it and keep it warm and teach it to fly." He found an eyedropper, and filled it with water, and when the little bird opened its beak he squeezed it in. The poor wee thing convulsed once, and fell over, dead. Kyle shrieked and screamed he'd killed it, and then cried for hours and hours, utterly inconsolable, until at last he fell asleep clutching the shoebox. The next day, it took Maggie until nearly nightfall to persuade him the bird needed to be buried. She told a story about how it would grow new, special wings, the way a plant grew leaves, and fly away to be with the bird-fairies. He hadn't believed a word of it, she didn't think, but at last he let her take the box, and stood beside her at the little grave, crying huge, silent, oily tears. She used to call him Little Brother of the Sparrow.

Oh, Kyle. My Little Brother of the Sparrow.

Maggie sobbed, and stuffed her mouth with the blanket to stop from screaming. Badger whined and licked her face, and she hugged him as she buried her face in the pillow. *Follow me . . .*

follow me . . . follow me . . . the words echoed. She finally fell asleep when the burden of being awake simply became too much.

MAGGIE DREAMS . . .

Kyle is a small boy, sitting by a window, looking out onto a field of moonlit snow. A single flake drifts down from the night sky and lands on the windowsill. It grows larger and larger until it turns into a woman, dressed in the finest white silk, shimmering like a thousand stars. Her long hair is the colour of the inside of a prism when the light strikes it just so, full of fire. She is delicate as an icicle, and her eyes are all that is dark about her. They are bottomless, full of nothing but hunger. Kyle stands transfixed, and Maggie tries to call out to him, to tell him to beware the beautiful woman, for surely she is evil, but Kyle either can't hear her or else he ignores her. The ice woman bids him to open the window. As soon as he does the woman reaches inside the snow-swept folds of her gown and when she lifts her hand something sharp flashes. A shard of ice . . . lethal as steel. Maggie is behind the glass now, while the ice woman stands inside next to Kyle. Maggie pounds on the glass, trying to warn her brother, but he pays her no mind. The woman will stab her brother in the heart, and there is nothing Maggie can do to stop it. Harder and harder she pounds on the window. And then, in a great explosion, the glass shatters and fragments fly everywhere . . . one of them to the centre of Kyle's chest, where it disappears deep beneath the skin and his white nightshirt blooms with a red rose as he falls to the ground . . . and the ice woman laughs and laughs.

It was still dark when Maggie woke in damp, twisted sheets. Badger sat at the end of the bed, whining. The dream hung in the air – the metallic smell of the cold, the grate of the woman's laughter. It was Maggie's heart that was pierced, shot through with slivers of ice. She cried out and sobbed again. It was impossible. The guilt would kill her; crush her beneath its frigid heel.

The room seemed smaller. Sharp talons of fear gripped her throat. Yes, the window, the door frame, everything slightly tighter, more compact. Whatever was happening in the streets, and outside in her garden, was happening now in the Grimoire. Not only was the shape altering, but she was sure there were fewer lights flicking on in the shop below, and more flames turning books to ash. At first she hadn't really noticed, but the last few days she was sure of it. More stories were dying than being born.

"Oh, Badger." She drew the dog to her. She buried her face in his soft fur, smelled the good clean doggy smell of him. Were these things connected? The messages, the slippery shrink of space, the dimming light, the elysium, the Forest? It was just a gut feeling, but the connection sat solidly inside her.

There was only one thing for it. She'd go into the Forest, a sort of reconnaissance. She'd get through the day, and at twilight, when the Pipers came out to play . . . She rose and went to the desk, sure it took her a step less than it should. She stared at the photo of Mr. Mustby, pleading for a sign.

The Forest, where Pipers congregated, was an area located in Old Toronto, bound by Shuter Street to the south, Gerrard to the north, Parliament to the west and River Street to the east. In the mid-1800s it had been called Cabbagetown, because of the vegetables people grew in their front yards, although that quaint name now referred to the wealthier area to the north. By the time the Second World War rolled around, it was the worst of Toronto's slums and in 1947 the whole place was razed and Regent Park, the "garden city," was built. With abundant green space, paths and walkways instead of streets, it was largely inaccessible to traffic. It should have been a haven, but from the beginning, people who didn't live in Regent Park had no reason to go there. As it grew evermore isolated and neglected by the rest of the city, gangs took hold. It was the perfect place for a thriving trade in elysium. Ten years ago the drug first appeared, and since then it had taken over.

Maggie stood in the doorway of an abandoned storefront on Queen Street. Across the street was the laneway Fee Place, one of the ways into the Forest. All along the walk here she'd passed gaggles of police in their dark blue uniforms and combat boots, with their nightsticks and guns in their belts. They loitered on street corners, urging the occasional pedestrian along, and not, Maggie noticed, answering questions. The police were never terribly good at answering questions but, judging from the tension on their faces, they had no more idea what was causing the spatial shifts than anyone else.

It was hard to explain what was wrong. The roads themselves hadn't changed – it wasn't as though the Forest was creeping into the city by taking over more streets, but still, it seemed closer, and the roads leading to it smaller, even though there were the same number of streets, the same number of buildings. Nothing was actually missing; it was just that everything outside the Forest felt *diminished*.

A group of police stood down the road, but they weren't bothering, it seemed, with Fee Place. Maggie remembered it as a small lane, but now it seemed little more than a crevice between closed up brick buildings, the one to the east five or six storeys, the one to the west an old Victorian. All the Pipers knew Fee Place and made dark jokes about how everyone had their price. The twilight hadn't yet darkened into night and light still ventured a few yards into the opening, beyond which the Forest spread, a sort of unmapped non-space.

A man, skinny as a ferret, slouched toward her, his shoulders hunched against the wind, a cap pulled low over his features. The police ignored him and as he neared her he dashed across to the Forest side. He took his hand from his pocket and held the collar of his jacket closed as a gust shook him. His skin was practically radiant with silver swirls. He glanced her way and she bent down, fussing with Badger. When she looked up again the man was disappearing into the lane. She waited a few minutes as the light dimmed.

"I guess it's time," she said. Badger tilted his head and whined.

She crossed the street, Badger at her heels, and stepped into the laneway. The sickly sweet stench from garbage piles created a barricade of odour. She wrinkled her nose. City workers didn't bother to collect the rubbish here. No one complained. The buildings were derelict, the windows long broken. Some boot-scarred doors still existed, but many simply had boards nailed over openings.

Badger sniffed and sneezed. He pressed against Maggie's leg. "It's okay, boy."

She turned left. Had she really lived here? And was it really in a broken-down, tilting and treacherous shack like that, held together with rope and tar, that she'd slept through all those freezing nights?

Badger's hackles rose, he rumbled. "Easy, Badger."

Something flitted at the corner of Maggie's vision. She swung her head around but saw nothing in the shadowy alley but rubbish bins, an old mattress, a busted television. Rats probably, or cats . . . although whatever it was seemed larger. She prayed no feral dogs scavenged, but Badger wasn't reacting as though other dogs were about. He was, however, nearly electric with odour overload. "Heel," she said. "Heel." But he was already plastered to her leg, his hackles up. Maybe she was wrong. Maybe there was another animal in the alley. "Leave it," she said.

She kept her pace brisk. She turned onto one of the unnamed laneways, only to stop in her tracks. Dead end. But she was so sure this was the way. And maybe it was, once, but now a make-shift hovel barred the path, part tent, part tin, several timbers, planks and boards; a thin trail of smoke seeped through a hole in what might be considered a roof. A trollish bulk hunkered in the shadowed entrance, past a glowing brazier. Something metal glinted. She muttered, "Sorry, friend," and began to back out. The bulk shifted. Badger growled.

"That dog comes at me, I'll snap its neck."

"Stay, Badger. No worries, he won't attack unless I give the word."

The mass shifted again, swelled up and moved forward.

"We're on our way; just a wrong turn is all." Her heart scattered everywhere in her chest at once.

"I'll be damned. That you, Mags?"

Maggie squinted, trying to make out the form as it stepped from the opening. Huge. Arms too long for the body, legs bandy, head bald as an egg. It clamped a hand on top of its head, and then the other on top of that. It was a gesture she knew.

"Is that you, Lumpy?"

"None other. What are you doing back here? I thought you were gone for good." He lurched toward her on those ridiculous, nearly circular legs. His army-surplus coat was a little too small and a wide belt around his formidable middle held it shut.

Although he wasn't as tall as he was round, Maggie still had to look up. Lumpy had once been a boxer but, unlike Alvin, he wasn't a very good one, and the resultant facial bone structure was the source of his nickname. The skin was covered in so many swirls it was almost a solid shade of silver. His eyes – the whites not white at all, but bleary red – were sinister in contrast.

He put his hands on her shoulders. "You weren't supposed to come back. I bet on you."

She shrugged, or tried to, under the weight of his hands. "Stuff happens."

"It does." A tremor shot through Lumpy's limbs and he jerked his hands back. "Do you hear that?" He spun around. "Goddamn weasels! Get away, ya bastards!"

He picked up a brick from a pile and threw it onto the tin part of his roof. It made a terrible racket and Badger barked. Lumpy picked up another brick and for a moment Maggie feared he might throw it at Badger. She clamped her hands around the dog's muzzle and quieted him. Lumpy dropped the brick and put his hands back on his head, a look of anguish on his face.

"Sorry."

"It's okay, Lumpy. You have the visions?"

"Weasels, of all things." He looked abashed and began to tell a story about when he was a boy walking home from school, in a northern suburb, where the fields began. "This weasel darts across the road in front of me. I picked up a stone and threw it. Knocked the thing over. Grabbed another rock and was going to brain it, right? Dunno why. Just did it." He hunkered down and held his hand out for Badger to sniff. When the dog's tail wagged Lumpy scratched him under the chin. "I got close enough to kill it and it sprang up and ran right up my clothes to my throat. Teeth and claws everywhere. I threw it to the ground and stunned it, but another sprang from the side of the road, I guess it was the first one's mate, and it came at me. Then they were both on me and I was the one fighting for my life. They were like razors in fur, and I can still smell 'em." Lumpy stood and crossed his arms over his chest. He recalled how he finally knocked one out while the other ran into a hole in the stone wall skirting the road, how he killed the wounded animal with a stone, then went home and got his father's rifle. "I came back and shot the other one. It was easy enough to find, for there it was, sitting next to the body of the first, like it was mourning." His eyes met Maggie's. "I guess I felt guilty. They looked small, you know."

"You were just a boy, Lumpy. Boys do stupid things."

"Well, I'm paying for them now."

That was the way of elysium; it demanded a price for the beautiful visions. It burrowed into your darkest crannies – your memories, your heart – and found the things you regretted most, the things you feared, the things of which you were ashamed, and dragged them out into the world, first in dreams, and then in hallucinations. "You thought about cutting back?"

"Tried. Even went clean for a few weeks. Don't help."

Maggie's heart sank. He was too far gone then. It happened. Pipers got to a point where the visions leaked into the real world. No road but madness or death then. They forgot to eat. Even if they wandered out of the Forest and to hospital, it was no good. They forgot to breathe, eventually. Her face must have showed her sorrow, for he managed a smile and chucked her under the chin with his anvil hand, carefully, so as not to knock her head off.

"I'll be alright a good while yet. Weasels are pretty manageable. Good thing they ain't lions, or dragons." His expression became serious. "Right, you. What are you doing back here?"

"What's anyone here for?"

He shrugged. "Well, I'm no one to give advice. Still, it's a shame. You looking for Srebrenka?"

There was no other way, of course, but still, it made her sick to think of it, and it must have shown on her face.

"I better walk you over there. Wouldn't want you getting lost."

"I'd be grateful. I thought I knew the way."

"Things shift. It's that sort of place, isn't it? Always has been, but lately, lots more. Whole place seems larger than it was, larger every week. Hard to keep up. Come on."

Night fell fast now. Lumpy picked up a flashlight. He led her through one fetid lane after another, edging around makeshift shacks and giving wide berth to pitch-black doorways. Every once in a while, from the corner of her eye, Maggie glimpsed something small streak past, but could never catch sight of what, or who, it was. Badger's ears lay flat and his fur bristled, but he didn't bolt. Maggie was quickly disoriented, wanting to turn left when Lumpy turned right, feeling they'd gone too far, or were circling round and round. The very streets and buildings had moved since her last time here, re-formed in new, baffling configurations. It was as if the Forest was larger on the inside than the outside. It felt like some insect world, some ant colony or wasp hive – intricate, claustrophobic. She looked up, eager to see some patch of star-blown sky beyond the dangerously leaning walls and rooftops. For several minutes scrabbling shadows danced in the flashlight's beam, rustlings, murmurs, the sensation that Pipers surrounded her in the dark, watching, coming closer. She reached out now and then to touch the slightly oily fabric of Lumpy's coat. She only realized how shallow her breathing was when at last she caught a glimpse of moonlight, a sliver of white above the roofs. She almost laughed; it was foolish, but for a moment she'd been afraid they'd been buried.

When Lumpy stopped suddenly, Maggie and Badger nearly collided with him.

A bulb burned over a door Maggie recognized – the blue wood, the silver knocker in the shape of a bear's head, shining so brightly in the dismal neglect surrounding it. She scanned the dark laneway. She recognized nothing. "Did Srebrenka move?"

Lumpy's laugh was like grinding gravel. "Nothing stays where it's supposed to here, Mags."

"Will you wait for me? I don't think I could find my way back."

"You couldn't," he said, his voice serious. "Not without me."

Ah, so that was it. Everything in the Forest was a transaction, even among so-called friends. "I'll make it worth your while."

He nodded and lifted the knocker and let it fall in a quick pattern. A new code. The sound of silver against silver was musical. Maggie had always wondered why none of the Pipers stole that valuable little bear head, but then again . . . The door opened and there stood Goran. His shoulders were massive, and his head oddly small for his size, perched on the top of his neck like a spare part. His scalp was shaved, save for a topknot of white hair that fell midway down his back. He wore a black leather vest laced over his gargantuan chest, a pair of brass wrist clasps, jeans and steel-toed boots. No matter the weather, this was Goran's uniform. Maggie fancied his head was so small there simply wasn't room for the part that registered sensations like hot and cold. He towered over even Lumpy and fixed his eyes on her – those strange eyes, nearly all-black iris.

CHAPTER SIX

"**M**AGGIE. I SAID YOU'D BE BACK." GORAN SMILED, revealing worn, yellowed teeth and gaps where teeth had once been.

"You going to let us in?"

Goran gestured, with exaggerated courtesy, that they should enter the hall. Maggie went first. Badger tried to sniff at Goran's boots, and then yipped when Goran kicked him.

"Hey! Leave the dog alone," said Maggie, petting Badger. "He won't bite."

"But I might." Goran laughed.

Maggie ignored him. If he'd wanted to hurt Badger he would have broken his ribs, or worse. "Come on, boy."

Maggie and Badger climbed the stairs with Lumpy behind them. They stepped into a cavernous space, the ceiling barely visible. She stopped, startled. She'd been here, or somewhere very much like here, hundreds of times, but it had never looked like this. It seemed older, as though it had been built centuries ago, rather than decades. It had always been a large room, but this was impossible. The entire building could fit inside this room. Pale blue velvet curtains hid the windows, which appeared large enough to drive a streetcar through, and murals of clouds, starry skies and snow-capped mountains covered the walls. The floor was painted black and shone in the light of hundreds of candles. Harp music played from an unseen source, a gentle, repetitious, drowsy air. Smoke, heavy with cloves and sandalwood, drifted in an amber cloud.

Maggie's temperature rose, her heartbeat accelerated. Her heart was a coal of longing, of hunger . . . for the blending, the melding, the melting of herself into the elysium.

A transparent tent, made from some glimmering, diaphanous material, stood in the centre of the hall. Maggie walked toward it, her footsteps echoing. The tent vibrated like a mammoth hive of bees. Despite her longing, she willed herself to stop. Inside the tent a dozen low couches ringed a central space. There, on an ebony table, a lamp with a silver shade, cut and pierced so the light from the candle within shone through, turned in the hot-air draft of the flame, scattering stars and crescent moons along the walls.

She couldn't blink, couldn't turn away. On each couch lay a Piper. Seven men and five women – all but two with glistening silver swirls on their faces – dreamed deep, their eyes closed, their mouths slightly parted and their brows placid. Now and then a hand moved languidly in the air as though touching a face, perhaps, or inviting a wren to land on a finger. Sighs and soft whispers rose and fell.

As Maggie watched, one of the dreamers' eyes fluttered and the skeletal man's arms and legs paddled like a dog dreaming of chasing squirrels. He was ice pale, silver tinged, his hair matted, his clothes stained and rough. The man blinked, raised his hands before his eyes and regarded them as if not quite sure to whom they belonged. Then he sat up and his eyes met Maggie's. The expression in them was of inconsolable loss. Tears welled, and he wiped them away angrily with the back of his hand.

"I see there's a couch opening up, my dear. Your timing is impeccable."

Maggie turned to face the voice. Bobbed, glistening silver hair with kiss-curls on her unlined forehead and cheeks. Kohl-rimmed blue eyes. Alabaster skin. Eggplant-coloured lips. A perfectly tailored man's suit.

Srebrenka smiled, ever so slightly.

"Hello, Srebrenka." Her heart thumped, thumped, thumped, but was slowing.

"Well, well. What a surprise." Srebrenka's intonation meant it was anything but. She ran the back of her fingers along Maggie's cheek. Maggie shivered under her icy touch. Badger stretched his neck to sniff. Srebrenka patted the dog's head, but Badger pulled back as if slapped and growled. "Such a pretty beast."

Goran appeared in the doorway and pushed through the tent flaps to the Piper who had just woken. "Time to go."

The man looked for a moment as though he'd appeal to Srebrenka, but instead wiped his face with his sleeve and stood, a little unsteadily. "I'm thirsty," he said.

Goran shoved him forward. Badger barked, and Maggie hushed him. The doorkeeper half carried the man to the doorway before shoving him so he stumbled down the steps. "Please," said Goran, "come again soon."

"Lumpy, I didn't see you," said Srebrenka. "It seems as though you just left. Pickings must be good. Maggie, does it not amaze you what a deft hand our rather – what is the word – *conspicuous* friend has? They tell me he can slip gold out of politicians' teeth without getting caught. Such a talent, no? But you will have to wait your turn. Pretty Maggie claims the couch before you."

"Thanks, but I'm only here for information," Maggie said.

Srebrenka pulled a lighter and a long black cigarette from her inside jacket pocket. She put the cigarette between her lips slowly, circling the filter with her tongue, her eyes on Maggie. It took everything Maggie had not to break her gaze, and the hot blush rising up her neck infuriated her. Srebrenka chuckled. "I am not in the information business. I am in the dream business. And after the way you treated me the last time we met, I am not inclined to be helpful."

"I apologize for my behaviour. I was rude." The words left a sour taste on her lips.

"You hurt my feelings."

"I'm sorry."

Srebrenka blinked slowly. "Yes. I'm sure you are."

"I'm looking for my brother."

"Ah. He is also a pretty one. Although perhaps not so pretty now. So impetuous. An adventurer."

The flush of a moment before turned to frost. "Where is he?"

Srebrenka shrugged. "The last time I saw you, sweet girl, you were very clear. Very, how shall I say it, *precise* in your desire to be done with me. Why should I help you when you refuse my hospitality?"

"I'm not going back on the pipe, Srebrenka, not even for my brother, so if that's the price you want, you can forget it." She turned to go.

Srebrenka put her hand on Maggie's sleeve. "You think I'm heartless? That I want to separate such loving siblings?"

"Tell me or don't."

Srebrenka sighed heavily and put her hand to her heart. "Such a headstrong boy, always wanting to go his own way. Each of us has our own path, our own destiny, and the road is longer for some than others." She blew three smoke rings, one dancing after the other, then two dashing through the enlarging ring of the first, before all three raced for the ceiling. "And you, Maggie, are you planning an unusually long journey? Do you need a pocket full of white stones to find your way back?"

The air was heavy and filled with an ever-increasing amount of smoke. Maggie's head swam. "White stones?"

Srebrenka's laugh sounded like tin wind chimes. "Just an old tale of two children lost in the wood at night, following stones made white in the moonlight, one stone after another, until they are home again. Of course, the nasty stepmother, she takes them back into the woods again, yes? With pockets only of bread crumbs this time, and then things are not so happy. What kind of mother would do such a thing, Maggie, what kind of mother?"

"I can't imagine."

Lumpy stepped into a corner and swatted at something. He cursed under his breath. Weasels again, Maggie suspected.

"I ain't got time for stories," he said, stomping at the floor.

"So wise, dear Lumpy. My time is also limited. I am all about enterprise," said Srebrenka.

"How do I find Kyle?"

"You can't. Even if you went where he did, you'd never be able to return, and if you returned . . ." Srebrenka pointed her index fingers to her temples and formed circles. She reached out and grabbed Maggie's hands in both of hers. "Forget your brother. It's hard, I know, but you have no choice. He wanders, timeless, from one tale to the next. Stay here with me, where you are safe and where pleasure is only a silver pipe away. Nothing bad will happen to you when Srebrenka stands guard. Your guardian is dead, Kyle has forgotten you and you are hurt, come to gather peace . . ." Her lips were almost black against her white teeth. Her tongue glistened pinkly.

The air was thick and warm. Maggie breathed through her mouth, for it was difficult to get enough oxygen. She tasted something like molasses and ginger. It was soothing, comforting . . . She blinked and pulled her hands away. "Kyle hasn't forgotten me. He's sent me a message."

"He did what?" Srebrenka's mouth formed a little moue.

"How inventive. He must need you very badly. How he must need you."

"I've come to find him. Any information . . ."

"He is a greedy boy. Wanting so much, never satisfied, always saying how no one loved him and he was all alone."

That stung, and Maggie saw Srebrenka knew it. It would feel quite good to slap her, but the chances of getting information then, no matter how slim they were now, would reduce to nothing. And besides, Goran would pummel her to ground meat.

"Do you know where he is?"

"I know where he's gone."

"And where is that?"

"Someplace you do not want to go."

"Try me."

Lumpy said, "She's talking about the door."

Srebrenka massaged her temples as though the conversation gave her a headache. "How is it you manage to get so much information out of me, and without making even a token purchase, my little Maggie?"

"What door?" It was odd how, even as she spoke the word, something familiar ran through her, as though this door they spoke of was some memory she'd forgotten.

Srebrenka tapped the end of her cigarette in a marble bowl. "Yes, Lumpy, will you tell your friend?"

"I might."

"Then you are not the friend she thinks you are."

What did they mean? Maggie felt dizzy.

"She's a grown woman. Makes up her own mind. Why do you care?"

"It amuses me to see what lengths lovely Maggie is willing to go to for her brother. It amuses me to see how hungry she may be."

Maggie said, "And of course we all live to amuse you, don't we?"

Srebrenka's eyes flashed darkly. "You came to me."

"Will you help me or not?"

"I have helped you. You want to know where your brother has gone. He has gone through the door."

"And what is that? Where is that?" How warm the air was. How good it would feel to lie down.

Srebrenka put her palms together and rested her chin on her middle fingers. "This much I will tell you: when the dreamer comes so very close to their heart's desire they come to a door and through that door . . . well, so many more things are possible. You must remember, pretty girl."

She remembered. At the end of elysium dreams . . . a door . . . always beckoning. Every Piper swapped such tales. "You're telling me the door is a real, physical thing?"

"What is real and what isn't, when one talks of the elysium?" Srebrenka shrugged. "Surely such silly distinctions are beneath you now, having walked in the Silver World."

"And how do you know what's on the other side?"

"A reasonable question. Let us say simply that the door is in my trust, just as the elysium has made me its special friend."

Maggie felt as if the floor was giving way beneath her. "There has to be another way."

"No, there doesn't," said Srebrenka. "You cannot swim in the ocean without getting wet. You cannot go where Kyle has gone without going through the door. Of course, you could always forget your brother. You wouldn't be the first to wipe their hands of difficult relatives. Why, I bet you'd hardly give it another thought. Your life is so good now. So safe. What do you care about a little brother, a little lost sparrow?"

"Sparrow? Why did you say that?"

"No reason." She shrugged. "It just popped into my mind."

Maggie looked down at Badger. He cocked his head and whined. "I have to think about this."

"Don't take too much time, Maggie. The door is here for

the moment, who knows when it will disappear again. Goran, see our guests out, will you?" Srebrenka chuckled and sat in a nearby black velvet chair. Her smile made Maggie think of cats and canaries.

The diaphanous walls of the tent seemed more water than cloth, as though Maggie looked at creatures swimming. How soft the couches looked – the cloth the colour of a full-moon midnight sky reflected on the sea. The pillows fluffy as foam. The pull of the elysium was tidal, full of undertow. Another moment and her feet would move against her will. Maggie shook her head. She turned away. She must keep her eyes on the floor, away from the tent. Her legs felt as if they were tangled in seaweed, yet although she practically dragged them, they did her bidding.

"Come again soon, I hope," said Srebrenka.

CHAPTER SEVEN

"THIS AIN'T THE PLACE FOR YOU NO MORE," Lumpy said to Maggie once they were outside.

He sounded miffed. Doubtless he was eager to be rid of her and get back to the couch at Srebrenka's. Maggie considered. Her body felt lead encased. She wanted to go home and stay home. Kyle's face as a twelve-year-old – tearful, red with frustration – flashed before her, saying if she left him and went to live with her boyfriend, Lenny, he'd hate her forever. "Don't leave me here with *them*," he'd cried. Don't leave me. Little Brother of the Sparrow.

Badger sat by her side, gazing up into her face, so trusting. "I'm coming back, but . . . the dog. I can't bring him back with me."

"Pity. Looks like a scrapper to me. Why not take him?"

Badger looked up at Lumpy and wagged his tail. Maggie didn't want to admit she was afraid of what might happen to Badger, more concerned about him than Lumpy. Badger would die trying to protect her. Lumpy might well turn heel and abandon her, might race back to the pipe. It's what she would have done, once.

"Let's face it, once I come back I might never leave." At least Lumpy didn't insult her intelligence by denying this. "Give me the day." She handed him some money. "Go back to Srebrenka's and take a journey. Meet me tomorrow and when we're all done, I'll give you enough cash to make sure Srebrenka's good to you for as long as you want."

"Long as I want?" His eyes glittered. "How can you do that?"

Telling a Piper one was wealthy was imprudent. "I've never lied to you, have I?"

He regarded her for a moment, then grunted. "Fine. But I don't like you thinking I'm only helping because of the elysium. Got a soft spot for you. Didn't think I'd see you back here. It's a bit upsetting. I've half a mind to walk away from this whole business."

"I need you." She looked around at the weirdly unfamiliar streets. "I'd be lost without you. You're about my only hope – Kyle's only hope."

He spat colourfully on the stones near his feet. "Like I want to be a goddamn hero. I must be nuts. But come on."

Badger padded along in front of them. Every few yards he stopped and looked back, checking they were keeping up. It was very cold, and Maggie kept her hands plunged deep in her pockets. Their breath puffed out ahead of them. As they rounded a corner, Badger stopped, sniffed the air and ran back to Maggie's side. His tongue flicked, and he cocked his head first this way, and then that.

"What's the matter, Badge?" She tried to make him sit, but he refused, his eyes fastened on the corner.

What was that sound? High pitched. Voices? Maggie looked to Lumpy for clues.

Lumpy scowled. "Kids."

Badger barked, and the voices got louder. Around the corner skittered a jumbled mob of small bodies. For a moment, it appeared as though they were one large body, low to the ground, with many legs. The mass stopped and separated into individual shapes. A boy stepped forward as though protecting the rest. It took her a moment to recognize him. It was Peter, with the plaid jacket. He looked different here, more feral, dangerous.

Badger growled, low and long. "Hush, hush," said Maggie. "What are they *doing* here?"

"Trying to find their parents," said Lumpy. "Used to be only one or two of 'em, but now, look, six, seven … Parents are Pipers and the children left to scrounge till they get back, but some of them never come back, do they? They go too deep and never come home for little Billy, so little Billy comes here, thinking Mummy'll turn up one day." The big man snorted. "They can be a nuisance."

Peter Pan, thought Maggie. The lost boys.

Peter rocked side to side, his hands dangling loose by his sides. "Evening, Lump."

"Ain't got nothing for you tonight, Pete."

"Come on, there's always something." The boy rubbed his nose on his sleeve. He jerked his chin in Maggie's direction. "Hey," he said. "Guess I should have expected you, sooner or later."

"Where are your parents, Peter?"

Lumpy elbowed her. "You know him?"

"He brought me the messages from Kyle."

"Don't trust what he tells you. He runs errands for all sorts, if you know what I mean."

The boy drew himself up and scowled. "You saying I'm not honest? I'm no Piper. That's why I get to do errands, because I can be trusted. More than I can say for some."

Lumpy took a step forward and so did the boy. Badger barked and edged forward, sideways, as though putting himself between Maggie and the mob of children. Just as Maggie called him back one of the smaller kids – a girl with a butterfly barrette in her wheat-coloured hair, a Toronto Maple Leafs jacket and pink boots with pompoms – broke from the pack and hurled herself at the dog. Her lashes and eyebrows were so pale she looked like a little rabbit.

"Puppy!" She wrapped her arms around the shocked canine. Badger's hackles sprang up and his ears flattened.

Maggie lunged for the dog, sure he would snap.

"Puppy, puppy, nice puppy," the child cooed as she buried her face in Badger's ruff.

"Oh, for crying out loud," said Lumpy.

"Come on, there, let go of the dog," said Maggie as Badger rolled his eyes, pleading with her. "He doesn't know you. He might bite." She put her hand on the child's arm and tried to pull her away.

The little girl looked at her, big brown eyes full of tears. "No. No. He won't bite. I had a puppy at home. I love puppy."

Badger's lip curled, and his tongue flicked. "Badger, gentle."

"That dog bites Mindy and I'm gonna kill it," said Peter, who had picked up a brick.

"Let go of the dog, Mindy." Maggie tried to pry the girl's fingers loose, but she held on tighter, and then suddenly pulled back, so her face was level with the dog's muzzle. Before Maggie could stop her Mindy kissed the dog on his nose.

"See, nice puppy. Good puppy."

Much to Maggie's astonishment, Badger licked the child's face, just once, as though, Maggie feared, tasting her, and then again, and again, tail wagging. The child giggled and said, "Nice puppy, silly dog, good dog."

"Okay, that's enough. That's enough, the two of you," Maggie said.

With that the little girl tipped backward on her bottom, still laughing, and Badger looked up again at Maggie, tongue lolling. "Sit," she said. "Good dog. Enough."

The not-terribly-clean children had gathered round. Several of them sucked their thumbs. They fidgeted in their ill-fitting coats and jackets, clearly scavenged hand-me-downs. A couple reached to pet Badger, but he moved beyond their grasp.

"I'd leave him if I were you. He isn't used to children."

"Stand back, you little monsters," said Lumpy.

How did these children survive? What did they eat? Where did they sleep? Maggie had an appalling urge to gather them up into her arms, to soothe them, brush the hair from their eyes, wipe their snotty little noses. She shivered.

"Give us something," said Peter.

"Didn't I already give you something?" asked Maggie.

"You see how many mouths I got to feed?"

None of the rest of the children said a word, not even the previously dog-drunk little girl. They merely stared their despairing stares, dull eyed and mute.

"Get lost." Lumpy waved his arm around as though to sweep them all away with a blow of his anvil-like hand.

"Hang on." Maggie reached into her pocket. She feared in their need they might swarm, trying to steal everything, and there was a limit to Badger's tolerance. "Be good and I'll give you something." The children waited, taut as bowstrings. She handed Peter a few bills; she wasn't sure how many.

He snatched the money and it disappeared into the folds of his clothing.

"You'll make sure they're fed?"

"I take care of my own!"

And with that the little tribe disappeared down an alley so quickly they might never have been there. Maggie was taken aback by how differently the boy behaved, but doubtless he had to be tougher here. Could he really be taking care of all those children? Children caring for children. She felt sick.

"You're a soft idiot, aren't ya?" said Lumpy.

"Probably."

They retraced their way through the twisting lanes. Maggie gave up trying to find familiar landmarks. It occurred to her

Lumpy might be leading her deeper and deeper into the heart of the Forest; he might be quite content to steal the rest of her money and go back to Srebrenka's. However, at last they turned a corner and Lumpy stopped and pointed.

"That's the opening, there."

She squinted. Yes, she saw they had, in fact, returned to the border. Street lights on Queen Street twinkled welcomingly, never mind that the street itself looked, well, shorter. Queen Street ran for miles and miles and yet looking toward the west, and then the east, Maggie fancied she could see from Spadina to Coxwell. That couldn't be. Apart from the fact it was.

"You'll be all right now." Lumpy's eyes darted back the way they'd come and his fingers twitched.

"I'll be fine. Thanks." She reached to at least shake his hand, but he was already loping back into the shadows, probably to Srebrenka and her silver dreams. "Tomorrow night, then?" she called.

He turned. "Mags, don't come back if you can help it."

THE ROADS HOME WERE BOTH FAMILIAR AND UNFAMILIAR; space truncated, shrunken. She remembered what the boy had said about the Necropolis having shifted to a spot near the Forest. It was a place she knew well.

Kyle was ten, and they hadn't been living with Horace and Phyllis Gallagher all that long. It was dinnertime and he hadn't come back from school yet. Phyllis sent her to look for him. It was mid-winter and had been dark for hours by the time she pulled on her boots and headed out to hunt for him, slouching, more irritated at being pulled away from her book than worried.

She went up and down the street but saw no one. She went around the school, thinking he might be in the playground. It was then, standing in the shadowed, deserted playground, that she started ever so slightly to panic. What had he been wearing when she saw him that morning? He'd said nothing about staying late anywhere or about going to someone's house. He had no friends she could think of, who might have invited him to dinner. Perhaps he'd gone to the Necropolis. Lots of kids went there to play among the headstones. Kyle liked it there, although he preferred to go alone. In another family, children his age might not be left to wander the streets alone. In this family, they were.

She turned back the way she'd come, passing the house. She popped her head in to see if he'd turned up, but there was no sign of him. Phyllis stood in the kitchen, opening a can of spaghetti sauce. She wore a sweatshirt on which rhinestones spelled out the word *Paris*. A cigarette dangled from her mouth, dropping ashes on her chest. Past her, in the living room, Maggie's cousins Ben and Brian were watching some violent movie and pummelling each other.

"I'm going to look in the cemetery," Maggie said. "Do you think we should call the police?"

"What for?" Phyllis said. "He's only being thoughtless, as usual. No point getting everyone in a flap. I'm not ruining dinner for him. We're eating. Brian, Ben, get your sisters."

"I'll find him," said Maggie. She grabbed a flashlight hanging from a string near the door.

She jogged to the Necropolis and ducked into the entry between the Gothic revival pavilion and the chapel. Inside, last night's snow softened the landscape and brightened it. She called Kyle's name and listened. Nothing. She noticed a ghostly trail of children's footsteps and followed them deeper into the cemetery, past stone angels and urns and obelisks and Celtic crosses. "Kyle? Kyle!" She stepped toward something dark on the ground and shone the flashlight on it. A stain in the snow. Her heart skipped. It appeared more black than red now, but how red it must have been when first it was spilled. And quite a lot of it. There was so much disturbance in the snow it was hard, for a moment, to tell . . . but yes, there, the footsteps went that way, spots of darkness here and there, splattered against the snow-muffled graves.

She half ran and called his name, picturing his body frozen and twisted. And then she heard something. She stopped and held her breath. Yes, it was something . . . "Maggie! Maggie, I'm here," and the catch and sob in his voice clawed at her.

Calling, she ran toward the sound and stumbled over a hidden root and went sprawling. She picked herself up and she kept going and calling, following the sound of his voice and the path of trodden snow. She saw him, and for a moment he was standing so nonchalantly against a tree next to a gravestone with a carved harp on top that she thought he might be playing some wicked game just to frighten her and fury squirted into her stomach and she was about to tell him what an evil boy he was . . . but then she saw he was tied to the tree, his arms at his sides. Ropes bound him from shoulder to shin. His gloveless hands were blue with cold, his hair, which must have been wet at some point, was frozen into wild spikes and on his face . . .

"Oh, Kyle, who did this?" She pocketed the flashlight and worked furiously on the knots. Her own hands were cold, and the knots were strong. She feared she'd have to run home and get a knife. "Who did this to you?"

"Get me out of here. Get me *out*." He sobbed, and his face was covered not only with blood, but with snot and frosted tears. One eye was swollen with the beginnings of a black eye.

So much rage, she thought, as her fingers finally got purchase on one of the knot's loops and pried it up and under . . . one down and three to go. She unwound the rope on his chest and he squirmed and thrashed until his arms were free. He wiped furiously at his face and squealed with the pain.

"I hate them. I hate them," he wailed.

"Stay still. You're making the knots worse." She undid another, and the rope whipped round the tree, striking her on the cheek as he flailed and freed himself.

Kyle collapsed. "I can't feel my feet."

She rubbed his legs and he moaned and gritted his teeth against the pins and needles as the blood began to circulate. She rubbed his hands until they looked like flesh and blood again and not like marble carvings. He shook them and cried and shook his feet and cried.

"Come on, climb up and I'll give you a piggyback home."

"No," he snapped. "No. I'm going to walk. I have to walk." He looked at her with panic. "If any of them see me being carried . . . No. I have to walk."

"No one will see you. There's no one here."

"I have to walk!"

She helped him to his feet and he didn't stop her when she put his arm through hers. "Who did this and why? Why?"

"They think I'm weird," he said through clenched teeth.

"I'm sure that's not true. Who's 'they'?"

"What difference does it make?"

"They have to be punished."

"I'm not going to tell you, or anyone else, so stop asking."

How resolute he sounded and how very much older than his age. He leaned on her less now; his steps surer. He stopped and looked at his sister. "Is it very bad, my face?"

"No, not very." She saw the disbelief in his eyes. "It's a bit bad."

Kyle bent down and picked up handfuls of snow. He rubbed his face with it and didn't make a sound although Maggie thought it must hurt terribly. He did it again and again and finally turned his scrubbed face to her. "How does it look now?"

"There's some blood in your nostrils."

He repeated the procedure and asked again. The blood, snot and tears were gone. His lip was swollen, and his nose was as well, although she didn't think it was broken. There was that eye. It might be closed by morning. "Better," she said.

"They invited me with them. Right from school. They asked me. Said there was something they wanted to show me and then they set on me." His eyes were wide with the injustice of it. "They ambushed me. Four of them. Said I was to be taught a lesson."

"What for?"

"You don't think I *asked*? They wouldn't say."

No matter how she pressed, or, later, when Phyllis did, Kyle wouldn't say who'd been responsible, or what had started it. He never did have friends after that. He said he couldn't care less, that the neighbourhood kids were about as sharp as a sack of wet wool and he wouldn't waste his time.

Little Brother of the Sparrow. How could a boy be both so tough and so sensitive? She'd never forgotten the look on his face, tied to that tree.

THERE WAS ALMOST NO ONE ON THE STREETS, SAVE THE police patrols. One questioned her and accepted her excuse for being out so late – Badger had run off and she'd only just found him, they were heading home.

"Don't loiter," said the cop, an older man who kept his hand on his nightstick. "Easy to get lost these days."

At the Grimoire, she took off her boots and coat, but the stench of the Forest seemed to linger. Badger leaned into her legs. "Good boy," she said. She fed him and quickly ate some toast and scrambled eggs. When she finished, she left the unwashed dishes in the sink, and climbed the stairs, Badger padding alongside. She thought she wouldn't sleep, so many thoughts careened around in her brain, but Badger jumped up on the bed and lay his head on her chest in a way he usually didn't. Dogs knew when something was up. Somehow, between his comforting weight and warmth, she drifted off.

MAGGIE DREAMS . . .

An old woman with skin white as bone and wrinkled as crumpled paper stands before a fire. Maggie hides in a cupboard, knowing only that she must be very quiet. The woman must not see her. Maggie bites her knuckle.

The woman's hair is weeds. Her lips, grey worms. She is wrapped in stinking furs. She plucks the body of a small rodent from inside a skin pouch and begins to gnaw it, tiny bones cracking. Behind her is a window and on the outside sill two ravens perch. One stretches its wings and the other taps on the glass. Both birds stare not at the woman, but directly at Maggie in her hiding place.

KYLE FOLLOWS A WOMAN DOWN, DOWN A LONG, DIMLY LIT stone hall, ever deeper into the heart of an enormous stone structure. The woman's skin is white as a dove's wing, her hair glitters like quartz, her lips are ripe strawberries. He gazes at the large black owl embroidered on the back of the frost-toned gown she wears. It seems to cock its head this way and that in the light of the torch the woman carries. Shadows flitter along the walls like velvet bats. At last they come to a door, heavy with iron hinges. The woman opens it, looks coyly over her shoulder and beckons with her pale, slender fingers to Kyle.

Inside, all is firelight and golden, the air scented with lavender. The woman leans over a bench on which are displayed glass vials, baskets of various sizes, twigs, small bunches of herbs, and the desiccated bodies of mice, moles and shrews. The woman grinds something with a mortar and pestle. When finished, she picks up a withered apple, smears the paste she's made upon it. The apple glows and plumps and the woman laughs with a sound like tinkling icicles as she holds it up to the torchlight. It is shining and red as blood. It looks like ruby candy. "Eat, sweet boy," she says. "You must hunger so." The apple is sweet as cider fermented with honey. It effervesces on his tongue. He closes his eyes as ecstasy wraps him in its arms like a cloak. She leads him to a fur-covered bed and draws him down. Kyle leans against the woman and listens to the purr of her breathing. No matter how much he eats, the apple never grows smaller and his hunger is never quite sated.

CHAPTER EIGHT

MAGGIE HAD PUT IT OFF AS LONG AS POSSIBLE but just before four o'clock the next afternoon she and Badger entered the Wort & Willow Apothecary. Finnick scampered out of the back, claws clicking on the wooden floor, to greet them.

"Maggie, my dear, how lovely to see you." Mr. Strundale popped up from behind the counter. He was the sort of person who often seemed to be exactly where you didn't expect him to be. And, as with the Grimoire, the Wort & Willow attracted a most specific clientele, people needing advice as much as a poultice or herb tea. As the Grimoire's clients were folk looking for answers to mysteries in their lives more than entertainment, Mr. Strundale's clients were seeking relief from far more than just physical pain. Just now, for example, he held in his hand a jar labelled *Dream Walker Tea, for the incorporation of Shadow.*

Badger and Finnick meandered over to their usual spot near an air vent and flopped down. Finnick curled up beside Badger with a satisfied little huff. From a basket Maggie carried she pulled a book and held it out. "I think this might be the book you wanted?"

Mr. Strundale cradled the slim leather-bound volume. "I'd completely forgotten. Age of course, wretched condition. Can it really be?" He looked at Maggie with something like wonder. "Thirteenth century? *Mel Vinum Loco Anima*. Honey wine for the soul, memoirs of a vintner." His eyes returned to the book. "Oh my. Oh my. How I shall treasure this. The wine I shall make! Is there no end to the wonders in your bookshop, Maggie?"

"You should know." Maggie chuckled.

Cradling the old book, Mr. Strundale said, "I don't know how I can ever repay you."

"Well, there is one thing . . ." She patted Badger on the head. "I have to go away for a bit."

Mr. Strundale stared at her in that way of his. Did the man never blink? Was it some glamour he used to make her talk?

"It's my brother, I'm afraid." She hadn't meant to say that.

"Oh dear. The old trouble?"

"I don't think I'll be very long. A day – or a few days at the most."

"He's ill, then?"

"Well, missing . . . but I think I know where to find him." Her mouth went dry.

"I'm not sure I like the sounds of this." Mr. Strundale crossed his arms and scowled. He succeeded in looking more constipated than stern. "There are strange doings these days. Neighbourhoods shifting size and so forth. I don't believe it's safe. And we don't want you going back into neighbourhoods where you're liable to be tempted. It wasn't that long ago you came in here, saying someone from your past was chasing you. Now you're going to look for trouble?"

"I'll be all right." She shrugged. "What can I do? He's my brother." She bent down and ruffled Badger's ears, escaping Mr. Strundale's glower. "Would you mind if Badger stayed with you while I'm gone?" Badger's tail thumped the floor. Maggie indicated the bag she carried. "I've got food for him here. Enough for a few days."

"You know I love Badger as you do, and my friend," he waved his arm toward the little fox nestled in the dog's embrace, "would be as delighted as I to have him visit, although I don't know if Badger will appreciate being left behind. And frankly, I don't think Mr. Mustby would much like whatever this plan of yours is."

Her cheeks flamed at the mention of Mr. Mustby. She stood. She was taller than Mr. Strundale, although just then she felt smaller. "A day, maybe two, and Badger can't go where I'm going."

Mr. Strundale snorted. "You'd be surprised what a determined love can do."

"He'll hardly miss me. I won't be long."

"Maggie, dear girl. Do not dissemble. You and I both know you can't promise that."

And she understood from the look on his face that Mr. Strundale knew more than she wanted him to. He and Mr. Mustby had always been like that: always knowing more than seemed possible. When she had first come to the Grimoire and, in true Piper fashion, bent the truth in the assumption the bald facts would do her no good, she discovered it was quite impossible to get anything past either of them. They would simply look at her, just in the way Mr. Strundale was doing now, and all her lacy lies would unravel. "Fine. You're right. I can't. But say you'll take him anyway, please."

He regarded her for a moment and then sighed. "I am worried about you. I care for you deeply. However, I doubt I'd be able to change your mind. You must make your own choices and learn in your own way. In truth I don't see the full picture here. I must admit it. You might very well be part of a more intricate story." She must have looked puzzled. He waved his hand. "Never mind that. Of course I will look after Badger. I only wish I were looking after *you* better. Mr. Mustby will not be pleased with me."

She might have asked him what he meant by that, but assumed he had intended to say, "*would* not be pleased." Then Badger, knowing they were speaking about him, walked over to Maggie, and Finnick dashed to Mr. Strundale and stood on his hind legs, wanting to be picked up. Mr. Strundale complied, and the animal settled around his shoulders like a living stole.

She knelt and took Badger's face in her hands. She could tell by the nervous flicking of his tongue, and the way he leaned up against her, that he knew something was up and he didn't like it. "Now, Badger, you be a good boy and stay with Mr. Strundale. I have to go away for a bit. Not for long and I will be back, I promise." He licked her face and whined, batting at her with his paws. "It's okay. Take care of Mr. Strundale and Finnick."

Maggie stood and put her arms around the old man. Under his smoking jacket he felt as though he were constructed of odd bits of ill-cut lumber, all angles and hard edges, but he returned her hug with surprising strength.

Then he pushed her away to arm's length. "I must tell you, Maggie – you are unlikely to find what you're looking for, and the chances of you coming back aren't good. I feel as though I'm letting my old friend down here, by being in any way complicit. However, I want to ask you one thing: Are you sure there is no other way?"

"I've asked myself that. I'm sure. Whatever waits for me will be no worse than what will find me if I do nothing." She dropped her head. "I couldn't live with myself, you see."

"I do. And I respect you as much as I fear for you. It's decided then. And who knows, you may be able to do something about the ooze and expansion." Just then, Finnick barked three times. "What? Oh! Yes." Mr. Strundale clapped his hands and said, "There is one thing I can do. Wait here."

He disappeared behind the ornately embroidered screen

and returned a moment later with a small blue enamel box. "Take this and keep it with you. Inside are certain things you might find useful on your journey. First, a pomegranate seed, although not the usual sort of seed. It grants wisdom and learning to whoever eats it. Second, the tooth of a bear, which is useful for those who have lost things, and finally, a sprig of mistletoe for warmth. If you need them, you'll know what to do when the time comes."

She took the little box in her palm. It was strangely warm, as if it contained bits of burning coal. She might never understand the magic that emanated from Mr. Mustby and Mr. Strundale, from the Grimoire and the Wort & Willow, but she had come to trust it.

Maggie returned home and went over her preparations one last time. From the trunk of cash in the closet she took what money she thought she might need, separating it into two pouches. Clothes were simple – she'd take only what she wore: boots, jeans, turtleneck, gloves, scarf, hat and coat. She put the hat, gloves and scarf in her rucksack. From a drawer in the sideboard she took a photo of Kyle, taken a few years back, during one of the periods he'd managed to stay away from the elysium. He looked defiant, with his chin stuck out, looking down his nose at the camera. She understood why girls found him attractive and why they had, on more than one occasion, supported him, let him steal from them, overlooked his moods and his bad behaviour. The blue eyes. The black hair, shaved close to his head in this photo. The air of a bad boy, a very bad boy, just waiting to be saved. She sighed and tucked the photo into an envelope. She wrapped cheese and bread in a cloth and this, along with a tin of dried berries, she placed in the pack. Clean undergarments and socks. A bar of soap and a

toothbrush and toothpaste. She could think of nothing more.
It would have to do.

CHAPTER NINE

THE WALK BACK TO THE FOREST SEEMED EVEN shorter than the day before. Lumpy waited for her in a doorway just inside Fee Place.

"Hoped you wouldn't come," he said.

"No choice."

"Always a choice," Lumpy grunted. His watery eyes had the wistful, longing expression of a Piper recently returned from a journey.

"Good night?" Maggie asked.

He sighed. "Let's get going."

Lumpy set a fast pace through narrow lane after narrow lane, each giving the impression of being piled up on top of the other. She thought, once or twice, she spotted a child's face, but it was gone before she could be sure. Lumpy paid no mind. She kept her eyes on his broad back. While of course the people who lived in a place affected the life of that place, she hadn't until now considered what effect so many people living with one foot in another world might have on a landscape. She lost track of time, along with her sense of direction. A small, squeaky voice in the back of her head said that if she didn't find

Kyle, and if she couldn't find her way out, well then, she might as well just dream with the pipe again. Why not? Shut up, she told the familiar voice. Shut up.

Lumpy lumbered toward a flight of uneven stairs that appeared to run directly into a brick wall. Perhaps, Maggie thought, there's a hidden door. Had they arrived? No. The stairs turned at the last minute. Lumpy scrunched, making his misshapen bulk as small as possible and ducked through an archway leading into a long narrow passage. The walls were damp and sprouted patchy, fungal-looking moss. After a moment, they came out into a square surrounded by uniformly grey concrete-block buildings she'd never seen before. It was a sort of parody on the village square. The buildings were chained and battered architectural ghosts. Three fires burned in the square, and around each one stood figures warming their hands. Men and women. At the nearest fire stood a woman in an obviously expensive leather coat and boots. She was still quite beautiful, even with deep shadows beneath her eyes. Instead of a purse, she carried a plastic Eaton's bag with string reinforcing the handles. Up until recently she'd probably been living in posh Rosedale or a condo by the lake. She had her arm hooked through that of a tall man sporting an only slightly stained Canada Goose parka. Maggie guessed they hadn't been in the Forest long. A couple of months from now that parka, the expensive coat and boots would be gone.

On the stoop in front of one of the surrounding buildings, Maggie saw four children. One of them waved. The little rabbit-pale girl from yesterday who had loved Badger. Mindy, that was her name.

"Puppy?"

"Not today, hon," said Maggie.

"And no more money, either," said Lumpy, as a little boy started forward, hands outstretched.

Maggie hurried after Lumpy. She reached into her pocket,

pulled out a handful of coins and tossed them toward the children. They scrambled in the dirt after them.

"You do them no favours," said Lumpy over his shoulder. "Without Pete around they're a pack of feral dogs. Even if she catches it, they'll take it away from her and leave her worse for it."

A high-pitched yelp, and then wailing. "Wait," Maggie called after his rapidly retreating back. "Stop!"

"Living on the other side's made you weak."

He didn't slacken his pace, and if Maggie wanted to keep him in sight, she had to leave the children. She cursed. He was right. She had to harden. She had to focus. What had Srebrenka said about children lost in a forest, trying to follow a trail of bread crumbs home? She hadn't even crumbs. Only Lumpy. The children, on the other hand, had each other.

The night was thick as a boiled-wool cloak around them. Here and there vapid lights flickered from busted-out windows. Just when Maggie feared she might run off shrieking, Lumpy stopped so abruptly she slammed into his back.

"Jesus, Lumpy, I almost knocked myself out." She rubbed her nose.

"Should watch where you're going." He stomped at the ground to his left. "You're here then, as promised." He jerked his head in the direction of a door to his right. Sure enough, there was the bear knocker. Maggie shook her head. This wasn't the same building as the day before, knocker or no knocker. Lumpy seemed to be tracking something on the ground. He picked up a rock and threw it. "Yeah, run, you little bastards. I'll not let you get my eyes." He turned to Maggie. "Wouldn't last a minute without my eyes."

"There are no weasels, not really. You have to remember that."

"Really?" He pulled open the collar of his filthy coat. There, on either side of his silver-streaked neck, blazed five deep raw wounds, too small to be made by his own hand.

"How did you do that?" They looked angry, red around the edges, starting to fester. Given the way Lumpy lived, the chance of the wounds becoming infected was high.

"I didn't do it myself, did I?" He pulled his collar back into place. Holes at the tops of his woollen gloves revealed dirt-clogged fingernails. "Dreams can come true, don't you know?" His chuckle held little humour.

What he was saying was quite impossible. Then again, she was standing on a street she'd have sworn didn't exist a few years ago. It seemed the mysteries of elysium were more complicated than she'd previously considered. She wouldn't think about that now. "You said we're here? What happened to the door?" The door, which was little more than a collection of boards nailed together, was certainly not the same door as yesterday. But there was the bear-head knocker.

Lumpy sniffed and wiped his nose. "Lots of entrances, not many exits, mostly depends on what you're coming for. This one's for what you want, the place you want."

She reached out, lifted the knocker and let it drop. The knock was loud and echoed like a ricocheting stone. She fought the impulse to duck. One of the boards slid back, revealing a cleverly disguised peephole.

"What?" said a man's voice.

"Want to see Srebrenka, she's expecting us."

"Maybe she's not available. Maybe she's having tea with the queen." He had an English accent, cockney, to be exact.

"And I'm the Earl of Asswipe. Let me in, I've business."

"It's *because* I know you I'm not opening the door. Not after last time."

"That wasn't my fault." Lumpy glanced at Maggie. "Weasels. I paid for the damages," he said to the hole in the door.

"Don't know your friend. Don't like strangers. Get off the stoop."

The peephole slammed shut.

"You sure about this?" asked Lumpy. "Maybe she changed her mind. Maybe you should, too."

"You promised."

"Said I'd get you here. No more."

Maggie didn't like the argent glint in Lumpy's eyes. He seemed to be wrestling with some internal dilemma. Her heart beat faster. It would be nothing for Lumpy to throttle her and take her money. She understood his struggle. The blue couches, the silver slide into sweet dreams . . . For that matter, they could *both* lie on those blue tufted couches, close their eyes and . . . a memory. Kyle as a little boy, coming into her room in the middle of the night, wringing his eyes, whispering he'd had a terrible dream: he was lost in frozen winter woods, hunted by wolves. "Their eyes were yellow," he said, his own glassy as marbles. *"Don't let them get me, Maggie."*

"I know what you're thinking, Lumpy. I don't blame you. You've kept your promise. You're a good friend. I've always known you to be a man of your word. A man I could trust."

The silvery glint dulled. His eyes were just his eyes, reddish and watery. "Always been fond of you." He stuffed his hands under his armpits, as though afraid if he didn't pay attention to them they might act of their own volition.

"And I of you. If you want to go now, I'll pay you and that'll be the end of it, no hard feelings. But, if you stay I'll do right by you. You know you can trust me, just as I can trust you."

He considered, and then said, "I'll get you inside, but I ain't getting caught up in no pointless quest. Clear? If I was smart, I'd drag you back to the border and leave you there. Stupid pipe dream."

"Well, pipe dreams got us all into this in the first place, right?"

Lumpy laughed and, to Maggie's relief, pulled his hands out from under his armpits, apparently deciding they were no longer a threat. "Must be nuts," he said.

He pounded on the door so hard every board shook, and the nails rattled. After a minute of this abuse the peephole flew open and the same voice as before shouted, "Keep doing that and I'll sic the demons of the underworld on your silvered soul!"

"Listen. This is Maggie and she's a friend and that means something, even in this scabby, vermin-infested, mouse-turd-reeking, piss-soaked cauldron of disease. She's already talked to her ladyship, who's got a soft spot for my friend here, and you don't want to piss that one off now, do you, or you might find yourself without even this farty excuse for employment. Now, don't make me reach in there and grab you by your warty neck, Colin. You don't let us in, I'm going to wait out here until you come out and I don't care if it takes a year and I starve to death in the process, I'll be waiting for you and when you come out I'll jam my own thigh bone up your ass and make you dance like the puppet you are." He took a breath. "So, you going to open this door or am I coming through it? Your choice, by God."

Maggie's mouth, she realized, was hanging open. In all the time she'd known Lumpy she'd never heard him say so many words in a row.

There was a period of silence from the other side of the door and then the voice said, "Such ructions. Such bad manners. You surprise me, Lumpy."

"Really? I'm surprised you're surprised, Colin."

"I'm thinking it would do you wise to apologize. Ever heard you catch more flies with honey?"

"I offer you my deepest regret. Now open the goddamn door."

A kind of snorted laugh came from the other side of the door and then the sound of metal against metal. Maggie imagined bolts and chains and latches and hooks. The door swung open. There stood a surprisingly small grey-haired man. He was closer to four feet tall than five. An impressive assortment of weapons hung from his belt: two revolvers, an unsheathed serrated dagger, a set of brass knuckles and a leather sap. He wore overalls, like the kind painters wear, and heavy boots, and he appeared to be made essentially of sinew and tendon, giving the impression of a well-armed, possibly psychotic leprechaun. He smiled, revealing teeth filed to points. A stool was next to him, on which he'd apparently stood while speaking through the peephole. Behind him a steep set of rickety stairs led to a second floor.

"Well, aren't you a pretty thing." He looked Maggie up and down. "What kind of present are you offering? Maybe a little left over for old Colin?" He smacked his lips.

"Don't make me slap you, Colin," said Lumpy.

"You could try." With astonishing speed, Colin pulled his dagger from his belt and went into a crouch, jabbing upward, toward Lumpy's groin. "Just like a wild boar, I'll split you cock to belly. You'll be dead before your blood pools on the floor."

Lumpy stepped around him and said, "No need to get all testy. I'm reaching for my own knife, gentle as a babe, right?" He pulled the knife from behind his back, holding the blade by two fingers, and handed it to Colin. "That's all there is."

Colin took the knife and placed it in a basket near the door, which already contained several knives and three handguns. "Oh, I'd love to take your word for it, but forgive me."

Lumpy held out his arms. "Have at it."

Colin put the dagger back on his belt. He patted Lumpy down, standing on his tiptoes to reach under the big man's arms, although how he expected to find anything under all the layers was a mystery. When he was satisfied, he said to Maggie, "Over here, girl, and let me give you the once-over."

Maggie did not like Colin's greedy, sharp-toothed grin, or the thought of his hands on her. She opened her coat. "I've no weapons, you can see that."

"Manners, Colin. Manners," said Lumpy.

"What do you think this is, the governor's mansion? I search her or out she goes." He pointed at her rucksack. "That first."

She handed him the sack and watched as he pawed through her belongings. "Get your arms up."

Maggie did as she was told and refused to give the little troll the satisfaction of a wince when he pinched the inside of her thigh or ran his hands under her breasts.

"You'll do," he said at last.

"Come on, Mags." Lumpy ushered Maggie past the grumbling little man.

Halfway up the stairs, Maggie turned. Colin stood on his stool, glaring after them. To Lumpy she said, softly, "He's a bit small for a doorkeeper, isn't he?"

"He might be small, but he's right about that wild boar trick and he can move fast as a cricket."

At the top of the stairs they entered a claustrophobically narrow hall. The smell was sweet, heavy, musky. Doors on either side were boarded over. There was no option but to go forward. Maggie thought it a clever layout. Any enemy who got through the front door would be forced to walk single file in one direction, giving whoever needed to escape plenty of time, especially if there were, as she suspected, an anthill of hidden tunnels and passageways behind the walls.

The silence made the hair on the back of her neck stand up. It was like walking into a crypt. The musty-sweet smell might be that of decay. A sign of any living thing, even a rat or a roach, would have comforted her. At least it would prove life hadn't abandoned this place. She tried to imagine Kyle walking this hall, money clutched in his fist, desperate for silver dreams.

As they neared the end of the hall they faced another door, which opened at their approach. A coil of dark smoke wafted out, curling up toward the ceiling as though searching for something in the rafters. She followed Lumpy and expected to step into the same vast hall as the day before, thinking this was simply a different entrance to the same place.

It was not.

The octagonal room was small and windowless. The walls looked as if fashioned of obsidian and lanterns hung from metal posts. The thick smoke roiled on the ceiling like thunderclouds. Maggie squinted up into it. It didn't just roil, it formed shapes, a hand here, another there, a face pushing outward, turning this way and that, as though looking for her. The face seemed familiar but before she could place it, it dissolved. A prickle ran along her skin.

"Srebrenka told me to expect you."

Maggie turned. On a sagging loveseat in front of a black velvet curtain sat a man of enormous girth, a bloated toad, his head blending into his shoulders as though he'd eaten his own neck. A drawstring shirt billowed over his massive, drooping chest. His brown jacket was missing all but two buttons, as if the task of keeping all that fat enclosed had simply been too much for the others and they'd popped under the strain. Folds of flesh rolled under his big ears. His lips puffed out like plump sausages. He wore multiple rings – all nearly buried in his fingers. His eyes were glittering slits and his belly hung so far between his monstrous wool-clad thighs they were forced wide apart.

"Hello, Trickster," said Lumpy. "Wondered if you'd be here. Where's Srebrenka?"

Trickster patted the front of his shirt, smoothing the oddly feminine garment. "She's away on business just at the moment, but told me you might stop in."

"I'm looking for my brother. His name is Kyle."

"Everyone's looking for something."

"Is the door here, or not?"

His eyebrows flicked and then his face settled into an impassive custard-like stillness. "Oh, of course it is, sweetie."

Maggie's stomach clenched. "And did Kyle go through it?"

"Now, you see, that's the piece of information that's going to cost you."

"I have money."

"How much?"

"Name a price."

He named an astronomical figure. She laughed. "Name a real price."

Trickster shifted, causing the seat to creak dangerously. He placed his hands on his knees and pushed himself into a standing position. He was slightly taller than Maggie, and three times as wide. As he waddled toward her a miasma of sweat and something yeasty preceded him. Lumpy stepped to her side.

Trickster spoke to Lumpy. "How much does she know about the way this place works?"

Lumpy shrugged. "She used to live here."

"But things have changed." Trickster studied her. "You don't know Srebrenka at all."

"I do," said Maggie, meeting his gaze steadily.

He snorted. "You only think you do. Like you think you know this place. I know things nobody knows and if you want to find your brother – though why you would I've no idea – you've got to know what I know. I'm the Trickster, right? I know all the tricks. You want to know a trick or two? That's gonna cost you, toots."

Maggie named a counter figure, less than she was willing to pay, but enough to let him know she was negotiating in good faith. They went back and forth until they arrived at a figure she considered criminal, which was only appropriate. She reached into her pocket and drew out one of her money pouches. She handed him the money. "What do you know?"

The room had become hot, and smokier. The curls of smoke, which had festooned the rafters when she entered, drifted downward.

The money disappeared into the loaf of Trickster's fist. "Pretty. Oh, yes. I am pleased with this." He winked at Maggie. His smile grew, pushing his mashed-potato cheeks upward slightly. "Maybe you'll even give me the rest of what's in your money pouch to pay for dear Lumpy's dreams. After all, he's been a friend to you."

"Fine." It seemed quite reasonable now to give him everything. She held out the cash. "But no more stalling or I'm gone."

"Yeah, that'd be a great loss," Trickster snorted. "Fine. Here's what I know."

The smoke was filling the room, although no one else seemed to notice. Maggie felt as though her insides were ripping in two. One part wanted to strike out, to swat at the smoke as one would a swarm of wasps. The other wanted to open her arms, throw back her head and let it in, that familiar sting in the nostrils. She wondered, at some emotional distance, if she were about to faint.

Trickster sat on the loveseat. "I liked your little brother. Even though he was a pain in my ass. Thought he was a tough guy, didn't he?"

"Are you going to take me to the door or not?" Under the guise of brushing her hair from her forehead, she swiped at the smoke.

"Impatience. Runs in the family." Trickster chuckled. "Don't rupture a blood vessel. Your brother always wanted more. No journey was enough for him." He scratched the back of his neck. "Things progress. One thing leads to another is what I'm saying."

"What are you talking about?" She waved her hands in front of her face, trying to banish the haze she now looked through.

"Srebrenka knows." Trickster put his palms together and pressed them to his lips. "You sure about this, toots?"

Why did everyone keep asking her that? "Forget it. I'll find him without your help."

"No, you won't, but then again I doubt you'll find him *with* my help either." He moved with more speed than she thought him capable. In one smooth motion, he was standing in front of her.

The smoke smelled so sweet – like lavender and burnt sugar. She wanted to lie down and dream. Right now. And keep on dreaming and dreaming.

"Mags, you all right?" Lumpy's voice cut through the silver mists swirling round her vision.

"Oh, Srebrenka likes you, she does," sneered Trickster. "And you ain't seen nothing yet."

"She's ready. Show her," said Lumpy.

"Not quite yet." Trickster pulled open her coat and plucked the second money pouch from her pocket.

Maggie wanted very much to stop him. In fact, she wanted very much to kick him in his probably inaccessible private parts, but the silver smoke had wrapped around her arms and legs and she moved as though through water, heavy water, as though through molasses. She could only be grateful Trickster didn't find the little blue box of strange gifts Mr. Strundale had given her. She wondered if this was the moment she should eat the seed, hold the tooth, wave the mistletoe . . . She stood like a tree rooted in this unhallowed ground.

Trickster bowed. "Step this way, girlie, and may I wish you all the best . . ."

He pulled the loveseat away from the wall and yanked a rope beside the curtain.

CHAPTER TEN

T HE CURTAIN OPENED, REVEALING A WIDE ROUGH
tree trunk. It didn't seem possible that a tree grew on the
second floor of a Forest tenement, and yet there it was. Its roots
grew through the floor, or perhaps they became part of the
floor. It was difficult to tell where the tree ended and the building began. Had the tree grown with the building around it, or
was the building built around the tree? The tree's trunk disappeared into the ceiling seamlessly, without any sign of a hole in
the surrounding wood. It must go up into the third floor, or the
fourth, Maggie thought, if there was one, or perhaps it grew out
of the roof. Well, it must do, in order to get light.

Her vision dazzled, sparked, flared. She was entering the
Silver World. Was she a Piper again? Despair was a rock in
her chest. How had this happened? And why was she standing,
not lying on a couch? Or perhaps she was lying on a couch and
simply didn't know it. No, it was only the smoke in the room
making her light-headed. Only? That was dangerous enough.

"Go on, girl," Trickster said. "You wanted to find Kyle, well,
go on, follow him. Open the door."

What was he talking about? What door?

There was, in fact, a door in the middle of the tree trunk. How could she have missed that? The door was black wood, nearly twice her height, and another tree was painted on it, all swirls and strange symbols – circles and crowns and eyes. A pair of ravens perched on the branches, one with wings outstretched. Both appeared to stare directly at her. She moved her head. Their gaze followed. The painted tree trunk shimmered with gold, the leaves sparkled emerald. Fruit the colour of rubies hung heavy and one formed a door handle. Flowers like glittering opals and diamonds twinkled near the roots. And what roots they were. From the middle of the door downward, the roots below were as vast as the branches above, so that the entire tree seemed perfectly balanced.

That door; it drew her like an enchanted flame. *Kyle's in there!* The thought came to her as though someone screamed it. She put her hands over her ears, it was so loud. *He's in there! Open the door! Open it! Open it now!* Her bones sang with the knowledge. Kyle was behind that door, and if she had any hope of bringing him home, she was going to have to open it.

Someone moved her hands from her ears. "Go on, Mags. It's what you came for ..."

Although the compulsion to open the door was fierce, she fought it. To open the door was a dangerous, probably fatal, thing to do, and her heart flapped and fluttered in her chest like a swallow trapped in a stovepipe. The doorknob pulsed slightly, reached for her.

The voice was right. It was what she'd come for, nothing could be simpler. Accept and surrender to the path. Kyle, I'm coming. Come out, come out, wherever you are.

Maggie touched the doorknob. It was smooth and warm and fit into her hand as though moulding itself to the shape of her palm. She had the distinct impression that if she tried to pull back, the doorknob would engulf her fingers and she'd grow into the trunk and become part of the tree. She took a deep breath.

She pulled, and the door gave itself to her, leaped toward her. She had only a moment to register a dark void through the opening. It might be an empty shaft for all she knew. And then someone from behind pushed her and she stumbled forward. The world spun. Up was down and down was up and it felt like being rolled in a huge wave. Her arms flailed, and her stomach flipped. But then her foot landed. She was at least on solid ground. She swung around to defend herself in case more than a push followed shove, but a wall faced her. She put her palms on it, trying to find evidence of the doorway, but felt only cold, flaking brick and crumbling grout. They'd been on the second floor, and from the outside, when she and Lumpy entered, the street was level. There'd been no hill. If she'd stepped outside from the second floor, logic dictated she should fall to the ground. Logic? She snorted.

Fine. Her head was clearer. Whatever the smoke had been, elysium or something else, walking through the door had banished its effects. She was where she was and the most sensible thing to do was to determine in what direction she ought to set off. She surveyed the scene. A narrow laneway. A pile of refuse – scraps of tin and plywood, old cans, broken bricks. It must have snowed while she was inside, and quite heavily, too, for she stood in an inch or more. No footprints, not even that of a rat or a dog or a cat, marred the white surface. The brick walls on either side sported not a single window or door. They went on a long way, receding in either direction into impenetrable darkness. These must be large buildings indeed. She looked up. The walls loomed for several storeys and she saw nothing but the sparkle of stars in the sky above her. Was she still in the Forest? Or had she come out somewhere else? Warehouses? What and where were these buildings? Her mouth was dry, and her thoughts bounced around. Of course, Trickster might simply have tossed her into the street, or perhaps he'd drugged her and moved her while insensible to some other part of Toronto, to some other city entirely, for that matter. Perhaps he knew nothing of Kyle. Srebrenka might have arranged the whole thing.

Wet snowflakes began to fall. Maggie pulled off her pack and in it found her black wool scarf and gloves, which she put on. The snow fell heavily enough now to make it even harder to see in the darkness. She looked right and then left and tried to decide which way to go. If she went to the right, that would, theoretically, take her back the way she'd come with Lumpy, although given the way the geography behaved in the Forest, it was just as likely to be the opposite. Assuming she was any-where near the Forest.

She would have given a great deal, just then, to have Badger with her. Perhaps she'd been foolish to leave him behind. She wished, too, that Alvin was with her. His confidence in the wide world, of which she knew so little, his wry humour; she could use a dose of that. Maybe she should simply sit down with her back to the wall and let the snow cover her, silence her, bury her in its chilly embrace.

"Not another one," said a voice. "You'd think this was the bloody public terminus the way people have been popping up willy-nilly of late."

Maggie's heart skittered. "Who's there?"

"Just the question I should be asking you." A flap opened in the pile of what Maggie had initially taken to be refuse. As it did, the snow slid from its sides, revealing a makeshift dwelling. From the opening stepped a small grousing woman. "Fine thing for you to be asking, when I'm the one who's always been here."

"I didn't realize anyone lived here."

"Shocked," said the woman, flatly. "I'm shocked."

She barely came to Maggie's waist and wore a collection of tattered grey rags, knotted and tied and slung and wrapped in an impossible-to-follow pattern. She had a sharp, wrinkled little face, with a distinct overbite. She certainly looked poor as a tenement mouse, but she didn't have any of the telltale signs of a Piper. Her nostrils flared as she tilted her head in Maggie's direction, as though scenting her. In fact, it appeared this was precisely what she was doing, since after a second she sneezed and harrumphed and said, "Another from over there, then."

"Over where?"

"Oh, well, that's typical. Doesn't know where she came from. Probably doesn't know where she is. Doubt she knows *who* she is, but then, who does, I always say. Not that anyone listens. Oh, no, not to such as me."

"It is a bit confusing."

The woman pulled an already lit pipe out of her clothing and puffed on it. The nails on the end of her long, finely articulated fingers looked quite sharp. "Well, life's like that. Don't suppose you have any cheese on you, do you?"

Maggie thought the woman's olfactory power considerable. "I do as it happens." She took the package of food from her pack. "Would you like a piece?"

"She's got decent manners, at least. Not like some I could mention." The tiny woman plucked the cheese from the cloth in which it was wrapped, broke it in half and handed the rest back. "Mustn't be greedy, now, must we?" she said. She nibbled the cheese and hummed contentedly. "What's your name, then?"

"Maggie, Maggie Marchette. And you?"

"I'm called Mother Ratigan."

"Pleased to meet you, Mother Ratigan. So tell me, this place . . ." Maggie said, looking up and down the laneway. "Are we in the Forest?"

"Well, only in the same way the inside of an oyster is inside the oyster's shell, if you catch my meaning."

"Not entirely, no, I don't think I do."

"Pity."

Since the woman appeared disinclined to say more, Maggie thought for a moment and said, "The Forest shifts about, doesn't it?"

"Nothing stays the same, nor ever will." The woman's dark eyes were bright as she talked with her mouth full of cheese.

"I suppose it wouldn't be a jump to think if streets move about of their own free will, they might fold over on themselves, too." Maggie looked at the woman for any sign she was on the right track.

"Very few things, or people for that matter, do anything of their own free will." Mother Ratigan smacked her lips and swallowed the last morsel of cheese.

"Meaning?"

She folded her sharp-nailed hands over her belly. "You should stay here. At least the night. Come on in and have a cup of tea by the fire."

Fitting into such a tiny dwelling, Maggie thought, would be impossible, even if she were so inclined.

As though reading her thoughts, Mother Ratigan said, "Oh, many things are bigger inside than out, you should have learned that by now."

"It's very kind, but I'm looking for someone," said Maggie.

"Aren't we all? Come and go and more gone every day without going anywhere at all."

Maggie had no idea what that meant but knew enough to understand that trying to make sense of what someone with mental health problems babbled was futile. Still, you could ask a mentally ill person something you might not ask a sane person without fear of being thought crazy yourself. "Are we in Toronto?"

The woman laughed, sharp and brittle. "Silver, silver, silver bright, cross over from the dark to light! Pipes and smoke and tricky doings."

Maggie simply stared at her, letting this information sink in. The Silver World. Land of the elysium dreams. She thought she might throw up.

"Look at you, all green at the gills. Bend over. Hands on

knees. There you go. Don't want you passing out or puking on my stoop."

It took a few minutes of deep breathing for the nausea to quiet and the world to stop spinning. Maggie stood up again, slowly. If that was true . . . "I'm looking for my brother. His name is Kyle." She described him and a little of how she came to be there, how she had walked through Trickster's door. By the way the old woman nodded when she talked about Trickster, Maggie concluded she knew the man, or at least knew *of* him. "Do you get many people passing this way because of him?"

"Thanks to him or with him to blame, take your choice. There's been a few."

"And was Kyle one of them?"

Mother Ratigan tapped the ends of her fingers together and turned her head in what might be said to be a coquettish manner were she fifty years younger. "Is an old woman expected to give up everything she knows, the only thing she has to trade, standing outside in the cold? You'll be old yourself one day, and all alone if you're unlucky. All the children gone and left me, more than I can count, and I loved them all, each one, and fed them sweet cherry pie, although the recipe's so much better now. Come in, girl. Pity the lonely."

Who knew what rules of hospitality applied here? "I'd be happy to visit a while, if you'll help me."

"And if I won't help you?" The woman raised a faint eyebrow.

How hard life must be for an old woman alone in an alleyway. Maggie shrugged. "I'll do it anyway."

"You are a good girl, aren't you?" It didn't sound like a compliment.

Mother Ratigan smiled. "The pie's awaiting and a cup of tea as well." The old lady held back the flap of hide that served as a door. "Come on, step lively, you're letting all the heat out."

Although Maggie saw no way she and Mother Ratigan would fit inside the structure (if such a tumbledown collection of odds and sods could be called a structure), she took a deep breath and placed her foot across the threshold.

No sooner had her foot touched the inside of the dwelling than she felt another vertiginous shift such as she felt at Trickster's door. She ducked, hoping not to hit the lintel and cause the hovel to collapse, but to her surprise, there was lots of space. In fact, she found herself stepping into a room, quite a proper room. High windows with different coloured panes of glass – red, blue and yellow – shone with light, although the source of this light was puzzling, since it was night outside. Jewel-tone patches of that light covered the wooden floor like a rich carpet and, for that matter, the floor *was* covered in a thick carpet so that Maggie sank a little in the plush. Instinctively, she stepped off it onto the wood, not wishing to mar it with her dirty boots.

"Don't worry about that, lamb. Just slip your boots off and make yourself at home. This is a place of comfort and safety. Just like the home you dreamed of when you were a little girl, am I right?"

A stove stood against the far wall, all bright tile and brass. Next to it were two comfy-looking reading chairs, covered in pink-and-yellow chintz. Each had its own footstool, on which blankets were neatly folded. In the middle of the room stood a round table and two woven-cane chairs.

"How is this possible? It's crazy."

"I like to keep a low profile on the street. It wouldn't do to draw attention to oneself in a neighbourhood like this, now would it? Go on, put the kindling in the stove and let's get a good blaze going, shall we? Take the chill off."

A fragrant cherry pie sat in the centre of a white-lace cloth on a round table. The sweet plump cherries rose through the latticework pastry and the smell of it filled the air. Saliva filled Maggie's mouth. The table was set for two, with a pot of tea and cups and saucers and forks and plates.

"Poor girl," said Mother Ratigan, "why, you're quite famished, aren't you?"

She was ravenous. Her belly pressed up against her spine. She'd never been so hungry. "Perhaps just one piece."

"As soon as the fire's going, lamb. First things first."

Maggie built a fire in the stove, but all the while her mind was on the pie. When the fire crackled and the warmth began to radiant, she turned to her hostess. "Now, could I please have a little bit of pie?" There was something else Maggie had meant to ask Mother Ratigan, but to save her life she couldn't think of it.

Mother Ratigan pulled out a chair for her guest. The old woman had changed her clothes. She wore a kimono, made of shimmering pink silk. Her grey hair looked clean and shiny now, braided and coiled on the top of her head. Her face was still wrinkled, although not quite *so* wrinkled perhaps, but her overbite was just as pronounced.

"I've been so lonely here all by myself, but now you're here I do feel all shall be well. You may have quite as much pie as you like; there's always more where that came from, and will you have a little tea as well?"

Maggie sat at the table and waited, feeling quite dizzy, while the old woman, who was nearly the same height as Maggie now, cut a spectacularly generous piece of pie and set it on a plate. The pastry flaked beneath Maggie's fork, and the cherries were the colour of rubies. The scent was of every good thing, full of promise and delight. The taste, oh the taste was an explosion of sweetness, thick and smooth, like cherry honey, with a little spark of sharpness. It rushed to her head, it made her immediately want more, and so she ate more, another piece and then another and finally almost all the pie was gone and she was suddenly so very tired it felt as though her bones were made of heavy wet sandbags.

"Poor dear, you're quite exhausted, aren't you, and why not, after all you've been through."

What had she been through? It was so difficult to remember.

"Why not tuck up in bed for the night and I'm sure everything will look well in the morning."

With that she led Maggie to a room with a great soft bed and a mountain of eiderdown comforters. She helped Maggie out of her clothes and slipped a soft cotton nightgown over her head. It smelled of lavender, as did the covers on the bed and the feather mattress itself. Maggie sank down as though into a cloud, a lovely white warm cloud where she floated off to sleep.

MAGGIE DREAMS ...

Alvin tells her there is a castle behind a great wild hedge, in which a boy has been asleep for a hundred years. Many have tried to rescue him, but all have died, lost and bloodied in the hedge.

Maggie stands in front of the hedge full of thorns and presses her way through, her skin tearing, the blood flowing. She goes on.

At last she comes into a courtyard. A horse sleeps near a trough, and a cat sleeps by the well, and mice sleep near the cat, and flies sleep on the walls. She walks farther and passes two ravens asleep on a perch. She walks still farther and sees a bed carved from oak. In the middle of the bed, under a blanket of dried leaves, lies Kyle. She calls out, bends and kisses him, but as she does he crumbles, his body turning into nothing but dried leaves that blow away in a sudden gust of wind.

KYLE WEARS FINE LEATHER BOOTS, AND A TWEED travelling suit the colour of oak leaves in autumn. He speaks with an old man, huge and shaggy-haired, with enormous hands and feet. The old man tells him of a great, impenetrable thorn hedge.

"There is a castle back behind," he says, "and a beautiful woman asleep on a bed of stone. Many have tried to rescue her, but all have had their flesh shredded from their bones on the thorns, for they are made from shards of broken glass. She's worth the effort that one, though. And if you make it through the hedge, she'll be yours, to do with what you will, for all the hours of eternity."

And Kyle says, "I'm not afraid. I'll have her."

He stands before the hedge made of glass-splinter thorns. He puts his hand against the first thorn, which trembles at his touch and then turns to dust. Forward he goes, as the thorns shiver and fall.

At last he comes into a courtyard. A horse sleeps near a trough, and a cat sleeps by the well, and mice sleep near the cat, and flies sleep on the walls. He opens the tower door, on which is painted a great tree. Inside is a bed carved from stone. In the middle of the bed, under a coverlet embroidered with blue swirls, lies a woman, her hair as pale as clouds, her breast alabaster. He bends over and kisses her . . . runs his hands along her form. How can she be so cold and so hot at once? She opens her eyes, blue as the ice at the centre of a glacier, smiles, her teeth like pearls, and wraps her arms around his neck in an unbreakable embrace.

CHAPTER ELEVEN

"**W**AKEY-WAKEY, LITTLE LAMB," SAID MOTHER Ratigan. "Here you are sleeping the day away when I've made cherry pies aplenty. Get dressed. Your clothes are on the chair, all fresh and clean."

Maggie was starving. Wasn't there something she was meant to be doing? She put on the pale blue dress with the puffy sleeves. She slipped into pale yellow slippers, made from the softest leather. She looked in the long oval mirror on the wall near the bed. Her hair was curled and fell softly around her shoulders. Her lips were tinted with cherry juice. The sunlight filtered through the stained glass windows scattered garnets and sapphires and emeralds all along the floor and the walls.

Maggie ate her fill of pie, and Mother Ratigan poured her tea sweetened with lavender honey. When she was finished eating and drinking Maggie felt sleepy again and the old woman helped her to a chaise where she reclined in the bejewelled sunlight. She dozed as Mother Ratigan brushed her hair with a silver brush. "You must call me, Mother, little lamb."

And Maggie replied, "Yes, Mother. You are very good to me."

"Think nothing of it, little lamb," said Mother Ratigan. "I

live for you and you for me and so now always we shall be."

And so the day passed until it was time to eat again and rest by the warm stove and have a little smackerel of something before dinner and that night, when she fell into the soft warm bed, Maggie didn't dream at all, but woke to another pretty dress and pretty shoes and a day of sweetness and dozing in the prismatic light.

Maggie was doing just that, dozing on the lavender-scented chaise, with Mother Ratigan brushing her hair, when the old lady jumped. The brush clattered to the floor.

"What was that?" Her eyes snapped to the doorway. "I heard something."

Maggie kept her eyes closed, for opening them took a great effort.

But then she did hear something. It sounded like . . . yes, it sounded just like a bark. Was there a dog nearby? Had Mother bought her a dog? Such a lovely mother.

"I don't like this," said Mother Ratigan. "Stay here. It isn't safe."

"I'm sure nothing's wrong. Whatever could be wrong here?" Maggie turned her face to the pillows. Mother's voice sounded so harsh.

The barking became sharp, urgent. Although it took a great deal of effort, Maggie opened her eyes. That barking. How familiar it sounded. It occurred to her she loved dogs. She remembered she loved one dog. A black-and-white dog. Badger. The dog's name was Badger. Her eyes flew wide. *Badger!* It couldn't be. Badger couldn't be here. But where was *here?* Why was she wearing this ridiculous dress? There were yellow bows on her shoes, for the love of God. Where were her boots? Her jeans?

A whirlwind in the form of a black-and-white dog exploded through the room, stopped, shook itself, spotted Maggie and ran to her, his head down and his lips pulled in a grin. He leaped at her, knocking her off her feet, which, she thought as she landed on her rump in a flounce of blue silk, would never have happened if she'd been in her boots.

"Badger! Good boy, what are you doing here?" What, for that matter, was *she* doing here? Her mind was clouded as milk. The dog licked her face and whined in joy.

Mother's voice called, and how angry she sounded. Well, no, that wasn't right for, of course, Maggie's mother had died long ago. Images flashed into her head: a sickeningly sweet pie, a ratty little woman in a tiny shack, a door, Trickster, Srebrenka . . . And then she remembered Kyle. Her gut twisted. How had she forgotten him? She jumped to her feet, tearing the blue fabric of the dress, and kicked off the yellow-bowed shoes. Badger danced around, barking. How the hell had he got here? How had he found her? He turned to the door just as Mother Ratigan appeared. He snarled and bared his teeth.

"You'd harm a poor old woman, would you?"

Maggie felt a fool in this absurd dress, and more so when she noticed her fingers covered in cherry stains. Her head hurt, and her stomach, too.

Mother Ratigan said, "Don't leave me, little lamb. You'd leave me here to starve and freeze to death?" She reached out to embrace Maggie, a silver brush in her hand.

Maggie stepped out of reach. "Where are my things? My clothes, my boots, my pack?"

"I don't know what you mean," the woman pouted. "You have such a lovely dress and a closet full of others."

Badger growled. It was Mother Ratigan who bared her teeth then, but catching herself, she wrung her hands and said, "I don't like dogs. I don't like them at all. Make him go away."

"Badger, come, boy. Find my boots, find my things; find them." Badger cocked his head and then raced around the room, sniffing as he went. "Good boy. Find them!"

Badger dashed into the bedroom and Maggie followed, leaving Mother Ratigan to pace and hurl curses. "May you freeze in a snowbank with your eyes under an inch of ice! May you die of hunger at a king's feast!"

Badger ran for the armoire. Maggie opened it but only saw a row of fussy dresses hanging from a rod and a row of fussy shoes lined up beneath. Badger scrambled at the floor of the armoire and Maggie realized there was a hidden drawer. She pulled it open and, sure enough, there were her things, balled up and stuffed inside. She ripped the dress from her body and dove into her jeans and turtleneck, her heavy socks and boots. Mother Ratigan still raved in the other room. "May you break out in boils the colour of cherries! May mice feast on your bones!"

Badger stood in the doorway, barring Mother Ratigan's entrance. Maggie grabbed her coat, checked the pockets to make sure the little enamel box Mr. Strundale had given her was still inside. It was. She snatched her pack. She felt as though she'd slipped back into her own skin.

They stepped into the main room to find Mother Ratigan sitting at the table with her hands over her eyes, weeping. "Leave me, they all leave me in the end."

"We had a deal," said Maggie. "You promised if I came inside, you'd tell me what you know about Kyle."

"What makes you think I know anything, you ungrateful girl?" Her voice was harsh, self-pitying.

Mother Ratigan was frail, thin as a stick, her skin nearly translucent. Her white hair was fine as spiderwebs, in a thin braid down her back . . . Or was it? Hadn't her hair been in a bun just a moment before? Hadn't she been wearing a pink kimono? Maggie blinked and shook her head.

"We had a deal. I hold you to your part."

"Oh, what do I know of boys who come and go and won't help an old lady?"

"Stop talking in riddles. Did you see Kyle, or didn't you?"

"I saw him. And he just walked on like I was so much trash in the street. Not like you. You're a good girl, aren't you, and you ought to be rewarded. You and your friend both should be rewarded."

A huge pie appeared on the table in front of her. Badger sniffed the air. The scent full of burnt sugar and buttery pastry and sweet cherries. Saliva once again rushed to Maggie's mouth. Just a bite, she thought, just a wee bite.

Mother Ratigan smiled, and there was something so triumphant and so greedy in that smile that Maggie felt her skin prickle from her toes to her scalp. She looked at Badger. He inched toward the pie.

"Oh, you have time for just a wee slice of pie, to please an old lady, don't you? Just a little one?" asked Mother Ratigan.

"Badger! To me!" Maggie took his face in her hands and turned his gaze toward her. His eyes were glassy. He drooled.

She knew they had to run and could think of no way out except the way they'd come in. "Come on, boy! Hurry! Hurry!"

They dashed for the door, while Mother Ratigan screeched behind them. As they stepped over the threshold another dizzying swoop overcame Maggie and then she and Badger stood in the strange endless laneway. It had stopped snowing and the stars shined brightly overhead in strange constellations. She turned to the hovel. It didn't look like Mother Ratigan would follow. In fact, the hovel hardly seemed even a hovel now. It was just a pile of garbage, an assortment of tins and planks and frozen vegetable scraps and something that might once have been a chair, or a commode. Nothing that vaguely resembled a cottage with stained glass and enchanted pies.

Which way? She scanned first right and then left. Neither direction looked promising. "Where's Kyle, Badger?" She wished she had something of his to give the dog for scent. He'd met Kyle a few times, but how much could a dog reasonably be expected to remember? Badger cocked his head one way and then the other, trying his best to figure out what she wanted. "Kyle? Can you find him?" It was a ridiculous plan. "Oh, Badger.

How did you find me? How did you get here?" Badger thumped his tail. And then she heard a *caw-caw.* There, perhaps a hundred feet down the wall, perched two large ravens. They bounced their heads and clacked their beaks. Ravens at night? Well, why not? One of them hopped a few feet farther, and the second followed. More cawing and clacking.

"We'll go that way, I guess," she said. "Come on, boy."

She began walking, with Badger running ahead. The ravens seemed to taunt him but kept in sight. Maggie kept glancing back to see if the old woman was following, but the fourth time Maggie turned round there was no sign of anything behind them, not even a pile of garbage. The lane just petered out after a few hundred feet, into a sort of misty nothingness. There was nothing to do but go forward.

As she walked she wondered what Mr. Strundale must be thinking. Surely, he'd be worried. Who knew how long she'd been Mother Ratigan's *guest* . . . She wished she could send Badger home, but she couldn't, having no idea how to get back herself. She wondered if Mr. Strundale would try and find her. And then, of course, she thought of Alvin. She should have left him a note. If he returned and she was gone, he'd be frantic. And furious. Why hadn't she confided in him?

The extent to which she really hadn't thought this journey through was disturbing. If Mr. Mustby was alive he'd lock her in the shop. Probably Alvin would have if she'd told him her plans. Just then she rather wished someone *had* locked her up.

The ravens wagged their heads and cawed. Badger barked. She had slowed down apparently, lost in her thoughts. Badger appeared to trust the birds, and if she wasn't much on trusting people, she trusted him. So she would trust the birds as well.

Badger padded along, running ahead a few paces toward the birds and then waiting for her to catch up. Now and again she looked back. The path behind ended in that strange mist, always a hundred or so feet away. She stopped. Waited. The mist came no nearer. She began to walk again and the mist advanced. It was like a broom at her back, sweeping her along. It didn't feel malevolent; it felt like nothing at all.

Maggie imagined Alvin walking beside her – broad shoulders under his olive-green duffle coat, the curl of hair on his collar, the lines around his eyes, etched by sun and wind and laughter. Just the idea of him, even glowering, glaring or scowling, was enormously comforting. She pictured him standing in the Grimoire, looking for clues as to where she was, worrying about her. The idea warmed her.

Her boots crunched on the hard snow, the ravens cawed occasionally and Badger panted. It was a good sign, how much Badger seemed to be enjoying himself, for surely if there was trouble, he'd sense it. Maggie had the odd sensation that the laneway was unfolding before them as they walked, that it got longer with every step, and yet at the same time they made no progress. She concentrated on her feet until the feeling went away. The steady pace, the quiet all around . . . she fell into a sort of walking trance . . .

IT HAD BEEN WHAT? TWO YEARS AGO? KYLE HAD BEEN clean for a while and was living in rooms on a small street between Dundas and Shuter, adjacent to the Forest. Maggie had bought some chicken, potatoes, carrots, celery, eggs, milk and a few odds and ends. She found his address, a squat, three-storey brick building with a cracked stoop. The air smelled of diesel fumes. Someone tooted a trumpet in one of the buildings across the street. Off-key and blatting, it was enough to take the enamel off one's teeth. A man, huddled in a too-big coat, sat on a chair near the door.

Maggie nodded as she climbed the stairs. "Hey."

"Who you looking for?" asked the man.

"My brother. Kyle. You know him?"

"Nope," he said.

Inside, the hallway smelled of rising damp and onions and the light was dim, but not so dim Maggie couldn't see the rodent droppings. An unlit stairway took her to the basement where several padlocked doors graced one wall, across from which was an unnumbered door without a lock. Maggie knocked. Someone moved around inside. She knocked again. Something broke, shattered – glass from the sound of it. She used the flat of her hand on the door. "Kyle, open up. It's Maggie."

It took a few minutes before the door opened. Kyle held a wadded towel to his left eye and the knuckles of his right hand were abraded. He wore a not very clean pair of jeans, socks and a T-shirt. His skin was swirled with silver. He smelled unwashed.

"May I come in?" Maggie tried to keep her voice steady, keep things calm. Best not to mention the eye right off.

Somewhat to her surprise, he stepped aside. He moved as though exhausted. An iron bed hunched against one wall and in front of it a low table on which was strewn a crust of bread, melted candles, a fly-speckled bowl of what appeared to be honey and a ragged paperback with a frog-like alien on the cover. A kitchenette of sorts took up the opposite wall – a porcelain sink and a wooden table with a little microwave. A collection of chipped mugs and plates stood in the sink, which glinted with shards of glass. Above the sink was a mirror, or what was left of it. Watery grey light seeped in through the shoulder-level, grime-streaked single window above the bed.

"What have you done?" She put the bags of groceries on the table and tried to pull Kyle's hand away from his eye.

"Nothing. I got something in it." He shied from her.

"Let me look, Kyle." Maggie tried to smile. "You know I won't give up."

Kyle plopped down onto the bed and dropped his arm. The eye was red, inflamed, but not bleeding.

"Tilt your head back." Maggie positioned Kyle's head toward the window. "Is there a piece of glass in there? We should go to the hospital."

Kyle snapped his head away. "I'm not going to the hospital." He stood and moved to the sink. He ran the water and splashed some on his face. "There's nothing in there, or if there was it's gone now." He turned to Maggie. "What are you wearing? You look like an undertaker."

She wore her usual black jeans, turtleneck, boots and coat. The same thing she'd worn, more or less, for years. Why he would remark on it now was strange. "Well, at least I don't look like a corpse."

He scowled with an expression of contempt so thick she could have scraped it off her shoe. And then, unexpectedly, he laughed. He laughed for quite a long time, and then the laughter turned to tears. She tried to touch him, but he held his hands up. "I'll hit you if you come any closer, I swear I will."

She stayed long enough to make him some soup and see he ate it.

IT WAS STRANGE, THAT INCIDENT WITH KYLE'S EYE. Hadn't she had a similar dream recently? Kyle behind a glass wall? A shattering, and a splinter in his eye? No, in the heart, not his eye. Just before she set out on her journey, she'd dreamed that. How strange.

Just then Badger stopped, stepping slightly into her path, legs braced, chest out, sniffing the air. The ravens had disappeared. At first she saw nothing, and then two figures appeared out of the darkness, dressed in uniforms with long white double-breasted coats and fringed epaulettes on the shoulders. Badger wagged his tail, then sat by her side. The two men walked briskly and stopped in front of her. Whatever they were, they were well trained, walking in step, nodding their heads precisely at the same moment. They looked as though they might be father and son – the same red hair, the same blue eyes, the same neat moustache.

"Good evening," the older of the two said. He wore a red crest on his lapel, which the younger man did not.

"Hello," said Maggie.

"This is not where you should be," said the red-crest man.

"We agree about that." The men did not return Maggie's smile. "I'm not sure where I am." She waved her hands around. "I mean, is this . . ." What should she ask? Are we in Canada? Are we in Ontario? How crazy did she want to sound? What if it wasn't the Silver World? "We're here only because I'm looking for someone, but there doesn't seem to be any way off this road."

"You are looking for your brother," said the man.

She glanced down at Badger, but he showed no signs of fear. "How do you know that?"

"We know only what we are told by Miss Tilden, for we are in her service."

"Do you know where Kyle is?" asked Maggie.

"We do not. We know you are to come with us."

CHAPTER TWELVE

THE TWO MEN DIDN'T APPEAR DANGEROUS, and Badger wasn't growling, but after the way the last invitation turned out, she wasn't sure she wished to accept another. "And what happens if I don't care to go with anybody just now?"

"The road will only get longer and longer, and sooner or later you'll want to arrive somewhere, and unless you come with us now, you won't get anywhere at all."

Maggie remembered the sensation she'd had that the pathway unrolled in front of them with every step, leading nowhere. "Where to, exactly?" she asked.

A quick smile flicked over the younger man's face. The older man said, "Why, to Miss Tilden, of course, wherever else? You're on her road, you do know that much at least, don't you?"

"I didn't see any signs."

The man snorted. "Signs indeed. Who else's road would it be? Are you coming, or do we leave you to keep walking until you regain your senses?"

Maggie shrugged. "It's either forward or back, I suppose."

"There's no back," said the man. "Not from here."

Maggie looked behind her and all she saw was exactly what

lay in front. The mist had disappeared, but the road behind was so formless it didn't matter. They might as well be rats running on a wheel. "I don't suppose either of you know the way back to the Forest, to Toronto, do you?"

"We know you are to come with us or we are to leave you here. That is all we know."

"For God's sake," said Maggie, "if this Miss Tilden turns out to be a witch like the last one, I swear I'll not be as polite as I was."

The young man blinked and wiggled his moustache. "That old rat? Not likely."

The older man shot the younger one a look of reprimand, then turned to Maggie. "I can assure you, Miss Tilden is nothing like the vermin who lives among refuse. The very idea is insulting, but we won't dwell on that since clearly you know less than nothing about a great many things, and Miss is a forgiving person. Now, come along, or not, the choice is yours."

Maggie looked down at Badger, who wagged his tail, making a snow-fan behind him. His mouth opened in a grin. "We'll come with you," she said. "I don't suppose we've got much choice."

"There are always choices," said the red-crest man, "just not always good ones. Come along."

After they'd walked for a short while Maggie began to hear noises – a low bustling sort of hum at first, and then as they walked along, the unmistakable sound of music and voices. "Beautiful violets!" "Best cheese – creamy and sweet!" "Silk fit for a queen!" Before she could register the change, she realized they were no longer walking on a snow-packed lane, but on cobblestones. Maggie swung round, but behind them the lane had disappeared; nothing but cobblestones remained. She turned back and found they stood in a market square lit by dozens of torches and oil lamps. It bustled with hawkers, despite the late hour. (Or at least what she assumed was the late hour, since who knew whether day or night actually existed here. Perhaps it was always night. An unsettling thought indeed.) They were in front of a jeweller's window, in which glittered a treasure chest of pearls, topaz, amethysts, emeralds, opals, dangling earrings, and sparkling chains and bangles. Next to that was a bakery. The cakes and cookies, muffins and pies, and tarts and croissants seemed no less alluring than the jewels. In fact, every storefront, doorway and lamppost glittered and shone as though made of crystal and gold. Stalls set up in the open space offered flowers and cheeses and silks; copper pots; walking sticks topped with cunningly carved faces, both human and animal; china teapots and an assortment of exotic teas. There were handkerchiefs, silver buckles for boots and belts, jams and jellies, umbrellas, hats, books, bowls of swimming fish, singing canaries in cages . . .

Behind them were only storefronts; the lane was gone. It was warmer in the square, too. The trees boasted leaves of vibrant red and marigold and pumpkin. People wore light jackets and shawls. There was no snow. Maggie removed her scarf and gloves. Badger seemed untroubled, nose quivering at the scent of roasting chickens, chestnuts and cheeses, his eyes almost closed in sensual bliss. Maggie rubbed his ears. He must be hungry, she thought, and walked to a man selling roast chickens. She reached for her money pouch, wondering whether they'd take Canadian currency. Nothing. Where had her money gone? Something on the edge of her mind . . . Trickster, his hand in her pocket . . .

"No need for that, Miss," said the red-crest man, as though reading her mind. "If you'll just follow me. Lots to eat for everyone inside, even your dog. Oh, yes, Miss Tilden's very fond of dogs and so forth. Nice big marrowy bone waiting, I shouldn't doubt."

Badger trotted forward as though he understood every word. At the other side of the square Maggie found herself

mounting wide marble steps that led to four enormous polished bronze doors, intricately engraved with peacocks. In front
of each door stood a man very similar to the red-crest man and
his younger image. They were mustachioed, wearing the same
brass-buttoned coats and black boots, although both the coats
and boots seemed a bit too warm for the decidedly autumnal
air. As they approached, the middle set of men opened the middle set of doors and bowed to let them pass, saying in unison,
"Welcome to the Tilden Hotel. Enjoy your stay."

The lobby was a vast space of pink marble and gold. The
floors were inlaid with jade and lapis lazuli flowers. Corinthian
columns rose to a vaulted ceiling festooned with gilt garlands,
cherubim and seraphim. From the centre of the ceiling dozens
of candles burned in a chandelier composed of life-sized naked
figures. At each corner of the lobby, harpists played in perfect
unison. Enormous vases, taller than Maggie, stood along the
walls, filled with equally enormous palm fronds, birds of paradise, ostrich feathers and strange fleshy flowers she couldn't
identify. The room smelled of jasmine and sandalwood and
musk. Badger sneezed.

Maggie tapped the young man on the shoulder. "Excuse
me. This is all very nice, but I can't stay here. I have no money."

"Pay? Oh, Miss, you'd only insult Miss Tilden if you tried
to pay. You're invited."

"Am I?"

"Oh, certainly."

They advanced through an archway. Chaise longues were
scattered throughout the room. On these, men and women
reclined, some having what seemed to be quite intimate
conversations involving hands and fingers searching beneath
garments. Others did no talking at all, but kissed or embraced.
The clothes they wore, regardless of sex, revealed more than
they covered.

Maggie flushed and looked at the floor. If this Tilden person thought she'd be doing any of that, she had another thought coming.

A young man with the same ginger hair as the others, although clean-shaven, wearing a sparkling white uniform, rushed forward and said, "Your luggage has been taken up. I'll escort you to your rooms."

"I don't have luggage," said Maggie.

"Everyone has luggage here. Yours is in your rooms. Miss Tilden's orders," said the young man, bowing and gesturing for them to follow. "You must hurry and dress, for Miss Tilden requests the pleasure of your company."

"Does she now?" Maggie watched two women, one raven-haired, the other with hair the colour of cream. The raven-haired woman nuzzled the neck of her companion and both were clad in no more than the palest of pink chiffon sarongs, which were tied around their shoulders and clung so it appeared the air around their naked bodies was blurred (not very effectively) for modesty's sake. "I'm not wearing anything like that, so you can just tell Miss Tilden no thanks," said Maggie. She couldn't help it, she felt like a prude, like an offended schoolgirl.

"Of course, Miss," said the young man. "Miss Tilden only wants her guests to be comfortable. Rest assured."

"I'm not sure I want to be Miss Tilden's guest."

The young man blanched. "Oh, I wouldn't tell her that, Miss. No, I wouldn't. Will you come now, please?"

It was clear from the way he twitched and wrung his hands that the thought of a waiting Miss Tilden made him very nervous, which did nothing to soothe Maggie's frayed nerves.

The couples (and at least two sets of triads) she passed on the chaises ignored her completely, so rapt were they in their activities. Badger walked past with his nose in the air, as though he were a wolf who cared little for the opinion of sheep. Maggie thought this a little odd, since even she could smell, well . . . the *sex* coming off them. It floated around the enormous room like trailing ribbons. Even if he was a sophisticated dog of incontestable good manners, she thought it would have demanded just the slightest bit of interest. Perhaps Badger understood the way things worked here in a way she did not.

The uniformed man led her to an elevator where his apparent twin waited. Once inside the elevator operator worked a lever like a ship's telegraph, although instead of words such as *ahead* and *astern, full* and *half* on one side it read, *up a little, quite a lot, just about* and *couldn't ask for more.* On the other side were *down a smidge, mind the drop, not quite there* and *that's all there is.* The man pushed the lever all the way to the top, to *off we go* and then over to *couldn't ask for more.* The elevator jigged and jostled, as though shaking itself out of a deep sleep, and up it went.

As they passed different floors – and there were far more of these than the words on the brass controls accounted for – Maggie glimpsed long, dimly lit hallways, with shadowy figures flitting and floating along them. Badger's ears perked up. At last, with the gentlest of taps, they stopped at a floor and the elevator operator said, "Here we are then, couldn't ask for more. Enjoy your stay." He smiled so broadly it was impossible to resist smiling back.

"Thank you," said Maggie.

"Oh, it's my pleasure, really it is."

She followed the bellboy along a hall that differed from the others only in the quality of the light. This floor was brightly lit, and the walls shone with gold paper. The white carpet underfoot was so thick Maggie sank into it slightly – an unsettling sensation, as though the floor wasn't quite solid. At the far end of the hall double brass doors, similar to the ones at the front of the hotel, were decorated with the same peacocks. They passed other simpler doors at regular intervals, although these, too, were graced with golden peacocks. Again, Maggie had the strange impression the hall was lengthening in response to their walking and she closed her eyes for a step or two to banish the feeling. When she opened them, she saw several shadows on the wall and turned to see who was following them. Even Badger tracked one of the figures. There was no one at all behind them.

"Excuse me, but what *is* that?" she asked.

One of the shadows danced along the wall. It made Maggie want to turn in circles, sure someone, or something, was sneaking up. Badger sniffed and cocked his head. He ran a few paces, following what appeared to be the shadow of a small horse, but it disappeared when it came to a door. Badger whined.

"What's what, Miss?" asked the bellboy.

"The shadows without bodies."

"Oh, don't mind them."

A shadow-band of what looked to be hunters ran by.

"I'm afraid I do mind them," said Maggie.

"But they're just dreams, Miss."

"I beg your pardon?"

"Dreams, Miss. Everyone who stays at the Tilden can order up the dreams they'd like and what we don't have in-store we order in."

"You order in." Maggie raised an eyebrow as the silhouette of a woman in a canoe paddled along the wall.

"Will you come this way, please?"

They walked to the door closest to the great double doors at the end of the hall. The bellboy noticed her staring at those and said, "Oh, yes, Miss. You're very lucky indeed, for your rooms are right next to Miss Tilden's. She holds you in the highest regard." He ushered her inside.

The door opened onto a small oval foyer, painted a peacock blue, with white marble on the floor and a mural on the ceiling. It was this last that nearly made Maggie stumble. The mural was identical to the one on the door through which she'd come to this strange place. A huge tree, all swirls and symbols – circles and crowns and eyes – with a pair of ravens in the branches. The eyes of the ravens glimmered.

From this foyer, three doors – these undecorated and open – led into three different rooms. Badger trotted into the one directly in front and Maggie followed. It was a sitting room, with a fireplace, a lamp behind a comfortable-looking brown leather chair, a fully set tea table and a plush burgundy-coloured carpet into which was woven golden peacocks. Badger sniffed around, tail wagging. Maggie shrugged out of her coat and pack and laid them on the chair, but no sooner had they hit the leather than the bellboy plucked them up and took them, via a connecting door, into what looked to be a bedroom.

"When you're ready, refreshed and so forth, perhaps you'd be so kind as to dress for dinner – Miss Tilden has left appropriate attire in your bedroom – then ring the bell," he indicated a velvet cord by the fireplace, "and someone will come to escort you." He cleared his throat gently. "Miss Tilden is waiting and I'm sure you're hungry."

"I'll be along."

"Very good, Miss. I'll just make sure you have everything you need. Say, an hour?"

"Say what you like," she said, and then, when the bellboy gasped, added, "Yes, fine then, an hour."

"Oh, very good, Miss. Thank you, Miss." He scurried away.

Bookshelves filled with leather-bound volumes covered one wall. All the literary classics were there, as well as novels by Jane Gardam, Linda Hogan, Hans Fallada, Magda Szabó and James Baldwin, her favourite authors. There were books about dream interpretation, histories and several books on the care, feeding and amusement of dogs. In short, they seemed chosen especially for her.

Maggie crossed the room to the French doors, bordered by large casement windows. Outside a terrace led to a rolling meadow dotted with sleeping sheep. Neat split-rail fences marked off the pastures and a little stream sparkled in the moonlight. The grass on the meadows was verdant, one could tell that even in the moonlight, and the trees were in full leaf. A perfect late spring evening, from the looks of it. Winter in the lane. Autumn in the market square, spring out there. What was this? Another dream? Not to mention they were on the fifth or sixth floor, but outside was a ground-floor terrace. She was getting a headache. No matter how she tried to keep her mind on the purpose of her journey, so far everything seemed a digression intended to keep her from finding Kyle.

Badger followed his nose to a tray set on the floor between the sitting room and the bedroom. On it was a bowl of water and another of minced meat and vegetables. He began gulping it down, tail wagging. She poured herself a cup of bergamot-scented tea from the pot on the small table. She sipped. Deliciously refreshing.

Maggie's thoughts swirled. Part of her wanted to rush out the door and down the hall and into the elevator and out of this dream-riddled building, but to where, since *back* was apparently impossible? Badger, finished his meal, placed his head on her knee and burped with gusto. "Oh, very well mannered," she said, and couldn't help but smile.

"Come on. Let's see what this luggage business is about."

In the bedroom she found clothes, including silk and linen undergarments, laid out on the bed. A black silk gown encrusted at the neck with sparkling crystals. They couldn't be diamonds, could they? Surely not. Shoes, too, in the same silk as the dress, with matching crystal buckles. She decided she needed a bath, for she still felt a bit cherry-pie-sticky.

The third room was, as she expected, a bath, although she had not anticipated the tub to be already filled with steaming water. The whole room smelled of gardenias and three blossoms floated on the water. Fluffy white towels hung from a rack heated by the nearby copper boiler.

CHAPTER THIRTEEN

MAGGIE LOLLED IN THE BATH, HER MIND SLIPPING back to Alvin. The weird sensuality of Miss Tilden's hotel sent visions of Alvin's body, his collarbone, the long stretch of his legs, his two tattoos: a nautical star on his right shoulder so he'd always find his way home and the Vegvisir on his left, the Icelandic compass said to ensure he would never lose his way. She thought of that particular crease at his hip, the inguinal crease she'd learned it was called. It pointed a *V* down his body to the root of him, the place she so loved, the velvet-iron feel, the smell, the taste . . . and so she drifted and dreamed and . . . then surfaced from delight and dressed and breathed deeply and kept her smile to herself.

Maggie followed the bellboy, whose name was Jacob (Maggie had at last thought to ask and he had blushed furiously when he told her), to their hostess's door. Maggie tried not to mind the pinching caused by the hard bone stays of the black gown's built-in corset. If Miss Tilden wanted her guests to be comfortable, this was an odd definition of comfort. Badger had gone outside onto the meadow for a brief after-dinner consti-tutional, returned and promptly fallen asleep on the bed, lying on his back with his legs in the air, possibly dreaming of chasing rabbits, and seemed quite content to be left behind.

Jacob rapped gently upon the great peacock-decorated doors. Almost instantly the doors flew open. The walls of the room were shades of aqua and turquoise, cream and gold, in such swirls and ripples that they gave the impression of being under sunlit water. Candlelight glowed from tapers in flower-shaped wall sconces. Maggie looked down, for a moment overtaken with vertigo. The floor was glass and under the glass goldfish swam in pools and candles floated on lily pads. In the centre of the room stood an enormous pillar, like the trunk of a golden tree. The leaves, made from jade, emerald, peridot and tourmaline, formed the ceiling, and more candles flickered from leaves. Two beds, designed to resemble monstrous lilies, one white and one red, hung from the branches on thick golden stems. In the white one, on plush cushions and thick white pelts, reclined a woman with translucently pale skin. Her eyes were the colour of the walls – now blue, now green, and shot through with gold – shifting and changing as she moved her head. Her hair was as pale as her skin, pale as the petals of the bed on which she lay. It was straight and fine and rippled about her shoulders. Her full mouth was the colour of roses, as was the blush on her cheeks. It was difficult to tell her age – older than Maggie, certainly, but by ten years or twenty was impossible to say. There was a kind of sheen around her, as though she was viewed through gauze. Her gown, fashioned from an opalescent material, flowed with subtle varieties of pink, yellow, green and blue. The diadem on her brow boasted a large opal. She held a glass in her hand.

"Maggie, I am Wallis Tilden and I am so pleased you've found your way here." Her voice sounded like water playing over pebbles.

"Since the road led only one way, you weren't hard to find," said Maggie, and then, fearing she sounded ungracious, "It's very kind of you to extend your hospitality."

Wallis Tilden said, "I know your friend Mr. Mustby well."

Maggie's stomach fluttered. "He never mentioned you."

The radiant woman smiled and revealed teeth as white and dainty as pearls. "You must call me Wallis, since I know we will be great friends." She picked up a green grape from a bowl resting on a little tray attached to her bed and tossed it into the red-lily bed that hung several feet lower than her own. "Jimmy, wake up. We have guests."

The body in the red-lily bed stirred and made small noises of protest. Wallis Tilden threw another grape, this time more forcefully. "I said, wake up. You have the manners of a rodent."

A rather mussed head of curly black hair rose above the lip of the bed. Its owner ran his hands through it and yawned. For the briefest of moments, Maggie's heart did a little double dutch, for the hair looked like Kyle's before he shaved his head. The young man was shirtless. His oiled skin made his already-impressive musculature more pronounced. He spotted Maggie and smiled. Slanted green eyes, high cheekbones and ears that were, if not pointed, quite prominent; the face of a mischievous elf. Yes, there was a resemblance to Kyle, save that Kyle's eyes were blue. Maggie couldn't help but wonder if Wallis Tilden had a soft spot for young men such as this, and if so, had Kyle once slept in that very bed?

"Hiya," said Jimmy, stretching. "What did I miss? Anything good?"

"He has, I am afraid, the wit of a wheel of cheese, but he's such a pretty thing. Down," she said, to no one in particular, although someone, or some*thing*, must have heard because the beds began a slow descent until they arrived at the floor. Jimmy hopped out of his – Maggie was relieved to see he wore loose-fitting trousers – and extended his hand to Wallis, so that she stepped from the bed as one might from a boat.

Wallis was taller than Maggie expected, and she towered over Jimmy. The gown she wore, although it technically revealed nothing save for her arms and one shoulder, managed to draw attention to every curve, slope, hill and valley of her body's landscape in a way that made Maggie feel as sexless as a lump of suet. She must have worn bells around her ankles, or else they were sewn invisibly into her dress, for when Wallis walked – as she now did toward Maggie – a tinkling silver sound came with her. Her scent was of roses.

"I was quite worried about you when you fell under old Mother Ratigan's spell. Dreadful woman. She hijacks more of my guests than I like to admit. Thank heaven for that dog of yours." She took Maggie by the hand. Her skin was as soft and cool as satin. "But come, you must be famished."

She led Maggie to an alcove behind a black lacquer screen where a table was laden with fish and fowl, meats and salads, steaming green beans and peas with melting butter, sweet potatoes, rice with raisins, sugared plums and apricots, dates stuffed with rich cheese and flaky baklava oozing honey. Decanters of red and white wine and a silver tea service stood on a side table. Candlelight and fine linen. Plates and cutlery of gold. Maggie bit her lip. She realized she was indeed hungry, but more importantly, she wanted to ask about Kyle. As soon as they were seated, waiters appeared from out of the shadows and set to filling the wineglasses.

Jimmy picked at a fig, nibbling it and licking the bruised-looking skin. He sat with a leg tucked up underneath him and now and again he stretched, arching his back and moaning softly. He appeared more animal, otter, perhaps, than human.

Maggie was aware of the stays and heavy material of her dress. If Wallis's gown fondled her, Maggie's reprimanded. Maggie imagined how liberating it would be to wear less . . . restrictive clothing. She understood how one might be talked out of one's clothes here and suspected Wallis designed her guests' outfits for precisely that reaction. She tried not to squirm.

The waiters served consommé and paper-thin rosemary-infused crackers. It was beyond delicious – delicate as a whisper and yet so rich, like velvet. Wallis said she hoped Maggie liked it.

"It's very good." Maggie cleared her throat. She would not be lulled here as with Mother Ratigan. "You'll forgive me, Wallis. I have so many questions. I assume you know I'm looking for my brother."

"Of course."

"I'm not sure how to continue. The roads here have a bad habit of only leading one way."

"Exactly. And so, the only course of action is to proceed."

"You're saying I couldn't go back even if I wanted to, until I find him?" Maggie put down her spoon and pushed her soup away.

"I'm saying if it's Kyle you seek, it's Kyle you must follow."

"You do know him?" Maggie's pulse quickened, and her chest tightened.

"Who really knows anyone else? But yes, Kyle was my guest. And no, he is not here now. He, unlike you, wandered straight up the lane, spending not a single second worrying about Mother Ratigan."

"That makes him the smart one."

"Do you think so? One might conclude from her behaviour that no good deed goes unpunished, but if I believed that I wouldn't be able to run this little inn and be made so happy by the pleasure of my guests, now would I? Well, no mind. Your brother didn't linger here."

"Where did he go? And he was all right when you saw him?"

The soup was replaced by smoked trout with lemon and asparagus. Wallis picked up an asparagus spear with her long delicate fingers and bit off the tender tip. "He was . . . how shall I put this? He was *focused*. Yes, that's precisely the right word." She looked quite pleased.

"Focused on what?"

"Your brother has been called. Someone has taken a fancy to him."

"Who?" She knew she should be paying more attention to the conversation, but this trout was sweet, as if candied, and the lemon sparkled on her taste buds. The asparagus was slightly nutty, crisp, the very essence of spring.

"I believe you've a more than passing acquaintance with Srebrenka."

"Srebrenka?" Maggie shook her head, trying to take it in. If Srebrenka had taken a fancy, as Wallis put it, to Kyle, sending Maggie here, helping her find him made no sense. "What's she got to do with Kyle? Other than selling him elysium?"

"My dear, don't be silly. Kyle is bait. You're the one who got away. Srebrenka does not take rejection well."

Srebrenka was after her, not Kyle? Guilt was an arrow in her gut. If it was true. Who to believe? "But she isn't even here. She's back there, in the Forest."

"She has more back and forth than most of us."

"I don't understand."

"It's complicated and Mr. Mustby didn't educate you half as well as he might have. There are, you see, certain thin places in the world, certain spots where what seems normal enough turns out to be, well, normal in a different way."

Thin places. Mr. Strundale had called both the Grimoire and the Wort & Willow thin places.

"Srebrenka has," Wallis continued, "through sheer dint of desire, managed to travel quite freely between your world and this one. Generally, it's a one-way street, as you've found out. It's quite impressive really; I never could do it."

"So where is Kyle?"

"That I can't tell you, at least not in specifics. I don't go where she is. There are certain territorial imperatives, you see. Just as in your Forest, where I understand she controls the trade in elysium." Wallis snorted. "Her little handmade gift to you all."

"Srebrenka *manufactures* elysium?"

"In a manner of speaking. Did you think it appeared of its own volition?" Tilden's laugh sounded like wind chimes. "What sweet innocence."

Maggie blushed. She'd never really considered the source.

"Srebrenka has her little hobbies," said Wallis. She reached out and ran a fingernail along Jimmy's bare chest, causing the boy to shiver and giggle. "We all have our pleasures. Mine are mutual. Srebrenka takes pleasure from the pain of others. She feeds off their hunger. She is unhappy you can fill your hunger with anything other than her potions. Your brother is a very hungry boy, a hungry little ghost, with a splinter in his eye."

"And what does that mean?" Maggie rubbed her fork between her thumb and forefinger so forcefully the silver was warming. She made herself stop. She didn't want to let on how frustrating she found Wallis's way of speaking *around* a subject and never quite getting to it.

Wallis regarded her with an arched brow. And then Maggie recalled the dream she'd had. The splinter of glass impaling Kyle. The woman made of ice.

"Srebrenka is a cold woman," said Wallis, as if reading Maggie's thoughts. She ate a bit of trout. "I can't tell you much more, only that he was here, that against my advice he left and that he's looking for her."

"But where did he go?"

"Why, north, of course. Where else do the cold things live? But you don't have to follow. You could stay. Some do, you know. You saw my guests in the lobby. They seem happy, don't they?" Wallis lifted a finger. The plates were cleared again and replaced with quail stuffed with grapes.

"What is this place? 'Thin places'? I don't understand," said Maggie. The quail was crisp-skinned and fragrant with morel mushrooms. The grapes lent a playful bite of acid. "I don't know where I am. This place seems, well . . . different." She realized this was a bit of an understatement. How difficult it was to keep one's thoughts on the subject at hand when food played a symphony in one's mouth.

Wallis dabbed at her lips with a napkin. "It's a contrary place, isn't it? You might think we're in the Forest, but we are inside the Forest in the same way the Grimoire is inside your city, your Toronto." She chuckled, pronouncing it Toe-Ron-Toe, the way no Torontonian would. "Come, Maggie, glowering like that will only upset your digestion." She smiled and blinked in her somnolent manner. "When you say of the Grimoire, 'it is not that kind of place,' what do you mean? You mean it's both what it seems to be and more than it seems to be. It's a bookstore, but it's also more than that, for it has a design and an intention all its own. Those who come to the shop are meant to do so. This is its nature. Why and how is this so? And who decides? Well, these are the great questions of all creation, are they not? All the world works to fit Creation's desires, the desires of the one you call God. What is the Plan? How can we know? The most important question is: Do we trust our experience or not? Do you think you came into Mr. Mustby's care by a random roll of the dice, or were you meant to find your home there?"

"How do you know so much about me?"

"We all have our special talents, and besides, I read."

"Meaning?"

"Books, my dear. Surely you noticed books have a life of their own, that they bring different things to different readers? You must have noticed the books in your shop aren't always the same books."

"There are a lot of books to keep track of."

"More all the time, wouldn't you say?" Wallis laughed. Waiters cleared away the quail and replaced it with lamb in mint jelly. "Well, I have my own little library here, as you may have noticed. The books fit my needs, as I like to put it, perhaps a little more than they do the ordinary reader. Oh, dear, I can see by your face I'm only confusing you. What I can tell you is that the way one reads the books of the world has much to do with what one can learn. But you haven't answered my question. Do you feel you were meant to find your home at the Grimoire?"

"How can I deny it when only those who are meant to find the shop find it?" Lamb and mint jelly. Succulent and sweet.

"Could I find it?" asked Jimmy, munching on a chop.

"Probably not, my dear," said Wallis. "But you always have a home here, don't you?"

"Look," said Maggie, "I'm all for philosophical discussions but . . ."

"You surprise me. Do you really want to play this ignorance game? You've taken Mr. Mustby's place. The Grimoire, the stories of your world, are now your responsibility." Wallis sipped from her wineglass. "Did Alvin never speak of these things?"

"Alvin? What's this got to do with him?"

"Oh, dear. So much you've been left to find out on your own." She sighed. "I find it distressing Mr. Mustby didn't educate his nephew, although it's true the young man was more interested in life on the water than the written word. Still, I suspect his nature will catch up with him. The ending to that story has not yet been written. But as for you, Maggie, how and when you leave here – both my hotel and the Silver World – is entirely up to you, or rather, to the story writing itself for you. For it's your story being told now. That's what a story is: a kind of spell we cast over our lives, and the lives of those close to us; it's the effect we have on our world and the effect that world has on us. You came through the door at Trickster's because you were meant to. What will happen, where you will go and who you will meet along the way is part of the Plan, that which is written in the books, and that which is *being* written even as we sit here. The choices you make along the way are your contribution to the writing of that story, the spells you weave within the greater spell of the *Book of Life* itself."

"I don't get this," said Jimmy. "And I'm very tired. Can I go to bed?"

Wallis waved her hand. "Do as you like, silly boy, your dreams await." And with that Jimmy pushed away from the table and said good night.

Maggie rather wished she could follow him and toyed with her fork. "Alvin did say his uncle told him he had certain responsibilities toward the stories in the books and that Alvin was expected to assume those responsibilities. Caretaker, sort of. I didn't think much of it, given that I'm there now, and the way the Grimoire behaves, well, it just seems like the store's nature to behave like that."

"Nature is quite the right word." Wallis ran her fingers through her hair, creating a sort of rainbow around her head. "Being a guardian of the books is a kind of quality. A character-istic. Like having green eyes or brown. It's a family trait."

"But I'm not family to the Mustbys."

"Oh, there are families and then there are families, or hav-en't you noticed?"

Maggie remembered how, just after Mr. Mustby died, Alvin had told her of the arrangement he'd had with his uncle. If someone else came along to take over the shop, Alvin could do as he pleased, as long as Alvin, in turn, took care of the person who came along – meaning Maggie. She had felt a little miffed at the time and said she didn't need taking care of. He'd smiled and told her that although he was quite sure she didn't, still, he was content with the deal. She wasn't quite so sure any longer about her ability to care for herself. What would Alvin, who had travelled to so many far-flung lands, make of all this? In the old Anglo-Saxon, his name meant *wise friend*. What advice would he have? He had been to South Korea once, and had been offered sea slug in soy sauce to eat, apparently a delicacy.

She'd asked him what it had tasted like and he'd said, "Much as you'd expect; like an eraser dipped in mucus." He could always make her laugh. Not only pain, but joy, surely, was part of the plan.

Salad sat in front of them now. Crisp and clean, sharp with dill.

"None of us escape our destiny," said Wallis. "When Mr. Mustby took you in, he and Alvin became your family. And the Grimoire is your family's obligation."

"But there must be others –"

"There are no others. Alvin is the last of the line."

It began to dawn on Maggie just how little she really knew about Alvin, or his family. She put her fork down. "Look, all this talk of stories and one-way doors and so forth aside, I'm still determined to find Kyle and it seems, according to what you're telling me, Wallis, that I am intended to do so –"

"After our conversation here, I believe you are intended to try."

"Fine, which means I have to go north."

"But not tonight. Tonight, you must sleep and dream and prepare yourself." Wallis licked a bit of sugar from a candied plum off the ends of her fingers. "Tonight, rest. See what dreams will find you."

With that she stood, and servants appeared again from the shadows. Dinner was apparently over.

CHAPTER FOURTEEN

MAGGIE WAS ESCORTED BACK TO HER ROOM BY one of the servants, a tall man with an alarming amount of hair in his ears. She thought the escort unnecessary, as she was next door, for heaven's sake, but he was all gallantry, holding open doors and bowing. As she stepped into her room he said, "'Scuse me, Miss, but I met your brother when he was here."

"You did? Did you talk to him? How did he look?"

"A bit worn out, Miss. And a bit tugged on, if you know what I mean, like he was a fish with a hook in his mouth, being reeled in. But more than that I don't know, except for one thing." He paused and looked a bit bashful. "He's lucky to have you. Takes some knack to get here, and you handled yourself well with Miss Wallis. She telling you things the way she did, well, she doesn't do that with everyone." He touched his cap. "You sleep well, Miss. Sleep well."

And with that he closed the door. Maggie's head was reeling. *Kyle as bait. Bait!*

Badger raised his head, and thumped his tail, but didn't rush to greet her as he usually did. Maggie wondered if he was feeling the narcotic effects of all this luxury. She removed her dress and rubbed the itchy red imprints left by the stays. A linen night-gown lay on the bed and she picked it up. Her bones thrummed with fatigue. Oh, that bed, that beautiful bed ...

MAGGIE DREAMS ...

The air around the bed takes on a silver tinge. The bedposts turn mother-of-pearl and the wardrobe shines like moon-stone. The windows appear glazed with mercury. Whispers scurry about the room like mice, singsong and slightly mock-ing. She grips the sides of the bed as the world tilts, and then settles.

But this is strange ... she is in her own room, on the second floor of the Grimoire. The air has the argent glow of the Silver World, but it's her normal world, isn't it? She sits up and places her feet on the floor. Her boots, her legs in her black jeans, no changes there. She's sure she's been somewhere else. She won-ders where Alvin is.

The air shimmers as if moonlit. Where's Badger? She looks around; the room isn't really hers. The bed is made from birch, not oak; the rag rug has turned into a silken pattern of orchids; the wardrobe is deepest indigo, adorned with scattered stars. She goes to the window, which is a most peculiar opalescence. It's impossible to see through the panes. She opens the window, sticks her head out and gasps. It might be twilight, or it might be dawn. A large white moon hangs in the grey sky, but she can't tell if it's rising or setting. All around her are gently rolling hills, covered with a metallic frost that turns the grass into white lace. In the distance lurks a black line of trees where a forest begins.

Surely this is an elysium dream.

Scritch, scratch, step, tap.

What?

A cough, or someone clearing his throat.

Maggie jumps up and dashes for the door, but it's not her door. Her bedroom door is black. This one is purple, the colour of an eggplant. And the handle isn't her simple glass handle. This handle is green and carved in the shape of a leaf.

Knock, knock.

There seems nothing else to do. "Come in."

The door opens, and there stands Mr. Mustby, wearing the same brown corduroy suit he'd always worn, but how warm the brown looks. "So, it is you," he says in a voice thick with disapproval. "I was told to expect you, but I hoped the message was wrong. You always were a proud and stubborn girl, but to do this . . . Maggie, I am incandescent with anger."

Maggie's hand flies to her open mouth. She makes a mental note to ask who had told him to expect her. But not now; now she only wants to hug him. Before she realizes she's going to do it, she throws her arms around him. "I don't care that you're angry with me. I've never been happier to see anyone."

He smells of leather and open fields and fresh bracing sea-drenched air, a scent quite unlike the old paper, candle wax and pipe smoke scent he used to carry.

He pats her back in a fatherly way. "All right, what's done is done." He gives her a squeeze and then removes her to arm's length. "Despite this idiocy, you look well."

"As do you." In fact, for a dead man he looks brilliant. "Do you know where Kyle is? How I can find him?"

"I know only what you know: that he has gone north."

Her heart falls. "Then I don't mean to be rude, but what are you doing here?"

"What am I doing here? What an odd question. Where else would I be? Although you're taking wonderful care of the old place I still consider it home, you know."

Then she understands. "Right, of course, it's my dream and I've conjured you."

"Not precisely." He winks and says, "Wallis Tilden has

certain powers of . . . shall we say, introduction? Why don't we go downstairs and have a cup of tea?"

He turns and steps into the hallway, which is much brighter than the real hallway, and decorated with a mural of lush green ivy, dotted here and there with butterflies and tiny birds. It's cunningly done, such perfect *trompe l'oeil*. Maggie reaches out to run her fingers across it, which is when one of the butterflies – blue as a sapphire – flies off a leaf and flutters up to a higher one. Maggie jumps back and then touches the vine with her finger. Real. Or as real as anything is here. Mr. Mustby's head disappears down the staircase and she hurries to keep up with him.

Downstairs is just as surprising. For one thing, it's so . . . tidy. Not a speck of dust, every book perfectly aligned on shelves sparkling in the light of a hundred candles burning from wrought-iron candelabras hanging from the ceiling. Bright blue and green rugs lie on the floor and the whole place smells not of dust and mice, but of apples and cinnamon. The kitchen is the least changed of the rooms, but then it's always been rather cheery – the yellow walls, the wooden chairs and table, the blue cupboards. The only odd thing is a vase of flowers in the middle of the table. They are like lilies, pink and white and yellow and blue. They turn in Maggie's direction as she enters, nod and then huddle together, as if discussing her.

"Bizarre." It's hard to believe her mind has created such a homey, pretty place and that is, in a way, even more worrying. How will any of this lead her to Kyle?

Mr. Mustby pours boiling water from the kettle into a pot, stirs the tea leaves and then brings the pot and two mugs to the table, where a sugar bowl and a milk jug stand next to the whispering flowers.

"Don't they know it's not polite to whisper?" Maggie says, and as soon as she speaks the flowers become still.

"Oh, they don't mean any harm." He taps the side of the vase, much as one would a fishbowl, and chuckles. "They do think themselves quite important."The flowers turn their heads away, giving the impression they're pouting.

She feels light-headed. "It's good to see you, although talking to ghosts, even dreamt-up ones, is a bit disconcerting."

Mr. Mustby hands her a cup of tea. "Death isn't what you may imagine."

Maggie reminds herself she's talking to a dream image; one can't expect it to make a great deal of sense. "Right," she snorts.

Thwack! Maggie nearly drops the teacup when Mr. Mustby slams the top of the table with his palm. "You have not dreamed me up, girl!"

He's never spoken to her so sharply. "What are you talking about? Of course I have."

His bushy eyebrows shoot upward. "You are a smart young woman, Maggie, even if you have done something remarkably stupid. No . . . silence! There's little time and I must tell you several things. Drink your tea; you're going to need it. Now, obviously, things are not normal, beginning with your brother's ability to send messages from the Silver World. If he's the one who sent them."

"The Silver World. So, this is a pipe dream."

"It is not."

"It must be . . . or else how could I –"

Mr. Mustby cuts off her words with a wave of his hand. "It's not supposed to happen. And to many of us it is deeply worrying that it has."

Maggie's curiosity snags on the word *us*. Whomever does he mean?

"I imagine you'd like very much to know who *us* is, but we don't have time," he says. "Suffice it to say you have not been alone prior to this and you are not alone now. The world is far more complicated than you or I know, and when I say *world* I mean the several levels of *world* you and I are aware of and a few we aren't. There is, of course, the world you live in, which

I also used to live in, known as the Immanent World, because it is the core world, the one which contains in microcosm all the other worlds, and all the intentions of God. Then there is this, the Silver World, which is not for the uninitiated. No one from the Immanent World should be here, outside of sleeping dreams, and you wouldn't be, had not Srebrenka unleashed certain substances." He clears his throat. "Third, there is the Below World, which is where all this present trouble originated. Most important of all, of course, is the Bright World, where the Ineffable resides, cause and root of all other worlds. There are more, but they don't concern us just now."

Maggie tries very hard to follow what he says, but it isn't easy. Multiple worlds? Present trouble? Uninitiated? Immanent? What on earth? Or perhaps more accurately, what not on earth?

"The Forest," Mr. Mustby continues, "became a thin place between worlds some time ago, when elysium first arrived. Now it's more than a thin place. It started as a doorway into the Silver World, which is expanding, becoming more of the Silver World, and less of the Immanent World. You've gone through a door that shouldn't be there. They're overlapping. The borderland you entered, where Mother Ratigan found you, is a kind of boundary place, which ended when you entered the market square of Wallis Tilden's hotel. At that point, you entered the Silver World proper, and you shouldn't be here, just as there are things in the Forest of the Immanent World that shouldn't be there. Things come up from Below. We fear the rest of the Immanent World will be absorbed into the Forest, and the boundaries between worlds will dissolve completely, which must not happen, for all worlds have their purpose, and are not interchangeable. A person is in one or the other, depending on their needs and their talents. In the wrong world, a person may never learn what is necessary to find their way home – back to that sacred source from which we all came. Srebrenka does not want anyone going home. She wants to draw the broken to her, rather than to the sacred, since misery most definitely loves company, and elysium is her wedge, her battering ram. Mother Ratigan answers to Srebrenka, of course. A sort of crossing guard.

"I can see I've baffled you. Well, there's nothing I can do about that. One must go on. In a nutshell – there are things in the Below World that are supposed to stay in the Below World. Srebrenka has dragged elysium up from Below. She is an envious, restless, irritable and discontent soul. Always wants what isn't good for her or anybody else and is never satisfied. She is, to be blunt, nothing but a bottomless pit of insatiable hunger, the essence of addiction."

If Maggie was dizzy before, now she also had a headache. Wallis had said Srebrenka fed on hunger, hadn't she? Maggie tells Mr. Mustby of the shrinking garden.

"She's focused on you especially, then. Things are urgent." Mr. Mustby raises an eyebrow. "And then there's the matter of the mirror. She was apparently rather displeased with her reflection in a mirror one of her wights stole from the Bright World, and that's when the trouble began."

"How so?"

"The mirror, being a truthful sort of mirror, showed her reflection as she truly is, not as she pretends to be, and I understand it was not a pretty sight. Srebrenka smashed the mirror. To punish the world for not being as she wished it to be she fashioned her own mirror out of some pretty nasty materials – spite and malice and bile. Then, in a fit of what can only be described as selfish bloody pique, she smashed it into countless pieces and scattered those shards on the wind that blows between the worlds so that they made their way to the Immanent World. For a long time now, those shards have been floating about, attracted to a certain kind of person as metal shavings are to a magnet."

"What sort of person?"

Mr. Mustby drops his head and purses his lips. "Sad souls, lost, insecure, selfish, broken –"

"Isn't that all of us, in one way or another?" asks Maggie.

Mr. Mustby drains the last of his tea and sighs. "Yes, I suppose, but some, perhaps those protected by love, or grace, or an innate sense of empathy for others, seem to repel the shards. It's most curious."

Maggie gasps and nearly drops her cup. "Kyle! I had a dream about Kyle and a shard of glass." Quickly, she relates the dream of a single flake of snow turning into a beautiful woman, with terrible, hollow eyes. She tells how the ice woman tried to stab Kyle, but in the end Maggie herself had broken the window, which sent a shard of glass deep into Kyle's chest.

Mr. Mustby looks grim. "That does sound like her all right, and she does like to blame others. But this isn't your fault, although she wants you to think it is. Hence that bit about the broken window. Srebrenka would like you to feel guilt and shame and resentment, since these powerful emotions so quickly undo us."

"She's in my dreams?" Maggie shudders.

"That's what happens, my dear, when elysium has become part of your story. Srebrenka is impatient; not content to let the shards float about willy-nilly, she sent elysium into the Immanent World." Mr. Mustby's face had gone quite red and his eyes spark with fury. "Some people, you may have noticed, are not susceptible to its allure. But we suspect those who suffer from an acute sensitivity to . . . well . . . yearning. They're born with a sense of incompleteness, of being outside, of not belonging. From the expression on your face, may I conclude that sounds familiar?"

"Well, again, doesn't everyone feel that way, to one extent or another, at some time or another?"

"Perhaps, but not everyone becomes a Piper, do they? For those who are susceptible, elysium breaks down resistance, releases those selfish, self-serving tendencies that otherwise a person might be able to control. Once you've ridden the smoke, you send a beacon into the mists between the worlds and the shards come flying. They catch sight of the beacon and latch onto you."

"And that's how she got into my dreams."

He nods. "Indeed. And once the shard is embedded, it changes your perspective on everything. Beautiful becomes ugly, good becomes absurd and cruelty becomes pleasure." He rubs his hands along his thighs and blows his cheeks out as though trying to calm himself. "And once you've ridden the smoke, Srebrenka and her wights always know how to find you. You can lock them out by staying away, but they'll never forget about you."

Maggie thinks back to how Kyle changed from the little boy who grieved over the dead baby sparrow to a slouching, cruel man who looked upon beauty and saw only flaws. He wrapped himself in squalor and called it comfort. He told her she dressed like an undertaker. He considered the book of poems she gave him no more than cheap sentiment. Maggie has a terrible thought. "Why wasn't I infected by the mirror, then?"

"What makes you think you weren't?"

"I'm not like that. I don't see things in such a horrible light."

"That's exactly what you did, when you first came to me."

She feels cold. What he says has the ring of truth. "Was it?"

"You cried so many tears, for so many weeks, if it was a small shard, it might well have been washed away. We shall hope for that. Tears have their own power, especially when they're shed in humility and remorse. But remember, Maggie, in the end, Kyle is responsible for his own actions, just as you are responsible for yours."

"What choice do I have, except to follow Kyle?"

He regards her calmly. "Only you can answer that, my dear. I merely seek to warn you. But it's time you were on your way." He stands and walks out of the kitchen into the shop.

Maggie follows, noticing again how much tidier, how much brighter and newer everything looks in this Silver World version of the Grimoire. "Mr. Mustby, why is the shop here? I mean, this world is all about made-up things, myths and dreams and so forth."

"This world is about things that tell the truth, although perhaps not the facts, which is why you are not supposed to be here unless you're naturally asleep and dreaming."

"Am I not doing that now?"

"Under Wallis's roof?" He snorts. "Not quite a natural dream. You saw the figures flitting through the hallways."

"Which doesn't explain the shop at all."

"Does it not?" He turns to look at her, surprise on his face. "I would have thought it made everything quite clear. This is a place full of stories, Maggie. There are some who say it contains all the stories in the world, although I've never had the time to go through every book since new books keep appearing." Mr. Mustby harrumphs. "Well, being a place, being *the* place of stories, it is in all worlds, expanding with every story told and contracting with every story lost. It is, in other words, a doorway, a liminal space. It is that kind of shop." He smiles as though that clears the matter up completely, and perhaps it does. The smile doesn't last, however. "You have been summoned, called by someone – it may be Kyle, but it may not be – and you have chosen to answer the call. This means powers from Below have infiltrated your world and the Silver World. No one knows how far this infection has spread, but I suspect at least some of what you'll find here has been put here not only with you in mind, but with an intention of strengthening the infestation." They are at the front door now, which is made entirely of silver engraved with shifting images. Mr. Mustby notices her staring. "The door of tales. Story is alive." He sighs. "You will not be alone." He takes her hands. "Just be sure, whatever you do, to be true, not in the way of plodding facts, but in the way of soul knowing."

"I do wish you'd speak clearly."

Mr. Mustby opens the door. A path runs up a slope into the meadows. The landscape is bleak, sunless and coldly silver.

"Do you know at least how long I have?"

"I suspect it will be as long as you need and much longer than you'd like. I only pray it isn't too long." With that he embraces her swiftly, and gently pushes her out the door.

CHAPTER FIFTEEN

WHEN MAGGIE WOKE IN THE LUXURIOUS surroundings provided by Wallis Tilden, Badger was lying at the foot of the bed, tail thumping. She rolled over. Dreams, she thought, dreams . . . Badger whined and then shook himself awake. She sat on the side of the bed and he put his head in her lap as she petted him. Had Badger had his own dream?

But . . . she cocked her head, trying to remember . . . Mr. Mustby. The Grimoire . . . And then it all returned, everything he'd told her.

A pang of longing gripped her. The Silver World. The Forest. Borderlands. The Below World. The Bright World. Her head hurt. And Kyle was bait.

She smelled food and noticed a silver tray with a pot of tea, a cup and saucer, and plates of buttered toast, poached eggs, jam and cheese. She ate with determination and as she finished she licked the butter, which had a note of clover and roses, off her fingers and walked to the window. Outside, the rolling springtime meadow was gone. The window looked out, with the view of a third- or fourth-storey window, on a small walled garden tidily planted with bushes wrapped in burlap.

Brown leaves gathered in corners by the stone wall. The limbs of the four plane trees were bare. Beyond the garden lay houses and shops, all the buildings made of grey stone, and looking as though they'd been there for hundreds of years. The roofs were tiled, and vines, as bare as the trees, covered many of the walls. The windows were glazed, and some were shuttered. As far as the eye could see nothing but walls and roofs and streets as the land rose gently into the distance.

Reality was apparently quite plastic. A disturbing thought. One could go mad thinking such thoughts. She decided the sensible thing was to wash her face and do what she normally did in the morning.

A short time later she opened the door to find the bellboy, Jacob, standing at attention in the hall.

"How long have you been here?"

"Miss Tilden says she hopes you slept well and had pleasant dreams," said Jacob.

"I slept very well."

"She hopes you will consider staying with her a while longer."

Wallis Tilden might be useful, and less dangerous that Mother Ratigan, but this garden of earthly delights held its own perils. "No, with thanks. Long journey ahead and I have to get started."

"Miss Tilden does understand and suspected that might be your answer. She waits for you now in the lobby." He bowed slightly and gestured. "Will you follow me, please?"

No dreams flitted about the halls, and the lobby was deserted, the only evidence of the previous night's escapades being the now-empty chaise longues and a certain musky scent. If Mother Ratigan lured her guests with promises of childlike security, the promises Wallis Tilden made were decidedly more adult.

The hotelier herself waited for them by the door. Her dress was blue silk trimmed with ermine, wrapped tightly around her breasts and rib cage and although of a heavier material than the pearly confection she had worn the night before, it clung just as closely to every curve.

"I trust you slept well," she said.

"Very well, thanks."

"Everyone does here. I make sure my guests are comfortable. Whatever dream you had, however, wasn't one of mine. I sensed an old friend wanted to speak with you."

"Then you know whom I dreamed of."

"Yes, I believe so. Did you learn many things? Knowledge can be such a pleasure."

"It can also be alarming."

"You mustn't be afraid of your dreams."

"I'm not afraid, but I'm not a slave to them, either."

"What an interesting concept." Wallis bent to let Badger sniff her open palm and then scratched him under the chin while she gazed into his eyes. "He is a very loyal dog. He would die for you."

"And I for him, but I'm hoping it won't come to that."

Wallis smiled. "Of course, we pray for only wonderful things."

"Would you mind answering a question?" asked Maggie.

"If I can." Wallis tucked her hands into the ermine-trimmed sleeves of her dress and looked mildly amused.

"About the view from the window in my room . . . it doesn't look out on the same thing this morning that it did last night."

"It's so restful to sleep in the country, don't you agree?" Tilden smiled. "Although some people do prefer the din and clatter of great seaports, or the hum of traffic, I knew you'd enjoy a little solitude."

Maggie's eyebrows rose. "You changed the view? How did you do that?"

"Things are generally what they are, no more and no less. Perception, however, is rather more fluid."

"So I'm beginning to see," said Maggie.

"It is my pleasure to make pleasure for others, happy only for the bonds of affection. You must be careful not to assume everyone is like me."

"I can't imagine anyone else like you."

Wallis laughed. "No one is quite like you, either, now are they? The journey is entirely your own, and I hope you won't mind, but I'd like to give you a little present. It's just outside." She turned and the doormen opened the great double doors as she approached. "To ease the journey ahead."

Maggie stepped forward and saw what awaited her. "Oh my God!"

It was an open carriage, black as night, decorated with silver stars and an ornately drawn *T* and *W* on the doors. A gleaming dapple-grey horse stood harnessed to the traces. His breath steamed in the chilly air. Thick bearskins covered the seats and a hamper full of food was tucked in the footwell. One footman held the reins, and another the carriage door.

"It's very kind," said Maggie. "In fact, it's beyond generous, and don't think I'm not grateful, but I don't know where I'm going and who knows if the roads will even accommodate such a thing." She blew out her cheeks. "I might be better on foot."

"It's true, you won't be able to travel all the way in a carriage, but it will do until the weather shifts and the snow lies too deep for the wheels. If it rains, as you can see, the hood can be put up and you'll be dry. And you needn't worry about the horse. Percival knows his way home. Simply unharness him when the time comes."

"I don't know."

Badger had approached Percival and the two were sniffing each other. From the wag of Badger's tail, he was in favour of the plan.

Wallis said, "If time is of the essence, you can travel quicker by carriage."

"Yes, there is that, it's true."

"Excellent then, off you go and good luck." She embraced Maggie and, with a twirl, turned and disappeared into the hotel.

"I guess we're riding in style," Maggie said to Badger.

They climbed in, and Maggie took the reins.

The footman clicked the latch on the carriage door closed and said, "Percival knows you are going north. He's a bright one and will lead you right."

"There's just one problem," said Maggie. "We didn't see a road out of here when we arrived last night. The square's self-contained."

"Oh, no, Miss," said the footman. "Just keep straight on in the direction you're facing and you'll find the way."

"Really?"

"You'll come to a fork. The choice, as always, is yours."

"Oh, wonderful." She clicked her tongue and jiggled the reins.

They were off. At first, she feared the footman had lied, for the road past the hotel took a sharp left, which they had no choice but to take, and Percival trotted along quite happily. Then another turn, in front of the same shops they'd passed the night before, the same bakery and candle shop and market stalls, which momentarily blocked the view of the hotel, and then another left . . .

"Well, I'll be," said Maggie as the road opened before them.

Percival paced along the road, which had not been there the first go-round, and they rolled down a modest street of brick and timber. The scene was more nineteenth century than twenty-first. Several men and women and a few children walked along and waved at the carriage.

Maggie looked at Badger. "I feel ridiculous having them wave at me like I'm some sort of royalty. On the other hand, we don't look in the least like royalty, do we?"

It had grown warmer and she slipped out of her coat. She

noticed leaves on the trees. Spring? Summer? Perhaps like space, time had its own rules here. The road was narrow, and Maggie wondered what might happen if another carriage approached from the opposite direction, but none did. There were only the people walking and waving, and then fewer and fewer of those, and the houses were spaced farther apart, and now they had little plots of garden out front, filled with morning glories and climbing peas and tomatoes and roses. And then the plots grew so that the cottages were set back from the road, with small enclosures for pigs and a meadow behind for sheep. Finally, after they had travelled for several hours, there were only fields and still just the one road, leading in the only direction it seemed there was.

Behind them the road ran for about a quarter of a mile, but beyond that was a wood, dense and dark. The road apparently came to an end at the edge of it. It looked as though the world had rolled itself up again. Maggie thought of Alvin, and how he hadn't wanted to take over the Grimoire. Perhaps he was wiser than she. She clicked encouragement to Percival, who just keep plodding along. Badger jumped from the carriage and trotted beside the big dapple-grey, an arrangement that appeared to please them both.

She remembered a conversation she and Alvin once had while she lay in his arms, sleepy and safe, and asked him about his inheritance. "I've always had the feeling it was only a matter of time," he'd said, "before I got drawn in somehow. It's what our family's *for*, if you know what I mean." She wished she'd paid more attention, asked him more questions. She wished he was with her. Master navigator who ate the world in huge gulps of wonder, while she huddled behind a fortress built of books. She opened the basket at her feet and selected a meat pie. It was still warm and the pastry was buttery and flaky. She racked her memory, trying to remember bits and pieces of what Alvin and Mr. Mustby had said over the years. She remembered she'd once complained to Alvin that she sometimes wasn't sure what the point was of anyone living in the Grimoire; they had a modest clientele and the books – their coming and going, their shelving and cataloguing – took care of themselves. What was her purpose?

"Nobody understands," he said. "But that doesn't mean it's not still our responsibility, does it? I mean, the books are there, and they keep on coming. I suppose that's why I love the water so much. The movement, the constant travel, it helps to turn down the volume, if you know what I mean. But it's always there, this feeling that my life on the water is a holiday from what I'm supposed to be doing." He'd said he found it interesting she fit in so well. More than once he'd said she seemed made for the place.

She missed the Grimoire. Her home. She munched the pie. It was comforting. If she was meant for the Grimoire, was she also meant for Alvin? She wondered if she'd ever see him again. It was difficult not to think she was being a complete fool. She watched Badger and Percival walk along companionably. The warm sun glinted off the metal on Percival's bridle. She thought about the mirror Srebrenka had made and then shattered, about the way things look different to different people, much in the way some people found the Grimoire and others couldn't. She thought about Kyle. Even when he was a little boy he saw things differently. So, for that matter, did Maggie. Neither of them, she mused, could be called happy children. But whatever the reason, both she and Kyle were glass-half-empty people. Always had been. They expected the worst, and that's what they got. Or at least that's what Maggie got until Mr. Mustby took her in. He wasn't like anyone else she'd ever met. He didn't judge her or think she should be different than she was. Which is not to say he thought she was a perfect little joy when she first arrived. She chuckled, recalling when she overheard him telling Alvin he had "acquired a malodorous, rather damaged young person."

Well, she had been malodorous, and suspicious, and prickly, and full of self-pity. But somehow, being around him changed that. He was ... is ... How did you classify a man whose dead body she had found but now seemed to pop up, full of knowledge, in the dream world? Perhaps the distinction didn't matter as much as people thought. Perhaps being dead was like being in the other room.

Such questions were out of her area of expertise, surely.

But there was no denying she had gotten a chance Kyle didn't. If she had once been infected with the mirror, and given what Mr. Mustby had told her, she presumed she had been, then Mr. Mustby's love had healed her. Kyle had no such love, and it should have been Maggie who gave it to him.

Hadn't she said as much to Alvin? And what had he said? "You can't blame yourself for everything. Frankly, you're not that powerful, Maggie. Really. You can't save those who insist on hurling themselves repeatedly back into storm-tossed seas. You made the choice to do whatever it took to get off elysium, and you had nobody's help, either, did you?"

"I had your uncle," she had said.

"But you'd already made your choices by the time you found your way to the Grimoire."

Maggie heard a noise, which brought her back from her thoughts. The landscape had changed again, with more and more trees appearing along the edge of the road. Maggie looked in the direction of the sound and there perched the two ravens, bobbing and spreading their wings. Something joyful bubbled up in her. They looked so proud of themselves, so puffed up with self-importance and, quite bluntly, they looked remarkably happy. If Maggie let herself, she could easily imagine them telling her to cheer up, that she wasn't alone, that it was all going to be all right.

Badger had also spotted them and ran up to the tree. He put his paws on the trunk and barked a greeting. The ravens cawed and chattered right back, and then fluttered to a tree up the road. Badger followed. So they went, playing a game of follow-the-leader until, some minutes later, they came to a fork.

Maggie waited for the ravens to make a choice. "Which way?"

The birds groomed, running their beaks and talons through their feathers.

"Really?" She sighed. Fine, then. She stood and tried to see down the paths, but they looked identical, each just a path through endless trees. She thought she might go down one for a while and then, if it didn't work out, double back and try the other. The path was narrow, though, and she'd never be able to turn the carriage around. Besides, if the road rolled up behind her, there'd be no doubling back. It would be awful to lose the carriage . . . the birds.

"Badger, come on." She jumped down and strode toward the right-hand fork. It had been the choice last time, why not this? She took a few steps, and went to take another, but found her feet stuck, as if in mud. She turned and saw Badger several feet back. His tail was down, and he whined. "It's okay. Stay." She struggled to free her foot. The back foot came free with a pop, but only because she was stepping back. She moved the other foot back. Tried to go forward again with the same result. Fine, not that way, then. She moved to the left-hand fork, but the same thing happened.

"So, neither?"

The ravens cawed. Maggie wondered if she was giving the birds too much credit. They puffed up and clacked their beaks as though insulted.

No, not neither. A path. But apparently one didn't get a sneak preview. Choices had to be made, not researched. Perhaps it didn't matter one way or the other. Perhaps, just in the way the road only went forward, they all led to the same place. Or maybe there was no way forward. Perhaps this was the end of the road and she'd be trapped in this forest limbo.

Well, she had to try. She hopped back in the carriage. She tugged gently on the left rein and Percival dutifully altered his trajectory. As she neared the fork, she became less and less sure. Perhaps right. That's the way the ravens went, so perhaps that was the best way. She pulled on the reins. "Stop." She didn't know. But she had to do something. She jiggled the reins. "Okay, let's try." As Percival neared the branching-off point, he stopped and shook his head, making his bridle jangle.

"Come on, then." Maggie clicked her tongue and lightly snapped the reins.

Percival refused to move, stamping a front hoof. The ravens set up a racket. Were they telling her to go the other way? She pulled back on the reins and tried to set the carriage on the right-hand path, but he still stalled. She climbed down and took the bridle, trying to lead him. Nothing. She stamped her foot. She looked behind her. The path was disappearing so quickly she could see it. What would happen when it overtook them? But she wasn't sure! She wasn't sure!

Could it be a question of confidence? If she was resolved would Percival move for her? Horses, she had read, responded to confidence and clarity. She set her shoulders, breathed deeply. She stroked Percival's nose. "It's all right, boy. I've decided. Off we go." She stepped into the left-hand path. Percival came along. Badger ran forward. The ravens zipped over to a branch a few yards past. They moved along and as they did the forest thickened and Maggie was surprised to see how quickly the path behind them disappeared. There was no sign of the fork at all. The forest seemed darker, the roots more twisted, the vines encircling the trunks more sinuous and muscular.

Maggie climbed back into the carriage and pulled her scarf around her neck. It was getting colder. The scent of snow drifted on the wind. The light began to fade, and the long yellowish rays slanted through the tree trunks. The road seemed narrower and Maggie, who had never until now suffered from claustrophobia, found herself thinking of closets, coal cupboards and coffins. Badger jumped into the carriage and leaned against her, panting. The ravens hopped from branch to branch, keeping abreast of the carriage rather than leading the way as they had done. Even Percival shook his head and chewed his bit. The wind whistled through the trees as through a hollow bone. Soon, flakes of snow began to fall, fat white flakes of the sort that made Maggie dizzy when she looked up into the sky, and she was uncertain for a moment if the snow was falling down or if she was falling up.

They would camp at the first likely spot. The snow worried her, and she was exhausted. She wouldn't have thought simply sitting in a carriage all day would have made her so weary, but in some ways, sitting was more tiring than walking. At least walking kept the blood pumping. In the carriage, it was easy to drift off, to be lulled by the clip-clop of Percival's hooves and the jingle of the harness.

Having made the decision to stop at the first opportunity, the woods appeared to respond, for it wasn't more than twenty feet before the ravens squawked and sure enough, there, just ahead, the path veered onto a clearing of evergreens. The ground was covered in a thin blanket of snow, but the area beneath the fir boughs was sheltered enough and looked not too hillocky or stone strewn. The moon shined through a circle of clouds, tinted yellow and grey and foretelling of harder weather to come.

She broke a few pine boughs and fashioned a makeshift lean-to and firebreak and before long she was wrapped in the bearskins before a small fire, thanking God for all the books in the shop about surviving in the wild. She ate sausages warmed over the flames, and bread and dried apples. There had even been a meaty bone for Badger, which he now happily gnawed while lying across her feet. She heated tea in the iron kettle Wallis Tilden had included in her basket. The ravens perched on a low branch, their feathers puffed up and their heads drawn into their necks. Maggie had released Percival from the traces and fixed a nosebag, filled with feed stored in a tin trunk on the back of the carriage, to his bridle. He stood, tethered to a nearby tree, his eyes half closed, his tail flicking with pleasure.

Maggie snuggled up with Badger, and as she watched Percival she remembered another horse.

EVERY SUMMER SHE AND KYLE HAD GONE TO THE Canadian National Exhibition. The only thing he wanted was to go on the pony rides. There was this pony – same one every year – a fat little dapple-grey thing called Derwin; the most mean-tempered pony Maggie ever saw. He regularly tried to bite any child who came near him, and if the old man who owned the ponies didn't keep a firm hand on the lead he'd try to buck the children off and then stomp on them. Maggie could never figure out why the old man used him, since he clearly hated children. Maybe the old man did as well, but, to be fair, he only used the petulant pony when all the other ponies were busy. She sometimes suspected if he didn't like a child he gave him or her Derwin. But Derwin was the only horse Kyle ever wanted to ride.

The first time Kyle went near him the horse nipped his shoulder, but Kyle didn't even flinch. He was seven and he turned to Maggie and said, "He's just frightened. He has to know I won't hurt him." It was as if he identified with the pony. It was like the pony was *his* pony. And he rode it, too. Around and around the little track. Then the time was up and Kyle would have to get off and he wouldn't. Maggie tried to bribe him with the Ferris wheel or the shooting games, or even cotton candy, but he would not have it. Just him and that malevolent pony. For hours. The old man liked Kyle and so he should have, for the pony cost Maggie every penny she had, every year, and when the money ran out Kyle did chores, just so he could stay. But he never did get bitten again, and the pony never kicked him, either, not like it tried to do to everyone else. Kyle cried and cried when the fair moved on.

It was the fourth year, when the fair came back and Derwin was gone. The old man said he'd sold him to a nice little girl on a farm, but he was lying. Maggie saw it in his eyes and so did Kyle. It broke his heart and he screamed and cried and picked up a handful of dirt and threw it at the man. Maggie had to drag him away. He cried so much he threw up. Made himself sick as anything. Took him weeks to get over it. Little Brother of the Sparrow.

HER THROAT CLOSED OVER AND TEARS SPRANG TO HER eyes. There was nothing to it but to see what tomorrow would bring. She curled up with Badger under the bearskins. The ground didn't feel hard or cold and the moonlight and starlight silvered the air. The snow had stopped falling now and it glittered, clean and quiet.

MAGGIE DREAMS ...

Something in the deeper forest calls her. She walks along the path and then she is alone in the wood. She is not afraid but feels the pull of something nearby. The path leads to the trees and as she nears, her fingers and toes tingle and she smells warm earth and fresh leaves, roses and what? Peony? Gardenia?

She steps a few feet inside the forest and then stops. Is this the same wood? It is warm here, and the trees are in leaf. The soft earth yields underfoot. She turns, intending to step back out of the wood, but when she does there is no end to the trees.

"So that's the way it's going to be, is it?" she asks aloud.

"Oh, yes, it's the way it ever was," says a voice, small and whispery.

Maggie spins, looking for the source, but there is nothing save the trees, the undergrowth, the scatter of flowers. Not even a squirrel or mouse . . . but wait, those flowers . . . Maggie places one foot off the path toward a patch of yellow flowers growing under an old oak. She fears wandering from the path completely. The flowers dip and wave encouragingly. Maggie takes a deep breath and walks several paces, then looks back. She lets the air out of her lungs in a relieved rush. The path remains.

In a patch near her foot the flowers make a sound very much like giggling. Maggie bends down. They resemble daffodils; the centre cups are bright yellow, but silver edges the rims, and the perianths are like rubies. As she puts her face close, the flowers pull back.

"Do you mind?" they say in a chorus that sounds like a cross between tinkling bells and a squeaky violin.

"I have a question I'd like to ask you."

"No harm in asking," they trill. "And since we know all sorts of things we rarely get credit for, you could do much worse than asking us. It's the benefit of roots, you see. We are all connected, don't you know, under the earth, just singing with important things and almost no one pays any attention, more pity on them. What do we know, you might ask? Well, we know, for example, that this time tomorrow a flock of starlings will fly overhead so thick you'd think it was the middle of the night, and we know the skunk in the burrow by the river has had five kits and that no matter what they tell you, you simply can't trust the violets."

Maggie's ears itch from the ting-pinging and squeaking of their voices, but they are such happy things, so full of life, she doesn't mind. "Well, I'm sure you're a great authority on many things, so I wonder if you've seen my brother? Have you seen Kyle, and can you tell me where he is now?"

The flowers bend together and confer. As they do the flowers all around ripple as though a pebble had been tossed in a pond and after a moment the ripple returns, and the flowers turn back to her.

"We know where he's been, and we know where he's gone, but we don't know where he is."

Maggie's heart skips. "Tell me where he's gone then."

"You know that already. He's gone north. Isn't she silly?" They say this last to themselves.

"I know he's gone north, but I don't know how to get there myself."

"Why would you want to go there?" they shriek.

Maggie rubs her ears. "I want to bring him home."

And oh, how they laugh at that. "Nobody comes home. Silly, silly, silly."

Maggie thinks she might cry.

"Hold on now. No cause for tears, we're not on *her* side, you know. We're just saying. But if you're set on it, and you seem to be, silly girl, you just need to follow the river and you'll find the door right enough."

"Where's the river?"

"Between the banks and the moon, of course." They laugh and laugh until the whole forest floor is trembling.

KYLE STANDS IN THE MIDDLE OF A GREAT SILENT FOREST. He cannot remember how he came to be here, only that he is lost. It is cold, and he has a coat made of beaver pelts. It smells of warm cider and woodsmoke. A woman gave it to him; a woman with eyes the icy blue of celestine. He walks along a path and smells something sickly sweet, like cut flowers left in a vase too long, the water gone rancid and vile.

"I want to go back to the woman," Kyle says to no one in particular. His voice is thin and weak, lost among the pine trees.

"She's waiting for you," says a raspy voice.

In a patch near his foot are flowers Kyle has never seen before. They are fleshy and look something like daffodils, but the centre cups have sharp edges, and the perianths are like blackened, burned sticks. They crackle with each movement.

"Do you talk?" Kyle thinks how absurd they are.

"We do and have better manners than some."

"You said she's waiting for me."

"We did, and she is. Waiting for you like a silver fox at a mouse hole. Be careful, little mouse."

"You're idiots. She is everything beautiful, not like you grotesque things."

"Grotesque, are we?" Their voices are like rusty hinges, like the squawk of protesting soon-to-be-beheaded chickens, like bones popping in a fire. "We're not the ones in that putrid old skin. We are blessed with beauty."

The fetid scent of them turns Kyle's stomach. "How do I find her?"

"Find her? Fool." They laugh again, their fleshy, sticky heads bobbing with mirth, and it's all he can do not to stomp on them.

"You've already found her," they say, quickly, as if they've read his mind. "Yes, you have. Just hurry along the path and she's right there. Always waiting. Silver fox, you know."

"I hate riddles," says Kyle, and he raises his foot to crush them, but they pull back into the earth so quickly his foot comes down only on the hard ground.

"Good boy," says a voice like silver bells. "And so hungry, walking all this way in the dark wood."

He turns to find her, nestled in fox furs, in a silver sleigh pulled by a great white bear. He runs to her and clambers into the sleigh. She opens the furs and lets him snuggle next to her.

He nuzzles her neck. Her skin is electric, sparking into him with something that feels almost like heat.

BADGER WAS GROWLING.

Maggie did not want to wake up, for she was sure the flowers had more to tell her, if she could just figure out the right question to ask.

Badger growled again. She opened her eyes. The hackles on the dog's back bristled. She put her hand on his neck. "Stay," she said. Her head was muzzy. "What is it? What do you hear?"

Badger scrambled from under the bearskins and stood, every muscle tense.

Maggie stood as well. "Heel, Badger, heel." The dog trembled at her side, his lips curled, showing teeth.

The ravens had disappeared. Percival shied and before she could grab the reins, he reared, snapped the tether and galloped off into the night in the direction they'd come.

Maggie stepped out of the lean-to and backed against the tree, cursing herself for not bringing a dagger or *something*. She picked a branch, as thick as her forearm, from the ground. Better than nothing. Yes, there was movement out there on the far side of the carriage. Her knuckles were white against the dark bark of the branch. Badger jerked, as though about to dash and she grabbed his collar. "Steady, boy. Steady."

CHAPTER SIXTEEN

A BIG MAN STEPPED OUT OF THE SHADOWS into the moonlight. He wore a wide-brimmed hat and the high collar of his coat covered much of his face. His arms were spread, and his hands held no weapons.

"Now, why would a horse run off like that?" The voice was incongruous for the body out of which it came. It didn't sound like a man.

"Can't blame him for being spooked," said Maggie.

"By me? I can't imagine. Now, by *them*, well, that's another story."

Seven figures stepped out of the darkness. Badger barked madly, snapping, straining under Maggie's hand. She looked to her right and left. Men ringed them. The branch was slippery in her palm.

"I'd tell that dog to stand down, unless you'd prefer I have him shot."

Yes, the voice was unmistakably female, never mind the speaker was Alvin's size.

"Badger! Enough. Enough." He stopped barking but continued to growl. She didn't know how long she'd be able to hold him. "I've got nothing you want," she said.

"Is that so?" The woman, for a woman it was, took off her hat, revealing a shock of choppy red hair. An owl was tattooed on her cheek. She ran her hand along the carriage. "This is a pretty buggy. Not much use without the horse, though. Be that as it may, no one comes here in such as this without they've got money, and lots of it. Why, look at these hinges. That's not brass, now is it, my brothers?"

Brothers? The faces, the eyes, the noses, yes, there was something familial about them. The shades of reddish hair, a certain set of the shoulders . . .

"Looks like gold," said one.

"Pretty," said another.

"Are we still talking about the carriage?" asked the first, and they looked at Maggie and laughed.

Badger snarled.

The ring of men closed in until they stood between the carriage and the tree against which Maggie and Badger held their ground. "Don't come near us, or I'll set the dog on you."

Out from the folds of their coats, the men pulled a collection of guns and knives.

"Now, why don't you put that toothpick away, missy. If you value the dog, you'd be wise to tell him to behave."

Maggie dropped the branch. "Badger, sit. *Sit*, I said."

"Oh, much better," said the woman. She asked Maggie if she had a belt and when she said she didn't, the woman ordered one of the men to remove his and give it to Maggie. "Now, use that and fashion a lead for the dog, right? And muzzle him with something."

"There's no need. He won't bite unless I tell him to."

"Call me untrusting," said the woman. "Do it. Or I'll tell one of my brothers to handle it."

Maggie knelt beside Badger, held his face in her hands and whispered, "Be a good boy, sweetheart. I'm sorry. It'll be all right." Badger whined, and tossed his head, but let her loop the belt through his collar. She stood, holding the belt. "I don't have anything to muzzle him with."

The woman fiddled at her neck and drew out a sweat-stiff bandana. She balled it in her fist and tossed it at Maggie. It was a sign of how filthy it was that it stuck together and sailed like a rubber ball. Maggie prayed Badger wouldn't gag at the smell of it. She kissed his nose and then tied the bandana, but not tightly. He pawed at it for a moment and then sneezed. The men and the woman laughed. "Sit. Good boy."

As soon as Badger sat, three of the men rushed to Maggie. Seeing they were about to bind her, she begged to have her hands bound in front so she could keep hold of Badger's leash.

"What do you say, Beth?" one of the men asked the big woman. He had very bright blue eyes.

Beth approached and stood so close Maggie could smell her meaty breath. "I don't think she needs to be bound. Where would she go?" She touched Maggie's hair. It was very hard not to pull away. She yanked, and laughed when Maggie managed not to shriek.

"Got a bit of heart, eh?" Beth said. In her hand she held one of the silver birds Maggie wore pinned to her braid. "Pretty." She plucked the other one out as well. "What's your name?"

"Maggie." She tilted her head toward the dog, "And he's Badger."

"Well, Maggie, I'm Beth Castoff, and these here are my brothers, and we're all one big happy family, so let's go home and meet Mother, shall we?" She turned to her brothers. "Tab, mark where this carriage is, and come back for it with a horse later. It'll be first light soon. Turner, grab that basket of food out of the carriage. Put whatever's in it in your pack."

The brothers grumbled, saying they could use some kip, but did as they were told. They began marching along, Maggie and Badger in front of Beth.

"Maggie," called Beth after a few minutes, "what brings you to our woods? Rude of me not to have asked." When Maggie declined to answer, Beth laughed. "Come on, you can tell me. If I'm not mistaken that carriage comes from Tilden's place."

"You know Wallis Tilden?"

Beth snorted. "It's not like we have tea. I've heard tales. I've a mind to visit there one day. But you chose this road at the fork and not the other, so there's a reason you're here. What is it?"

Maggie tucked that piece of information away. It was possible this world worked the same way the Grimoire did. You walked the roads you were meant to walk. What of choice, then? She stumbled on a bit of root. This wasn't the time for philosophical exercises. Although Maggie questioned the wisdom of telling this ragtag pack of thieves her business, Beth was probably right. "I'm looking for someone."

"And who might that be?" Beth's tone was that of a friendly neighbourhood shopkeeper. "No one comes this way without our knowing, isn't that right, my boys?" They avowed it was. Beth drank from a flask she pulled from her pocket.

Badger turned and growled low at Beth. "I don't think your dog likes me," she said.

"You haven't given him any reason to."

"I'd have thought not killing him would have counted for something. Now, come on, who are you looking for?"

"I'm looking for my brother."

"Well, why didn't you say so? I'm partial to brothers, aren't I, boys?"

Her brothers avowed she was.

"His name is Kyle."

Something flitted across Beth's face, but too swiftly for Maggie to know what it meant. "And what might his business here have been?"

"I'm not sure."

"Oh, come on, smart girl such as yourself. I don't believe it.

Do you, boys?"

They avowed they did not.

Beth poked Maggie in the back, making her stumble. "What's the point, Maggie? What's the point of all this palaver? You'll tell me eventually, what with the way you care about your doggie. I'm patient only to a point and thus far you've seen the best of me."

"I'm not being evasive. I honestly don't know. He wandered in here from the Forest, if you know where that is."

"I know it's a place neither here nor there."

Maggie considered this an entirely apt description. "Yes, well, my brother's lost, and sent word for me to find him."

"Did he? Huh." Beth said no more to Maggie after that.

Eventually the path turned into a cobbled road, and ahead loomed a great stone manor. The pewter-coloured dawn rustled her skirts at the edges of trees and the high ground on which the stone house stood.

A stone wall enclosed the manor house and iron gates in the centre opened at their approach. Half a dozen women and four old men came to greet them. Inside the gates, chickens scattered and a great grey hound bounded out. The mammoth whiskered beast practically bowled Badger over and then ran in circles sniffing him and barking. The dog stuck her hindquarters up in the air and wagged her tail, inviting Badger to play. Well, thought Maggie, at least someone's friendly. Badger let the dog sniff him but showed no desire to frolic.

"Well, if it ain't Lady Beth," said a woman with a third eye tattooed in the middle of her forehead. "What's this then?"

"Just a little bird for my collection, Bridget." Beth adjusted the pair of curved knives in her belt. "Dog! Oso!" At the command, the hound's ears flattened. Her tail curled between her legs. Her back hunched and she urinated slightly. Beth ignored her. The dog rushed to her side and sat, shivering.

"Bridget, girl, got something for you," said Beth.

Whereas the names of the men all seemed to begin with the

letter *T*, the women's names all started with *B*. Bridget, Betty, Blossom, Brenda, Beverley, Bunny – the smallest. They flocked around Beth and the men. The younger ones wanted to know what Beth had brought them, and she took Turner's pack and tossed things from Wallis Tilden's basket – jars of jam and candied plums – as well as trinkets she pulled from her pockets – coins and handkerchiefs and a string of amber beads. Maggie saw one of the silver bird clips from her hair go into the pocket of the woman named Blossom. The men handed out more presents, and although none of them seemed of any true value to Maggie, the women shrieked with delight.

With the present giving done, Beth ambled over to Maggie, the dog at her side. "Seems we both like dogs." The shaggy hound squirmed submissively at her side. Beth raised her hand as though to strike and the dog dropped to her belly.

"Down," said Maggie, and Badger lay on his belly, too.

Beth laughed. "We each have our methods." She put her arm around Maggie's shoulders. "Come on, you're with me."

They crossed the courtyard. Ducks and chickens scattered. Around the walls stood pens of livestock – goats and sheep – as well as stacks of wine casks, trunks and suitcases. Maggie wondered if the latter came from other unwary travellers. Mounds of musty straw and manure produced a thick funk. The half-ruined manor lay before them. Pigeons and swallows nested in the exposed beams and openings in the walls. It seemed unnaturally dark; even though the sun was beginning to caress the landscape with buttery fingers, the manor remained shadowed.

When Beth pushed Maggie through the doors she found herself in a large hall. It felt like a place daylight never fully reached. Cooking fires burned at various places on the stone floor. Long shadows danced on the walls and cinders rose. Without a chimney, smoke wafted to the ceiling, seeking escape through the many holes in the roof. This was only moderately successful, and the grey haze gave the space a murky quality.

Daylight should show through the roof holes, but it was only void beyond. The entire place smelled of cooking, unwashed bodies and soot. Maggie thought this once might have been a quite wonderful hall, but now it was so dirty and dark and neglected that the very walls seemed to lean away from the inhabitants. Women, children and old men sat on stools at trestle tables, drinking from cups. Beer, from the smell. In an alcove in the far recess of the hall, several thin, unattended children played with sticks or bones.

An enormous woman in a long dress and apron and stout boots crusted with muck stood near the largest cooking fire. A scarf round her head covered her hair. Her face was red and sweating.

"Come on," said Beth. "Introduction time. But first, let's deal with your dog. Bunny! Bring me something to tie this dog up with, a rope or something." Bunny, in the same sort of dress the enormous woman wore, ran into the courtyard and returned with a length of rope. "Good girl," said Beth. She handed the rope to Maggie.

Feeling she had no choice, Maggie tied the rope to Badger's collar and knotted a loop into the other end. Beth snatched the leash from her and dragged Badger away into the shadows, Oso following, with her tail between her legs.

"Don't hurt him," Maggie called.

Beth laughed, but Maggie heard no cry from either dog, which gave her hope. When she returned, Beth shoved Maggie in the direction of the enormous woman. The woman examined her in such a way – lifting Maggie's arms, running her hands over Maggie's thighs and back – that Maggie feared she was deciding which part of her to throw in the bubbling cauldron hanging over the fire. The woman then stood back and regarded her. Maggie felt very much like a heifer at a fair.

"What have we got here?" asked the enormous woman.

"Maggie," said Beth. "And I claim her. Winnie meet

Maggie. Maggie, meet my mother, Winnie." She put her hand on Maggie's shoulder.

Her mother cracked Beth across the knuckles with a wooden spoon. Beth shrieked and dropped her hand. "I say who gets what, where and when. You'll obey and behave."

"That hurt," Beth mumbled.

"As well it should." She stirred the great pot, which had begun to boil over. "Now, Beth, tell me what you brought me, and how." Beth recalled the story of Maggie's abduction, adding a great many flourishes about how difficult it had been to track her and how fierce the dog was.

Winnie put up her hands. "I'm too hungry for this folderol." She regarded Maggie. "Most people have the sense not to come through our woods, or they've the good sense to run when they see us coming. Those who don't, well, we've got work for 'em, don't we, children?" Her sons and daughters avowed they did.

Chickens and rabbits roasted on a spit turned by a podgy young man. Winnie checked the meat and pronounced it ready. The smell of the sizzling fat was mouth-watering, even under the circumstances. Winnie told them to get their bowls.

Beth ordered Maggie to sit and stay put. She fetched bowls of food, while Maggie tried to catch sight of Badger. She heard whimpering, and laughter, and then a yip. Maggie's veins turned to fire and when she heard another yip she could stand it no more. She'd rush them and grab a knife. She'd hold a knife to the fat woman's throat and . . . Seeing nothing but red mist, she leaped from the stool. Her hand closed round the skillet's handle, but no sooner did she feel the heft of it then something that felt like an oak tree landed between her shoulder blades and she was face down on the stone floor.

Beth hauled her up by the collar. "See what you made me do? Here I am being all nice and polite and you act like an animal. Oso acted like that at first, but she doesn't now. Damn near wore myself out beating that dog." She shook Maggie like a baby squirrel. "You do something like that again and I'll cut the tendons on your ankles." She brandished one of her knives close to Maggie's eyes. "Understood?"

Maggie nodded. "Badger . . ."

"What? Oh." Beth turned and yelled, "Leave that dog alone or I'll throttle the lot of you!"

She dropped Maggie, who fell to her knees, pain spiking up her thighs. It was her fault the dog was here, just as it was her fault, apparently, that Kyle was here. She deserved the pain. Beth put her hands under Maggie's arms and lifted her back on the stool. "Stay," she said. Maggie hung her head. There was copper-tasting blood in her mouth; she must have cut her lip when she fell. She wiped her face with her sleeve.

"Eat," Beth said.

Maggie chewed on a piece of rabbit meat. It was tough and stringy.

"Right, then." Winnie, her hands on her hips, stood in the middle of the room and the firelight made a gargantuan shadow on the wall. "Should Beth be given the girl to keep as a pet?"

Beth looked so angry it seemed sparks flew from her eyes. She stood and addressed her mother. "Given? Am I not Beth Castoff, eldest daughter of Winnie Castoff, and the one you have chosen to take your place when the time comes, may it not be for a long time yet?"

"It is true."

"And so, as the next Robber Queen –"

"You're not Robber Queen yet, my girl," said Winnie.

"But I am the chosen of the Castoff Clan and as such I claim this one as my servant, as is right." She nodded at the podgy boy turning the spit. "You have Steven there, and I, too, should have someone to help with the work, to care for my fire."

Although some arguing went back and forth about the nature of Castoff laws and the right uses for a woman, in the end it was decided. Maggie would be given to Beth. The band of Castoffs drank and ate. Tim produced a harp on which he played plaintive airs until complaints from the others persuaded him to play something festive. The children in the alcove, six in all, came forward at last. They crawled into laps and were petted like kittens and fed scraps of food. They were handled roughly but not without kindness and, with their wide-open curious stares, seemed unafraid.

People wandered off to various corners of the hall. Although Maggie thought it should be late morning now, the darkness inside the hall made it night again, or, she suspected, always. Perhaps these people slept inside, during the perpetual night, when it was day outside, and woke when the sun set. Some people claimed spaces portioned off from the main hall with blankets, others simply fell onto blanket-covered straw. "Come on," said Beth. "We're over here."

She picked up a torch and a bowl of scraps and led Maggie to a far corner of the hall where a heavy blanket served as a sort of doorway.

"After you, my pet." Beth held the flap up and winked.

The room's walls were stone and wood, ramshackle and bowed, but they afforded more privacy than the blankets many of the others used. A straw bed, covered in quilts, hunkered in the corner. There was a leaded window through which no light passed, encased almost completely in vines, and stone stairs that ended at a pile of rubble, with a cushion and a few candles on the lower step. A trunk and a chair upholstered with what once must have been a soft-blue brocade but was now a patchwork of grey and rusty stains stood next to the stairs. Inside a series of cages on the wall by the entrance pigeons perched on branches. Several books sat atop a stool by the bed.

The pigeons startled as the women entered. Beth put the torch in an iron holder on the wall. There, at the back of the alcove, were Badger and Oso. When Badger saw Maggie, he jumped up from where he'd been curled and dashed forward, only to jerk back when he reached the end of a chain fastened to his neck and secured to a link in the wall. Maggie went to him, knelt and took off the scarf tied around his face. She let him kiss her face while she rubbed his ears. "Good boy," she whispered. "Good boy." It was hard to keep the tears back.

Oso wriggled and whined, but dared not come forward until Beth told her she might. The dog ran to her mistress and sat at her feet, chin tilted up, her eyes blinking. Beth grunted and rubbed the top of the dog's head roughly.

"You'll sleep with me and my little pets tonight," said Beth. She looked at Maggie and Badger, who was in convulsions of wiggling joy. "You can unchain him. It's just a latch. But if he tries to run I won't be responsible."

Maggie unlatched the chain from Badger's collar. Badger tried to crawl into her lap. Even Beth had to laugh. "He seems to like you, all right." She looked down as Oso, still cringing at her feet. "Maybe I should get a better dog."

"I think Oso's a fine dog."

"Always running off. That's why I keep the pigeons in cages. Man who had them first said they'd come back home if I let them fly, but when I let some of 'em out they just disappeared." She seized a bird from the nearest cage, held it by its feet and swung it about. "I hate it when things run off." She kicked Oso and the hound rolled away, whining.

"Well, maybe if you didn't treat her like that!"

Beth whirled and raised her hand. "You mind your mouth, or I'll feed you your teeth."

Badger's lip curled. "Easy. Beth's not going to hurt us."

Beth stuffed the flapping bird back in its cage and then sat on the leather trunk and regarded Oso, who slunk over to her on her belly. She pulled her knife from her belt and held it against Oso's throat. "I do this every night, don't I, girl? I tickle you with my sticker and remind you who your mistress is." The dog trembled and panted. Beth put her knife away and turned to Maggie. "And on what do you base your opinion that I won't hurt you?"

Maggie noticed her pack lying near the trunk and wondered what was still inside. "I don't think you'll beat us," she said, "because if you do, you might make us do whatever you want, but you'll know we do it because we're afraid, not because we respect you, or like you."

"You talk too much." Beth set the bowl of scraps on the floor and Oso looked at it, trembling, but didn't move. "Let your dog eat if you want."

"I'd rather they both ate."

Beth snorted and made a small gesture with her chin. Oso dove on the food. Maggie gave Badger the signal and both dogs hungrily gulped the meat and vegetables, but they minded their manners and didn't snap at each other.

Maggie said, "It seems our dogs have become friends. We might even do the same."

Beth stood and, turning her back, stripped off her heavy sweater. The shirt she wore underneath pulled up. Her back was a mass of scar tissue. Maggie's hand flew to her mouth. Crisscrossed white ridges where the flesh had healed unevenly, and what looked like burn marks. A lot of them. Beth quickly pulled her shirt down.

"What are you gawking at?"

"Nothing." Maggie felt as though she'd seen something more intimate and fragile than skin, something she had no right to see.

Beth went to the pile of straw and kicked it until she was satisfied. "You lie next to the wall."

"I'm happy on the floor, if you've a blanket to spare."

"No need. There's room for two." Beth picked up a candle and held it to the torch until it lit. She extinguished the torch, using a large tin snuffer hanging from a chain and placed the candle in a hurricane lamp with a mirrored backing. From its perch on a delicate table it cast a surprisingly bright and comforting glow.

Maggie lay down and scooted as far over to the wall as possible. Badger curled up at the end of the straw, keeping his eyes on Beth. "Is it okay if he sleeps there?"

Beth looked over at Oso, who had squinched into the far corner. "Come," commanded Beth. Oso's head came up and she looked questioningly at her. "Come, stupid." The dog crawled on her belly. Beth snapped her fingers and pointed to Badger. "Go. There." For a moment, Oso didn't seem to understand, and it was plain the not knowing put her into fits. She trembled even more.

"Useless dog."

"Tell her it's okay," said Maggie softly. "She wants to please you. She just doesn't know how."

From the look on Beth's face, Maggie feared she'd beat her and the dogs bloody.

"S'all right," mumbled Beth to Oso. Still the dog did not move.

"She's not allowed to sleep near the bed, am I right?" said Maggie. "She's just afraid she'll do something wrong."

"Soft, that's what you are." She pointed at the spot near Badger. "Get over there, you."

Oso did as she was told, with her tail between her legs. Beth then flopped down on the straw next to Maggie and pulled the blanket over them both. "My little pets, all here together and safe, and grateful for it, too, aren't you?"

"Of course," said Maggie. The woman smelled like she hadn't washed in months. "But, do you always sleep with your knives on?"

"Always." Beth's smile, missing a tooth on the left side, flashed in the candlelight. "You never know what's going to happen around here." She sat up, leaning on an elbow. "Hey, I'll bet you can read, can't you?" Maggie said she could. Beth reached for one of the books on the stool. "Good. You can make yourself useful. Read this to me."

The book was a collection of folk tales. "Any story in particular?"

"I don't care. Just read a damn story."

Maggie opened the book at random. It was a story called, "The Snow-daughter and the Fire-son." "What about this?" She held the book so Beth could read the title but, rather than reading the words on the page, she told her, "It's called 'The Frost King.'"

Beth looked hard at the illustration of a young woman in a diaphanous gown with her arms raised high over her head, in the middle of a snowstorm. From the woods a man wearing a crown, riding a horse, watched her. Beth pointed at the title on the drawing, which said, *The Snow Maiden*. "Is that what that says? The Frost King?" Maggie lied and told her it did. "Read it then. That's a good picture."

Maggie tucked away the knowledge that Beth was illiterate and read the story. It was about a brother made of fire and a sister made of ice and how no matter how they loved each other, they were doomed to do each other harm.

Maggie's voice caught on the last sentences and she shielded her face in the blanket so as to hide her tears.

"What are you blubbering for?" asked Beth.

"I'm thinking of my brother, of Kyle."

"Oh, I wouldn't worry about him," said Beth.

"I can't help it. I'm here to find him, and I keep making a mess of it and making everything worse and I'm afraid I won't find him at all and even if I do, I don't know what I can do if he's with *her*." She fairly spat the last word.

"Well, he was fine when he left here."

CHAPTER SEVENTEEN

MAGGIE STOPPED CRYING AND TURNED TO BETH. "He was here with you?"

"I found him, half frozen in the woods, waffling on about being called by *her* – the One Who Lives in the North." Beth chewed on her lip. "Thought he was daft. Not that it mattered."

"Did he tell you about elysium?"

"He did. No time for that nonsense around here, and he didn't have none or I'd have found it. Told me that's what caused those pretty silver swirls on his skin. I liked them." She sounded wistful, then scowled and cleaned her thumbnail with the tip of a knife. "I didn't want no man pushing me around and they're apt to get like that. I wasn't having it. He wanted to go so good riddance."

Maggie had to keep her wits about her. "You did the right thing."

"How do you figure that?"

"It's not right to keep something that doesn't want to be kept."

"What a load of horse droppings. Something belongs to you, you keep it tied up tight." Beth snorted. "Your brother wasn't much in the end. Thought only of himself. Running off to his woman in the north. I know you're fond of him, but he thinks only of himself. I've done you a favour. He was pretty, though, I'll give him that. He don't want to stay, well, to hell with him. I kicked his ass out into the snow and no regrets." She tucked the knife back into her belt, blew out the candle and rolled over, kicking Maggie in the shin in the process. "Now, go to sleep. I don't want to talk about it."

Maggie stared up at the ceiling and after a few minutes Beth fell into a deep sleep, snoring like an overfed bear. The darkness felt like an imposed, unnatural thing, perhaps the heart of despair made manifest, sucking all the light. If it was always night here, what regulated the days, if you could even call them that? They had arrived, she was sure, near daybreak, so presumably the sun rose outside. She had seen the silvered gleams on the horizon. But here, it was impossible to tell what time it was, only that it was dark.

High overhead, up in the exposed rafters of the ruined roof, something moved. Maggie strained to see. Two things. Dark. Barely visible. Her heart beat more quickly. One of the things grew bigger, stretched out. Could it be? It was. Ravens, two of them, stretching their wings, bobbing up and down. Letting her know they were still with her.

MAGGIE DREAMS . . .

She tries to reach the prince, trapped in a tower atop a glass mountain. She has tried once, and twice, and a thousand times more. Each time she falls, tumbling and twirling in the unforgiving air. She falls to her knees, atop a mound of bones, and screams and screams and then looks down at her feet and sees they have turned into the feet of a lynx, with razor-sharp claws.

Her hands, too, are lethal paws. She places one in front of the other, and starts up the glass mountain again.

The sun is setting and she's only halfway up. She can hardly draw breath she's so worn out, and her mouth is parched. Her back paws are torn and bleeding, and she can only hold on now with her front paws. Evening closes in, and she strains to see if she can behold the top of the mountain. Then she gazes beneath her – a yawning abyss, with certain and terrible death at the bottom, reeking with the half-decayed bodies of horses and riders.

It is almost pitch-dark now. Only the stars light up the glass mountain. Maggie clings as if glued to the glass by her bloodstained paws. Then, the eagle who sits atop an apple tree, guarding the prince, spots her and swoops down. The eagle digs its sharp claws into her flesh, but she seizes the bird's feet. The creature, with a cry, lifts her high up in the air and circles round the tower, which by the pale rays of the moon looks more like ice than gold. In a high window she sees Kyle. She struggles and shakes and lashes out until the bird releases her and then vanishes, shrieking, into the clouds and she falls into the branches of the apple tree.

The apple tree is no longer an apple tree, but a pomegranate tree and when she rubs the juice against her wounds they are healed.

KYLE SEES HER. SHE SITS AT HER WINDOW IN A SILVER room in a marble castle, atop a mountain made of mirrors. She waves languidly to him, trailing frost from her fingertips. A tree full of golden apples grows in front of the castle. He must bring her one and then she will reward him. He is astride a splendid horse, white as the moon. She has a silver pipe in her hand now. He will reach the top of the mirror mountain; he will pluck an apple from the tree and thereby gain her favour and the dreams she offers.

Knights have gone before him. Some shod their horses with sharp nails, and some tried to loop ropes around the crags with which to haul themselves up. They all fell back to the bottom of the steep, slippery hill. The cries of the men and the horses, broken into pieces as they tumbled, sliced to ribbons, were terrible to hear. Now, nothing is left except their bones, which rattle in their battered armour like dry peas in a gourd.

Kyle, though, wears a suit of golden armour. He clings to the horse's mane as they climb over the heaps of corpses, both equine and human, at the mountain's base. He spurs the horse and makes a rush at the mountain and scrabbles halfway, then he turns the horse's head and comes down again without a slip or stumble. Again, and again he does this, and sparks fly from the horse's hooves. People gaze in astonishment, for he is almost at the summit now.

An eagle flies above, riding the thermals. It spots Kyle and his moon-horse and prepares to dive, but the woman in the window plays a single note on a bone flute and the eagle returns to the heavens. The horse opens its wide nostrils and tosses its mane, then rears high in the air, allowing Kyle to pluck a golden apple from the tree.

A lacy handkerchief flutters from the window, white as a dove. "Well done, sweet boy. Now bring me the fruit of my desire," says the woman. Her laugh is like wind chimes made of bones.

BETH POKED MAGGIE IN THE RIBS AND TOLD HER TO GET UP.

"I'm awake," said Maggie. "But it's still dark. Is it always dark?"

Beth used a match to light the candle, then turned back to Maggie, leaned on her elbow and grinned. "You get used to it.

Outside the hall's different than inside. Inside suits us. We like the shadows. Keeps secrets." She scratched her head.

Maggie and Badger followed Beth and a still-cringing Oso through the torchlit hall. The fires burned low and the floor was strewn with bones and apple cores and crusts of bread – remnants of the last meal. A partial staircase in the corner, which Maggie had not noticed the night before, led halfway up the wall to nowhere and then abruptly stopped, just as the one in Beth's room did. She wondered if there had once been a second floor, now fallen. There must have been, for the ceiling looked very far away indeed. It was hard not to think of how grand it all must have been once. Now vines crawled in through the windows and clung to the walls. Bats hung from the beams. There was no sign of the ravens.

Beth led her through a back doorway into a small courtyard with a privy and a water pump. In the far stone wall, Beth used a large key on the lock on an exterior gate and opened it to let the dogs out. Beyond the gate the day was blindingly bright, the sky blue, and Maggie caught a glimpse of snow. The day, however, stopped dead at the threshold. Maggie's legs twitched with the desire to dash toward that light and Beth must have sensed it for she slammed the door shut. "Oso'll bark when she wants back in," she said. The women relieved themselves and washed and then Oso barked. Beth opened the door just enough for the dogs to bound in and led Maggie back to her room. No one else stirred. Either they were still sleeping, or they'd gone out.

Beth dressed, making sure to keep her scars hidden.

Maggie took the opportunity to check her pack. What was left in it? Her undergarments, yes; Kyle's picture. The little enamel box Mr. Strundale had given her.

"You think I'd steal out of your pack."

"Forgive me, but you did take the carriage, and I think a lot of other things, no?"

"Castoffs are outcasts. Castoffs take what's been cast off by others, and if they come on our turf, then it's fair game." Beth picked up the book from the stump, sat down and rubbed it between her palms. "Wanted by none, welcome by none, invited to no one's table, we're stronger and tougher for it."

"I thought I was an outcast, too, once, but it turned out I was wrong."

"And what would you know about being an outcast? You in the fancy carriage, with the dog and the silver birds in your hair."

"Believe me, I haven't spent much time in carriages." Maggie sat on the floor with her back leaning up against the trunk. "What do you know about elysium?"

Beth poked at the birds, making them flap and squawk. She then looked at Maggie with a raised brow. "Part of the trouble from *her* in the north." She stood. "You can tell me while we're walking. We've got work to do."

After a few handfuls of bread and cheese, and while the rest of the band was beginning to rouse, Beth and Maggie stepped past the gates of the main courtyard into the brilliant day. Snow had fallen, and glittered as though strewn with crystals. Being outside the resolutely night-filled hall was like taking off a heavy, wet cloak. From the position of the sun, Maggie judged it to be just past noon.

"I don't understand this at all," she said.

"Winnie says when she was a kid the old-timers told tales of it being different, but gradual-like night fell on Castoff Hall." Beth shrugged. "Just the way it is."

She took Maggie into the woods to check the traplines for rabbits. And as they walked, Maggie recounted her story, about her addiction and the Grimoire, and about how the message had come from Kyle. She talked about Mother Ratigan, and how Badger saved her, and about Wallis and her hotel of delights. "So that's where the carriage came from. It wasn't mine at all."

Beth, who had listened thoughtfully as they walked the snowy trails, grunted. "We've all got our troubles, I guess."

Maggie thought this response a little thin but remembered the scars along Beth's back. It was possible her story sounded not so very bad after all.

They walked a few more minutes and found three rabbits, which Beth stuffed into a stained satchel slung over her shoulder. Maggie asked, "Do you want to tell me your story?"

"Nothing to tell."

"Well, how did your people come to live in the hall?"

"I don't know. Our people came here a long time ago. Don't know why. Found this place and moved in."

"What about your father?"

"He died. No loss, believe me. He was a fist-happy bastard."

They walked for several hours, checking all the traps. They walked through fields and hollows, through woods and by rivers. There was no path here, just animal trails, and Maggie wondered where it had gone.

They collected eight rabbits, and Beth's satchel was full when she finally said they were circling back to the hall. Maggie had thought they were going in a straight line. How would she know which way was north?

Beth watched Badger and Maggie. Finally, she said, "So, show me how you make your dog, you know, be the way he is with you."

"Well, you can't *make* a dog love you. That's just what dogs do, if you give them half a chance."

"Yer daft. Can't be that simple."

WHEN THEY ARRIVED BACK AT THE COURTYARD, DARKNESS again enveloped them the moment they stepped across the threshold. The dogs cared little about such things apparently and romped ahead. Beth looked into the hall and called out to Blossom and Betty, "Where's Winnie?"

"She went out for a walk in the woods. Says she's done with us."

"What have you been up to, then?" asked Beth.

As her eyes adjusted to the light, Maggie noticed the women looked dishevelled, bruised and a bit battered all over.

"We don't see why we should share if you don't," said Blossom. "I want my own friend, too."

Beth spat on the ground. "And I want to have wings and fly, but it ain't likely, is it? You get what you earn around here, have you forgot? And it isn't like any of you are good for much. Winnie decided and that's that, or do you want to tell her she's wrong? Oh, Winnie'd like that fine."

"I'd like what?"

Winnie stood at the entrance to the courtyard. She held a clay pipe between her lips, puffing away furiously. She wore a man's coat, tied in the middle with a piece of rope, and stout boots. Her grey hair escaped from a red bandana and the tattoo of a cat on her cheek gleamed with sweat, even in the cool air. "What's going on here?"

The women began to talk all at once, sounding like a gaggle of angry geese. Winnie held up her hand and they went silent. "Beth, what's going on here? Where are the boys?"

"Seems the sisters don't like the way things are. And I don't know where Tim and them are. Probably gone back to get the carriage with Tab."

"I'll skin him if he's off in the woods getting drunk." Winnie turned to the women. "Since when do you question my decisions?"

Blossom mumbled, "Just don't seem fair, is all, Beth getting presents when we don't."

Winnie frowned, then nodded. "We'll see what Tim finds. Any luck, you'll have a new toy, you sisters. If not, well, maybe Beth should share."

"Wait now," said Beth. "What belongs to me stays mine."

"You telling me the way it's going to be?" Winnie puffed up to monstrous proportions. "You dare?"

Beth looked like fury. "Maybe I do. Maybe it's time."

"I give. I take away," Winnie bellowed, and then stalked over to Maggie and backhanded her. As Maggie fell to the ground she heard Badger snarl and then yelp.

"That dog tries to bite me again I'll rip its head off. You lot," Winnie turned to the sisters, "you've got work to do so bloody well do it. And Beth, if you're not with Tim then you can skin them rabbits I see in your basket." Winnie jabbed the air with her pipe. "You pull your weight or you'll find yourself on the road out of here and no never mind about it." She barrelled past them into the hall.

"You're getting old, Ma," called Beth. Her face was blood red and the owl on her cheek jumped as she ground her teeth. She grabbed Maggie by the arm and pushed her forward. "Go on, get inside." The dogs bounded after them.

Beth led Maggie to her room and kicked the trunk as she entered.

"Gonna have to be some changes around here," said Beth, her head hanging. Absently, as though she wasn't aware she was doing it, she reached round and ran the back of her hand over her scars. She looked as though she might explode, but Oso, who had come into the room with Badger after the women, lay her head on Beth's knee. Beth stroked her dog. Oso's tail wagged and wagged. "You're not such a bad dog, are you?" Oso's tail thump-thump-thumped on the floor. Her whole behind wagged. It was impossible not to smile.

"She loves you," said Maggie.

"Nobody loves me," said Beth, so quietly it was little more than air passing between her chapped lips. Oso put her paws on Beth's knees and began licking her hands and her face, her tail thumping away. Finally, Beth chuckled and told the dog to stop, which she refused to do, just went on licking, and Beth turned her head this way and that, trying to avoid the great slobbery affection. "You daft thing. Cut it out," said Beth, but she held the dog in her arms. Oso laid her head on Beth's neck and seemed to faint from love.

It was shocking to see the big, muscular woman hanging onto the dog as though drowning, but it gave Maggie just the wedge of hope she needed. She had to persuade Beth to let her go. She waited until Beth had somewhat recovered. Oso sat between her legs, her head resting on Beth's thigh. Beth was gentle with her, and even bent down to kiss the top of the dog's head.

"Seems dogs are better'n most people."

"It's true, I rather prefer dogs to most people," smiled Maggie. "But people can be pretty good, too. Take yourself, for example."

"Me?" Beth sneered, but it wasn't a terribly convincing sneer, rather it looked as though she wore it more out of habit than conviction.

"Of course. You let my brother go, didn't you?"

Beth pulled back from Oso and folded her arms over her chest. "So?"

Maggie ducked her head, trying to look as submissive as Oso. "I just meant, well, dogs understand loyalty, and so do you, so maybe you understand the loyalty I have to Kyle."

The muscles in Beth's jaw worked. Oso moved away from Beth, lay down, put her chin on her paws and looked up at her mistress. Badger sat at the end of the bed. He cocked his head, as though he knew something of import was about to happen.

"Maybe I do," said Beth.

"Beth, you're strong and have insight, but you're apart. You have this room, and you aren't – you'll forgive me – quite like the rest of your family."

"Maybe. I guess."

"Is it possible there's something new waiting for you?"

"You're new."

"I mean something much bigger than me. I think you have a calling, a vocation, if you like."

"And what might that be, Miss Know Everything?"

In the hall a child cried, and a woman told it to be quiet or she'd give it something to cry about. Someone dropped something metal on the stones and cursed. "Not for me to say."

"Is it not?"

Oso took herself off to a spot under the pigeon cages. Maggie stayed quiet. To try and persuade Beth of her honesty would do nothing but make her sound less honest, and besides, she didn't trust herself not to sound desperate. Beth got up and, moving aside the blanket at the doorway, gazed out into the torchlit, perpetually dark hall. She ran her finger over the owl tattoo on her cheek. Then she turned to Maggie and said, "I want you to teach me to read."

"Yes, I can do that. But," Maggie hesitated, "it takes time."

"And you're thinking you don't have much time, is that it?"

"Not if I want to find Kyle alive. You and I both know if he's with Srebrenka for long, he'll be past healing." She kept her voice as calm as she could.

"You're thinking you're tough enough to rescue your brother from *her*?"

Maggie kept her head high. "I just know I have to try."

Beth snorted and looked down at her boots. "Teach me to read." She stood and opened the trunk. Inside were piles of books. "They're mysterious, especially the ones without pictures. I don't like it."

Maggie knelt by the trunk and picked up a leather-bound botanical study of something called the Qualsat Mountain Range. It was filled with drawings of plants and herbs, mosses and lichens. They were precise and rendered by an expert hand, the petals, stems and leaves fairly jumping off the page. Qualsat Mountains? They must be a range of mountains in this world, as they weren't in hers. She picked another book: *The Evaldian History of Cerlian City States*. Apart from not knowing what a Cerlian City State was, she had no idea what *Evaldian* meant. Was it a person? A school of philosophical thought? Here was a book of poems by someone she had never heard of. And here, what looked to be a geological work about the Great Rift Valley of Collana.

A strange shifting sensation went through her and made her a little dizzy. Worlds within worlds. Her chest tightened. She'd never find Kyle. The darkness spreading through the Immanent World would keep going, until there was nothing but elysium-haunted Forest, with Srebrenka ruling over a kingdom of suffering. Badger pawed her leg. She snapped back to the present. Oh, what a good dog. She kissed the top of his head.

Beth sat on the brocaded chair and watched her through narrowed eyes.

"Sorry, it's just that you have a lot of books here. They're a bit advanced, even for me."

"I know my alphabet," said Beth.

"Do you? How did you learn?"

"I made your brother teach me. I know my *A*s from my *R*s, but I just can't see what sense they make all jumbled up together."

"I'm sure we'll find something." Maggie kept digging, and there, yes, she found several children's books. More folk and fairy tales, and oh, thank God . . . a child's reader. She opened it to the first page. *The Eclectic First Reader for Young Children, consisting of progressive lessons in reading and spelling, mostly in easy words of one and two syllables.* "But where did you get this? It's perfect!"

"Wanted some books, you know, and so there was this teacher, got lost on his way to Waterton, and wandered over into here. You'd be surprised how many people get lost." Beth grinned. "Course, maybe the fact we're handy with road signs accounts for that."

"Are there more?"

"Might be. He had a bunch of books. I looked at the pictures, but they were pretty dull."

Maggie dug in the trunk. Yes, there were more readers. Along with this, *The Eclectic First*, were the second, third and fourth. As well, she found the *Pictorial Primer*. As helpful as this was, it seemed an insurmountable task. To teach someone to read in a few days? Impossible. It was like a fairy-tale task, where the maiden must spin straw from gold, or empty the sea with a slotted spoon.

"Can you pull your chair over? I'll sit on the trunk. That way we can both see the book." She picked up the candle and put it between them. "All right, let's see where we stand. Do you know the sound of letters? If I point here, do you know what the letter is?"

"It's a *B*."

"Yes. And the one after it?"

"An *O*, two *O*s."

"And the next?"

"A *K*."

"Can you tell me what a *B* sounds like?"

Beth made the sound. "Buh."

"Yes. Good, now the *O*s, what do they sound like?"

Beth looked puzzled and said, "Is it the same if there's only one?"

"What would one sound like?"

"Same as it's called?"

"Close, sometimes it sounds like uuhh, so the *B* and the two *O*s would be buuhh . . ."

Beth practiced the sounds, with her dirty fingernail against the page.

"It's a kind of magic, reading. The letters are like a clue to the sound, and then, when you learn to make a connection between the way a word looks and the way it sounds, it pops into your mind. So, if we take the buuhh and add a *K* sound onto it, what do we get?"

Beth started with the *B* sound and moved, with only minor difficulty, into the *O*s, getting them not quite right. At the *K* she came out with a word that sounded a bit like *bouquet*.

"Almost," said Maggie. "But shorten it. Just make the sound of the letter; don't repeat the name of it. Buuhh . . ."

Beth scowled. She pressed her finger into the paper, leaving a smudge. "Buh – uuhh –" Then she moved her finger to the top of the page, to the illustration of two little girls and a little boy. The girls were in long dresses and the boy wore short pants and a frilly collar. The girl in the middle was older than the other children and she held a book, from which she appeared to be reading. Beth's finger hovered over the drawing, as her brow furrowed and she made buh-buh-buh noises. Then, suddenly, she poked the book the older girl held. "*Book! Book*, it's *book*." She pointed at two more places on the page where the word appeared.

Beth shone with effort and delight and Maggie thought she looked like a young girl. The candle's flame sparked. "That's it exactly," she said. "Well done."

"Do it again," said Beth. "Give me another word."

"What a wonderful way of putting it. We'll begin. I'll read the page aloud, and then you can try."

Beth nodded and chewed on her lower lip. "It's hard."

"Once you get the hang of it, you'll be amazed at what lies between the pages of a book," Maggie began. "Lesson one. The New Book. Here is John. There are Ann and Jane. Ann has a new book. Ann must keep it nice and clean."

Beth said, "I smudged it."

"That doesn't matter," said Maggie.

"Yes, it does. I want to wash my hands. You stay here. Don't move."

Maggie thumbed through the books and found charts of sounds and discussions of diphthongs and exceptions, regular and irregular sounds. It was confusing. She'd never teach Beth to read in time. Books on history, geography, biology. She wasn't sure what she expected to find . . . something magical perhaps. A book with a red botanical illustration on the cover caught her eye. It was a compendium of properties contained in different fruits, seeds, plants and trees. The cover drawing was a pomegranate, cut in half so that the tough outer rind revealed the sweet red seeds within. Pomegranates? That reminded Maggie of something, but what? Pomegranate seeds! The dream . . . healing pomegranates. The little enamel box with Mr. Strundale's gifts to her, one of which was a pomegranate seed.

CHAPTER EIGHTEEN

S HE DOVE FOR HER PACK AND FOUND THE BOX. She shook the seed into her palm. It wasn't an ordinary seed. This was firm as glass, more like a bead than a seed. But what to do with it? Beth would be back any moment. She picked it up and held it between her thumb and forefinger. It glowed like a little ruby heart, lit from within with the tiniest of flames. Should she eat it? Get Beth to eat it? As she lowered her hand to the book in her lap, the seed flared brightly. Of course. She could already read, but Beth could not.

Beth's footsteps sounded, and Maggie tucked the tiny seed in her pocket. Beth entered and held out her hands for inspection. From the redness, Maggie thought she must have scrubbed them with a wire brush. The nails gleamed.

"Beth has a new book," she said, grinning. "She must keep it nice and clean."

"Excellent. Let's get back to work," said Maggie.

A while later, Maggie said her throat was scratchy from so much talking, and surely Beth's must be as well. Did she want something to drink? Perhaps some tea, and with honey, if they had such a thing.

"I'd rather have beer," said Beth.

"Well, it's best to concentrate when doing such hard work." Maggie wasn't sure what it would be best to hide the seed in but thought putting it in something hot and sweet might help it dissolve, or do whatever it was supposed to do. Beth grunted and said Maggie would find what she needed in the storeroom. They acquired all sorts of delicacies from travellers, and she might even find some biscuits. Beth said she'd take the dogs out for a break.

Maggie headed for the storeroom and as she neared it, Winnie called out. She sat on a stool near the front entrance, working a churn. "Where do you think you're going, missy?"

"Beth wants me to make tea and look for biscuits."

"Tea and bloody biscuits, is it? Aren't we la-de-da? What are you two doing in there, anyway?"

"I'm telling Beth about what I saw in Wallis Tilden's town. Is it all right? And would you like a cup of tea? I'd be happy to bring you one."

Winnie snorted. "Tea? Not likely." She stopped churning, picked a wineskin up from the floor, held it above her head and sent a stream of red wine into her open mouth, only a little of it trickling down her chin. "Go on, then," she said. "Back to what you were doing."

Maggie stepped into the storeroom and stopped short. Shelves lined the room, four rows high, and on them were flour, sugar, pecans, honey, molasses, candied ginger, pickled eggs, coffee, tea (six canisters of various blends), dried beans, salt, smoked hams, cans of smoked oysters, jams (quince, strawberry, rosehip and blackberry), bottles of wine and spirits, pickled beets, pears in wine, sardines, wheels of cheese ... The robbing business must be going well. She picked a canister of strong tea, as well as lavender honey and a tin of cardamom-scented shortbread.

Back in the hall, she made tea over the fire, boiling the water in a smoke-scarred kettle. Four little boys in filthy leggings and soot-blackened shirts raced around near her, the braver one – a red-haired boy with a face full of freckles and two missing front teeth – dashing near to touch her, as though on a dare. Maggie opened the biscuit tin and held one out. There was much poking and jostling, but finally he tiptoed over, much as an untamed fox would, snatched the cookie and raced back to his siblings. He stuffed it in his mouth and from the astonished look on his face Maggie guessed he didn't get cookies very often. Maggie held out a handful of cookies and after a moment's hesitation, the boys rushed her, nearly knocking her into the fire. They grabbed the cookies and retreated to their lairs in the shadows.

Poor wild things, Maggie thought, which is when another idea began to form. She made the tea, strong and black, and poured it into two earthenware mugs. She stirred in the honey and slipped the pomegranate seed into Beth's cup. It sank to the bottom, as any seed would, and for a moment her stomach pitched, thinking she'd wasted it, but then it floated to the top and blossomed into a small golden drop of light, which for a second illumined the inside of the cup, and then, *poof,* it was gone.

She returned to Beth's room, with the biscuit tin tucked under her arm. Maggie sipped her tea and handed the other cup to Beth, who blew on it and then drank. Maggie held her breath. She put down her cup and opened the tin. "Have a biscuit?"

"Don't mind if I do," said Beth. She dipped the biscuit in the tea and then ate it in one bite. "Good. Give us another."

"You have so much food in the larder," said Maggie. "Why bother with the rabbits?"

"You never know how long it's going to be between travellers." She took a big mouthful of tea. "We had an awful hungry winter a few years back. Best to keep the stores full."

"Ah. Shall we get back to work?"

"The boys," read Beth, "rrrr – an . . . no, *run.*"

Maggie watched Beth from the corner of her eye, trying to discern any reaction, any difference. "Very good."

"'One of the boys,'" Beth continued, and then stopped. "Is that right?"

"It is."

"Huh. 'Th-th-they run as f-f-f-is' no *fast* as they can.'"

"Oh, excellent." Maggie's pulse began to race.

The big woman grinned and slurped her tea. "Feels a bit tingly."

Beth looked at the illustration of two running boys, taking a long drink. She said, "'One of the boys has no hat.'" And then she laughed, pointing at the sentence. "See, that's it, isn't it? 'One of the boys has no hat.'" She drained her cup and put it down on the floor.

"Yes, yes, go on!" Was it just Maggie's imagination, or did Beth's features seem less heavy, lighter somehow? And something else as well, the room didn't smell quite so fetid. She sniffed. Lavender? How bizarre. Must be from the honey.

"'Here is a small dog. He has the boy's hat. The boys . . .'" She tilted her head. "'. . . cannot get it.'" She flipped the page. "'The horse eats hay. The hay is on the ground. The hay is made of grass.'" She stopped and unbuttoned her jacket, flapping it to create a breeze. "Has it gotten hot in here?"

"It might be all that learning catching up with you." Maggie glanced around the room, looking for the source of the lavender scent. The window, which had previously been a hole to only blackness, was clear now. The light shone in through panes of green and golden glass. Her eyes widened. The walls no longer seemed so damp. The straw mattress was plump and clean looking, and from the way Oso sniffed it, was probably the source of the lavender.

Beth took off her jacket and tossed it on the straw. And then she noticed the changes in the room. "What's happening here?"

"I'm not quite sure. Could it be the reading?"

"Is it magic, then?" The dogs, sensing something was up,

whined, sat up and stared at her. Oso wagged her tail. "Let's see about that."

Beth pawed through the trunk – on which the brass fittings now shone – until she found another reader, *The Eclectic Third Reader*. She opened it and ran her finger over the page. Then she began laughing so hard she sputtered and wiped her eyes. "'One day his wife,'" she read, "'on going to the bath, left the in- the in- the infant to her husband's care. Begged him not to leave the cradle until she came back. Scarcely' . . . what's that? 'Scarcely, how- however, had she left the house when the king sent for her husband. To refuse the royal sum . . . mons, was im-impossible.' He's going to leave the baby? Though his wife said not to?" Her face, far cleaner than a moment before, was a mask of disapproval.

Maggie smiled. Beth was so involved in the story she didn't realize how impossibly well she was reading. But now Beth paled, her eyes on the brocaded chair, which was stainless, all stitching repaired. "What the hell? And look at my pigeons." The cages were clean, without any droppings or seed husks. The metal gleamed. The birds cooed. A shaft of sunlight pooled on the floor, so inviting even Maggie wanted to curl up in it like a cat. "What magic is this?" Beth stood and dropped the book.

Maggie picked it up and handed it back to her. She thought it best not to mention that not only did the room look much improved, but Beth herself was changed. Her clothes and face were clean. Even her hair shone. "I won't deny there's magic afoot here. And perhaps . . . well, I'm just thinking aloud of course, but is it possible you awakened it? I've never seen anyone learn so fast."

Beth scratched her head. "I know I'm smart, but . . . magic?"

"It's possible. And good magic, clearly. If I had to guess I'd say it's because the power of story has come here at last. Story has *such* power. Why don't you read a little more? I suspect there may be something in it for you. That's one of the great gifts of reading – to learn that others have felt as you have."

Beth frowned and ate another biscuit. "I don't know about that. But if it's magic it's about goddamn time we had some of that around here." She stood and pulled back the curtain on the door, peering into the hall. "Seems all the same out there."

"Why not read on, and see what happens?"

Beth took a deep breath. "'The husband, the-there-therefore'– Well, look at me reading the big words – 'went to the palace straight away, leaving the child to the care of his favourite dog. When the father returned from court the dog ran out to meet him, and as the man bent to praise him, he saw the dog was stained with blood and the man imagined he had killed the child.'" Beth stopped reading and glared at Oso. "Stupid dog ate the baby. World's so hard on little things." Her eyes glistened. "It's like this everywhere then, is it? Not just here with us?"

Beth looked so miserable, so deflated and beaten. Maggie touched Beth's shoulder. She flinched, but allowed it. Maggie kept her hand there for a moment and then took it away. "Pain is like the wind. It gets in everywhere, blows at every door."

Beth considered this. She looked down at her hands, at the cuffs of her shirt, worn and frayed a few moments ago, and now crisp and clean. She turned back to the book. "'The man rushed inside the house and found the cradle over-overturned, and the child gone. In fury, he struck the dog a killing blow with his walking stick. He turned the cradle over, fearful of what he would see, but there beneath he found the child safe, and a large snake lying dead in a corner, its head bloody and its neck broken.' I'll be trussed up and tarred," she said. "He should'a known. Poor dog. Saved the kid and what thanks does he get for it?" Beth crossed the room to where Oso and Badger sat. She crouched down next to Oso and took the dog's face between her hands. "You woulda protected the babe, wouldn't you?" Oso's tongue lolled and her tail thumped the floor.

"So, what do you think the story's asking us to think about?"

"Think about? Do I have to think about things as well as read them? More work than I thought, but the reading part's easy enough. Don't know why I couldn't figure it out before." Beth scratched Oso's ears and sat down on the floor. Oso lay down beside her and put her great bristly head in Beth's lap. She stroked her. "Well, it wasn't fair, and he didn't wait to think things through. He didn't trust his dog."

"I'm seeing certain similarities here, aren't you? No, really. You didn't trust Oso, did you? At least you didn't trust her to obey you unless you forced her."

"Maybe."

Maggie was quite sure Beth blushed a little. "Forgive me, but can you be trusted?"

This question seemed to surprise Beth. "I'm good as my word," she said. "Can't no one say different. I tell you I'm going to do something, I do it. I tell you I'm going to cut you open neck to nuts, well then, that's what I'm going to do."

"Not precisely what I was thinking," said Maggie. "But fair enough. Do you trust, say, Oso? To do what you tell her, like the dog in the story?"

"I suppose."

"So, if it appeared she'd done something out of character, would you assume the worst, or give her the benefit of the doubt until you discovered the truth? You wouldn't just condemn Oso, would you?"

"I guess not."

"Of course you wouldn't, but perhaps in the heat of the moment, up until today, you might have forgotten that. Now, since you've read this story, you're more likely to remember, and to take a minute to think before you hit her." Maggie held her palms open. "Stories give us tools we can use later, and they make us feel less alone, and sometimes help us see things from someone else's point of view."

Beth picked up the book of fairy tales and flipped it open

to the middle. "'Prince Milan rode on slowly with his bride without fearing any further pursuit.'" She smiled broadly. "I can read. Really read."

The soft light of late afternoon filled the room. "Yes, you can. I told you I would try and teach you, and I did."

The smile disappeared. "You're going to say I don't need you anymore."

"I was going to say you might do something wonderful. You might," she raised her eyebrows, "become a teacher yourself, and teach the little ones."

"Go on!" Beth guffawed so loudly the pigeons fluttered in their cages.

"They respect you. And you can read now, and you have these books." She picked up one of the primers. "You even have books on how to teach reading. Look, the lesson plans are all set out for you, all you'd have to do is follow them."

Beth took the book but didn't open it. "I'm no teacher. You should teach the brats. Make yourself useful."

Oso rolled onto her back, her paws held limply in the air, and Beth absently rubbed her belly.

"Beth, I have to go. I have to find Kyle and I think you want to help me."

"What I want, I get and what I get, I keep."

"But every hour that passes is another hour in which I might lose him."

Beth wouldn't look at her. "I had enough to deal with when he disappeared. If I were to let you go, too, Winnie might be angry enough to rethink making me her heir."

Desperation was a sharp-clawed ferret in Maggie's belly. "Look around this room." The wave of her hand encompassed the once-griseous window now lucent; the once-malodorous bedding now fragrant with lavender; the once-shit-spattered pigeon cages now polished; even Beth herself, skin shining, eyes bright with knowledge. "It's your reading that's done this, not me. And the more people you teach to read, the more reading you do, the more the magic will take root and spread. Consider this. With books you have everything. You have the whole wide world. You could learn any number of skills, you and everyone else here. You wouldn't have to rely on robbing people, which you must admit is a fairly uncertain living."

"Hey now, we're good at what we do. You've seen the larder."

"If you don't mind living alone in the forest in a broken-down ruin of a once-glorious hall."

"Is a bit drafty."

"Not to mention uncomfortable and smelly. When horrible weather sets in people must get sick."

"Lost two of the kids a couple of winters back." She ran her hands over the dry, sunlit stone. "Better now, though." She stood. "Stay here."

In her captor's absence, Maggie took stock of the room. While its condition was an improvement on what it had been, she really had no way of knowing if it was a glamour that would fade away in time. What was the quality of magic, in this place or any other? Perhaps it depends on faith, or work, or both.

Beth returned. "Seems to be just this room for now. But much as I hate to admit it, I think you might be right. It feels so," she tapped her chest with her fist, "in here, in my bones. But I only got the books in this trunk and most of them are just stories. If we're going to learn things – building and trades and so on – we'll need more than that."

"You can learn a lot from stories, but I see what you mean." Maggie thought. "There must be a town nearby. Waterton, you said, right? Surely if there are teachers, there are booksellers. You can buy more books."

"As though anyone's gonna do business with the Castoffs."

"They might if you didn't rob everyone you met." Maggie raised her palms in the air by her shoulders. "I'm just saying."

Beth began pacing. "We Castoffs are who we are and that's

the end of it." She began talking, as though to herself. "If I let you go, Winnie'll have my hide." She whipped the knives from her belt. "Then again, maybe it's time Winnie figured out I ain't no kid," she slashed the knives back and forth, "and she don't get to make all the decisions." She crouched and made jabbing motions. Oso slunk farther into a corner and Maggie kept her arm around Badger. "I can read, can't I? I can learn things, and that's all mine. I made the magic." She swung round to Maggie. "You kept your word." The blades made a whispering sound as Beth sheathed them. "I'll help you," she said.

Before Maggie realized she was going to do it, she launched herself across the room, threw her arms around Beth and kissed her.

"Get off, get off," said Beth.

THEY ATE THEIR EVENING MEAL OF RABBIT STEW, BUT this time with the addition of a smoked ham Beth insisted be brought from the larder. The fire was smoky and stung the eyes. The children fretted and cried. One of the little girls, no more than seven, wandered between the adults whining and wiping her snotty nose on her sleeve. When she neared Brenda, the woman reached out and pinched the child cruelly, making her shriek. The child ran to the shadows, snivelling. A moment or two later Beth stood up, dropped her bowl and spoon in a bucket and walked over to Brenda. She reached down and pinched her sister on the tender skin under her upper arm. Brenda's face went white as she struggled not to give Beth the satisfaction of hearing her cry out. The women's eyes locked. Beth's arm trembled with effort. Even through the sweater Brenda wore, it must have been like having your skin caught in a vise. At last Brenda shrieked and kicked until Beth let go.

"What was that for?" she screamed.

"Next time you feel like pinching someone, pinch me, why don't you?" Beth went back to her stool beside Maggie and sat down. "Goddamn bullies around here, the bunch of you."

Winnie took a long swig from her wineskin and then laughed. "What, had yourself a bath, put on some clean clothes and think you're special? Since when do you give a fart there, missy?"

"Since now. Time we stopped acting like a bunch of feral cats," said Beth.

"That so? That your opinion, is it?" said Winnie, who wasn't laughing any longer.

"It is, as a matter of fact. I've had it up to here, and I ain't gonna stand for it no more. You all better get used to it." She stood with her feet wide apart, like a tree deeply rooted. "I been doing some thinking, that's right, some *thinking*. And I do believe there'll be changes coming." She hefted her pants. "I'm gonna teach you all to read."

This was met with gales of laughter.

"Get the book," Beth said to Maggie, who ran, snatched up the book of fairy tales and brought it to her.

Beth began to read. "'There was once upon a time a husbandman who had three sons. He had no property to bequeath to them, and no means of putting them in the way of getting a living.'"

The room grew quiet. Then Winnie said, "How'd you learn it?"

Maggie held her breath. If Beth spoke her name it would be another reason to keep her captive.

Beth said, "I just learned is all. I've been studying. And," she drew herself up, "it's brought magic." Amidst a certain amount of derisive snorting, which died away as she spoke, she described the changes to her room, and to her person. Blossom and Brenda ran to peek behind Beth's curtain and when they affirmed that indeed, it wasn't the room it had been, the others crowded round to see.

"This come from reading?" Brenda asked. "From reading a book?"

"I want new clothes, too," said Betty.

"Then you must earn them by learning." Beth dangled her fingers on the hilt of her knives. "And I'm the one's got that knowledge."

Beth stared at her mother with her chin thrust out. Winnie opened her mouth and perhaps she saw something in her daughter's face, or in the casual way Beth rested her hand on the knives in her belt, but she closed her mouth. She turned away from Beth and busied herself with something in the bottom of her bowl. "Tim'll be back soon, you know," she said.

"Let him come," said Beth with a small, thin smile. "If he's good I'll even teach him."

Winnie stood and arched her back, her hand on her sacrum. "Magic," she snorted. "Who's to say you just haven't been cleaning?" She held her hand up to silence her daughter. "I'm stiff as a board and getting too old to be spending my remaining days doing nothing but herding you bunch of wildcats." Her back cracked and she bent side to side. "Might just be time I let the younger generation take the reins. You think you can do better? Let's see you try." She spat on the ground. "Disappointments, every last one of you. You and Tim can sort it as far as I'm concerned." Winnie wiped her hands on her skirt and said, "Go on, go to bed, before I do something I regret."

Beth stepped toward her mother, her hands in fists, and for a moment Maggie thought the two would come to blows, but Winnie turned her back, and Beth merely huffed and relaxed her fingers. Beth half turned to Maggie and, with a jerk of her chin, drew Maggie's attention to the pot hanging from the tripod over the cooking fire. It gleamed, the copper radiating like a miniature sun. Maggie grinned. Beth told her to go back to the room and take Badger with her; she was going to check on the hogs.

In Beth's room, Maggie sat on the step (on a now-plump pale yellow pillow) under the window. Beyond the clear panes, the stars looked so familiar and yet so utterly strange. The apple tree in the neglected orchard reminded her of home.

A few minutes later, Oso scampered through the curtain door and ran to Maggie, wriggling, nuzzling and pawing at her. "Good girl, stop it now." Badger joined in and it took a moment to get the dogs settled down. Oso sat for a second and then jumped up and whined, standing at the doorway.

"You want me to come?"

Oso play-bowed, tail wagging.

"Shush, then, shush. All right." Instinct told Maggie she should take her pack. She also had to avoid people and so wouldn't go out by the door. She called Oso to her, opened the window, heaved Badger up and out, then Oso, and then jumped down herself. If she was wrong she'd have a hell of a time explaining it to Beth, but she hoped it wouldn't come to that. She and Badger followed Oso to a large pigsty enclosed by a fence. Beth sat on the topmost rail, a long pole in her hand. Maggie could make out four enormous hogs. Three lay near a slop trough. The eyes of one glinted in the dark. The other rooted in the earth near Beth. He flicked his tail and ears. Beth turned to Maggie as she approached.

"I think Oso wanted us to come with her," said Maggie.

Beth grunted. "That dog might amount to something after all." She prodded the hog at her feet with the pole and the beast grunted. "I come out here to think sometimes. The hogs are peaceful creatures."

Beth swung her legs to the open side of the fence and jumped down. She propped the pole up on the fence and rubbed the owl on her cheek with her thumb. "You see this owl, right? When I was a little girl Winnie's aunt, who saw things, said she saw this in me. Wisdom, she said. And secrets. And death.

Well, I've had my share of some more'n others. But until you came," she pointed her thumb at Maggie, "I wouldn't rightly say I had much wisdom. This reading business, I don't know how you managed it, since I've been looking at those letters for years and getting nothing back but sore eyes. Some magic underpinning it all, I'm sure. Yes, you might well blush. Keep your own counsel, but answer me this, and mind well your answer – does it wear off?"

"I honestly don't know. But I don't think so. It seems to be spreading, don't you think? Even into the hall. I believe if you keep reading, and if you teach others to do the same, the magic will grow."

Beth's gaze on her was steady, examining, probing, more like a dissection than query. It was entirely possible the magic was working on an even deeper level. Wisdom. Perception.

Beth blinked at last and nodded. "I agree. I made a decision – yes, I'm going to teach the little ones."

"They might not learn as quickly as you. You'll have to have patience."

"They'll learn. And when they do things might be different. In time."

"I'm glad for you, for you all. But what does that mean for me?"

"Speaking of patience, you might be better at it yourself."

"Fair enough," said Maggie.

"It means I owe you, and I pay my debts." She tucked her thumbs over her knife hilts. "I expect you should be on your way."

"Thank you," said Maggie, quickly. "Will you get in much trouble?"

"I'd like to see anyone try and give me trouble. Winnie's ready to step back, that's clear or she wouldn't have let me get this far. She knows what's up. She's a crafty old biddy. She'll back me. Tim'll fall into line and that'll be that, or it won't," she tapped her knife with her thumb, "and then we'll have a little fun." Beth took a piece of jerky from her pocket and fed it to Badger. "This kindness thing is getting to be a habit. I just hope it won't be a bad one. All right, I see it comes as no surprise to you, given as how you've brought your pack, but if you're going, we best get on with it."

Maggie hugged her. "You won't regret it."

Beth led them to a track between the sty and another shed. The track led steeply down and even in the light of the full moon (was the moon *always* full here?) one had to take care not to slip. As the path descended, the ground rose on either side until they were walking through a narrow canyon between rock walls. Maggie grabbed the moss growing on the stone to keep her footing as the shale shifted beneath her feet.

Then, quite suddenly, the walls ended, and they stood in front of a mirror-calm lake. The moon's light was a silver streak along the surface. A fish jumped and the circles seemed to flow outward forever. It was a pebble beach, and behind them the great rock face loomed. Tied off to a large boulder was a boat. The bow curved up and over, reminiscent of a stem, and indeed there were two smaller curves, like sprouts, so that the entire boat looked like an overturned, deeply concave leaf. From the two sprouts hung lanterns.

"That's the prettiest boat I've ever seen," said Maggie.

"It's a nice little thing, ain't it?" Beth lit the lanterns. The flames' reflection twinkled on the water.

"Did you build it?"

"I might have," said Beth. "Bit of a hobby."

Maggie whistled through her teeth. "You've a real talent. I have a friend who knows boats, and he'd love this." She pictured Alvin running his hand over the gunwale from bow to transom, clucking his tongue and saying, *Oh, yes, a handsome piece of work. Look at the hull on her, deep and smooth as can be. Rudder strong and true.* "He'd say, 'Goddamn, woman, I am impressed!'"

Maggie laughed, thinking of him, and there was a pang in her heart.

Beth beamed. "Ah, just put it together from scraps and such."

High up, about halfway on the cliff ledge, something moved. A determined tree had taken root in a crevice and a large raven flapped its wings as it settled on a branch, making the whole thing shake precariously. It sharpened its beak on the wood.

"Right, I've wasted enough time on you." Beth fumbled in her pants pocket and then pulled out a silver bird hair clip. "Might as well have this back; it's not like I'm going to wear it."

Maggie took Beth's hand in hers and closed the woman's calloused fingers around the small figure. "I'd be honoured if you'd keep it. Perhaps if you don't want to wear it yourself, you'll find someone you want to give it to one day."

Beth snorted, but pocketed it. "Well, take the boat and keep straight with the moon-river path, as we call it." Her face showed shadows of past sorrows. "That's the way he went. I think you're a fool for going after him, but you're right you can't stay here and there's no going back, as you've found. Forward's all there is."

"I'm sorry to take your boat, Beth," Maggie said.

"Don't be. Leave it at the other side, but don't tie it off. It'll find its way home."

And with that the big woman turned her back, crossed the pebble beach and disappeared into the crevice in the cliffs, Oso at her heels.

Maggie grabbed the lines, pulled the boat closer to shore and tossed in her pack. "C'mon, Badger. Faster and farther the better."

Badger jumped in as she untied the line and pushed the boat into deeper water before heaving herself over the side. As the boat glided across the water Maggie wondered what it would be like for Beth, reading those books without anyone to interpret what was in them for her. Surely learning without a teacher could be dangerous. On the other hand, books were a very good way out of a dark wood.

Maggie looked behind her. Apparently, she would not be going back. Although the moon-river path lay in front of the boat clear as silver on black velvet, behind them the blackness had swallowed the beach and the cliffs and all that lay beyond. Maggie felt as though someone had dripped ice water down her back and she shivered. Badger curled up under the seat, his nose to his tail, although he wasn't sleeping. A wind came up, pushing in the direction they travelled. There's a bit of luck, she thought. She unfurled the sail and adjusted the line as the wind filled it. This really was a fine little boat, she thought. It rode the lake like a bright horse.

From the portside two dark shapes flew toward the boat. The ravens landed on the bow's curling stems, next to the lanterns. Badger barked, and the birds clacked their beaks and cawed, then tucked their heads under their wings and promptly went to sleep.

She wondered if they'd been waiting for her all this time and then she pondered how much time had passed since she'd left home. How long had Kyle been in this strange world? It would drive a person mad. She looked at Badger, fast asleep. He was a wise dog. She realized how exhausted she was. Every bone ached as though weighted with iron. She tied the rudder in place with her scarf, slipped off the seat and curled up next to Badger. He heaved a great sigh and before she heard him finish the exhalation she was asleep.

MAGGIE DREAMS . . .

She and Kyle are walking in a deep and tangled wood. They have been wandering for days and they are terribly thirsty.

A spring of clear water appears before them and Kyle rushes toward it, bending his head to drink.

Just as he does, Maggie hears terrible growls, and the sound of claws scratching against stone.

"Kyle! Do not drink! Step back; if you drink you will be turned into a horrible beast and you will tear me to pieces." She sees it in her mind – the teeth and the shredding of her flesh, the pitiless eyes of the beast, part tiger, part wolf.

Kyle turns to her and smiles, and his teeth are red. Maggie runs to pull him back from the water's edge but he bends and his head is below the surface before she can reach him.

In an instant, her brother, the soft fragile boy she knows, is gone and in his place squats a huge yellow-and-black-furred creature, thick of haunch and neck, and snarling, turning toward her, hunching, ready to pounce . . .

Kyle is so thirsty. He feels as though he has been walking in this dark wood longer than the trail of his memory. Through the trees comes the sound of water burbling and he races to it, bending his head to drink.

Just as he does, he hears his sister calling to him. She stands on the other side of the spring. She is filthy, her teeth are rotten, her clothes tattered and stinking. Snakes curl through her hair. "Kyle! Don't drink! If you drink you will be lost to me forever!"

"No loss to me," says Kyle. He drinks, and the water is as sweet as the wine of frozen grapes.

Power surges through him, he is thrumming with it. His muscles bunch and flex; his member becomes erect. Maggie has disappeared and in her place is the woman he seeks. She wears only argent fog and her long white hair. He hunches, leaps and pounces on her, and she opens herself to him.

CHAPTER NINETEEN

DAWN WAS BREAKING IN A TANGERINE BLAZE, setting the landscape in harsh relief. The little boat floated toward a pier. Beyond, on the slopes leading from the lake's edge, village lights twinkled. The air was clear, but thick dark blue and orange clouds, like the rippled surface of an upside-down lake, adorned the sky. Such clouds signalled approaching hard weather and a bad day for travel. Maggie's breath fogged around her face. When she had woken a little earlier, the first thing she'd noticed was that the ravens were gone. Badger shook, rocking the boat, and then kissed her. She stretched her chin as the dog's hot tongue flicked her neck. "I don't know what you're so happy about." She scratched his ears. Badger cocked his head and perked up his ears. Maggie's teeth began to chatter. She held Badger close to steal some of his warmth and wrapped her scarf around her head and ears.

Badger hopped from the boat, sniffing around and lifting his leg against a pylon. Maggie stepped out, her pack slung over her shoulder. She held the line in fingers stiff with cold. The line went taut in her grip as the boat pulled away. The rope tugged. She was either going to have to let go or be dragged. "Have it your way." She let go.

The boat slipped back, turned and steadily, but without haste, returned the way it had come. The lanterns bobbed in a jolly sort of way. In a few minutes, it had disappeared.

"Well, that's that." She scratched Badger's head. "We've got to get in out of this cold or we're done for. I could use a cup of coffee, a bath and a long sleep."

She started toward the village. The pier had only two small rowboats tied to it, neither in good condition, and the pier itself was in dire need of repairs. Many of the boards were soft with rot and she had to watch where she stepped for fear of falling through. The pier ended at the same sort of pebble beach as on the other side of the lake, but instead of great cliffs, the land rose in a gentle snow-covered hill. Buildings faced the lake, and several lanes led to dwellings on the hillside that were constructed from mismatched boards of red, yellow, blue and green. Windows were of every size and shape. Chimneys tilted. The whole place looked as though it was built with odds and ends. Yet it was an oddly cheerful facade.

The wind whipped, and snow pricked her face. Her feet were numb, as were her fingers. She tucked her hands under her armpits. The village looked deserted and just as she wondered how she'd go about finding anyone she heard the ravens' caws. They swooped down and flew to a sign over a door, flapped their wings a few times and then flew off again, quickly disappearing. Maggie walked toward the building. It was a tavern. The sign read, *The Fish and Fiddle*. A painted flounder played the fiddle and smiled at the weary traveller.

The tavern was attached to a row of buildings and seemed not much wider than the door that came barely to the top of Maggie's head. She knocked. Badger sniffed along the walls and then the bottom of the door. His tail wagged. She knocked again, and the door opened to reveal a woman with a smiling face as wrinkled as a dried apricot. She wore a long burgundy skirt and a quilted jacket of the same fabric. A red scarf tied under her chin secured a red hat. The jacket, hat and scarf were all embroidered with yellow flowers and green vines. Her merry blue eyes held not the least surprise at seeing a strange woman and a dog upon her threshold.

"You're early on the road, my pets. Come in, come in. Weather on the way."

Badger sniffed the woman's skirt and wagged his tail. The old woman put down her hand and Badger licked it.

As the crone stepped aside Maggie thanked her and ducked so as not to whack her forehead on the lintel. The three crowded through a tight-fit hallway, with only enough space to walk single file. Badger kept trying to push past Maggie. She was afraid she'd trip on him and was starting to feel claustrophobic, but as they walked farther into the tavern the ceiling rose and the walls broadened. By the time they reached the end of the hall the beams were a good two feet or more over her head. Maggie followed her hostess into a room in which a cheery fire blazed on a stone hearth, filling the air with the scent of pine and cedar. Four well-used, overstuffed chairs crowded round the fireplace. Scattered about the room were chairs and tables, and a bar with three stools filled the far end. Emerald, amber, garnet and crystal bottles of various shapes and sizes glittered from shelves. Deep casement windows let in the early morning light, but when Maggie looked, she could make out nothing but cloudy grey shapes. She assumed the clouds she'd noticed on arrival had descended and the hard weather was about to begin. It was a bit unsettling, as though the tavern wasn't in the cramped, if gay, little town, but perched on the edge of some great cloud-hung mountain.

Maggie shivered. Badger sniffed here and there – along the floor, the baseboards, around the bar – and then plopped down on the carpet in front of the fire and heaved an enormous sigh.

"The dog seems at home, now let's make you feel the same

way and you can tell me all about your travels," said the woman. "Sit, sit."

Gratefully, Maggie sat by the fire and peeled off her gloves, hat and scarf, stretching out her fingers to the dancing flames. The woman brought her a tankard of hot spiced cider with a cinnamon stick in it. Maggie held the tankard between her hands and let the fragrant steam warm her face. She sipped. It was sweet and rich and ran like a little molten stream down her throat into her stomach. She thought she'd never tasted anything quite so delicious and said so. She was rewarded with another smile.

"Should banish the chill." The old woman sat in a chair next to Maggie and clapped her hands. "My name is Aunt Ravna, and who are you?"

Maggie told her.

"And what on earth brings you to Lake's End?"

"Is that where I am?" asked Maggie.

"If it isn't I'd like to know where I am!" Aunt Ravna laughed so hard at her own joke she had to wipe tears from her eyes.

Maggie didn't think it was that funny but thought it would be rude not to laugh along and so she chuckled lightly, and then the chuckle turned into a chortle and the chortle into a giggle. Her giggles turned into cackles and the cackles into belly-clutching guffaws and the guffaws into the kind of sound-less, open-mouthed, foot-stomping laughter that was very difficult to stop and resulted in tears and hiccups.

Maggie assumed it must be a reaction to all the strange things she'd been through, and the travel, and the fatigue, and she didn't really care why, in the end. It just felt wonderful.

When she finally caught her breath, the old lady said, "Oh, that's much better. I always find nothing warms a person up quite so well as a good chuckle. And if there's nothing to laugh at, it's just a question of laughing at what there is, don't you think? But where are my manners? I must be getting old, although that's what I said fifty years ago, I'm quite sure. You sit here and I'll bring you something to eat, shall I, which goes ever so well with something to drink, as does the reverse, of course, and then you can tell me all there is to tell."

Aunt Ravna slapped her hands on her knees and tottered off somewhere in the back of the tavern.

"Oh, dear," said Maggie, lolling in the comfortable chair and gazing at the fire. She wondered if this might not be another trick of a place like Mother Ratigan's. She felt herself sliding into sleep and pinched the back of her hands. Kyle's face swam before her. *I need you. Follow me . . .* As she stared into the fire she fancied she saw tiny figures with pointy shoes and pointy hats and sharp little fingers. They danced round a mirror and laughed and laughed . . .

"All right now, my possum, let's get some food into you."

Aunt Ravna wheeled in a butler's tray loaded with plates of scrambled eggs with cheddar cheese, and rashers of bacon, and toast and butter and jam, and a pot of apple cider to refill their tankards.

"Did you think I forgot you?" said Aunt Ravna to Badger, who'd woken at the scent of food. Aunt Ravna disappeared briefly and returned with two bowls, one of water and the other filled with stew that smelled so good Maggie wouldn't have minded eating it. Badger's tail thumped. "That's a good boy," Aunt Ravna said and he began eating.

Once Maggie began her meal, Aunt Ravna asked her to tell her story. Maggie did her best, and the more she talked, the more she found she trusted this ancient woman. There was a great calmness about her. The room was so homey and the old woman's demeanour so placid, she couldn't help but open her heart. Badger's deportment also reassured her, for he lay on the rug with his legs out behind him, completely at ease. Although she knew it would be prudent to keep a few facts back, she couldn't deny she felt a great relief at not having to keep it all bottled up.

"Oh, I know all about the Castoffs," said Aunt Ravna, sipping from a tankard of her own and making a tut-tutting noise. "Poor lambs. All the little ones, half wild, and the adults up to all sorts. There's no need for it. They'd be welcome here. Heaven knows I've plenty of room."

"Wouldn't your neighbours object?"

"They're good people here. You'll meet them later in the day. Most stop in for a wee chat and a dram."

"I don't think the Castoffs feel welcome anywhere."

"Yes, well, robbing people does lead to that. Although the truth is, from what I've heard, people on the other side of the lake often travel with a good deal of things they don't need, as a way to get supplies to people too proud for charity. But there is the issue of hostages, which is their new game, apparently." She tut-tutted again and looked serious. "If only there was some way to educate them."

"Well, that might change. The oldest daughter has learned to read."

"Oh? And did you have a hand in that?"

Maggie blushed. "A little, maybe."

"Did you? How extraordinary. How did you manage it?"

"I had some help."

Aunt Ravna nodded. "Well, however you did it, if there's a reader among them I think we'll see changes. Perhaps not right away, but learning does have a way of taking hold. You've done a good thing, young woman."

Maggie dropped her gaze and chewed her lip. Knowing she'd done it primarily because she was hoping to influence Beth in her favour didn't make it feel like a selfless act.

Aunt Ravna regarded her. "There are times when we are used in ways we can't understand. We must trust that. Our motives, even if they're not entirely pure, do not negate our usefulness, don't you agree?"

"I suppose." Outside the window a blizzard now blew. A hard gale.

"Good. Now, the question is, do you know where your brother is, precisely? All you've told me is that this drug caused him to travel here, to this world. The problem is, like all worlds, it's rather big. Do you think you can narrow it down just a tad?"

Maggie was loath to reveal too much. Who knew how Srebrenka was thought of on this side of the lake? "He was *called*, from what I understand."

Aunt Ravna put her tankard down on the table and leaned forward. "Called? Called by whom?"

"I was hoping you could tell me."

"There's only one person capable of that sort of thing, I'm afraid. Someone who feeds off pain. This is a bad business. *She* is bad business."

"You mean Srebrenka."

"Indeed. She who travels in both worlds, who dabbles in things she ought not." Aunt Ravna's eyes widened. "We should have known. You're telling me she gave your brother this drug ... this ..."

Maggie nodded. "Elysium."

"Yes. That does sound like her."

Badger came to Aunt Ravna and rested his head on her knee.

"I know the standard good advice is never to trust anyone who tells you to trust them," said Aunt Ravna, "but I hope in this case you'll let your very wise friend here vouch for my good intentions. You'll come to no harm here, and we'll do all we can to help you. It is our job, you see, just as caring for the Grimoire is yours. We are a way station for travellers, and we have a few other tasks as well, but principally, we are a refuge. When I retire as tavern keeper ... not for decades yet, of course," she giggled, "but when the time comes, my son, Guivi, will take on the title of Uncle." She petted Badger's head and he rolled over on his back, presenting his belly for a rub, which Aunt Ravna obliged, laughing.

Any fears Maggie had about this being another trap dissolved. "It's elysium that allows Kyle, and others, apparently, to move between the worlds. Perception changes. Ultimately, it's impossible to tell what's real from what's not. Madness. Death. It's caused more damage than you can imagine where I come from. No one, once they ride the pipe, escapes."

Aunt Ravna looked at Maggie. "No one? You have battled this, haven't you?"

"Yes," said Maggie in a soft voice. "But I didn't take it again to come here. At least I don't think I did. There was smoke in the room . . . so maybe . . . but I came through a doorway. I didn't take the pipe. It almost killed me, once."

"The point is it did not. Never forget that. Whatever it is you drew upon to save yourself, it's still with you."

"But I don't know why I was spared and so many others aren't."

"It's obvious, isn't it? You surrendered to life, no matter what it held for you, even abandonment, even grief and loss and pain."

Aunt Ravna spoke as though she knew more about Maggie than what Maggie had told her. She shifted in her chair. "I had no choice. It was give up or die."

"There was a choice. There's always a choice, even if not everyone makes it. Tell me about the moment you decided to surrender."

"I'm not sure it was any one moment. A series of moments, perhaps. Each more humiliating, more shameful, more soul-destroying than the next. Waking up in my own filth. Willing to do almost anything to get another pipe."

Aunt Ravna's face remained open, attentive and, to Maggie's relief, without judgment.

"But there was one moment," she said.

Maggie knew what the old woman was talking about. She'd

run out of cash and Srebrenka had thrown her out. She'd wandered through the Forest looking for some way to get more money, but everything, everywhere had been deserted, as though every single person had magically disappeared. At last she'd collapsed in a doorway and passed out. She woke some hours later, cold and sick and terrified. She'd dreamed of burning towers and madwomen in attics who tried to stab her with their long sharp nails. In a terrible moment of clarity, she knew if she spent another night this way she would die. Although every step felt as if she walked barefoot on glass, she dragged herself from the Forest. It took her hours and hours and she knew not how long, until she finally crawled into an alley in Kensington Market and found a stale heel of bread and a bruised pear in a refuse bin. She bit into it and nearly cried out it was so delicious, even as her stomach cramped. She chewed and chewed, and it took a long time for it to go down. She nibbled the bread and told the voice in her head, which whispered how wonderful it would be to lie on a soft blue couch and dream of paradise and plenty, to shut up, *please* shut up.

It was a lucid moment and, with a strange objectivity, she recognized it as such. As though someone had tapped her on the shoulder and said, "Pay attention, dear. Look and see things as they are." Something broke in her. All at once she saw how her life might be if she no longer wanted things to be different. What the world might look like if she didn't mind it being just as it was. This was no one's fault but hers. There was a sort of freedom in that. And so the choice was clear: she could lie down and die right then, and be done with it; or she could get up and keep walking, and see what would happen next, and no matter what is was, she'd let it happen. She stood, and she walked, and walked, and walked, and came to a bookshop she'd never seen before.

"There was one moment," Maggie agreed.

Aunt Ravna's eyes twinkled. "Good, remember that." She

put down her tankard and folded her hands across her middle. "You'll be wanting to go north, then."

"Yes," said Maggie. "Kyle came this way, I think. The Castoff woman said he'd stayed there for a while and then she sent him in the boat, as she did us."

"If he came here, he didn't stop in, and I do believe I know why. The one you want was seen some moons ago. It was remarked upon. She drove a white carriage pulled by an enormous white bear. She brings the snows with her when she comes and ice flies in the wind. Although she's not often seen, we feel her effects. We huddle inside for we're sensible folk. One of the farmers said he thought she wasn't alone, that a man sat next to her on the carriage seat. Although I wonder why she made him come all this way alone, if she wanted him so much. It does seem odd. Why not simply bring him with her when she returned?"

The fire and food were doing their jobs. Maggie felt a great warm weight come over her and feared she'd fall asleep in her chair. "I wonder if Badger and I might stay here tonight? I don't think either of us are up for a journey unless we get some sleep."

The old lady picked up a spoon and polished it with her apron. "Of course you may. The one you want lives at the edge of the world, where north becomes south again. You've a long way before you. Hundreds of miles."

"That far? But we'll never make it!"

"Not on foot. But there are other methods. I've a sled you can have and a caribou to pull it. They are the best for such things; feet as sure as suction cups." She stood up. "But that's for when you've rested."

Maggie was too tired to talk more. She roused Badger and followed Aunt Ravna along another hallway. As they passed a doorway, Maggie glimpsed a huge kitchen with a bank of stoves against one wall, each one with an enormous boiler on top, and each boiler vented out the wall. She wondered if this was how the tavern managed to stay so nice and toasty. Aunt Ravna continued on, and then turned right and stopped before a large wooden door. It opened onto a stone room with arched ceilings and furs on the floor. A great canopy bed stood against one wall and in the corner was a large stone bathtub with taps for hot and cold water.

"That bed looks like heaven," said Maggie. Badger immediately curled up on the fur rug. She put her pack and satchel on the windowsill. The windows looked out on the same thick, featureless whiteness. It made her a little dizzy, all that lack of shape. "You don't have much of a view," she said.

"It's the clouds. This high up the mountain it's mostly clouds, but I like it that way. It makes it rather cozy, don't you think?"

"We didn't seem to be that high up at the lakeside."

"The lakeside? Oh, no. Once you step into the tavern, you're stepping into the mountain."

"I don't recall seeing a mountain."

"Well, that's what clouds are good for – covering up what we don't want seen. Why do you think the Castoffs never raid this side of the lake? It's because we keep things well hidden from those with ill intent. We're very handy with clouds." She chuckled. "You'd be amazed how many people would swear there's nothing at all on this side of the lake except fog and cloud, cloud and fog."

Maggie thought of the great kettles in the kitchen. "You produce the clouds?"

"Bit of a family business. Secrets passed down and all that. We each have our jobs to do, don't we? I just have an affinity for clouds."

If she got home, what stories Maggie would have to tell Alvin. He might talk about the Komodo dragons of Padar, the fur seals of the Galapagos or the Hamamni Persian Baths of Zanzibar, but a cloud-producing tavern ought to at least match those. He might have escaped a scrap or two in Manila or the Yucatán, but she had escaped the Castoff band of robbers.

"But I found the tavern without a problem," she said.

"I'm also a rather good judge of character. People often miss the most obvious things. No fault of their own. The world can be confusing. A little breeze here. A little updraft or downdraft there. Smidgen of moisture in the air. Things can be hidden or revealed, as needs be. Your needs, I perceived, fell more into the area of *revealed*." She giggled and stepped out the door and, as she closed it, said, "Sleep as long as you need, and just pull this bell if you want anything. The others will be getting up soon, but you're off on your own in this wing of the mountain and won't be disturbed. We'll set your plans when you're rested."

And with that she was gone. Nearly comatose, Maggie kicked off her boots, stripped off her clothes and was asleep before her head settled on the pillow.

CHAPTER TWENTY

MAGGIE WOKE FROM A DREAMLESS SLEEP TO FIND Badger on the bed with his head on her legs. She hadn't felt so rested in ages. Judging from the light outside the window, either a full day had passed, or no time at all. She supposed she should get up and have a wash. She sniffed her armpit. Ripe indeed. On one of the chairs by the fire lay her freshly cleaned and pressed clothes and on the floor nearby, her boots, polished to a shine. Maggie got out of bed and held her clean turtleneck up to her face. It smelled of roses. "Heavenly," she said. "I could get used to this."

She bathed and dressed, and then she and Badger headed to the tavern's common room and found it crowded with people dressed in the same style as Aunt Ravna, mostly in embroidered red, the women in hats and scarves as well. Their faces were open, bright, curious and etched with the deep lines that come not only from a good deal of time spent out of doors, but also from smiling and laughing.

"Well, here's the sleeping beauty." Aunt Ravna stood behind the bar and pushed a tankard of spiced cider at Maggie. "Say hello, everyone."

A chorus of hellos and welcomes. "Good to have you with us." "Nice to drop in." "Heard nothing but good things." "What a lovely dog."

Maggie blushed and realized she could hardly think of another time when a group of people had been genuinely glad to see her for no other reason than that she was there. "Most grateful for the hospitality," she said.

"My name is Emel," said a man smoking a pipe, his blue eyes bright as a dragonfly's wing. "I fish the lake and the rivers hereabout. Glad to know you." He held out a calloused hand and Maggie shook it. "Sit down and have a bite."

"How long have we been sleeping?" Maggie's stomach felt like a deflated balloon.

"We didn't like to wake you," said a young woman about Maggie's age, who smiled shyly and fiddled with the buttons on her burgundy jacket. "It's been two days, more or less."

"Two days?" The suspicion must have shown on her face. The group began to laugh and Aunt Ravna told her not to worry, the length of her sleep had nothing to do with enchantments of any kind and only to do with the degree of her exhaustion.

"We did check on you a few times, and thought to wake you, for I know you're in a great rush to be gone, but I made the young ones leave you be. The body knows what it needs and we must listen to the wisdom of that and not be forever fighting it."

"Yes, I can see that, and I thank you. Is there somewhere I can take Badger out? Two days is rather a long time for a dog not to pee."

This struck the group as hilarious and they broke into more guffaws. It was quite contagious and Maggie couldn't help but join in. Badger, however, did not find it quite so funny, and walked over to the edge of the bar and lifted his leg. Maggie feared Aunt Ravna would be angry, but on the contrary, she howled with laughter and the rest joined in with hoots and knee slapping.

"Such a smart dog. How did he know he wasn't the first to do his business on that spot?" asked Aunt Ravna. "Quite right he is, too. Where are my manners?" She laughed some more. "Oh, I must get him a lovely big bone."

"Is there a rag, a bucket? I'll clean it up," said Maggie.

A girl came out of the back room with a sudsy mop and a big grin. "Never mind, I'll do it. I like dogs," she said.

"Eat," said Emel. "There are no worries here."

Women appeared from the kitchen carrying platters. Maggie ate roasted wild goose with stone-bramble jelly, lamb soup, pickled red cabbage and beets, and for dessert cream pancakes. While she ate the people asked her questions about where she came from and found everything amusing. When Maggie tried explaining hockey one of the men laughed so hard he choked and his neighbour had to slap him on the back.

The door opened and in came a roundish sort of man, slapping the snow off his clothes. "Afternoon, all!"

"Guivi! All's well out there?" asked Emel.

"Oh, sure. Mice, voles, all the little ones tucked up under the snow. Food out for the birds, some nice twigs and moss and so forth for the deer. The foxes are all sleepy and I suspect they'll go dormant until it warms up. And this must be Maggie?" He approached her and shook her hand vigorously.

"Sorry I wasn't here when you arrived. Hospitality here extends to the non-humans as well and Mother's a bit too old for stomping around in the deep snow. Pleased to meet you, awfully pleased, glad you're with us. I assume Mother took good care of you?"

He was rather like a young bear, sturdy and plump and ready for fun. Maggie took to him immediately. "Your mother has been wonderful. Everyone has. Thank you."

"Tell him about hockey!" said Emel, and much more laughter followed.

Only when the discussion turned to elysium did the laughter

fail. They bowed their heads, scratched their beards and jiggled their knees. Maggie told them what Mr. Mustby had said about Srebrenka. It wasn't until she was halfway through her tale that she realized she was speaking of him as though Mr. Mustby had stood right in front of her, not as a figure in her dream. Although now, what was dream and what was not wasn't nearly as clear as it had been, and in either case she no longer doubted he'd told her the truth.

"Srebrenka, is it?" Emel snorted. "Oh, she's a piece of work, that one." He stared into his cup of coffee. "We heard she was fiddling with things, experimenting. She always did want more than her fair share of everything, even as a child."

Maggie said, "You've known her since she was a child? Is she from here?"

"No," said Guivi. "Not from here, but near enough. Most people here know each other one way or another. This world is not quite as large, I suspect, as yours. She was always a greedy child and she has grown into a greedy woman. She had the gifts, that's true enough, but didn't want to wait for the wisdom age brings before she used them. She called up creatures we don't speak of, thinking they'd be her servants, but they've made ill use of her. She's caused great harm and has harmed herself."

Maggie told them how Srebrenka's distorting mirror made everything lovely look horrible, and vice versa; about the shards sailing on the wind that blows between worlds, infecting people, and drawing them to her in their pain and misery, using elysium to quicken the process. She told them how her world was changing because of elysium and tried to explain how the Forest was expanding. "I'm afraid it will swallow everything and everyone, that we'll all end up attached to the pipe."

The people of the lakeside now looked very glum indeed.

"I'm sorry to bring you such an awful tale," said Maggie.

"It comes as less of a surprise than you might think," said Aunt Ravna. "Although to you the mountain looks shrouded in mists, you'd be surprised what we see from up here. We knew about the mirror. We didn't know about elysium. She's an impatient one, isn't she?" She rubbed her palms together as though suddenly chilled. "There were millions of shards floating in your world, and many people infected, long before she created this elysium, as you call it. The shards are like magnets, seeking to regroup and rebind. Many of those afflicted come through one of the various doors between worlds, but none, until now, have survived for long. They're in a terrible state when they arrive and it's a long cold journey. The bits of mirror work themselves out, it seems, of their own accord when the host dies, and fly on the wind back to Srebrenka. We've seen some of the bodies. We've been told of others. These are not good things to see. Your brother has fared well, considering. I can't help but think she's taken quite a fancy to him. What do you say, Emel?" She looked at Maggie. "Emel here is nearly older than the mountain and that's a wee bit older even than me."

"Hey now," said Emel. "I'm at my prime, I am." And that gave them cause to giggle again.

"Fair enough, my spring chicken," smiled Aunt Ravna. "But you're the one keeps track of the goings-on here, of the way things work. We each have our gifts. Having heard our Maggie's tale, do you agree on my plan?"

The man considered the fire for some moments. He relit his pipe and puffed thoughtfully. "I would like to say I can think of another way, for it's a hard journey and what you'll find at the end will be, I fear, harder still. I'd like to say you should stay here with us in the mountain and we could teach you how to be happy, because it's the best thing we have. But you've been called just as your brother was, although my feeling is you're called by something far greater than Srebrenka." He reached over and squeezed Maggie's hand. "What Srebrenka's done, and is doing, is entirely wrong, and the expansion of the Forest won't stop at our borders. Her hunger will engulf us all if you don't stop her."

Maggie hadn't considered this. The responsibility was a great stone around her neck. She thought of the little kitchen at the Grimoire. Her blue mug, her kettle, a fire roaring, books to read . . . her own bed . . . Alvin. And nothing but icy waste before her. Mr. Mustby. The ravens. She sighed. It didn't matter. She was a cog in this great wheel. "I don't know whether I'll succeed, but I believe this is meant to be. I'll see it through, whatever that means."

The people raised their glasses and tankards and cups. "Well said," they murmured. "Hear, hear!"

"Right," said Aunt Ravna. "Here's my plan. You'll take the carriage and the caribou, whose name is Usko. He's a good animal and will bring you safely to my cousin Perchta. Many of Usko's relatives live with Perchta and he'll be glad of an excuse to visit. Perchta's a very wise woman, and because she lives so much farther north than we do, she'll be able to advise you more than we can."

"I'm grateful, Aunt Ravna. To all of you."

"There's no need to be rushing off. I know this all feels like a most urgent business, and of course it is, but you've been through a difficult time and I think one more good night's sleep would help you both, and another good meal before you go."

As much as Maggie was impatient to be going, she knew Aunt Ravna was right, and so she stayed another night.

Maggie dreams . . .

She is spinning dirty, tangled flax and must fill a bottomless barrel with water. Kyle must chop down a tree with a dull axe. A water nixie has taken them prisoner, and all she gives them to eat are dumplings as hard as rock. Kyle's hands are bleeding.

Hers are as well, from the nettles mixed in with the flax and from carrying the bucket, with its barbed handle.

Maggie and Kyle are crying in great sobs, but they keep on working because if they stop they will be given even harder tasks to do and be beaten until their bones break. And then, all of a sudden, Maggie senses the water nixie has gone off somewhere.

She grabs Kyle's hand and screams for him to run, run, run … and they begin to run through the clearing around the water nixie's riverside hut to the forest. It isn't long before Maggie turns and sees Srebrenka, in the water nixie's dress of green reeds, following them with long strides, barely touching the ground. Maggie takes a brush out of the pocket of her apron and throws it behind her. The brush turns into a mountain, with thousands and thousands of spikes. Srebrenka lets out a great cry and scrambles over it, cursing as she does, and her hands are cut, but finally she gets to the other side and her strides grow even longer.

"Faster!" screams Maggie to Kyle and she throws a comb behind her and the comb turns into another mountain with a thousand times a thousand teeth, but Srebrenka is able to keep hold of them, and finally get to the other side.

"She's going to catch us!" yells Kyle.

And Maggie throws a mirror behind her, which stands on its edge and becomes bigger than any mountain, and Srebrenka, shrieking with rage and horror, is stopped by her own reflection. She begins to pound her fists against the mirror, again and again, with heavier and heavier blows and then in a great shattering the mirror explodes, and shards begin to rain from the sky on Maggie and Kyle.

THE WOMAN SITS IN A LEAFLESS TREE BY THE RIVER AND her gown drips into the water so there is no telling where the water ends and her dress begins. Kyle sits on the bank with his feet dangling in the cold water.

"Would you like to see your sister?" the woman asks.

"Oh, I don't care," says Kyle.

"I think it might be good for you. Look across the river. Can you see her?"

Reluctantly, Kyle drags his gaze from the woman's white skin, and the dress that clings to it. Light sparkles through the winter-bare trees. Maggie sits on a rock, chained to a spinning wheel. She is crying, and her hands are bleeding. Drops of blood mix with the flax and ruin it, so she must always start over. Kyle laughs.

Maggie turns to him and calls out. "Help me, brother! Help me! The woman you love is not what she seems. She will kill us both."

Kyle laughs harder and points at his sister in her bloody dress. "What an idiot," he says, "she's got more nettles than flax."

Maggie cries out from the pain. There is something in that cry, like a pinprick of something sharp in his chest and he stops laughing.

"Make her go away," he says to the woman, who is no longer in the tree, but there beside him, her lips to his ear.

"Make her come over here and join us. It will be fun," the woman says, her voice like crystal.

"It's not fun with her here. Make her go." Kyle pouts and reaches for the woman, but she pulls back.

"No, my sweet. I thought you were ready, but perhaps I was wrong. So you must wait."

"Ready for what?" His hands move toward her but she slaps

them away.

"Your sister thinks she can fend me off with trinkets. Isn't she a silly girl?"

"She is. But you said I am for you, and only me?"

She holds out a mirror to him. "Look, sweet boy, look at yourself."

He is beautiful in the mirror. Skin of the palest alabaster, teeth like pearls. "I am like a statue," he says, "and might be adored."

"Of course, you are, my little poppet. Here, the pipe you long for. Breath deep and deep and deeper still."

THE NEXT MORNING AUNT RAVNA, EMEL AND GUIVI LED Maggie and Badger to a different door than the one through which they'd entered. The entire community had come to see them off and there was much chatter and laughter as they walked. They turned down a corridor just past the room with the great kettles in it, a corridor Maggie hadn't noticed until Aunt Ravna turned into it. Whereas the first hallway had felt smaller the closer one was to the door, this one got roomier and roomier until they stood in a sort of cave. Huge wooden gates secured the cave opening. Near the gates were stalls, and in each stall stood a caribou, their winter coats thick and grey. Bells tied to some of their antlers tinkled when they shook their heads.

Two young men shovelled fresh hay into the stalls. As the group approached they stopped, went to the gates and folded them back like an enormous accordion. Maggie gasped. Outside the gate a sleigh with a caribou harnessed to it stood on a snowy terrace, at the beginning of a pathway. Beyond the terrace, however, the drop was dizzying, and far below a river meandered through a snow-white valley. The river shone like mercury. All around the valley loomed gigantic snow-capped mountains. Hawks drifted in the thermals, in and out of fast-moving clouds. The sun flashed and disappeared, flashed and disappeared. When it flashed, the dazzle from the snow made Maggie shield her eyes. A waist-high stone wall edged the terrace, and for that Maggie was grateful. The drop, many thousands of feet, caused her considerable vertigo. She put her hands on the stones as she peered over.

Badger was fascinated by the caribou. He sniffed around the animal, back to front, keeping a safe distance from the wide hooves. When he reached the front, the caribou lowered its muzzle and the two met nose to nose. Badger barked once and then bowed playfully. The caribou shook his head, and the silver bells on his antlers chimed prettily.

"I don't suppose," said Maggie, "you'd like to explain how we got up this high? Doesn't seem possible from where we came in."

"Does it not?" asked Emel, his eyes twinkling. "How odd. Perfectly natural to me. What about you, Ravna?"

"Can't imagine it any other way."

They both laughed, but Maggie didn't get the joke. The trees below looked like stalks of grass. She was a little woozy, and had to turn away from the cliff. People crowded round, and some sat on the stone wall. Others hopped up on top and walked along it, secure as mountain goats.

Maggie kept her feet firmly on the ground and gazed along the downward-leading path. "It looks like it'll take us days just to get off this mountain."

Guivi chuckled. "Oh, you might be surprised. Usko knows all the shortcuts and is eager to see his friends and relations so he'll waste no time. Besides, the dear creature is so fleet and sure of foot, or *hoof* I suppose I should say, that no matter how long the journey takes it will be half as long as it would have been if you'd arrived twice as early."

"I beg your pardon?"

Guivi merely laughed and slapped his thigh. "Never you mind, my dear. Trust this noble beast and all shall be well."

Maggie and Badger climbed into the gracefully curved sleigh. Wide runners served not only to ease one's getting in and getting out, but also stopped the snow from flying up in the passengers' faces. It was painted black, with red and white roses and green vines. Fur blankets were piled high in the seat, making it not only comfortable but warm, and at Maggie's feet a covered brazier filled with hot coals ensured she'd be toasty. The back of the sleigh held her pack and some food.

"You should easily be there before the moon sets in the morning, but travel always works up an appetite, doesn't it?" Aunt Ravna said.

Maggie didn't see how they could possibly go so far in so short a time, especially in this terrain, but thought it would be rude to mention it. "I can't thank you enough for all your help."

Holding Maggie's hands between her own, Aunt Ravna brought them to her lips and kissed them. "Bless you, girl, but you're doing far more for us, I suspect, than we're doing for you. I hope you find your brother and put an end to all this nonsense. I wish we had the courage to do what you're doing, but it seems we are not that kind of people."

"I think you're perfect, just the way you are."

"Well, we all have our jobs to do, don't we?" The old lady smiled and stepped back.

Maggie fiddled around at the front of the sleigh. "I'm sorry, but where are the reins?"

That made them all laugh very hard indeed.

Usko shook his antlers so the bells rang and then turned his head to look at Maggie, as though to ask if everyone was settled in and ready to go. The people of the mountain waved and called out their good wishes. "Make sure you keep your hands and feet tucked in, and mind the dog," said Aunt Ravna. "You can trust Usko. He's very wise and knows the way."

At first Usko walked at a stately pace, and then, as the sleigh continued down the hill and they were no longer in sight of the entrance and the people, his speed picked up. Maggie sat in the middle of the seat, with Badger next to her. As the speed quickened, Maggie braced her feet and put her arm around Badger. Usko galloped, and the snow flew up from the sides of the sleigh like water from the prow of a ship.

Maggie wished Usko would slow down but had no idea how to make him do so. Badger's ears flapped in the wind and his mouth was open. He looked as though he was laughing. He barked once, an excited sort of bark. Without breaking his stride, Usko looked over his great shaggy shoulder and waggled his bell-bedecked antlers again.

The path began to level out, but their speed slowed not one bit. The mountain was to their left, and the enormous drop into the valley to their right. The path curved around the mountain. She began to relax. It was so much less steep here that, if one ignored the drop to the right, it felt almost safe, and there was no denying the exhilarating effect of speed. Two ravens flew high above, circling, keeping them in sight. She waved.

So they continued for some time, an hour, and then another hour, and the sun reached its zenith and began its descent, although the valley continued to look very far away indeed. She and Badger burrowed in the furs where it was warm, and she tried not to think about the great drop. Then, all at once, they came around a bend and there, perhaps a quarter mile before them, the path ended and there was nothing but air.

"Whoa, now!" she called.

Usko stretched out his neck and rather than slowing down, picked up even more speed.

"Stop! Usko, stop!" It occurred to Maggie this might all have been a plot on Aunt Ravna's part to kill them. Perhaps she was in league with Srebrenka. "Oh, stop!"

The caribou merely shook his antlers. Maggie swore. There

had to be a brake or an anchor or something. Where the hell was it? Maggie imagined them all mangled and torn, smashed into the mountainside, or hurtling sleigh-over-caribou off the path, falling thousands of feet to the valley floor below. She could feel her bones crunching, taste the blood, and prayed for a quick unconsciousness. The ravens dove and swooped. Badger whined. She held him close, buried her face in his ruff. She closed her eyes and prepared to die.

CHAPTER TWENTY-ONE

MAGGIE HAD TIME TO THINK, HERE IT COMES, and in the tight, icy instant there was Kyle's face before her, crying frozen tears, and she clutched Badger to her breaking heart, and . . . well . . .

It didn't come. She opened her eyes. It was very odd, but for a moment she couldn't see anything except blue sky. Vast, open, watery blue sky. There was Usko, running with the same ease he'd been running all this time. Badger was in her arms, wiggling a bit in her too-tight embrace. She couldn't make sense of it. Badger licked her face. Maggie assumed she'd just missed seeing the turn, which must have been awfully sharp indeed, but then, looking round, she saw that wasn't the case at all. For there was a drop to the right, as there should be, but there was also a drop to the left, as there shouldn't be. The mountain should be to their left. She looked in front. The road must be awfully steep here because she could only see the road just in front of the sleigh, and then . . . nothing. It gave the impression they travelled toward a drop-off, which was forever just out of reach. She turned to look behind them.

Between them and the mountain was a path, well, a bridge

really; a bridge on which they appeared to be travelling. Arches hung under the bridge, delicate and white as the snow. The only problem was the arches dangled far above the ground. The bridge was creating itself as Usko advanced. The ravens criss-crossed the air before them. She had the impression they were laughing at her.

As she watched, the part of the bridge connected to the mountain evaporated, leaving them suspended in mid-air. She'd half expected it; still, her stomach lurched. Usko's hooves moved over the ground (if you could call it ground) with hardly a whisper. There was nothing to do except sit back and tell one-self to remain calm. Remain ... she breathed in ... calm ... she breathed out. Repeat. Repeat.

The wind was cold, and Maggie pulled her hat from the pack and tugged it low on her forehead and ears. She snuggled under the eiderdown next to Badger, who rested his head on her shoulder and sighed. Remain. Calm. Remain. Calm. After all, if Usko hadn't sent them all crashing to their deaths by now, wasn't it best to assume he knew what he was doing, just as Aunt Ravna said?

She settled in. Whenever she remembered they were travel-ling on a bridge made of vapour, she shook her head and shooed the thought away. Remain calm. See where you are, she told herself, for this is an experience you are not likely to have again. Take note of this world.

And what a world it was. The thin clouds overhead flicked like horses' tails in the blue sky and the mountains reached as far as the eye could see – grey and black and white – sentinels of rock and ice. Far below the silver ribbon of river wound, shining blin-dingly when the sun struck it. A world entirely of ice and snow and stone and sky. It was harsh and hard, severe and lonely, with the ravens, those obsidian shadows, the only other sign of life.

The sun began to slide to the tops of the mountains and their gigantic, monstrous shadows crept along the valley floor, as though they were eating up the land below. The ravens circled closer, swooped ever lower, until first one and then the other landed in a flap of feathers on the front of the sleigh. Usko, without lessening his stride, turned around and shook his bells, and the ravens cawed. Badger barked, and the ravens bobbed in his direction.

"Good to see you both," she said.

They cocked their heads and clacked their beaks.

Maggie hadn't been this near to the birds before (even on the boat they had stayed up by the lanterns), but here they were in close quarters. They were so similar, as birds are, that at first glance it was hard to tell one from the other. When she looked closely, however, one was slightly smaller, and well, tidier. The larger bird, even when the wind was quiet, looked more rumpled. Their feathers ruffled in the wind and they had to grip the rim of the sleigh for balance.

"You probably know better than I how long we'll be travelling, but it doesn't look like we're going to arrive before nightfall. Do you want to hop down into the footwell? You'll be out of the wind." She arranged the eiderdown around her feet to make room and the birds jumped down. They preened and then tucked their heads under their wings.

Darkness came on quickly. Maggie opened the food packages Aunt Ravna had given her, and shared the meal of cold chicken slices, cheese, bread and water with Badger. The shadows consumed the valley completely and when the sky turned deep indigo, flashes of green and pale blue and orange began appearing. At first Maggie thought it must just be some trick of the sun, setting far beyond the mountain range. Then, as the lights grew, she realized something else was happening, but what? She gasped. Vast ribbons of green, higher than the stars, or so it looked, rippled over the indigo sky. Badger growled low. Usko shook his antlers, and the sound of the bells danced amongst the ribbons. Tinted with yellow and rose, they fluttered across the sky, wisps of living light, twirling and swirling. Maggie gazed open mouthed. The northern lights. Aurora borealis. Badger tracked them and growled.

"It's okay. I don't think they're dangerous." How could anything so beautiful be dangerous? Badger quieted.

Usko had changed course a little, or else the bridge, or path, or whatever it was, had shifted. They headed right for the dancing lights. A laugh bubbled in Maggie's throat. She found she wasn't in the least frightened. Her pulse quickened, and she had the urge to stand and reach upward for the ribbons, and she might have, too, but thinking of the ever-more-distant drop, she settled for letting her fingers play in the air. Badger's eyes followed the lights, as he would have fireflies. Oh, Kyle, she thought, picturing him as a giggling little boy, reaching for coloured streamers, how I wish you were here. And Alvin, too, who would no doubt have some tale about his time in the high Arctic and knowledge of what the Inuit knew about the aurora borealis.

Soon, they not only travelled *among* the light ribbons, but one of them, teal coloured, turned into the bridge. Usko slowed his pace, from a gallop to a canter to a trot to a walk, and yet they moved just as quickly. The light path carried them. Maggie laughed.

"This is wonderful!" Her heart rose like a spark on a warm draft.

The caribou sat, shook his bells and then lay down and chewed his cud. Thinking how hungry he must be after his long run, Maggie took an apple from her pack and moved to the front of the sleigh, thinking to climb onto the ribbon of light itself. When she stood up and looked down, however, she became quite dizzy. The world was a white ripple far below and she could see through the lights quite clearly. Although the sleigh and Usko were clearly supported, she didn't trust that if she stepped from the sleigh she wouldn't simply drop through the light as she would a cloud.

The crows awoke and cawed urgently. She felt something and realized they were tugging at the leg of her pants. "Okay, okay." Badger was on his feet. "Sit," she said, afraid he'd jump after her. She didn't need to be told twice. Aunt Ravna had been clear. Keep your hands and feet in the sleigh.

"Usko," she called. The caribou turned his great wide head toward her. His eyes were placid, deep and dark, and his muzzle looked soft. She juggled the apple in her hand. "Do you want this? Can you catch?" The animal rose and turned partway toward her. She tossed the apple and he caught it nimbly between his teeth. He munched, with a contented look on his face and jingled his bells.

"You're welcome," she said. "Thank *you*."

Usko settled down and Maggie curled up with Badger in the furs, both of them gazing at the light ballet. She watched and watched and soon her eyes began to grow heavy . . .

BADGER BARKED, AND MAGGIE'S EYES FLEW OPEN. The sleigh was on solid ground again, with snow shushing up on either side. The dancing lights were gone, and the sky was pre-dawn, with just a hoary violet edge along the horizon. It smelled of snow and the clean, slightly metallic scent of ancient ice. The ravens perched on the back of the sleigh's seat. Now and again they spread their wings for balance.

"Good morning, gentlemen," she said, and they bobbed.

She scratched Badger's ears. Maggie had no idea how far they'd travelled. If her experience was to be believed, they had flown the arc of the heavens. The thought made her tingle all the way down to her toes.

Now, however, they were back on terra firma and moving fast. Usko once again ran with sure-footed swiftness through the powdery snow. Maggie realized she'd have to stay under the furs if she didn't want to risk frostbite. Scarf wrapped around neck, woollen hat pulled low, gloved hands beneath the furs. Had anyone looked for her they would see only eyes. The empty landscape stretched on and on into the seemingly eternal not quite day, but not quite night either.

She tried to think of Kyle somewhere north even of here, in the frigid darkness. Kyle hated the dark. How many times as a boy had he called out to her because he was sure something scratched at the floorboards under his bed, or clung spider-like in the corner near the ceiling? "What colour is my hair?" he would ask her, and she would tell him it was the same as ever. Why did he ask? Because, he'd say, he'd read a person's hair could turn white if he was frightened enough. She'd reassure him there was nothing at all in the dark that could hurt him, but knew he never really believed her. Perhaps he knew something she didn't, after all. He was always cold, too, and had a hot water bottle in the shape of a rabbit. She could never get it hot enough for him and sometimes in the morning he'd have a red mark on his chest from where he'd clung to it, but he said he never felt the burn.

How could he stay warm? What was Srebrenka doing with her brother, right this moment? Srebrenka surely knew she was coming. What on earth – or *not* on earth – did Maggie think she was going to do against so formidable a foe? A spiky little worm of resentment slithered into her gut. If she didn't love Kyle so much – even now, even with all the dreadful things he'd said and done – she might have hated him for what was happening. Flying on bridges of dancing green light was all very well and good, but what was that worth when it ended with her frozen corpse next to his at the end of the tale?

The more rumpled of the ravens reached over and pecked her on the top of her head. "Hey!" she cried, and glared at him. He cawed, spread his wings and looked altogether too pleased with himself for her liking. Badger licked her cheek as though to make up for it, or to cheer her, or both. "Oh, fine. I'm not giving up, am I? Aren't I allowed a little ill humour?"

Neither the birds nor Badger answered, so she, too, fell silent.

After a short while a shadow appeared on the horizon. For a moment, Maggie thought it was a smaller mountain, but as they approached she realized it was a forest. How strange, she thought, that way up here in the north there would be trees like these. As the sleigh entered the woods, she noticed aspen next to fir, next to poplar, next to birch, next to spruce, next to Jack pine. She suspected someone had designed the forest this way. Left to naturally develop, one wouldn't find such trees side by side, and certainly some species would never, at least in Maggie's world, grow so far north.

In the distance was a clearing and in the clearing were many round shapes, like snow-covered boulders, and one larger structure, although Maggie couldn't make out what it was. Usko shook his bells vigorously and his gait slowed. He stretched his neck and made a loud bellowing, barking sort of grunt.

Like a ripple of wind across water, the smaller mounds shook and shifted and transformed. Caribou, as though growing out of the ground, rose from the hummocks, shaking snow as they did. An enormous herd, antlers everywhere. They turned in the direction of the sleigh and returned Usko's bellow, running toward their cousin. Maggie drew back, pulled the furs up to her chin and put her hand through Badger's collar. His hackles stood high and he trembled, lips quivering. "No, boy. Sit. Stay."

Within seconds the sleigh was surrounded by a sea of fur, hooves and antlers. Then the caribou circled so they faced the same direction as Usko, parted and walked on either side of the sleigh, bellowing and grunting. The ravens must have flown off in the excitement. The herd and sleigh neared a low-built hut with a steep turf roof that nearly touched the ground. They stopped before the hut's entrance, a small arched, purple-painted door tucked under the pitched roof.

A woman's head, with an old-fashioned white bonnet atop it, poked from the doorway. "You made good time. Come on, don't sit out there, come in, come in, and bring the dog, but slip Usko out of his harness first, so he can have a nice visit." And with that the head disappeared.

CHAPTER TWENTY-TWO

MAGGIE TOLD BADGER TO LEAVE THE CARIBOU alone, and he trotted a distance away to do his business. Maggie jumped from the sleigh and unharnessed Usko. She scratched him under the chin and fed him another apple. He jingled his bells and nudged her, then turned back to his friends and relations and merged into the enormous herd.

The small doorway meant Maggie had to duck her head to enter and she sent Badger in first because, even for the best behaved of dogs, an entire herd of caribou was difficult to ignore and the desire to chase them would be great. Still, he marched in without protest and she, with her pack slung over her shoulder, followed. The entranceway was stone-floored with red rugs, and the walls were smooth, the colour of Usko's coat, and made from earth, perhaps, or wattle and daub. From the timbered ceiling hung candles in copper and glass lamps.

The entrance opened into a good-sized room. The walls here were panelled in blue wood, painted with birds and flowers. Shelves over a wooden workbench were filled with herbs and liquids of some sort, and dried flowers and more herbs hung in bunches along the walls. A large cast-iron stove squatted in the centre of the room and cast off a lovely warmth. The oven door was open so the glow of the fire within shone onto the stone floor. Something wonderful smelling simmered in a large black pot. Behind the stove was a cabinet of blue and white that fit snugly from floor to ceiling. On the other wall were bunk beds, built from heavy round timbers, with thick, fluffy mattresses and quilts and pillows. The wall behind each bunk boasted a small round window to look out of. From the ceiling hung a chandelier made of caribou antlers and candles. The square table was set for two with bowls and plates, cups and saucers, and there were two chairs. More woollen rugs were scattered on the stone floor.

The old woman sat on a stool in front of a spinning wheel and next to her was a large goose. The woman wore a woollen dress and shawl, and black boots. Maggie noticed the sole of the left foot was built up a little, as though that leg was shorter than the other, or the foot shaped differently. A long white braid trailed from under her bonnet. Her skin was brown and deeply lined, and her lips quite red. Her eyes looked as though she were perpetually squinting, but if her face told of a hard life, her smile full of strong white teeth showed good humour.

"Welcome," she said and indicated Maggie should take the chair nearest the stove. Badger inched toward the goose, his neck stretched out and his nose twitching. The goose stretched out her own neck, a surprisingly long stretch, and hissed, a red tongue showing within her beak. The old woman laughed. "Go on, Gans, you silly. The dog won't hurt you, not here, so hop up to bed." The goose looked indignant but waddled over to a lower bunk bed and flapped up onto it. She waggled her behind into the quilt and then settled, keeping her bright eyes on Badger.

"Leave it, Badger," said Maggie and the dog flopped onto the rug near her.

Maggie took off her hat, gloves and scarf and undid the buttons on her coat. "Are you Perchta?"

"I am, and you've met Gans." The old woman's eyes were dark and glinted in the candlelight. Round and round went the spinning wheel, and up and down went the woman's foot, the one with the built-up shoe. Her fingers nimbly and firmly mated the fleece to the thread. How easy she made it look.

"My name is Maggie, and this is Badger. We've been sent from the people at Lake's End, from your cousin Aunt Ravna."

Perchta nodded. "I know who you are and why you're here."

"You do? Well then, will you help me?"

"How do you think I can do that?"

"I don't know. I just hoped . . ."

"Perhaps you had better tell me your story," said Perchta. "But before that, you must eat." She left her spinning and dished up stew from the pot on the stove, setting a large bowl in front of Maggie and a smaller one at the other place for herself. She gave a bowl to Badger as well, who gulped it up much quicker than showed good manners, but Perchta said nothing. She took a loaf of bread from the shelf, sliced it thickly and sat. "Eat."

Maggie spooned the fragrant stew into her mouth. Chicken and dumplings, scented with thyme and rosemary, enriched with cream.

"Eat more," said Perchta, serving her seconds. "It keeps you warm and you'll need warmth."

There was no need to tell Maggie twice. Perchta heated water in a battered kettle and made tea. Maggie didn't know what kind it was, but it tasted wild and sweet. With the steaming mug in her hands, she told the old woman her story thus far. Perchta asked no questions, merely nodding occasionally.

As she finished, Maggie said, "But I know so little of what to expect when and if I arrive at this woman's house, or cave, or whatever it is she lives in. I don't know how I can possibly rescue Kyle. I don't even know if he's still alive." Saying these words, she felt cold again, and terribly tired.

"I'm the woman who controls the caribou and they travel

far and return and tell me many things. And I have my own ways of seeing." Perchta winked. "Let me see what I shall see."

She went to the shelf above the workbench and picked up a small skin drum. She returned to her chair, held it in her lap and began to beat upon it with a long bone as she sang a strange song. It was high and keening and sounded like all the winds of the world twisted together into a single thread that blew first soft and then sharp and then in braids of air that seemed to enter and exit her throat simultaneously. The drum beat to the pace of Maggie's heart. Boom-ah-boom-ah-boom-ah-boom-ah-boom . . . The light from the candles and the stove's fire threw shadows around the walls. Badger lay with his chin on his paws and stared. Maggie, too, stared. The shadows looked like caribou, many, many caribou, running this way and that. It grew very warm in the hut and sweat streaked down Perchta's face. Badger panted. And now a shadow raven flew. A great bear. A figure . . . two . . . three . . .

"Drink your tea, Maggie. Drink it all up."

Maggie did as she was told and suddenly simply holding her head up involved a massive effort and after another moment she couldn't manage it. It was understandable, she thought, of course it was. How could she not be bone-weary? And she was safe here. So very safe. She put her elbow on the table and rested her cheek in her palm. Her eyes burned with fatigue. She had to close them. Just for a second. Just to rest her eyes.

"Maggie," said Perchta, "take off your clothes and lie on the bed." Boom-ah-boom-ah-boom-ah.

"Why?" Maggie found she could open her eyes again. It was so peaceful here and the drum was the sound of her heart.

Boom-ah-boom-ah-boom-ah . . . Perchta's face became hard. "Because I tell you to. Do you think everything is to be handed to you? Should I send a girl to do a woman's work? Prove yourself. Endure the testing. Do as you're told."

Still the drum droned on, making it hard for Maggie to

concentrate. She wasn't quite so tired now and felt completely reassured. Nothing bothered her, not even when she saw that it was now Gans, the goose, playing the drum, standing on it and stamping with her flat webbed feet.

Maggie looked at Badger, and only then did she feel a tingle of misgiving. Badger's eyes were closed, but his feet were moving as if he were running, and his lip twitched. "You won't hurt him. You'd never hurt Badger, would you?"

"If you think I might hurt your dog, you shouldn't do as I say." The old woman snorted. "You shouldn't lie on the bed. You shouldn't go north. You should go home." Boom-ah-boom-ah-boom-ah-boom . . .

"I didn't think the road went backward."

"It doesn't. Not for you."

"Then how would I go home?"

"The way we all do, in the end. Are you going to endure, or not? Decide. Now."

Boom-ah-boom-ah-boom-ah . . . "The way we all do in the end." Could this strange old woman mean what Maggie thought she did? Death. Well, death would indeed come for her eventually as it did for everyone. It might even come now. For that matter, she might already be dead. It would make as much sense as anything. Dead or living, though, it seemed she must, as Perchta said, endure a testing.

"Doesn't the fact I've made it this far mean I'm worthy to continue?" The drum sent vibrations through the room, right into Maggie's chest.

"You have no idea what's before you. Go, or don't. But it's now or never. Time is running out."

Boom-ah-boom-ah-boom . . . *Follow me* . . . *Follow me* . . . *Follow me* . . .

Maggie stripped off her clothes, even her shoes and socks, to the sound of the drum, and lay down on the bed as instructed. It didn't seem as odd, now that she was lying down, as she thought it would.

Perchta said, "Maggie, remember this: you must be soft to die."

"What does that mean?"

"Go to sleep now," said the old woman.

Maggie thought she would stay awake to see what Perchta would do next, but it was no use, the exhaustion was upon her again, and her lids closed. Her breathing slowed.

In the next instant she saw that she was standing outside the hut, but not in the forest. Rather she was on a frozen plain. She was wearing a long coat made from feathers, goose feathers perhaps, or no, possibly owl, or both. The sky above was a dome of blue-black dotted with diamond-bright stars. It made her dizzy, it was so vast. For a moment, she had the sensation she was utterly alone and sour panic rose in her throat, but the coat was warm and soft and she thought she would be able to stay outside for a long while, snug as a fluffed-up puffin. Not knowing what else to do, she sat down, cross-legged, and took a deep breath.

She waited. She breathed in and out. She waited. She began to drift off to sleep, and started awake, and waited . . . and breathed . . . and drifted. She opened her eyes and stood so she wouldn't be lulled into sleep. She looked up. She felt very small under the dome of blue-black sky, untethered, as though she could fall up into that glassy space and keep falling forever. She wished the ravens would appear.

She had the oddest sensation – as though someone was watching her. She swung her head around. A tall figure stood there, cloaked in black. A woman.

"Perchta?"

The figure said nothing but moved closer. It was Perchta, but her eyes were like frozen, dark stars, and she was barefoot. Her left foot was webbed, like that of the goose. Her hands were hidden by the long sleeves of her cloak. Her hair flew round her head, white and wild as a winter storm. Perchta spread her arms and Maggie found herself lying on the snow, her coat of feathers open, exposing her completely. She tried to cover herself up, but it was as though the sleeves held her arms fast. She tried to move her legs but they, too, were frozen. Maggie screamed when she saw the knife in Perchta's right hand, the long blade and antler handle carved with strange symbols along the edge.

"Hush, Maggie, remember what I told you," said the old women as she knelt next to Maggie's prone form. "Remember." "You must be soft to die."

Maggie bit her tongue to stop from screaming again. She was freezing to death, she was sure of it. The pain of the cold was like burning. She did not want to die. But would Perchta truly kill her? Would Aunt Ravna send her here only to be butchered like a seal on the ice? *Be soft.*

She must submit then? Be willing?

She felt like a sacrifice laid out beneath the distant stars, the witnessing moon.

Perchta put her hand on Maggie's forehead and her palm was warm. The warmth ran through Maggie, all the way to her toes. Not to freeze to death then. The knife glinted as Perchta raised it. Maggie could not even move her head to see where it would land. She did not want to see. She closed her eyes.

"Look up, Maggie. Look up."

She opened her eyes again and watched as the ribbons of blue and green and red and violet, the road that had carried her and Badger and Usko to this place, flew and twirled, with a great rushing roar. It was both beautiful and terrible.

And then the pain, from breastbone to belly. She knew it was the knife, that she was being slit open. She tried to scream, but even that was taken from her. All was taken from her, even breath, everything but the night and the stars and the moon and the dancing waves of roaring light. She felt her insides scooped out and tossed aside and in her agony, the flame-bite-and-tear of it, in the hollowness, the emptiness, she felt herself let go. She rose then, away from the sad, fragile, blood-ragged thing and the black-clad knife wielder, and rose, rose, rose, until she was in the midst of the ribbons of light and they embraced her, covered her, draped themselves around her and she was warm and safe and all was well.

She turned to look down again and saw her entrails spread across the snow, so dark they looked as black as Perchta's cape. And she watched as, from pockets inside that cape, the old woman pulled out some very odd objects and began to place them in the gaping wound of Maggie's stomach: a hive of bees, an acorn, a perfectly spherical stone with a hole in the centre, an egg, a piece of blue sea glass, a flint, a mirror . . .

Perchta was saying something over Maggie's body, singing something, and now she was sewing up the wound. Maggie felt herself spinning, falling, twirling, swirling . . .

Boom-ah-boom-ah-boom-ah-boom . . .

Bah-BOOM-ah!

The drum stopped. Maggie was on the bunk bed, naked as a trout. Perchta sat, wide eyed, as though looking at something far in the distance. Gans hunkered next to Perchta, her head cocked, watching Maggie.

Maggie sat up and her hands grabbed at her stomach. Skin. Muscle. The bones of her hips. Just a faint silver line from her breasts to her pubic bone, and even that seemed to be fading. Perchta moved her lips. Then the old woman closed her eyes. When she opened them, she appeared to have returned to herself.

Maggie said, "What happened to me? I was outside, and you . . . you . . ."

Perchta smiled. "I did what had to be done. Get dressed now."

Maggie hopped from the bunk, a little unsteadily, and pulled on her pants, her turtleneck, her socks and boots.

"You did well, Maggie," said Perchta.

Badger yipped, then stood and shook as though shaking off water. Maggie shivered and sat next to him on the floor by the stove, her arms around him. "What did you do to me?"

"You were carrying some things you no longer need, and I merely replaced them with things that will serve you, added bits to things you already have, a little more faith and courage, perseverance, steadfastness. Before I sent you on, I needed to know if your heart was large enough to do that which is required to stop the suffering of others."

"And you felt you had to open me up to do that? But it was just a dream. Something you gave me, in the tea?"

"Think of it as you will. Just know that not everyone survives the remaking."

Badger licked Maggie's face. It was odd. She ought to be exhausted and terrified, but she wasn't. In fact, she felt energized. Stronger.

"I learned something," said Perchta. "Your brother is where you think he is. He is not dead, but he's much changed. If he sent you a message he must have done so some time ago, for he's not now someone who'd ask you to save him. She has a great power, the one who has him, and she arranges things."

"What does that mean?"

"He has a splinter in his eye, you know."

Maggie said that she did and buttoned up her coat.

Perchta grunted. "Bad magic. People fooling around with things to which they have no right. She's made a world for him. And he's the centre of it, wanting for nothing, getting everything he demands. She gives him kisses too, oh, yes, she does that." She cackled and rubbed her thighs. "Gives him things he never dreamed of. Icy kisses, icy lies. Icy bed and icy food and icy halls of white delight and all the while he dies a little more. Soon there will be nothing left of him that you would recognize."

Gans honked as though in agreement.

"What can I do?"

"You have something with you. A bear tooth, do you not?"

One of Mr. Strundale's gifts. She nodded.

"There's nothing more I can do, except direct you and tell you to keep your intentions clear. You'll meet someone who's lost something. You'll know what to do. He may help you, or he may not."

"You're speaking in riddles."

The old woman shrugged. "You only think that because you don't know the answers. To me it's perfectly plain. Her powers are limited, you see, by how much you're willing to deceive yourself."

"More riddles."

"See things as they are, not as you wish them to be. It's wanting things to be different that gets us into trouble."

"I don't see how I can figure out what's real and what's not in a place like this."

Perchta snorted. "Don't be ridiculous. This is as real a place as any there is. Be practical. Think. Has your brother ever lied to you?"

"Yes."

"And did you know he was lying?"

She considered this. "Yes, I think I always knew."

"How did you know?"

"I'm not sure, the way he looked away when he talked, or I remember one time when I knew he was back on the pipe, even though he said he wasn't. We were in a café, sitting at a table, just the two of us, and he kept putting things between us – a cup, a vase, a fork, a book. It was like he was trying to barricade himself behind things."

"Yes, good. What else?"

Something came to mind, but she didn't want to say it.

Perchta said, "Come on, out with it."

"He stole some money from a friend, and when I asked him about it he said I'd never cared about him, that I never cared about anyone except myself." She saw his face in front of her now, all flushed and sweaty, all defiance and venom. "He wasn't wrong. I did care more about myself than about him. But," she looked straight at Perchta, "he didn't answer the question, and I knew, even though I'd hoped it wasn't true, that of course he stole the money."

"You might want it to be different, but there it is. It's wanting things to be different that puts the thorn under the skin." She clapped her hands. "Your instincts are good. Your head is clear. But you'll have to keep your wits about you, oh, yes, you will. Much will depend on how far the shard has burrowed inside him, and whether he wants it to come out or not. Someone pampers him." She made a grunt of disgust. "Rot and duplicity. But enough talk." She shrugged. "Get your things. It's time for you to go."

This took Maggie by surprise. She had thought, as before, she would spend a day or so in this place before moving on. Why was she not as anxious to get going as she had been? Was she afraid? Yes, she was afraid she wouldn't find Kyle, and she was afraid she would. Afraid it was all a fool's quest.

"The path only goes one way," said Perchta.

"I noticed."

"That's still the only direction. No point wanting things to be different."

Maggie reached for her pack, but Perchta stopped her.

"You don't need that anymore. Take the box your friend gave you, with the bear's tooth. Leave the rest. A change of underwear can't help you now." She cackled.

"I can't go off into the snow without anything."

Perchta pointed to the wall where a pair of boots and a coat made from the softest fur hung from an antler. "Take those.

They'll keep you warm. And the dog'll go with you. Oh, and tuck this knife in your boot as well. You never know."

Maggie looked at Badger. He had fallen back asleep and was lying on his back, feet in the air, belly exposed. "Perhaps he should stay with you."

"Not possible. He goes with you." Perchta's face softened. "You know it yourself: he wouldn't have it any other way. Would you, Badger?"

At the sound of his name he snapped awake, rolled over and yawned hugely.

Maggie took off her own coat and put on the new one, took the little box with the bear tooth and slipped it into a wide pocket. She looked into the flickering lamplight, thinking this might be the last time she'd be anything even close to warm. She'd taken warmth for granted, as she'd taken lamplight. What a fool she'd been.

She and Badger followed Perchta and Gans outside. The night – or day? – was the colour of dull tin, with the faintest opalescence along the far horizon. The caribou had returned. They stood or lay all around, a forest of antlers, like the thicket of thorns surrounding the sleeping princess of a fairy tale. The sky was an argent charcoal, and the green and pink and blue lights rippled against the darkness. It seemed as though they touched the top of the trees.

"Usko will take you part of the way, until you reach the stone marker at the boundary between her land and ours. But beyond that he cannot go. You and Badger will be on your own from there on in, do you understand?"

Maggie said she did. The blood in her veins seemed thick with ice crystals. She shivered. Perchta told her she couldn't take the sleigh, but must ride Usko, holding Badger before her. The herd of caribou parted and from the stately way Usko walked forward and the deference the other caribou gave him, it was clear he knew both his duty and its gravity. Perchta placed a hide saddle on his back, with stirrups made from horn. Maggie clambered up and Perchta lifted Badger to her. The dog was uncomfortable and struggled, but Maggie calmed him as best she could and he stilled, facing her, with his head on her shoulder.

"I don't ride," said Maggie. She glanced at the animal's great antlers, which looked very sharp and far too close to her face. "I've never even been on a horse, let alone a caribou. How do I stay on?"

"Use your legs. But don't worry, Usko is, as you've already discovered, a caribou of unusual talents. His gait is smooth. You probably won't fall off more than a dozen times or so, and the snow's soft. You'll get the hang of it." She must have seen the look of panic on Maggie's face. She put her hand on Maggie's leg. "Don't worry. Just make sure Badger doesn't jump off. Usko won't drop you, will you?" The caribou jingled his bells.

Before Maggie could voice more doubts, Perchta stood back and said, "Good luck to you, girl. Darkness is spreading and we depend on you." She looked up. "You're to have company after all." The two ravens circled above. "You have friends in high places." Perchta laughed at her joke, and slapped Usko on the hindquarters. "My prayers go with you." Gans honked, her head held high, her chest puffed out and her wings spread.

Usko ran, but his stride was so smooth it hardly felt like they were moving at all. Only the wind in her face, and rippling through Badger's fur, indicated their speed. Within minutes they were beyond the woods and the landscape became so unchangeable and so empty that had she not looked behind her and seen the trees dwindle to a speck with alarming rapidity, she could have fooled herself into thinking they moved at a slow walk. The only sound was that of Usko's bells and the occasional caw from the ravens. She watched them, swift as arrows, flapping furiously and then tucking their wings at their sides as though riding the wake of air from Usko's passing.

The path did not disappear behind her this time; there was no path at all. It was just empty white snow, without even Usko's hoofprints. It was as though he didn't touch the ground. The cold made her forehead ache and her eyes water, and she pulled the fur hood over her head. Badger's body shielded her and warmed her. His fur was thick, but he must have been cold as well, for he buried his face inside her hood, his wet nose on her neck making her shiver.

After some time Usko began to slow. Ahead stood what looked like a tall dark man. The figure was stout, with arms outstretched. He was motionless and the air behind him was oddly opaque. How, she wondered, could he stand so still? Surely, he must tire. Surely, he must freeze. As they neared, she saw it wasn't a living man, but rather a stone figure. Thick legs and larger, wider rocks for his body. Two stones were positioned in the centre of the top body stone, forming arms, and over the middle of these two, where they met, was another stone, set as a head. This, then, was the marker Perchta spoke of, the boundary between Srebrenka's land and this one. The stone man looked as though he was warning travellers to pass no farther.

Usko halted. The ravens perched, one on each of the figure's outstretched arms, facing into the strange thick air beyond. Badger jumped down, sniffing, his hackles up. Maggie slid from Usko's back and looked, or tried to, past the stone marker. She could see nothing. It was like a wall of cotton. The caribou's bells tinkled, and Maggie turned to him. He stamped his hooves. She rubbed his muzzle and laid her cheek against his nose. He smelled clean and sweet as grass. Usko stepped back and shook his massive head. He looked at her gravely, with deep solemnity, and appeared to be waiting for something. She nodded, giving him permission. He ducked his head three times, then turned and sped off, leaving no prints in the snow.

He vanished. There was nothing to see except miles and miles of undulating snow, a white ocean, deceptively placid, undeniably lethal. She turned back to the stone marker. One of the ravens, the more rumpled of the two, cocked his head, fixing her in the glitter of his eye.

"This is it, isn't it?"

The raven bobbed.

Oh, Kyle, she thought, what have you done to us? She saw him as he'd been that day in the greenhouse at Allan Gardens (it seemed like years ago), when he'd asked to stay with her and she'd refused. His dark eyes glinting with need, the lines around his mouth so hard. He'd been so thin.

So many strands, a spider's web of links and connections, making everyone responsible for everyone else, tied to them, wrapped up and snarled.

Kyle's hands reaching up for her when he was a little boy, frightened by a dream. The look of disbelief on his face when she left home and left him behind to fend for himself. Little Brother of the Sparrow.

She tucked her hands inside the front pocket of the fur coat. The box from Mr. Strundale, with the tooth and bit of mistletoe, felt warm and comforting, but still her heart pounded. "Oh, Badger," she said. And then she turned her face skyward and stared into the vast emptiness.

"You wanted me here," she shouted at the sky. "And here I am. Now do your part. Do something. Do anything. I don't want to do this. I want to go home!" She wiped tears away. She listened. Nothing. Just Badger beside her, whimpering.

Well, to hell with it. Standing here wasn't going to save either of them. They'd freeze and become a pair of markers to stand next to this one. Just let it be done, one way or the other. She supposed there were worse things to die for than love.

Maggie stretched a hand into the whiteness, half expecting her hand to freeze instantly, but whatever it was seemed no more than a veil. The ravens squawked loudly and beat their wings as though urging her on. She was afraid she might lose

Badger in the fog or mist or whatever it was and so she took her scarf off and fashioned it into a leash, tying it to his collar. He danced nervously, straining forward.

"All right. Here we go."

CHAPTER TWENTY-THREE

A S SHE STEPPED FORWARD, THE RAVENS FLEW
straight into the whiteness, and then she lost them. It
was snow all around. But the snow didn't fall from the sky, nor
was it snow as she expected it to be. It was snowflake *creatures*.
Plural. Hundreds of them. Thousands? They dashed at her,
each flake as big as a cat. They threw themselves at her, hitting
her like snowballs. Some looked like huge quilled rodents,
others like snakes tied into knots with their heads ready to
strike, others like bats. They nearly blinded her they were so
white, so bright.

She swatted them with one hand and with the other clung
to Badger's scarf-leash. She had no doubt at all who sent these
things, nor who controlled them. She pulled Perchta's knife
from her boot and sliced and stabbed at them as Badger, at
the end of his leash, snapped and bit. But it was no good; the
creatures were too many and too swift. As soon as she sliced
through a creature, it fell, but then re-formed and came at her
again. Their touch felt as if they had teeth. Badger yipped and
yelped but fought on. Somewhere in all the whiteness, the
ravens cawed and shrieked.

Soon she and Badger would either be battered to death, buried or frozen, or all three. It was becoming harder and harder to walk as the snow thickened. Badger, snarling, plunged through the drifts as through deep water. Both did what damage they could to the things assailing them, but she began to lose what little hope she had and battled on only through the instinct to survive. She needed some sort of protection, but there was nothing she could use. A spell, a charm. Force wouldn't work against these creatures. She needed magic and power. Something, something . . . What had she read about charms? What could she use? Winter. Protection. And then she knew. While she continued to slash and fight, she remembered. Druids. Winter rites. Mistletoe. With her left hand, she reached for the box Mr. Strundale had given her, and it was warm. And it moved.

She pulled it out and, nearly blinded though she was, she opened it. As soon as she did a tendril of mistletoe inched out, tipped with waxy, nearly transparent white berries. She pulled the sprig from the box, making sure it hadn't attached to the bear tooth, and put the box safely back in her pocket. Even as she watched, the sprig grew and grew. The snow creatures around her shivered and pulled back slightly. Badger stood next to her, growling, but he wasn't snapping at anything. Indeed, he didn't need to, for the snow creatures retreated before the mistletoe. It grew ever faster, so that now it spread along the ground, forming a circle around her and Badger, a line the snow did not penetrate. She looked up. High above her, stars glinted, but outside the circle, all was still white and wild. And then the mistletoe slithered rapidly along the ground and the snow backed away so that a path opened up, wide enough for Maggie and Badger to walk side by side. The ravens stood on the path in front of them. They preened their feathers and looked quite indignant, and horribly ruffled, but no more damaged than that.

The ravens flew ahead and Maggie and Badger started along the path, their sides heaving, their breath ragged, and the snow did not touch them. Indeed, they were dry and quite warm. The creatures tried time and again to breech the mistletoe's force field, but were frustrated. It was impossible to forget they were there, but after a few minutes Maggie's breathing normalized and she stopped flinching every five seconds. The ravens flew and then stopped on the path, checking to see that Maggie followed, and then flew on again.

A set of gates appeared. They were made from ice or glass, so that it was hard to see them until one was nearly upon them. The ravens perched on a snowbank. As Maggie reached the gates the birds flew over and disappeared from view. She feared she would have to climb over, leaving Badger behind. Perhaps she could dig through the snow walls surrounding the gate. But when she put her gloved hand on the latch, it swung open easily.

There stood a great palace, made entirely of snow and ice. The thick slabs of carved ice that served as doors opened as easily as had the gate. It was as cold inside as out, although being away from the wind was a relief. It was possible to see through the thin panes of ice that acted as windows, but the view was blurry. Besides, beyond lay only snow and more snow. She walked through one enormous empty hall after another, staircase after staircase and room after room . . . Chandeliers hung from the ceilings, but instead of candles, they were lit by strange blue lights, like tiny stars trapped in frozen cages.

Maggie wandered from room to hall to staircase to hall to room, but found no sign of Kyle, or anyone else. The silence was thick, as was the fog from her breath. She lost all sense of direction. She hadn't seen the ravens since she'd opened the gates. Badger padded by her side, the scarf-leash slack.

"Can you find Kyle, Badger? Can you find him?"

Badger looked at her and sniffed. Maggie wanted to call out, but didn't want to alert Srebrenka if there was a chance her entrance had gone unnoticed. It occurred to Maggie this palace was nothing more than an elaborate labyrinth, a trick to keep her wandering until she froze. How long would that take? She couldn't last long, not without fire and food.

The walls glinted, and the floors glimmered. Beneath the silver-blue lights the ice flickered. As Maggie exited another room she looked down a long hall and there, at the end, something moved. A dot of black among all the white and crystal. A small white fox with a black nose and black eyes. Predatory. Skulking. Dangerous. Badger growled. "No, Badger. Leave it." The fox trotted close to the wall. Then another Arctic fox appeared from a side door, and then another. Badger, unable to control himself, lunged, but Maggie kept his scarf-leash firmly in her grip, telling him to stay. He barked madly. Five foxes, six, seven, all of them slinking along the wall, turning to stare at Maggie and Badger, as if teasing the dog, tempting him.

That was probably exactly what they wanted. To lure Badger away from her. Well, if Srebrenka wanted her and Badger to go that way, she'd just turn and go the other. She pulled Badger and began to run in the opposite direction. He resisted at first, but then ran with her. She turned and looked back. The foxes were gone.

Panting, she halted. The hall branched into three passageways: to the right and left, stairs led down; in the centre, a grand staircase rose. Right or left? Badger was on her left. She would go that way. Up or down? She would go down, if for no other reason than she didn't want to climb stairs. Down she went, and once she was on the staircase, there were no more hallways, no way to get off the stairs. The strange blue stars, now in small torches affixed to the wall, shed a weak light. She ground her teeth and continued downward.

With several more turns, Badger's fur bristled and he began sniffing madly. Then Maggie smelled something over-ripe, rotting even. She imagined the carcass of a whale, or a walrus, putrefying in a cellar below. Fishy, yes, but also musky, oily, meaty. She covered her nose with her hand and breathed through her mouth in an effort to stop the stench from turning her stomach.

The staircase grew darker with each turn as the torches dimmed. Badger pulled on the leash and Maggie ran her hand along the wall to keep from stumbling. What if this stairway never arrived anywhere? Aunt Ravna's tavern flashed through her mind – the people, the fire in the hearth, the apple cider. And then she thought of home. Home. To sit in a quiet room, surrounded by books, surely that was paradise. And Alvin. Yes, to have Alvin's big warm body next to hers in her own soft bed. To smell the good water-and-wind scent of him. She thought of his forearms, the muscles and the down. She thought of his laugh, that deep, rumbling chuckle. To sit across the table from him again, to share a bowl of stew and to talk of silly things. Her eyes stung and her throat constricted. She couldn't help but cry. A vast sense of the nothingness all around her – the ice, the snow, the endless sky – mile after mile of cold and dark, and here she was with Badger, two infinitely tiny sparks in a sea of white and black and grey.

Badger growled. A bluish light wavered far below. Small, fighting against shadows, but a light nonetheless. She stopped crying as her breath quickened. Something, someone, was down there. What now? What horror? A sound . . . and yes, again . . . She couldn't be sure but it sounded like one of the ravens cawing. She straightened her spine and wiped her face. *Caaaw*. Yes, it was the ravens. If they hadn't disappeared, perhaps there was hope yet.

The smell remained, but at least it grew no worse, or perhaps she was growing accustomed to it. Whatever was down there, at least something *was* down there and she wasn't walking into a bottomless abyss. There was an end. Even as her heart threatened to break through her ribs, it was a token of solace.

One turn of the stairs, another and another. There were no torches now, but the light from below seemed to creep up the stairs toward her, more liquid than light. She thought of the phosphorescence one sometimes saw on waves at night. And then, the last turn. Maggie and Badger found themselves in a chamber of sparkling, glistening crystal stalagmites and stalactites. The smell was very strong, thick with decay, and in the centre of the room stood a fountain – the light source. Luminescent water flowed from the mouth of three bears carved from ice. The light was silver and blue and white; a cold, hard light, offering no warmth. Pipes ran in a ring round the base of the fountain, catching the liquid and carrying it into the walls. Even at the entrance, an atmosphere of despair and hopelessness rose around Maggie. It took all her will not to crumple to the floor.

No sooner had they stepped into the chamber than Badger began barking wildly. A huge shape, which Maggie had taken to be a mound of snow, separated from the whiteness around it. It shook and reared on its hind legs. A bear. A polar bear, at least ten feet high. Badger went mad and Maggie shrieked, struggling to hold him back. The bear, apparently the source of the stench, fell onto all fours and lumbered forward. Maggie thought to run back up the stairs, but when she turned she was met with nothing but a wall of ice with a railing sticking out of it.

The bear snarled, revealing . . . well, not much at all. Gums and a tongue. It seemed the bear had not a tooth in its head. *The bear tooth!* The bear swiped at them with its enormous paw. What it lacked in teeth, it more than made up for in claws. Badger would be eviscerated, as would she. Trembling, she reached into her pocket, grabbed the box and pulled out the tooth. It was curved and as long as her middle finger, with a lethal point at one end and a hollow at the other. She held it up. The bear paused, closed his mouth and sniffed.

"Do you want this? Is it yours? Have you lost it?" she asked.

The bear swayed back and forth as though unsure. He was a terrible mess, marked with malodorous goo and stains. His muzzle was not white but brown and red. Maggie noticed a mound of rotten seal carcasses in the shadows. That, more than the bear itself, was the cause of the stench. His food source? Liquefying seal? Perhaps that was all he could eat, given his lack of teeth.

The bear could, of course, simply kill them and take the tooth, if that's what he wanted. So why didn't he? He tapped the ground with his paw. Badger, although his hackles were still raised, making him look like a porcupine, stopped barking. The bear sniffed and Maggie held out the tooth, letting him get a good look at it. He became practically cross-eyed and then, with a kind of slow dignity, as though this were the most formal of gestures (and perhaps it was), he lowered himself onto his forepaws in a bow, keeping his eyes on the tooth.

Badger sat. Something flapped behind Maggie and, loath as she was to take her eyes off the ursine hulk, she glanced behind her. The ravens were settling on the stair railing. How they got in was a mystery. They cocked their heads and cawed. When she looked back at the bear, he had not moved. He put his head on his paws and looked, with his dirty rump in the air, very much like a monstrous dog asking to frolic.

She held up the tooth. The bear inched toward her, crawling. She would have backed up, except there was nowhere to go. Badger vibrated with tension. She put her hand on his head and stilled him. She was surprised the dog could control himself and wondered if he sensed something about this bear. The great beast inched nearer. Badger growled and, before Maggie could stop him, he snapped, his jaws a hair's breadth from the bear's nose. Maggie winced, picturing Badger's head under an enormous paw, but the bear didn't move. Rather, he gazed at Maggie and when his dinner-plate-sized foot was nearly resting on her boot, he opened his mouth and tilted it toward her.

It was evident he wanted the tooth. If she gave it to him, and it worked whatever magic she had no doubt it would, he might rip her head off. The rumpled raven cawed, twice, in short sharp bursts. Gingerly, she extended the tooth and as she did the bear stuck out his tongue. Not sure what the right thing to do was, she placed the tooth on it. He flicked it into his mouth, closed his eyes and flung backward with such force he slammed into the wall. Badger barked and Maggie screamed. The bear writhed and growled and bleated as though being flayed. He shook his head so quickly it blurred and then he threw it back and roared and roared.

His mouth was full of razor-sharp white teeth. The atmosphere of despair in the chamber lightened ever so slightly, even as the light from the liquid in the fountain dimmed a little. The air vibrated with the bear's roar and Maggie threw her hands over her ears. As she did, she dropped Badger's leash and the dog jumped forward, snapping at the bear. The bear, returning to himself, stopped roaring and looked down at Badger.

"Badger, come. Come to me!"

The dog ignored her and nipped the bear's leg. The expression on the bear's face was one of surprised amusement. Maggie chewed her knuckle, afraid if she made the slightest noise she'd spook the bear into attacking, but he sat down and let Badger nip at him until, seeing it had no effect whatsoever, Badger stopped. Then the gigantic beast lowered his head and sniffed at Badger and let Badger sniff him. Badger returned to Maggie and sat by her side.

The bear opened and closed his mouth, as though testing his new teeth. He put his paw in his mouth, then removed it. He picked up one of the putrid carcasses and roared, flinging it against the wall where it exploded, releasing a torrent of liquid matter and a reek so toxic, tears sprang to Maggie's eyes.

"You ought not to have done that," said a voice.

A figure sat at the shadowed far end of the chamber, in a sort of chair carved in the ice wall. It was so still, and of the same bluish white colour as the chamber itself, it was almost invisible.

She took a step toward whomever it was. Badger trembled, his tail between his legs. She stepped closer, her heart a panicked bird in the cage of her ribs.

Was it possible?

The figure stood. Thin as a birch tree, brittle as spun glass, his hair as frost, his skin bloodless and intricately swirled with blue, his eyes like oyster shells, but *him* nonetheless, the one she sought. Kyle, or what was left of him, stood before her, dressed in rime, shimmering and frigid.

"He guards me and now you've broken him. She won't like that a bit." His voice was like something heard on a distant north wind, all thin and hollow.

Something stopped her from throwing her arms around him. "Kyle, it's me. It's Maggie."

"I know who you are."

"I got your message."

"What message?" His eyes were dead. They looked but saw nothing. Like the eyes of some creature who lived far, far beneath the sea, beyond the reach of light.

"You sent a message. You wanted me to come and find you. You said you needed me. We have to get you out of here."

"I remember no message. You shouldn't have given the bear back his teeth. You'll be in trouble." His voice was so emotion-less. "He didn't need teeth. Not in here. She fed him. Now he's got teeth again he'll probably leave, and then she'll have to catch another."

Maggie reached out to touch Kyle, but he pulled back as though scalded. "Don't touch me. I don't want your filthy hands on me." He held his hand in front of his left eye, as though protecting it.

"Kyle, where is she?"

"She'll be back. She knows you're here. She thought the bear would capture you for her."

A loud thumping noise behind them startled Maggie. The

bear hammered at the wall with his enormous paws and his dagger-like claws. With every swipe a larger hole appeared, although it seemed they were so far underground it would take him forever to dig out. And then, with an earth-shaking thwack, the wall cracked and, with a shudder, crumbled, revealing a vast expanse of moonlit snow.

It was quite impossible, of course, since Maggie and Badger had walked down so many stairs they must, had they been in any place where the normal rules applied, be a long way below ground. Impossible or not, however, the bear sat on his haunches and gazed onto the ghostly plain. Then he turned to Maggie and made a low sound in his throat. She had the impression he was thanking her for breaking whatever enchantment he'd been under. He got to his feet and hesitated, as if waiting for her. She shook her head. She hadn't come so far only to leave without Kyle, and it was obvious he wasn't ready to leave. The bear growled, but then turned and sprang forward, bounding away over the snow.

"He wasn't very good company, anyway," said Kyle. He rubbed his eye.

Maggie positioned herself in front of her brother so he couldn't help but look at her. He regarded her blandly, appearing quite bored. The white of his eyes were silver, but in the left one something glinted. She couldn't imagine how he wasn't frozen to death. He seemed to be made more of ice than flesh and bone.

"Snap out of it," she said.

"You are dull," he replied and turned away from her. "But stay. Everything becomes as it should here."

He glanced at the hole in the wall through which the bear had escaped. It was closing up. Now it was less than a door's width. Now less than a porthole. Maggie's heart fell. She'd never have the strength to bash through. Kyle returned to his ice chair. He glided, rather than stepped. A silver pipe lay on the arm of the chair. He picked it up, drifted to the fountain and scooped the luminous water into his pipe. He lit it using a match with a blue flame that he pulled, already lit, from his waistband.

Although the concept of flammable water was baffling, Maggie understood then at least part of what ailed Kyle. The fountain was the source of elysium. "You're more elysium than human," she said.

"Being human was never much fun." He blew smoke to the ceiling, and still his fingers worried his eye, now rubbing it, now pulling down the lid, now tapping the socket. "You have no idea, you poor sack of skin, just what glory there is in the dreams, which aren't dreams at all, but surely you know that, now you're here. I have all the elysium I want, all the time. It pleases Srebrenka that I dream. She says the dreams make her stronger, and I do enjoy them so."

His wrist was hardly wider than a twig. His cheekbones stuck out. He was blue-swirled ice over bone. As he sucked in the smoke, Maggie fancied she watched it swirl into his chest and along his limbs. He was virtually transparent. And there, in the corner of his nearly opaque eye, the place he kept touching, was that glint. It looked sharp. It looked like glass.

"The stronger she gets, the weaker you get. Surely you see that?"

"I float." His hand trailed in the air as he sank into a reclining position on the ice ledge. "I float amidst the beauty and the plenty."

She stalked toward him. "What are you talking about? You're sitting in a frozen cellar, surrounded by putrefying seal meat."

This seemed to get a rise out of him. "Rotten meat." He laughed, and it was little more than wind whistling through bone. "Now who's crazy? Caviar and champagne, lobster and truffles . . ." He picked a piece of rancid meat from where it had stuck to the wall. He popped it in his mouth. "Served on plates of gold." His voice was dreamy and his eyes glowed with the same blue light as the match. "One dreams with eyes wide open here. All the world's a dream . . . Ah, delicious."

Her stomach heaved as she watched him chew. She swallowed to keep from vomiting. "Kyle, you're not seeing things as they are. It's the drug. It's this place. It's that piece of glass in your eye. It's an evil thing and we're in an evil place."

"You're the one who doesn't see. You never did. Selfish cow." He gazed at her with an expression somewhere between disinterest and contempt. "What do you know of love?"

"Love? You call this love? Left to freeze to death in the dark?"

"Her kisses are molten sugar. Her skin is warm honey. Impossible to freeze."

That shut her up. The woman was a vampire in more ways than one.

The ravens flew to the fountain and perched on the top of the ice-sculpted bears. Kyle looked at them with amusement. "Your guardian, I see. And isn't that your old neighbour? Fancy them bothering. They must have come in with you."

Maggie looked at the ravens. The rumpled one had spread his wings wide. His mouth was open as well. Surely not. But then, why not? Wasn't it entirely possible? She frowned and the bird bobbed up and down. "Mr. Mustby?" she asked. The bird cawed. Then he cawed again, and suddenly the other raven began as well, and the two became raucous and urgent. They flew into the darkest corner of the chamber where Maggie couldn't tell them from the shadows.

Badger growled and then barked. Srebrenka stood at the foot of the blocked stairs, bringing with her the same heavy scent of cloves, sandalwood and amber that had permeated her Forest den. It almost masked the stench of rotting meat. The bobbed haircut was gone and in its place were long, slithering tendrils. Her skin was as white as ever, and her eyes as blue, but her lips were no longer red – they were quite black. She wore a long dress that seemed to be fashioned from snowdrifts and icicles.

"Pretty Maggie, how resourceful you have turned out to be." Srebrenka glanced at Badger. "Stupid dog," she said and spit at him.

Badger began barking even more wildly. Srebrenka raised her hand as though to strike him, but Maggie stepped between them. "Don't hurt him."

"Hurt him? My dear, I'm going to kill him."

"No!" Maggie threw herself over Badger and made him lie down. "See, he won't bother you. Leave him alone."

Srebrenka shrugged. "Perhaps he'll prove useful. Perhaps he'll guard you as the bear guarded Kyle." She shook her thin finger and tsk-tsked. "I do not like what happened there. Where did you get the tooth?"

Maggie noticed Srebrenka's accent seemed to have disappeared. "You not only look different, you sound different."

"What adds a certain allure in one place is useless in another. But you didn't answer me, my girl. Where did you get the tooth?"

"I found it."

"Nasty little liar." Srebrenka smiled. "There may be hope for you yet. And I'm glad you got my messages."

"Your messages?"

"You don't think *he* sent for you, do you? Look at him. He doesn't want your help. He doesn't want to leave me, do you, sweetheart?" She walked over to Kyle and, with her finger under his chin, lifted his face so he looked in her eyes. She licked her lips and bent to kiss him. He shuddered and moaned with pleasure.

Bile-like revulsion rose in Maggie's throat. "But why? Why should you want me here? If Kyle's so happy?"

"Look at him. He's weak. Drawing pain from the weak is a limited pleasure and I am easily bored." She pushed Kyle away and turned to Maggie. "I like a challenge. I was so happy when you used to come and visit me, and so sad when you stopped. I miss you, Maggie. You were so close to being mine. You're the only friend who's ever left me. I'm just like anyone else, aren't I? I want to be loved, don't I? I want to be needed. But you cried so hard you washed the splinter from your eye, and you found someone to take you in, that ridiculous man. You forgot about me, but I never forgot about you. I never forget a friend."

Maggie recalled what Mr. Mustby had said about the creatures who were attracted to you when you used elysium, how you could keep them away if you stopped, but they never forgot. She remembered what he said about Srebrenka feeding off guilt and grief. Well, Kyle may not want to leave, but if he stayed he'd die. She had to find some way, but it was hard to think, hard to focus . . .

Smoke from Kyle's pipe was thicker now, as was Srebrenka's scent of cloves and sandalwood. A kind of fog hung low around the chamber's ceiling, descending . . . impossible not to breathe it in, if one was to breathe at all. The room grew oddly bright, and the fountain no longer ran with liquid, but with luminous smoke. Even Badger was affected. He lay panting on his side, his feet twitching. The walls expanded and turned into richly panelled wood, hung with tapestries. The floor was covered with thick red rugs. A long table was set with golden plates, goblets, platters of roast pheasant, green grapes, poached trout, pickled beets, plump olives, creamy cheeses, salads with lettuce and apricots and walnuts, strawberry tarts, pecan pies and carafes of garnet wine.

"Why not treat yourself to a little something?" Srebrenka said. "A little pheasant, an apricot? Help yourself, pretty Maggie." Srebrenka poured a glass of wine into a golden goblet. It glowed. It smelled of violets and plums.

Maggie's mouth watered. She could taste it on her tongue. Other people were in the room now. Men with eyes like sapphires and teeth like pearls, women with cheeks the colour of peaches and lips like cherries. They smiled encouragingly. They purred their approval. Maggie wanted them to like her, to accept her as one of their own. Even Kyle. He stood among them, and was no longer thin and brittle and frozen. He was her little brother again, no more than thirteen, his hair curling around his ears, the mischievous grin on his face, his eyes bright and clear . . . Maggie reached for the goblet, but kept her eyes on Kyle. There was nothing wrong with him after all. It had all been a bad dream from which she was now awakened, here in this warm and well-appointed room. Look, see the glimmer in his eye. Her hand touched the goblet. It felt so oddly cold.

"Drink a little, pretty Maggie."

Badger lay on the floor, panting. The way he was twitching didn't seem natural, not even for a dog dreaming of chasing rabbits, or whatever it was dogs dreamed. He kept raising his head as though struggling to wake. Maggie looked down at her hand holding the goblet. Or was it? For a moment, it appeared more like a hollowed-out hoof, on a stem of leg bone. She heard something, from a great way off. Like a bird's wings flapping. She stared hard at Kyle. What was that in his eye? He kept touching it, as though it bothered him. It made her own eye hurt, just to look at it. The faces of the people in the room shifted, melted and re-formed, but not in quite the same form. Their eyes were not quite so blue, their cheeks more bruised than blushing.

"Drink up, I said." The voice sounded vexed now.

Maggie looked at the speaker. She knew this woman. But she didn't look as she had a moment ago. Her hair was now black, with kiss-curls on her forehead, and now like a prism, full of fire, and now it was dull rust, and now it appeared as seaweed. There was something about dreams Maggie ought to remember. Things of importance depended on her remembering. Every thought flew away just as she was about to catch it. She stared hard at the woman and tried to focus. The woman aged, wrinkled, shrank, as her skin thinned and hung from her bones. Snow swirled around her.

Maggie was very cold. She wanted to lie down and dream. How she craved it.

The wing-flapping grew louder and Maggie remembered that such craving almost killed her once, a long time ago and very far away . . . She feared her chest would tear from the ragged shriek of craving building up inside . . . She hurled the goblet against the wall where it clattered and fell to the floor. As it bounced it flickered, oscillated, looked one second like a golden goblet spilling red wine, the next like the skeletal end of a caribou leg, spilling offal.

"What a tiresome girl."

Srebrenka no longer looked like an ethereal spirit of the winter, but haggard and worn and ancient. Her hair was white and scraggly, her skin pallid, her fingers bony and sharp. A black shape swooped past Maggie. It circled Srebrenka and dove toward her. She whirled and covered her head.

"What is that? What's in here? What is that?" The shape flew at Srebrenka again. "No! You! How did you get in here? I do not permit it!"

The flying and flapping caused the smoke to dissipate slightly. Maggie, from where she found herself sitting on the floor, watched as the ravens strafed Srebrenka. The woman held a long bone, and swung it around the room, trying to strike the diving, fluttering, zigzagging ravens. She kept screaming, demanding to know how they'd found their way in. What glamour had the birds worked, Maggie wondered, that Srebrenka hadn't noticed them?

"You should have killed them, you idiot!" Srebrenka yelled at Kyle. "Kill them!"

"I can't. They're too fast, and I'm dreaming such a pretty dream." The subject seemed to weary him.

Srebrenka swiped and swatted but the birds kept coming. "Useless piece of dog shit! I should have left you in the snow to die like the others!"

"I am not useless." He sounded just like a little boy. "You love me. You're not supposed to say things like that."

The birds cawed as Badger leaped into the fray, barking and jumping at Srebrenka. She struck at Badger and he yelped and jumped, snarling. She then drew back her arm and Maggie watched as the long bone she held came down in a great arc. She struck Kyle on the side of the head. It sounded like a rock hitting a hollow wooden bowl.

Maggie screamed.

CHAPTER TWENTY-FOUR

THE RUMPLED RAVEN LOCKED ONTO SREBRENKA'S head with his talons and pecked at her eyes as the other flew at her time and again, ripping and tearing the skin on her hands and face. Badger joined in and bit her legs and arms and belly. She shrieked and twisted and turned. She screamed but she could not shake them off. She stumbled and fell, blind and bleeding.

Kyle had slumped to the ground near the fountain.

Maggie stumbled to her brother and reached for him, but as her fingers met his he threw back his head and howled. She screamed as well for his flesh was so cold it burned. She pulled away as the ends of her fingers blistered. She knelt and called to him, but he convulsed, his back arching until it looked as though he'd snap in two. He let out a great cry and flipped over onto his belly, his hands clawing at the side of the fountain. Srebrenka groped for him, even as she fought the birds and Badger. She kicked at the dog and protected herself with one arm, pulling herself up to the lip of the fountain with the other. As she did, blood dripped from her wounds into the liquid silver, causing it to sputter and boil. Badger bit and tore at her belly and she shrieked, kicking more feebly. Maggie's mind splintered into a dozen parts. She pulled at Badger, for surely Srebrenka was no longer a threat and she couldn't bear to watch him savage her. The dog allowed himself to be pulled away, and then shook his head and whimpered. He stood panting and looking at her, his eyes hollow with fear.

Maggie picked up her scarf from where it had fallen from Badger's collar in the melee, and wrapped it around her hand to protect herself from Kyle's frozen skin, and embraced him. The cold instantly shot through the fur she wore and the clothes beneath, into her skin and bone. She gritted her teeth and refused to let go. The birds kept up their attack, scratching and pecking. More blood fell into the fountain and then, her arms windmilling, Srebrenka tipped over and fell headfirst into the silver water. She struggled for a moment, and then was still, her head under the liquid. The ravens flew into the shadows.

Kyle screamed. "My eye! My eye! I can't stand the pain. Get it out, get it out!" He held his hands up at either side of his head and turned to Maggie. Tears, silver and thick, like mercury, flowed down his cheeks. She could see the shard, right there in the corner of his eye. "Take it out! Take it out!" he screamed.

She wanted to but knew she mustn't. "I can't," she said, her voice hoarse. "It won't come out for me. It has to be you."

His face was that of some long-frozen corpse. He threw back his head and wailed like an animal with its foot caught in a trap. He tore at his eye until blood ran, and it joined that of Srebrenka's in the fountain, drop by drop. He let out one final shriek and a small, shining piece of glass tumbled, as though in slow motion, from his eye to the fountain.

As soon as it hit the surface of the liquid, something happened. The elysium began to change. Kyle fell backward into Maggie's arms. His eye, where the shard had been, was torn and bloody. His skin was cold, but no longer burned her. She held him and watched as the liquid roiled. She pulled him away from the splashing. It appeared to thicken, to become prehensile, and it shifted colour. No longer silver. Darker. The colour of tarnished pewter, and then of wet driftwood, and then of coal. It pulled at Srebrenka's corpse as though hungry for it, eager and impatient. It pulled her like a snake pulling a frog into its jaws, until she disappeared.

Badger sniffed at Kyle and Maggie and whined. He looked unhurt but puzzled, as though he didn't know what on earth had come over him. "It's okay," said Maggie, praying it was.

Kyle seemed baffled. "Maggie?"

"I'm here."

"Everything hurts." The look on his face was one of indescribable grief. "What is this awful place? What have I done? Am I to blame for all this? Oh my God!"

Maggie had no time to answer. The ground beneath them began to shake. A rumble rose from everywhere at once, and grew louder and louder, like eight freight trains coming from various points on the compass. Snow and ice tumbled down around them. Badger barked and barked.

"We have to get out of here," said Maggie.

She dragged Kyle to his feet. His colour was better, but he was thin as an icicle and she feared he'd shatter if dropped. She could see no way out. The ravens had returned and flew in circles near the crumbling arches of the roof. The black liquid in the fountain churned and began to flow in reverse, so that it did not run down from the mouths of the ice bears, but ran up their sides, turning them black, making them look larger and more ferocious, and then encompassing them so they disappeared beneath the pitch. The liquid did not stop there but rose up in a pillar from the fountain, reaching with tarry fingers. The stench grew as the liquid swelled – of offal and blood and the sweet-sour tang of decay.

Maggie sensed the liquid would reach the roof and then begin to fill the whole room until they drowned in its putrid grasp. "Do something!" she screamed to the ravens. To have come so far, to have found Kyle, and then to die here seemed impossibly unjust. Badger ran to the side of the wall where the bear had escaped and began digging, his front feet blurring with speed. The liquid ran down the walls and Maggie choked on the smell. She half carried Kyle to the wall. "Dig!" she said. "For your life, Kyle, dig!"

She dug, scooping out ice and snow and flinging it behind her. The birds flew and cawed, avoiding the black gush. Kyle was weak and listless, his head lolling, his eyes rolling.

They would die here.

And then she felt something. A great weight, like a sledge-hammer, pounded on the wall. She stopped her digging and put her palm against the ice. Yes. Someone was trying to reach them from the other side. The force was terrific. She pictured battering rams, catapults, some huge earth-moving machine. She pressed her face against the wall and it struck again, and the force knocked her back.

"Badger, come!" she called. Whatever was coming through that wall, for good or ill, would crush everything in its way. Kyle had crumpled. She put her hands under his armpits and pulled him toward the stairs, away from the fountain, away from the fluid slipping slowly but inexorably down the walls. She called Badger again, her voice sharp with urgency, trying to break through his panic. He stopped digging, ran to her and put his tail between his legs.

It was all she could do not to cover her face with her hands.

In a great burst of snow and ice, and with a mighty, ear-piercing roar, the bear crashed through the wall. Maggie stood, ready to do something, although she had no idea what. The bear looked at her and Kyle and Badger and padded to them. He stretched his neck and opened his mouth. Maggie held her breath, sure Srebrenka has magically reasserted her influence over the beast but, instead of decapitating him, he picked Kyle up by the back of his jacket, as he might do a cub. He turned and bounded into the hole in the wall.

The ravens squawked and flapped. "Badger! Come!" She ran, with Badger at her heels. She had to jump over a pool of black liquid in her path and Badger did the same. The liquid stretched toward them, searching, grasping. They dove for the hole, but instead of escaping to the outside, as the bear had done before, they found themselves in a tunnel. No sooner were they inside it then it closed up behind them, just as every path had done. The ravens swooped ahead. The bear's rump was just visible before her. The tunnel twisted and turned and closed behind her with each step, forcing her to run or be buried. There should have been noise behind her, some sort of cave-in rumble, but there was nothing, just a terrible silence. Her breathing and the pounding of her feet were loud in her ears. The only light came from the strange white glow of the great bear plowing on ahead.

And then, quite without warning, she was standing on a white plain, which stretched to the horizon. The bear had dropped Kyle and her brother sat between the bear's forepaws, leaning up against one of them. The eye in which he'd had the shard was torn, swollen to hideous proportions, and blood trickled from both corners. Even so, he looked human again. Broken, perhaps, but human. His skin showed not a single silver swirl. Maggie approached, keeping her eye on the bear. Badger kept by her side, but his hackles were down and he did not growl. As she neared, the bear nuzzled Kyle. Kyle reached up and patted the bear under his great jaw. The bear made a low sound in his throat and licked the top of Kyle's head.

Maggie knelt beside him. "Oh, Kyle, your eye."

He patted his face. "Can't see a thing out of it. But it's funny. I see more clearly anyway. Everything," he looked around, "is so sharp and clear. The colours so bright. I don't even mind the pain." He tried to smile. "It feels right to feel it, this kind of pain. I don't remember much. Bits and pieces. But I have the sense of terrible things, and of doing terrible things."

The air smelled of metal, of blue ice. Maggie took his hands in hers. "You're not to blame. Things were done to you."

"You know better than that. We who rode elysium have only ourselves to blame, especially for the pain we caused others."

Kyle's voice was weak, but clear. It was too calm. Too much at peace. Maggie would not have him be soft to death, as Perchta had said. Not after all this. His hands were red, and mottled. He'd freeze soon. They all would. Even Badger was shivering. But where to go? Behind them was nothing but a huge mound of snow, and if ever there had been an ice castle, it was gone. Srebrenka? The fountain that was the source of elysium? Buried. Disappeared. Eaten alive by its own essence? Who knew? She only prayed it was gone for good.

The wind blew up a swirl of snow, which danced across the surface of the plain like some sort of ghost before vanishing. The sky was a bluish dome, dotted with faraway stars. Her home might as well be on one of them. She stood up.

"We can't stay here," she said.

"There's no place to go," said Kyle. "And I don't mind, really. I could go to sleep right here."

The bear, who no longer smelled of rotten seal meat, but had a clean scent, as though he'd rolled in the snow until all taint was washed away, nudged Kyle, first with his nose, and then with his paw. It spanned Kyle's chest, but he used it gently.

"I remember you. Hey, Fluffy," said Kyle. "Good bear."

"Fluffy?"

The bear pushed Kyle again. "It's just what I called him."

The ravens fluttered down from wherever they'd been and settled on the top of the bear's head. They began to chatter and run up and down the bear's neck. The bear nudged Kyle and then turned to the birds and bobbed his head.

"I think he wants you to get on his back," said Maggie.

"Really?" Kyle looked into the bear's face with his one good eye. "Are you still guarding me, you old furball?" The bear rocked back and forth and nudged him again. "I suppose I could give it a try."

The bear lay down on the snow, but in Kyle's weakened state he needed help. Maggie let him use her hands as a stirrup and with him pulling and her pushing, they managed to get him seated high on the bear's shoulders. The bear then turned and looked at Maggie and made a grunting noise.

"Me, too, then?" The bear waggled his head. Badger would be able to keep up, if the bear went not too quickly. She climbed up. The bear was surprisingly comfortable. His fur was so thick, and so warm. She braced herself for when the bear stood and began walking, but nothing happened. The bear turned his mammoth head toward her and then to Badger and back to her. Well, it was the bear's decision. "Come on, boy," she said. "Jump!"

Badger jumped, and she positioned him between her and Kyle. He seemed utterly calm, as though riding on the back of a polar bear was the most natural thing in the world. She squeezed Kyle's shoulder and he half turned to her. "Are we going home? Will you take me home, Maggie?" He sounded about nine years old.

"I hope so," she said, hugging him around Badger. "But we'll stay together now."

The bear began to walk, and then to trot.

"Can you forgive me?" asked Kyle, keeping his face averted.

"There's nothing to forgive. It might just as easily have been me who got lost. And you would have come for me. I know you would have."

He said nothing. They both knew he probably wouldn't have come after her if their roles had been reversed. But he might have. They would both, Maggie thought, cling to that. Maggie couldn't help but notice Kyle's strange affect, the way he oscillated between stiffness, almost as though he were an automaton, and a childlike fragility. It was doubtless the effect of his confinement, and the massive doses of elysium to which he had been subjected. He'd been walking in dreams and nothing but dreams for so long it would take him some time to return to himself, if he would ever truly be the man he'd once been.

Badger hunkered down and Maggie wrapped the long white fur around her fingers as the bear began to canter. She asked Kyle if his grip was tight. He nodded, and it must have been for he didn't fall off when the bear began to run. The beast's muscles moved with the power of a locomotive. There was nothing behind them except snow and sky merged together into a featureless nothing. The motion of the bear was like that of a huge, gentle rocking horse, but his back was so wide that sitting astraddle became uncomfortable after a while. She cocked a leg up. Badger nestled in her lap, and Kyle stretched first one leg, and then another, and then sat cross-legged, his hands buried to the wrists in the bear's coat. The ravens, on the other hand, hunkered down one behind each ear, using them as a kind of windbreak. The less ragged of the two tucked his head beneath his wing.

They were silent. So much had happened, and so much was yet unsure, it felt as though there were no words ready, not yet. And so they travelled, as the stars slowly revolved in the black dome above them.

AT LAST, AS THE DAY FADED THE STARS AND TURNED THE sky nearly the same white as the snow, far away but approaching fast, Maggie noticed a black smudge on the horizon, and she thought it might be a rock. As they closed in on it, however, she saw that although it was made of rock, it was not a single rock, but a marker, perhaps, like the stone figure at the entrance to Srebrenka's country. Because the bleak landscape contained nothing with which to compare the structure, she miscalculated its size. It wasn't until they were quite close she saw it was a sort of doorway, built from large black stones. It stood high up from the snow on a slab of rock on which was carved spirals and hares. Steps led up to it. Maggie looked through the doorway but could see only blue-white light.

The bear slowed to a walk. The ravens had woken up and clung to the bear's ears, their wings spread as if in greeting, or respect. But of what? The bear stopped a few yards from the doorway. He lay down and they hopped off his back. The bear and Kyle stood face to face, and it seemed they communicated in some way Maggie didn't understand. How long had they been together in that ice castle? Kyle moaned, then reached up and embraced the great bear's head, his forehead on the space between the bear's eyes. The bear seemed to droop, and then reached up with one of its paws and drew Kyle close. Kyle nearly disappeared in the bear's embrace. They stayed like that for some moments and then Kyle pushed back and the bear let go. He made that low rumble in his throat, waggled his head and then turned and loped across the plain . . .

Kyle's gaze was pinned to his disappearing friend. "He feels awful that he kept me there so long. It was long, wasn't it?"

"I'm not sure," said Maggie.

"I told him he wouldn't have done it if it hadn't been for her and her tricks." He turned to Maggie, and tears ran from his good eye. "Why didn't I see her for what she was?"

"That's a long story and I don't think this is the time."

"I suppose not." He touched his face. "Funny, but my eye doesn't hurt anymore." He dropped his hand. "What do you think this thing is? We don't know what's on the other side. Should we go through, even so?"

"Even so."

Badger paced back and forth in front of the doorway. He turned to them and barked, his tail wagging.

The ravens, who had been circling high above, cawed and spiralled down over Maggie and Kyle's heads, and then, with a great flutter of wings, they dove into the centre of the doorway and instantly disappeared, as if they'd never been there at all.

"I'm scared to death," Kyle said.

"Me, too," she said, and held out her hand.

Together, they climbed the stone steps. Maggie took a deep breath. She looked at her brother and smiled. "We're in this together," she said. "Come on, Badger."

They stepped over the threshold. She expected the old vertigo, but there was none. She stood on solid ground, alone. Fog was all there was. Grey. Thick. A mass of nothingness. Her heart raced and she spun around. "Kyle! Badger!"

"It's all right, my dear. Quite all right," said a familiar voice.

Mr. Mustby walked out of the fog. He wore a black, rather rumpled coat, with a half cape around his shoulders. Behind him walked Mr. Strundale, wearing the same kind of coat, although not quite so rumpled looking.

"You've done very well, Maggie. Very well, indeed."

"Mr. Strundale! What are you doing here?"

"Oh, Mr. Mustby and I have gone on many journeys together, haven't we?"

"Indeed," said Mr. Mustby. "I did say you wouldn't be alone."

It was so obvious. "The ravens."

The two old men bowed. "At your service, my dear."

"Mr. Mustby I sort of understand, but Mr. Strundale?" She'd left Badger in his care, but he was here, and Badger had been, and Kyle . . . her head swam. "Where am I? Where's Kyle? I can't lose him now . . . And where's Badger?"

"All is well," said Mr. Strundale. "Kyle's waiting a moment for you and won't notice this little wrinkle in time. We wanted to have a chat with you."

"But where am I?"

"You're in between," said Mr. Mustby.

"But homeward, tell me we're homeward."

"You are homeward," said Mr. Strundale. "Rest assured."

She went to throw her arms around him, but he stepped back and held up his hands. "No, my dear, I'm afraid that's not allowed. We must keep a certain distance. It's only proper."

Mr. Mustby gazed at her sternly, his eyebrows bristling. "I wasn't in favour of this quest of yours, my girl. I admit it, wasn't sure you were up to it. Not quite sure we wouldn't lose you to Srebrenka, and I couldn't have borne that."

"She sent the messages."

"Oh, yes. Drove her mad to think you'd escaped elysium. She used Kyle as a lure. Besides, Kyle was easy prey, and you promised greater . . . entertainment."

"Did you know that? Before, I mean?"

"I'm not God, child. I don't know everything. Although I did deduce it along the way, only slightly ahead of you."

"Well, she's dead now," said Maggie.

"Death is a less final state than most people imagine, wouldn't you say?"

Looking at him standing there, she had to admit the truth of it and her face must have showed her fear of the implications.

"Not to worry. Her influence has been returned to quite insignificant proportions. The flow of elysium has been stopped and the Forest is stable again, although," he shook his head, "there's still much sadness. But without Srebrenka the mirror shards are merely bits of glass." He tipped his head to the side. "Apologies. I was utterly wrong. You've done more than any-one could have hoped, but that doesn't mean that everything is sorted, I'm afraid."

Maggie's heart fell to her knees. "You're joking."

"One thing you learn, my dear, is that things do not finish. Every door leads to a room within a room, each one larger than the one before. You have noticed?"

She considered. Yes, it did seem the world got larger, the deeper into it one got. At least this one did. "Are all worlds like this?"

"What does it matter?"

Maggie blinked. Mr. Mustby looked at little frayed around the edges, as though the fog surrounding them was thickening. Mr. Strundale, too, appeared less definite. She had things she must say. "Will I see you again?" she asked Mr. Mustby.

"I'm never far away." His voice sounded as though he spoke through a wad of wool. "Just as close . . . You always . . ." and she couldn't make out what he was saying then.

She had wanted to thank Mr. Strundale for the gifts, but she could do that later, if and when she got home.

She was enclosed in mist for a second, and then Kyle's hand was in hers and Badger was next to her and the furs she'd worn over her clothes were gone. Kyle wore regular old clothes as well – jeans and boots and a sweatshirt. They stood in Trickster's room, where the door of the great tree had been. The room was vacant, littered and silent. Neither Trickster nor Colin nor anyone else appeared to have been there for a long time. The air held no trace of elysium, although three pipes lay among litter on the floor. The black curtain's tattered remains hung from broken rods and the loveseat on which Trickster had sat was overturned and broken. Profane graffiti defaced the walls. There was no sign of the great tree and the door; behind them was just an ordinary chipped-plaster wall.

"What on earth is going on?" she said.

She turned to her brother. His damaged eye no longer looked painful, swollen and bloody. It was just a smooth sunken space where once his eye had been. Healed, if you could call it that. Her fingertips, too, which had blistered when she touched Kyle, were once again healthy flesh. "Your eye looks better."

He touched the socket. "Feels better. Odd."

"This is Trickster's place, part of Srebrenka's den, isn't it? We are back, aren't we?"

"Looks like it, but where is everyone?"

They picked their way through the broken furniture and scraps of paper and bits of dried bread and a left shoe and a torn jacket and so forth, into the hallway. The entire building seemed deserted, which Maggie supposed made sense. Without elysium, the Pipers would hardly come round for tea. They descended the stairs. Watery light spilled onto the floor; the door to the street had been torn off its hinges. These signs of violence. Who knows what she'd find at the Grimoire? Alvin. Mr. Strundale. What if they were all gone?

Outside the air was warm. So much so Maggie had to take off her coat. Weeds grew in the cracks in the asphalt. The street had changed, no longer the bizarre conglomeration of twisted, spatially conflicted laneways it had been. Now it was merely a rundown assortment of apartment blocks and empty lots, overgrown and scattered with plastic bags and cardboard cups and lost socks, the sort of debris one found in any poor neighbourhood. Gone were the dead ends and monkey-puzzle mazes. The only odd thing was the absence of people. Now and again, as they wandered in what Maggie hoped was the right direction, they heard voices from somewhere far off, but no more. There were no shacks, no fires burning, no shadowy half-seen figures and no Lumpy. Their footsteps echoed, bouncing against the buildings and fleeing into alleys. For the first time in her life she wished she had a cellphone. She longed to hear Alvin's voice, to hear he was all right.

"You think this is all because of what happened?" asked Kyle, with something like awe.

"I think it is."

The way the worlds were stitched together, the way things happened without one seeing them and being able to prepare was frankly terrifying, but, then again, she remembered how the dreams, the path itself, everything seemed to work in harmony. A complicated web. Too complicated. Best to focus on the small patch before her. One foot in front of the other. Each one, she hoped, leading home. She looked back and, to her enormous relief, the road was just a road, solid and inanimate. "When we get out of here, what are you going to do?"

Kyle didn't look at her. "I've no idea."

"Assuming it's still there, you can come to the Grimoire if you'd like. I'd like you to."

He cleared his throat. "Yes. I'd like that. Thanks." His voice was thick. "I promise –"

"Don't," she said. "There isn't any need. None. We'll just take it one day after the other."

Badger suddenly stopped and whined. Then barked. From a doorway stepped a little girl with very pale lashes and brows, and hair, cut in a choppy bowl cut, the colour of wheat. She wore a pair of ragged leggings and a holey shirt several sizes too big, the sleeves cut off and fraying. It was Mindy, the little rabbit girl.

"Puppy!" She called and ran to Badger. The dog winced, but sat quietly as the little girl threw herself on him. "I knew you'd be back," she said, turning her grubby face toward Maggie. "I told Peter!" Mindy pointed at Kyle. "Who's that? And what happened to his eye?"

"This is my brother, Kyle. And he got a piece of glass in his eye."

"That's awful. Must have hurt."

Kyle said, "It did. So much so I forgot what it was like not to hurt."

The little girl considered this. "I've been waiting for you ever since the stuff went missing. I knew you'd be back." She stood, wiped her nose with the back of her hand and looked pleased with herself. "Don't go," she said and disappeared.

"Who's that?" asked Kyle.

"One of the lost children."

Kyle arched his brow. It looked horrible over his empty eye socket. "Sounds like members of our tribe," he said.

Mindy reappeared in the doorway, pulling on Peter's arm.

"Thought she was kidding," he said. He scratched his head. "Suppose you had something to do with it all?"

"With what all?"

"With elysium going missing. All there one minute, all gone the next. People going crazy for a while, tearing everything up, beating each other up," he glanced at Mindy, "and worse."

"Elysium's gone then? For how long?"

"Couple of months or more."

It seemed like only hours, or a day at most, since that terrible time in the ice castle. "Peter, when did you see me last?"

"I dunno." The boy pulled into himself, as though he'd learned long ago not to respond directly to any question unless he knew why someone wanted the answer and knew the reason wouldn't put him in jeopardy.

Maggie stepped toward him and, when he took a step back, reached out her open hands. "I only want to know because we've been on a very strange journey. I've lost track of time. I may have been away longer than I think."

He looked unconvinced, by Mindy piped up. "We saw you a long time ago. Months and months."

There was movement at the doorway and three boys stepped out. They whispered and nudged each other and looked pointedly at Mindy. Maggie had the impression the little girl had been talking about her quite a bit.

"And what about Lumpy? Do you remember him?"

"Yeah," said Peter, "poor old Lumps."

"What about him?"

"Cracked up. Managed a couple of days without the stuff, but then went loony, yelling about weasels. Just kind of curled up, from what I heard. Dead. That happened to a lot of them.

Most maybe. Police were all over the place for a while."

Maggie looked at Kyle. He looked ill, but she suspected the time-shifts had healed more than just the wound to his eye. Given how much elysium he'd been doing at the end, he should by rights be as dead as poor Lumpy. But he wasn't. There was no explaining it. Then again, it was hard to explain many of the things she'd seen the past . . . how long? Never mind.

"I'm sorry about Lumpy," she said. "He was a good friend once."

The children shuffled round her, as though waiting for her to make some sort of decision.

"Where are your parents, then, if there's no more elysium?"

"Few came back. A couple took their kids with 'em." Peter glanced at the children behind him. "Most didn't. Didn't come back or, well . . . we're still here." He looked exhausted and tight with fury.

"But how are you surviving?"

He looked at her as if she was an idiot. And perhaps she was. Mr. Mustby had said not everything was sorted. He hadn't been joking. She sighed. "Right, then. You're coming with us."

"They are?" asked Kyle. Then, seeing her expression, "Yes, of course they are."

"I dunno," said Peter, puffing himself out and hiking up his too-big trousers on his narrow hips. "Dunno about that. What you got in mind?"

"What I have in mind is a hot bath and a hot meal and a safe place to sleep."

Mindy jumped up and down and shrieked, but Peter held a finger up and she went quiet. "Yeah," he said, "and what do we have to do in return?"

"You've been to the bookstore. There are always things to do. Dusting and such."

"Dusting?" He snorted.

"You can read the books, too, which will come in handy when you go to school."

"We haven't been to school, some of us, like, ever."

"Well then, we'll have some work to do together, won't we?"

"I'm going." Mindy ran and threw her arms around Maggie. It stabbed her, that did. The little girl smelled like a bouquet of sour milk and stinky hair and the vinegary scent of long-unwashed skin. Bath first, thought Maggie, and then thought she, too, probably smelled like an old boot.

"Coming?" Maggie asked Peter.

He grinned. "Coming."

Peter led them out of the Forest, through one quiet street after another, and within minutes they were on Gerrard Street, heading west. A huge billboard showed an artist's rendition of townhouses, green space and modern low-rises, all glass and steel. The wording said, *Regent Park Renovation Project, reconstruction to begin March 2018.*

CHAPTER TWENTY-FIVE

EVENING WAS SETTLING OVER KENSINGTON Market as they neared the Grimoire. The walk had taken just the time it ought to have. The scent of coffee, spicy Caribbean and Middle Eastern food, and incense, which wafted from the vintage clothing shops, smelled familiar and comforting. Even the graffiti sprayed on the brick walls looked like marks of celebration. People carried bouquets of flowers and mesh shopping bags full of vegetables. The smell of fish from the Coral Sea Fish Market made Maggie think of Alvin and her heart cramped. The children held each other's hands and Maggie herded them along like a gaggle of geese. They approached Mr. Strundale's apothecary. Maggie didn't know what she was going to say to Mr. Strundale, other than thank you, but she simply wouldn't be able to go home until she'd seen him.

"Wait a minute," she said to Kyle. "Stay with the kids. I won't be long."

Inside the shop it looked as it always had – the shelves, the jars, the chandelier. "Hello," she called. "Mr. Strundale?" She still had so many questions, and only he would be able to answer them.

A woman stepped from the back. She was tall, perhaps fifty or a little older and dressed in a mandarin-collared black jacket and matching trousers. Bright green silk adorned the turned-back sleeves. Her white hair was in a loose chignon at her neck. Finnick dashed out from behind the counter and flipped over on his back in front of Badger, chirping with delight. Badger, in turn, tail wagging and butt wiggling in paroxysms of joy, began licking the little fox's face.

"May I help you?" asked the woman.

"I'm looking for Mr. Strundale."

The woman's face became serious. "Ah, you must be Maggie." She walked over and put her hand on Maggie's arm. "I'm so sorry, my dear, but Mr. Strundale has passed away."

What Maggie felt wasn't precisely surprise. It was more that something she'd already known clicked into place. It explained things in a way, she thought, as the stone in her chest grew heavier. It explained how Mr. Strundale had come to be with Mr. Mustby. Even the raven shape. Somehow that made sense. And yet, of course, it explained nothing. She pressed the heels of her hands into her eyes.

"He was so fond of you. So proud of you."

"He was a dear friend."

"And so he considered you to be." The woman's touch on Maggie's arm was warm and reassuring. "May I get you a cup of tea? Something calming, lavender perhaps?"

"I can't stay. I'm just back."

"I understand." She looked out the window at the gaggle of children on the sidewalk and smiled. "I see your time away has provided you some new responsibilities." She held out her hand. "Let me introduce myself. I'm Clara Strundale, Mr. Strundale's niece. This business has been in our family a very long time and we trust it will continue so. I hope you and I will be friends. You'll find I'm quite good with children and I'm so fond of them."

A spasm of relief washed over Maggie. At least there would

be someone nearby who knew something about children. "Can't tell you how glad I am to hear that. I'll come back in a few days when we're all settled."

"I'll be here."

Maggie thought she had a lovely smile. Motherly, almost. It would be good to have a friend.

"You okay?" asked Kyle, when she stepped outside, wiping her eyes.

"A friend has died." Would she try to explain to him about Mr. Mustby and Mr. Strundale? No. She doubted she could explain it to herself. "Come on. We have to get the kids sorted." She'd find Alvin as fast as she could. Maybe he'd have answers. "Bath and toast and tea, I think," she said, because she had to say something or she feared she'd be overwhelmed. Her bones felt as if made of lead. Her feet felt like boulders.

The little parade reached the Grimoire, and never had Maggie seen a more beautiful sight. The place seemed to gleam, somehow, in a way it never had before. The flower boxes with red geraniums in them, they'd not been there before. Her heart thudded. Could it be that someone had taken over the shop while she'd been away? What would she do if it wasn't her home any longer? What would she do with all these children?

She opened the door and stepped in. She frowned, blinked. Things were different. For one, the place seemed cleaner, fresher, less cluttered than she remembered. And on the walls over the windows were *trompe l'oeil* of lush green ivy, dotted here and there with butterflies and tiny birds.

Alvin appeared from the kitchen and stopped in his tracks. His mouth opened, then closed and opened again. "Maggie?"

"'Fraid so."

How good, solid and real his arms felt.

"By God, you have a lot of explaining to do!" he said into her hair. "I don't know whether to yell at you or never let you go."

"I vote for the latter."

Alvin pushed her back to arm's length, his face a fluid mask of joy and fury. "Are you all right? Are you? Not hurt?" He patted her arms and head. He held something in his hand, but she couldn't see what it was.

"Yes, I'm fine. I'm not hurt. I'm all right."

He crushed her to him again and then stepped back. "Let me look at you." His hands were on his hips. He had a tea towel tucked into the waistband of his pants and a wooden spoon in his hand.

"What are you doing with that?" she asked.

"I'm cooking, but that's hardly the question." He glanced at Kyle. "Maggie, where have you been?"

"It's a long story. I was looking for Kyle."

"Hello, Alvin."

"I thought as much," Alvin said. "You're the worse for wear."

"I don't really know what I am, to be truthful." Kyle patted the ruined side of his face. "It's bad, I know, but not as bad as it could have been."

"Awful as that?"

"Worse."

"And who are all these?"

"Um, they're children. From the Forest. Orphans, or near as can be. Peter and Mindy and Billy and, well . . ." She realized she didn't even know the names of the other two boys. "I'll explain everything."

Alvin turned back to Maggie, "I've been worried. Strundale sent word to me after you'd left and he took ill. And Badger. I thought he was gone for good. Took off as soon as Strundale died. Oh God, sorry. Did you know?"

"I just found out. I met his niece."

"She's good people. I like her. We'll miss Strundale, though." He shook his head sadly. "Anyway, I tried to follow Badger, thinking he'd lead me to you, but he was too fast. Has he been with you all this time?"

"Most of it. I have no idea how he found me. I went through a strange door and found myself in another place entirely. Seems impossible. I was in such a strange place."

Badger sat and opened his mouth as if laughing. Maggie supposed she'd never know.

"Dogs know things we don't, I've always thought. See things, and such." Alvin frowned. "What kind of strange place?"

She tried to find a succinct way of explaining it. "Not quite this world. Another world entirely, I think." How ridiculous that sounded.

Alvin, however, did not laugh at her. "In the way the Grimoire is not like the rest of the street, the rest of the city?"

"Yes, I suppose. A bit like that, but more. I can't believe Mr. Strundale's gone. What was it?"

"Not sure, really. Heart? He just slipped away. Went into a coma and never came back."

The idea she'd never see him again hadn't quite sunk in. It would, she knew, in the days to come. And yet it didn't rend her in the same terrible way Mr. Mustby's death had, and not because she loved him less. Partly, she was simply too tired to feel much of anything, but also, Mr. Mustby had said death was a less final state that most people imagined. "He was a friend," she said. She almost said, *is* a friend.

"I looked everywhere for you," Alvin said. "I've never been so worried about anyone or anything. And when I couldn't find you I moved back in here. Assumed if you came back anywhere, it would be to the Grimoire."

He might have said more, but at that moment Mindy walked past them into the kitchen as if she owned the place. "I like it," she said.

Alvin's brows shot up. "Seems they're in the right place."

"She's bossy," said Peter, who, along with the other boys, followed Mindy.

"Is it their home now?" asked Alvin.

"I believe it is. How do you feel about that?"

He laughed. "Well, I suppose that explains it."

"Explains what?"

"I woke up with a sudden urge to cook soups and stews and pies, of all bloody things. All day I've been waiting for something to happen, and this seems to be it. I'd say we've just become a rather large family. I can't remember the rooms on the third floor – the old nursery – ever being in use but I guess they'll come in handy now."

Maggie laughed. "I could use a cup of tea, and I think Kyle needs to sit down."

"Come on." Alvin guided her by the elbow as though afraid he was going to lose her again.

"You've redecorated, I see. Did you do these?" she asked Alvin, pointing at the *trompe l'oeil* birds and butterflies.

"You haven't been gone that long," he said. "They've always been there."

She followed Alvin into the kitchen to find the five children around the table, eating buttered scones and strawberry jam.

Alvin looked a bit sheepish. "Seems I've got a knack for cooking, which I suspect is going to prove useful."

Mindy grinned and said, "I told them you'd come back."

"Would you make that tea as strong as possible?" Maggie sat on a stool by the window. She looked out into the garden. It was the perfect size, with the perfect tree and the perfect spot to sit.

THEY ATE SUPPER AND BATHED THE CHILDREN AND PUT them to bed in their rooms, which looked as bright and clean and fresh as did the rest of the shop – four boys in one room, and the delighted Mindy in a room of her own. The children wore some of Alvin's clean T-shirts.

Kyle paced from room to room, and through the stacks of

books for the longest time, unable to settle. He kept muttering that he didn't deserve any of this and would spend his life making amends. "Where do I start?" he kept asking. "Where do I start?" Maggie finally took him by the shoulders and told him to sit by the fire. Alvin pulled up a chair and joined them. She told Kyle she would never have learned the things she'd learned about herself – how she could resist temptation, and be patient, and trust others, and be brave even though she was terrified – had she not gone to find him. "It is," she said, "as far as I can determine, a matter of faith." She told him what she truly believed: that if it wasn't for him, elysium would still be among them, and Srebrenka would still be causing more and more pain to feed her insatiable hunger. "It's all so much more complicated, so much more interconnected, than we can see," she said at last. "We are all responsible for the mess in the world, and we are all responsible for cleaning it up. It's not *either-or*, is it? It's *both-and*. We harm and we heal."

Kyle laughed, and his face was brighter, the strain in his features less. "Well, look who got all wise."

And with that she was able to persuade him to climb the stairs, and eventually he slept in the room always destined to be his. She watched him from the doorway for a few minutes. He fidgeted and tossed in his sleep. Healing the body was one thing, healing the mind and soul would take time, with him as it had with her.

AT LAST, MAGGIE AND ALVIN LAY IN BED, THEIR ARMS around each other. Badger sprawled on Maggie's feet. They had spent hours talking, Maggie telling her story as Alvin listened and asked questions, and told her how it had been without her, and the dreams he'd had of his uncle telling him it was time to come in off the water.

"He gets around, your uncle."

"Uh-huh. Suppose I just took it for granted. It's the way he is." Alvin snorted. "It is a twist, though – here I thought I was the wanderer."

Even as she talked about all that had happened, all the places she'd been and the people she'd met – the flying caribou and robbers and Aunt Ravna who made clouds and the roads that disappeared behind her and the snow palace and the mirror and the fountain – she felt it slipping away, fading, becoming thin and vague. It would be easy, she realized, to forget it all, the way one forgets a dream during the passing of a day.

"If you told me I'd made it all up," she said, "I might be inclined to believe you."

"Except that Kyle's here."

She smiled. "There is that."

"You'll have to decide if you're going to believe your experience or not," said Alvin.

"You sound just like your uncle when you talk like that."

He hugged her tight. "There are worse things."

"We're a family, I guess," she said. "Do you mind?"

"Nope. But there's going to be some legal stuff, paperwork and so forth, getting them into school, if we're going to be able to keep these kids. It'll be a long haul."

"They're supposed to be here, though, surely. Since they're here."

"You brought them."

She hadn't considered that. "But it seems like the nursery was there just waiting for them, and then your sudden culinary instinct."

"Yes, there is all that. And I suppose if the social workers and so forth find their way here it will be meant to be."

"So, it's back to that, to faith, then."

"Seems so."

"You didn't answer me. Do you mind?"

"I never thought I'd want to be here," Alvin shifted a bit. "But when you disappeared, and I thought of never seeing you again, all I wanted was to be where you'd been. Now, I can't imagine not being here. Kids and all. Besides, it seems like all the real adventure happens around here, doesn't it?"

Maggie nuzzled into his shoulder and drifted off to sleep. Adventure? Maggie dreams . . .

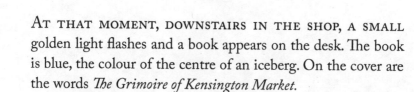

AT THAT MOMENT, DOWNSTAIRS IN THE SHOP, A SMALL golden light flashes and a book appears on the desk. The book is blue, the colour of the centre of an iceberg. On the cover are the words *The Grimoire of Kensington Market*.

Tomorrow, when Maggie notices it she will open it and read, with laughing astonishment, the opening line:

People didn't wander into the Grimoire. It wasn't that sort of bookshop.

ACKNOWLEDGEMENTS

To begin, although surely some readers have already noticed this, I took inspiration for this tale from Hans Christian Andersen's "The Snow Queen," a story that has stayed with me since I first read it as a child.

This book has taken me longer to write than any other work. Ten years. And so, of course, there are many people to thank.

First, I'd like to thank Sister Rita Woehlcke, who encouraged me to go and sit by the ocean for a while and allow my soul to heal after the suicide of my brother, Ronnie. It was there, in 2008, that the first glimmers of this book appeared. Sister Rita continues to be an *anam cara* if ever there was one.

Hat tip to Kate and Joe Zuhusky, who allowed us to rent their beautiful house by the sea time and time again. So much inspiration has come from that place. Ron and I feel you are family.

And a tip of the teacup to Paul W. Meyers for that story about the Korean sea slug. Just can't make this stuff up. You and Debbie must come for dinner. Tell me more stories!

I would also like to thank early readers Maria DiBattista, Susan Applewhaite and John Foster for taking the time to give me their excellent feedback. Much appreciated.

Many a dark night of the soul has been part of the writing of this book, birthed as it was by the suicide of my brother, Ronnie. I would be remiss, indeed, if I didn't offer love and thanks and deep respect to my parents, Bill and Carmen Seguin. Their ability to survive yet another loss and to keep their love intact has been a miracle in my life.

Also, I would like to thank Lily and Elliot Kraus, Lynne and Van Davis, Mary and Paul Gerard, Jill and Felix Aguayo, Angie Abdou, Michael Straw, Chantal Cartier, Bernard Applewhaite, Lynn Robinson and so many more friends for their patience, kindness, humour and understanding as I wrestled with this angel.

I bow to Natalee Caple for introducing me to Noelle Allen.

My agent, David Forrer, has been my constant champion and guide for a long time, and my affection for him only grows.

Most exuberantly, my gratitude to Noelle Allen, for giving this book a home at Wolsak & Wynn, and of course to my editor there, Paul Vermeersch, of the Buckrider imprint, who made the editing of this book such a unique pleasure. Paul, your gentle hand, your keen instincts, your humour and your knowledge of the craft have been a revelation. I hope we work together for a long time. A mighty hat tip to Kate Hargreaves for the wonderful cover design. I adore it! And finally, many thanks to Ashley Hisson, copy editor extraordinaire, who made sure my spelling mistakes and grammatical stumbles didn't make it into the public arena. Whew.

LAUREN B. DAVIS is the author of *The Grimoire of Kensington Market; Against a Darkening Sky; The Empty Room*, named one of the Best Books of the Year by the *National Post*, the *Winnipeg Free Press*, Amazon and the *Coast*; and *Our Daily Bread*, longlisted for the Scotiabank Giller Prize and named one of the Best Books of the Year by the *Globe & Mail* and the *Boston Globe*. Her other books include the bestselling and critically acclaimed novels *The Radiant City*, a finalist for the Rogers Writers' Trust Fiction Prize, and *The Stubborn Season*, one of the Top Fifteen Bestselling First Novels by Amazon and Books in Canada, as well as two short story collections, *An Unrehearsed Desire* and *Rat Medicine & Other Unlikely Curatives*.

Her short fiction has been shortlisted for the CBC Literary Award and the ReLit Award, and she is the recipient of two Mid-Career Writer Sustaining grants from the Canada Council for the Arts. Lauren was born in Montreal and now lives in Princeton, New Jersey, with her Best Beloved, Ron, and Bailey, the extremely spoiled rescue pup. For more information, please visit her website at www.laurenbdavis.com.